PRAISE FOR JASMINE SILVERA

The TOOTH & SPELL series is so fresh and broadly appealing, that even romance readers who don't normally read paranormal will be hooked. A perfect balance of wry humor and angst; sweetness and heat.

> — JEN COMFORT, AUTHOR OF *WHAT IS LOVE?* AND
> *MIDNIGHT DUET*

DEATH'S DANCER weaves suspense and romance into a story as smart as it is sensual... Silvera deftly choreographs the action using lush depictions of Prague's storied scenery and deliciously dark humor. A thrilling debut.

> — CAMILLE GRIEP, AUTHOR OF *LETTERS TO ZELL*
> AND *NEW CHARITY BLUES*

Silvera's worldbuilding is exquisite... a rollicking, romantic, riveting ride.

> — THE PINK HEART SOCIETY (*THE TALON & THE*
> *BLADE*)

A spellbinding urban fantasy.

> — BOOK BUB (*THE TALON & THE BLADE*)

ALSO BY JASMINE SILVERA

TOOTH & SPELL

Binding Shadows

Conjuring Moonlight

GRACE BLOODS

Death's Dancer

Dancer's Flame

The Talon & the Blade

CHARMING DAWN

TOOTH & SPELL
BOOK THREE

JASMINE SILVERA

First publication date November 2024

Published by No Inside Voice Books, Seattle, WA

ISBN: 979-8-9912670-1-4

Cover design by The Book Brander

Book Design by No Inside Voice

To those who know that hope is like the dawn, love is a verb, and the best realities begin as our wildest dreams.

PRAGUE, 2004

WHEN CHRISTOF VOGEL passed the old Vyšehrad Train Station on his way home from school and a shimmering bumblebee meandered into his path, he grinned and changed direction, accepting the invitation.

He hadn't seen Ofelia at recess, which meant she was probably in the library or being a teacher's assistant—a job no one truly wanted but was one guaranteed way to avoid the dangers of being a social outcast in the schoolyard. She had it almost as bad as him. That she trusted him with this small magic made his chest ache in that peculiar way he longed for. Something settled in him, leaving him finally restful after the long day spent trying to avoid the attention of the older boys.

Undeterred by the tall metal fencing, he headed toward the hill at the south end of the building, climbing the broken stone staircase cut into the slope. It ended at the changing house, and he crossed into the wild growth.

Ofelia had left him a path, and the brambles closed behind his heels as he went. She was as good with everyday plants as she was with magical bees. He found his way to a shorter chain-link fence and scaled it easily. He kicked a leg over and dropped into the high grass along the tracks.

The passenger station loomed, a three-storied beauty in sun-bleached shades of ivory that crumbled a little more every day, its boarded-up windows and doors relentlessly graffitied and the roof a patchwork of blue tarps nailed down with boards. It seemed to sigh at his arrival, reminding him of a tired old woman slouching over her handcart as she waited for the late-night tram.

The station was, everyone agreed, the most tragic eyesore in all of

Prague. As close as it was to home, he and his siblings had been told to stay away from it often.

He found the loose panel in a boarded-up door, scanning the rails and the grass to make sure he hadn't been followed. He slipped his backpack inside first, then wiggled into the narrow opening.

The terminal seemed far larger inside. He passed the corners of junk and trash left by squatters and vagrants. They'd claimed a few spots over the past few months, and he counted on the bees to help him find Ofelia. Each appeared irregularly but exactly when he would have taken a wrong turn.

He climbed a spiral staircase all the way to the third floor. Upstairs was remarkably untouched.

She had already made herself comfortable in a shaft of sunlight beneath a broken vent in one of the domed cupolas. She sat on the light spring jacket she'd worn to school that day, and a thick book filled her lap. She *had* been in the library at break. Her thick black hair was organized in a complex network of braids, and her deep brown skin shone in the dusty sunlight. She always dressed neatly, as though expecting to be presented for inspection. Today her dress was a pale blue with darker blue flowers around the neckline and a lace overlay on the skirt. Matching shoes, patent leather with little bows. Even the little ribbons tying off her braids were blue. He decided blue was his new favorite color.

He swiped at the smudges of dust and grease on his pants and rubbed his tousled hair back into place. She looked as immaculate as she had in the classroom earlier. He wasn't sure if there was a truer sign of magic than the inability of dirt to touch her.

When he looked up, Ofelia's dark eyes were on him, holding the smile she never let reach her mouth.

He gave up and flopped onto his belly with a sigh. "What is it today?" He angled his head to read the book in her lap. "*Dangerous Gardens: Poison through History*. They have that in the library?"

"Advantages of being a good teacher's assistant." She closed the massive book with a thud and tugged at his backpack. "Did you get them?"

"All yours." He shifted to make it easier for her to reach.

"My sweet, sweet babies." She drew the bag of gummy bears from the side pocket like priceless treasure, pressing them to her chest with a grin before tearing it open. Her parents didn't allow sweets.

"You going to eat them or what?" He rolled his eyes, trying to sound as though her simple pleasure barely moved him. While she lined up a neat, multicolored row of bears on her pencil case, he lifted the top of her backpack. He knew better than to paw through a witch's belongings uninvited. "What'd you get on the test?"

When the teacher had returned their papers, Ofelia tucked hers quickly beneath the stack of books on her desk.

Chris had allowed his to linger on top for too long, stunned by the teacher's brief praise: "Much improvement, Christof."

The chorus of jeers started as soon he turned back to the front of the room.

One of the biggest boys leaned over his desk and grabbed the paper, his meaty breath hot on Chris's neck. "Nice work, Christof."

Chris hunched, trying to make himself smaller as he tugged it free and mashed it into his notebook. Something small and wet hit him in the back of the neck. He didn't dare wipe it away.

A sharp wooden crack echoed through the room. The bigger boy shouted in alarm as a leg of his desk snapped, sending him tumbling to the floor. His elbow and cheek hit the boards with echoing thuds.

When Chris looked up, Ofelia was in her seat near the front of the room, focused on her exercise. Only her still-twitching finger gave her away.

In the train station hours later, Chris smiled. "Nice trick with the desk leg. But you shouldn't waste your gifts on those idiots."

"Mom says practice will make me stronger." She shrugged and produced the test from her backpack for him.

A perfect score. If she could have gotten higher, she would have. He compared the tests, seeing what he'd missed and frowning with the effort of committing the correct answers to memory. With his second-oldest brother away at Oxford, Ofelia was officially the smartest person he knew.

When he looked up, laughter obliterated his worry that she was too smart to waste time with him.

The smartest girl in their grade and witch in training was using magic to march a row of gummy bears up her arm to the back of her wrist, where they leaped into her mouth one by one.

"Want one?" she asked between bites.

"Yellow, please." He opened his mouth and closed his eyes.

"They all taste the same."

He opened one eye. "The yellow ones are the best."

"Whatever." With a little smile from her, a yellow bear took a flying leap sideways off her thumb.

It hit his nose and bounced off. He lunged to catch it before it hit the floor and rolled to his back with a grin and the gummy clenched between his teeth.

She frowned. "Working on my aim."

It was the only place outside his home he'd ever seen magic, and never used so mundanely. He'd tried to warn her about the dangers of being what they were so close to the necromancer Azrael's seat, as his mother had often warned his brothers.

Ofelia had listened patiently and then patted his head like reassuring a little dog afraid to cross the street before a noisy van. "Don't worry, Woof. I'll protect you."

Though everyone in the family tried to hide it from him and his sister, he knew what had happened to his brothers. He'd begun to have the dreams. Ofelia had seen it on the first day of school, her eyes growing wide with excitement and anticipation.

"Want to visit him today?" she asked Chris when she'd had her fill and tucked the gummy bears into a secret pocket of her bag.

Chris rolled onto his belly, worried. It was a lot of magic even for her. "Are you sure?"

"It's Friday. I can rest this weekend." She nodded briskly and dusted off her hands. "Close your eyes."

He would have obeyed even before her fingertips threaded through the hair at the back of his head, but that made it easy.

The air stilled so that even the dust motes froze their lazy spirals, and the delicate scent of her magic—fennel and citrus—flooded his nostrils.

"Can you picture it?" she asked.

The first time, she'd told him to think of a special place, a safe place. One he had been to in real life worked best. His mind went automatically to the clearing he hiked to with his mom on the weekends. Back when Mark and Toby lived at home, she'd take all the boys up to the family cabin on the edge of the Šumava Forest for the weekends.

His older brothers went into the woods. Camping.

Chris and Mom spent the evenings playing board games and the days hiking, tending to her garden, and gathering herbs in glades just like this one until his brothers returned Sunday evening, disheveled and weary.

When he could see the glade exactly in his mind, he exhaled with a nod.

She built a place between them, using his memory, until the last gust of dusty old train station was replaced by forest loam, rotting leaves, and wild trees. The gnarled trunks pushed through the undergrowth. City trees smelled different somehow—even the ones in the big parks and green belts. These trees had never been civilized.

It was that final hour of light before the dark that never truly came no matter how long he stayed.

At first it had taken what felt like hours to get his first glimpse of pale fur, but when Ofelia had brought him back, only a few moments had passed.

"It's like dreaming," she'd explained. "Not less real, just not bound by things like time and space. It's yours. You and Woof."

Today he was aware that he was being watched long before he caught a glimpse of a tail or the flick of an ear. It took effort to keep the smile off his face, not to give away the game.

The juvenile wolf came in a rush of silver fur, mouth open but tongue lolling. Chris dropped to one knee at the last minute, and the wolf tumbled through the space where the boy had been. He recovered quickly, spun with an unearthly grace, and Chris was waiting for him. They wrestled until Chris was muddy and the pup's pale fur was tipped with streaks of loam. It would be years before they were united in the tangible world, but Ofelia had seen the wolf in him and created this place for them.

Usually nothing reached them here. But today the young wolf raised his head, ears and gaze pointed at the distance over Chris's left shoulder.

"What is it?" Chris rubbed dirt out of his hair, thankful he wouldn't take any of this mess back with him. His mother would have killed him for ruining another pair of pants. She'd stopped wasting her magic on stains and rips years ago.

One ear flicked back to Chris, accompanied by the swift glance of smoky blue eyes, a mirror of his own. Usually when their time was over, the wolf would wag his body bonelessly in a playful goodbye and vanish into the woods.

This tension in his neck was new. The fur on his spine rippled and bunched.

Trouble. It wasn't a word so much as the sense of a threat.

Ofelia was unprotected and casting the enchantment that had brought him to this impossible place to bond with the animal inside him.

Chris lurched to his feet, face to the sky. "Bring me back now!"

The transition was rough, a yank that left him gasping. Her cool hand settled on the back of his neck, tingling with remnants of energy.

"You're fine. Everything is fine." Wide eyes the color of a deep wood at midnight met his, searching. "What happened?"

Chris rocked to his hands and knees. He longed for the wolf's senses. The wolf's strength. How could he possibly protect her as he was now?

In the silence, his gaze found hers. Confusion etched a line in her

brow, tiny furrows at the corners of her smiling mouth. The enchantment always made her seem weary in a way he couldn't place, as
though some of the vibrance in her deep brown skin and endless
woods-in-night eyes had dulled. He wished there was some way to give
it back.

He opened his mouth to speak. The distant creak of a board and the
squeal of rusted nails cut him off. Ofelia's face didn't change. She hadn't
heard it.

Maybe he had a bit of the wolf after all. Hope surged in his rib cage.

She started to speak, but he squeezed her hand.

They had been coming to this place since the fall when it became
clear that being together at school only doubled the attention they got
from their bullies. She reviewed the lessons he struggled with in school so
that he would pass a test or took him to the place where he could meet
his wolf or read to him from whatever magazine she had stolen from her
mother. In exchange, he brought bags of gummy bears, trinkets, smooth
rocks, strange leaves, and branches from his weekends at the cabin. They
came and went separately and waved goodbye at dusk.

He'd never held hands with a girl. Any girl. Never mind the most
beautiful—and the only magical—girl in his grade.

Her skin was warm and softer than he'd ever imagined. He had been
imagining this moment for months. His chest seemed to expand and
tighten all at once.

Their eyes met. His grip eased.

She laced her fingers in his and squeezed back. Her expression softened. Maybe it was his imagination, but some of the brightness returned
to her cheeks. The heat built in his neck. He was probably turning red. As
the fairest-skinned of all his siblings, his visible flush had been a source of
teasing since he was small.

She was going to laugh at him.

Instead, she smiled, her eyes darting to their clasped hands. It was as
if all the bees she'd ever used to summon him buzzed madly under his
collarbones. He forgot everything: the noise, the warning, the wolf.

When their eyes met again, the hundreds of wings settled, and he was
aware of every mote of dust in the air of the sun-drenched cupola moving
between them again, the tiny springy curls at her nape, and her smile,
warmer than any beam of light and a little shy.

Her free hand wrapped in his worn collared shirt, a hand-me-down
from Tobias, and tugged.

She kissed him—barely a touch of lips, featherlight on his own. He
tasted gummy bears and magic on her breath.

Another creak. This time a board snapped below as though forced to bear too much weight. Chris yanked away, eyes wide.

She bit her lip. "I'm sorry—"

"Someone's here," he whispered.

She released his hand abruptly and began stuffing her backpack. He helped, then shoved the last of his belongings recklessly into his.

"Where are you rats hiding?" A voice floated up from the lower floor, echoing off the broken walls.

The hairs on his neck rose in recognition—the meanest of the boys in their grade. The accompanying chuckles and heavy footfalls meant he wasn't alone. He never went anywhere without his cronies.

"What did you drag us to this old wreck for?" called a fourth voice, one of the boys from the grade ahead.

Their voices were distant, echoing. He wished for the wolf's ability to pinpoint people and things by sound and scent alone.

"They came here. I saw them."

Chris met Ofelia's gaze. Anger and a shining edge he'd never seen lit hers. He mouthed, "We have to go."

She held up a hand. Closed her eyes.

"There!" A shout rose below, and the footsteps moved away from the stairs and the broken door.

She opened her eyes, bright with victory but feverish. "Distraction."

He lurched to his feet. She wobbled. Whatever she'd done had drained her even more. When she reached out, his hand was waiting.

"Ready?" He forced a smile he hoped conveyed fearlessness.

She nodded.

He crept along the edge of the room, guiding her around the squeakiest spots on the stairs as they descended. Floor two. He considered turning there. This level mainly had offices and a central mezzanine overlooking the main floor. There was another loose window at the end of the hall, but that would put them on the roof, and he wasn't sure exactly how to get the rest of the way out from there, plus she could get hurt falling from that height.

Their best shot was the way they'd come in. At the foot of the staircase, he leaned out. He could just make out the boys at the other end of the terminal, following a glimmer of something bright, the vaguest outline. A glance at her face showed the strain of maintaining the illusion wearing on her.

Her fingers trembled in his.

He squeezed her hand. "Now."

They gave up on stealth, sprinting toward the broken board. The boys had ripped it almost entirely away. Daylight glittered through the splintered panel. Freedom.

A shadow crossed the door. One of the older boys blocked the path, his smile a threat.

Chris bared his teeth and let go of her hand. Without slowing down, he hurled all his weight at the bigger boy. They crashed into the wall, leaving the opening clear. Shouts echoed from the far end of the hall.

Chris stumbled to his feet, wild-eyed. The boy he'd hit lay on the floor, gasping for breath like a landed fish.

Ofelia stood on the other side of the opening, knotting her fingers together like she would spark a spell. Flares of color sputtered from her fingertips but winked out. Nothing.

"I can't—"

He'd never heard fear in her voice before.

He tossed her backpack through the opening and then gave her a shove after it. "Run."

She stumbled. The only way to keep from falling was to pull herself through. Ripped boards tore the once immaculate fabric of her skirt. She whimpered, one hand clamped to her calf.

She hesitated, eyes on the boys racing toward them at the end of the hall. "Come with me."

"They'll catch us." He tried to summon the wolf's authority. "Go."

She shook her head once, eyes shining.

"Please, Ofelia," he said. "I'll be right behind you."

Her chin wobbled, but she grabbed her backpack. Taking one last look at him, she sprinted down the platform and toward the tracks.

Fresh blood on a shard of broken board caught his eye. Her blood. He wiped it clean with his sleeve. A witch's blood was precious and should be kept safe.

Chris shoved the board closed as best he could.

Ofelia was small but fast. She just had to make it to the tram stop. From there she would be safe. She just needed a head start.

Chris dropped his backpack at his feet, hefted the nail-studded board, and backed himself up against the door to face the gathering boys.

"Out of the way, runt," the big boy said. "We only want her."

If he hadn't been afraid his voice would shake or squeak, he would have given them a line from one of Mark's old gangster movies. He decided silence was his best bet.

The boys from his grade looked nervous for the first time. "Thought we were just going to scare them."

The ringleader ignored him, addressing Chris again. "You'd get a cut of the reward."

Desperately, Chris called for the wolf. But the line between them was still solid. Perhaps in a year he would come quickly, but now?

Chris flexed his knees and lifted his upper lip, baring his teeth in what he hoped was a respectable snarl as he took a few trial swings with the board.

The older boy frowned at his classmate. "Look for another way out."

There wasn't one. Chris knew that. After the last time the city had cleared out the vagrants, they'd done an even better job of sealing off all the entrances and exits.

"What are you going to do?" His classmate looked at Chris, hesitating.

The bigger boy grinned. "Move this little piece of shit out of the way."

CHRIS MISSED A WEEK OF SCHOOL. His first day back, the tingle of Ofelia's presence was absent from all her usual haunts and her scent was old.

City workers boarded the train station up again—this time with metal bars.

He finally got up the courage to go into the office, waiting until the secretary who always smiled at him was at the counter.

"Ofelia?" She squinted at his whispered request. He nodded, stumbling over her last name. "Adjei."

She rifled through her desk for a file. "Oh. Yes. I prepared her transfer paperwork."

A great big hole opened in his chest and sucked his lungs into it. He tried to speak, failed, and tried again.

She smiled, a little curious, a little worried. "Last week. It was a bit of a rush."

"Do you know… why…? What school she went to?"

"Some fancy boarding school in Switzerland." The secretary shrugged, puzzled. "Her father was called back into service. A former embassy official, you know. Swiss."

Gone. Ofelia was gone.

She frowned. "You look a little pale. Would you like me to write a note to your teacher so you can go to the infirmary?"

Chris shook his head. He didn't even look at the decrepit old train station on his way home. All the magic that mattered in his life was gone.

CHAPTER ONE

CHRIS NEVER WOULD HAVE GUESSED a day that started in vomit would end in reconnecting with the love of his life. But there it was. Life was funny that way.

He woke up to the incessant buzz of the group chat on fire, his friends sorting out the evening's destination. He checked the time—at *eight a.m.* What was wrong with his friends? Knowing Luca, he was headed home from whatever girl's bed he'd wound up in. Ondrej had to be on the jobsite early. Klaus. Klaus just never slept.

@Luca3000: Tiny's?

@Klausmodious: What is wrong with your brain, man? The music is shit.

@Luca3000: But the girls are friendly there.

@Klausmodious: Pokojíček

@Luca3000: You are so predictable! That's way the hell out in 7.

Help me out here, @BigBird.

Chris rubbed his brow. Pokojíček was a solid choice, but if he sided with Klaus, he'd never hear the end of it from Luca. If he went along with Luca, Klaus would pout all night and probably get himself into trouble. Either way, he'd regret it. So he passed.

@BigBird: Ondrášek?

A second chime indicated a message on another thread.

@Klausmodious: Coward.

@BigBird: It's too early for this shit, man.

He tossed his phone and slipped out of bed. Might as well get something to eat. Then he'd go downstairs and do some work on the apartment. The one that was supposed to be his if he could finish it. He could get a solid chunk of work in before he had to be in the shop that afternoon, and he needed the money for building supplies. He dragged a pair of beat-up gray sweats over his hips, not bothering with a shirt.

As he lumbered down the hall, the din of small voices and the clatter of breakfast dishes grew. He squinted at the clock on his way through the living room. What were his brother's kids still doing here? They were due at nursery and preschool soon.

The chaos became obvious when he stepped into the dining room. His eldest brother, Mark, hurried around the table, collecting dishes as he barked orders in Czech into his phone. He was dressed for a jobsite.

It bugged him that Mark hadn't called him in on it. It's not like Mark didn't know he needed the cash.

Mark's four-year-old daughters shrieked with glee, bolting from the table over their father's demands to get their coats and shoes on. "Uncle Chris!"

"Hey, Pinecone." Chris scooped up Thyme obediently when she held out her arms. Lilach sprang directly off the chair, grasping his arm and climbing the rest of the way with a lupine grin. His wolf huffed a greeting, and Chris laughed. "Buttons."

From matching high chairs, a younger set of twins—Tobias's—clapped their hands gleefully and howled at him like the barbarians they were.

"Isaac puked in your shoes," Thyme informed him primly as Lilach mimed retching. "Your Nikes."

"My new—" Chris began as his mother herded his eldest nephew from the kitchen, a pot of tea and set of cups on a tray snugged against her hip.

"Sorry, Uncle Chris." Isaac gazed up at him, pale and on the verge of tears.

Chris dropped to one knee and turned the girls loose. They raced away, mock vomiting and giggling. "Hey, tough guy. No worries. Happens to the best of us. You okay?"

"I feel better." He nodded glumly. "I do."

Beryl shuffled the tray to her other hip and cradled the boy's shoulder. "You're staying home with Oma."

Isaac started to cry.

Chris rubbed a hand through Isaac's soft, dark curls. "Maybe we can go for a walk later, okay?"

"Library?" He sniffled.

"Sure thing." Chris fought the urge to smile: Had Tobias cloned this kid or what?

Chris rose, leaning in on his way to full height to catch the kiss his mom aimed at his cheek.

"Morning, sweetheart." She patted his shoulder. "We didn't wake you with all this commotion, did we?"

"Wake him?" Mark disconnected his call. "It's eight a.m. on a Thursday—what the hell is he still doing asleep?"

"Markus Vogel," their mother warned.

"It's fine, Ma," Chris said. "Why don't you get Isaac settled? I'm gonna grab something to eat, then go do some work downstairs."

Beryl nodded at him and herded her grandson to the living room.

Mark scoffed, yellow-eyed and bristly. The problems at the jobsite must have been big if he was ready to wolf out at the breakfast table. "You finally getting around to finishing the place or just getting started?"

Chris exhaled. He wasn't going to let his brother get to him. Not today. He had a plan for his day, and he was going to see it through. From the high chair, Barbarian #1 began to whine, clearly annoyed at not being given her due. Chris liberated her and tweaked her belly until she giggled and then tried to chomp his finger. For having two academics for parents, she and her twin were remarkably bloodthirsty. He gave her a knuckle to gnaw on and she went to it happily, drooling. "Where's Bebe?"

She mostly ran the mornings and possessed the precision of a drill sergeant who moonlighted as a lion tamer.

His middle brother, Tobias, emerged from the kitchen, arms full of lunches and daycare bags. "I think I got everything. Extra clothes, water bottles… Where is your shirt?"

Chris stared. *That's* what he was worried about? "I think you have something on your tie."

Tobias dumped the load on the kitchen table, bags and bottles scattering as he frantically studied his tie.

Chris guffawed. "My mistake."

"I have a meeting with the dean today, you little shi— turd," Tobias said as his twins locked eyes on him expectantly. "I don't have time to change my tie. And Barbara had to go to the shop early to deal with a finicky buyer. This morning has been its own circle of hell, and I don't need any shi— shenanigans from you."

Chris stifled his laughter as he started collecting the scattered stuff. "You forgot Philip's water bottle."

"Scheisse," Tobias muttered.

The barbarians in question, Octavia and Philip, howled gleefully in unison.

"Savages." Mark laughed, a little too pleased.

"Where are your little angels, huh?" Tobias muttered, hoisting Philip out of the chair for a wipe down.

Mark looked up, alarmed at the sudden silence. "Fuck. Girls!"

His brothers were clearly out of their depth. Chris sighed and marched into the kitchen, retrieved the missing water bottle, and replaced his knuckle with Octavia's spare teething ring. Her molars were coming in with a vengeance based on that bite.

In the dining room, he handed Octavia off to her father. "Hold this."

Mark was wasting time looking in the living room.

Chris found Lilach and Thyme playing in their grandpa's study, which was definitely off-limits, and leaned through the doorway. "I wonder who can get coats and shoes on fastest?"

"Me!" they screamed in unison and raced down the hall to the front door.

On his way past his parents' bedroom, he called in German, "Papa, remember to lock your office door or the girls are going to reprogram all your machines."

"Danke schon, meine kind!" His father thanked him over the buzz of his electric razor.

When he got back to the hall, Mark's girls were in jackets and shoes and swinging their backpacks into place. Tobias was losing the battle with Octavia, so Chris took over. Philip screeched a lot less. He did bite more, however.

Chris squinted at the clock. "There—everybody's ready, and if you hurry, there's a tram in five minutes that will get you there almost on time."

Tobias checked his watch. "I'm going to be late to my meeting."

"I'm already late. Shit's going down on the site today." Mark's phone buzzed. He turned, plugging one ear, and barked something about foundation stability in Czech.

"What do you want me to do about it?" Chris's stomach rumbled. *You couldn't even be bothered to call me in for the work on the jobsite.*

Mark and Tobias exchanged a look.

"I'm working on the apartment today." Chris lifted his hands. "You two should be happy. You give me enough sh— stuff for still living up here."

"It's only gonna take you an hour," Mark said. "Two tops. You've got plenty of time."

Chris shook off a brief flare of annoyance. "Fine."

Mark went back to his call, grabbing his keys.

"I really appreciate it. It's the dean. Huge meeting. Huge." Tobias handed off a set of backpacks. "Thanks, Christof. You're a lifesaver."

And then Mark had to open his damn mouth. "As long as you're not doing anything else with your life, you might as well help out around here."

Even Tobias stared.

"He barbers two days a week—the rest of the time he wanders around barely dressed, cleaning out the fridge, and partying with his friends. Rough life." Mark went back to barking orders into his phone.

Chris shut off his annoyance with his eldest brother. Mark couldn't help being what he was—an oversized worrywart with a savior complex.

Octavia and Philip gazed up at him expectantly.

"It gives me great joy to spend time with my nieces and nephews." Chris grinned. "I won't even leave anyone on the tram this time. Pinkie swear."

"This time?" Mark hung up, glaring at him. His phone buzzed again and he swore.

"A joke." Chris scooped up Octavia and Philip. "Grow a sense of humor and watch your mouth."

"He's got a point about your language." Tobias tweaked his tie and headed for the door.

When they were off, Chris surveyed his charges. Two sets of twins. Piece of cake. "Gonna need a shirt for this."

They barely made the tram, but he got everyone in two seats. He stood in the aisle, leaning in to play *I-Spy* until Lilach and Thyme got bored and started babbling at each other in their own private language. Philip dozed off on his shoulder. He checked the boy's forehead and the skin under his jaw, hoping he hadn't caught whatever Isaac had. So far his nephew was only toddler warm, nothing out of the ordinary.

When Chris looked up, a few overly long glances from women around his age slid away. Even women older than him in nice clothes with fancy jobs made full-on eye contact when he was with the kids. One winked at him.

Chris didn't mind the attention. Trouble was, somehow they were always looking for something serious and he never lived up to what they expected. Oh well. He glanced out the window at the old Vyšehrad Train Station before the view was blocked by buildings.

He passed the old station almost every day. Unlike the Municipal House, its more famous sibling, the art nouveau marvel had been lost to ruin and disrepair. Every few years, plans were announced for a restoration that never manifested. Today his gaze lingered on the boarded-up windows and the overgrowth. The graffiti was getting worse as the city seemed to lose interest in keeping the building free of mischief.

Once, he and Ofelia had imagined buying the old station and turning it into a café. A place where witches and shifters could meet and share gummy bears and tea. He wondered where life had taken her and if she ever thought of those sunny afternoons.

The announcement of their stop brought him back to the present. They made it to the school just as the principal began closing the door. Thyme grabbed Lilach's hand and hauled her sister into the building.

At nursery school, saying goodbye took more time. Octavia and Philip would be fine as soon as he left, but he indulged them, sitting cross-legged on the colorful carpet near the cubbies until Octavia wandered off on her own to the art table. One of the teachers came by to check on him after half an hour when Philip refused to unlatch.

"It's been a rough morning," Chris explained. "I've got him."

She smiled benevolently. "If you need to go to work…?"

"Nowhere more important than this." Chris shifted to let Philip get more comfortable.

By the time Philip had succumbed to the siren song of story time—of course—it was nearly eleven.

Early for lunch, but considering Chris had missed breakfast, he was overdue for a snack.

The streets buzzed with activity—old people and their shopping carts, young, surly-eyed men smoking beside tobacco shops, and students waiting for the tram. He took a shortcut through the Franciscan garden. Old men played chess while a goth girl in lug-soled boots coaxed a featherlight sonata from the public piano in the quiet hidden courtyard just off Prague's busiest and most historic thoroughfare.

He wasn't quite ready for the full press of Wenceslas Square, so he raced across the tram tracks and ducked into the Lucerna Passage. The statue of the king-turned-saint on his upside-down horse always drew a crowd. Their cameras flashed, never mind the racks of postcards ten feet away, loaded with much nicer images of the mocking modernist statement dangling in the elegant old shopping arcade.

Chris loved the strangeness of it all. He offered to take photos until a group of girls wanted a photo *with* him in it and one squeezed his butt. He begged off and hurried out into the square. Outside again, he dodged street performers and restaurant criers waving their menus at the clusters of tourists heading toward the National Museum.

Chris diverted to his favorite pizza stand at the Muzeum metro station, splurged on a half dozen slices, and checked the group chat while he sipped his Kofola and waited for his food. Ondrej had resolved the issue with a wildcard.

@Ondrej: Tresor

@Luca3000: The snob trap? You mad, man?

@Luca3000: Nobody gets in unless you're on the list or that tattooed Mussolini at the door likes your face.

@Klausmodious: We're out then. Nobody likes your face. Too bad. I heard they're doing a live Afro set. I live for that shit coming up from the motherland.

@Luca3000: That's because you hop on whatever trendy shit rolls around. Give me some Detroit any day.

@Klausmodious: 🦕

@Klausmodious: Wait. @BigBird didn't burn that bridge with the bouncer, did he?

@Ondrej: We don't need a pretty face to get in the door tonight, pigeons.

@Ondrej: 🥁

@Ondrej: I'm on the list.

The chat exploded into GIFs and emojis peppered with swearing that amounted to delight, awe, and wonder. How Ondrej, the youngest and newest member of their little merry band, had scored entry to one of the most exclusive underground clubs in the city was going to be a story for the ages.

Chris felt a burst of pride. He knew he'd been right to bring that kid in.

His order came up, and he slammed down two slices before returning to the thread. It had blown up again. He skipped to the end.

@Ondrej: We're doing a reno for Sasha and Geoff. I got started talking with Sasha and it just went from there.

Chris grimaced. How the fuck was Ondrej on a first-name basis with the club owners?

Ondrej worked for Mark's construction company. That meant Mark was doing work for two of the biggest names in the local club scene and he hadn't brought Chris in on the job. That *asshole*.

Klaus pinged him on their private thread.

@Klausmodious: Where the fuck you at?! Shit is going down. We're getting into Tresor.

@BigBird: I don't know, man. That place is played out.

@Klausmodious: Liar. Did the doorman get tired of your pretty face?

@BigBird: No idea what you're talking about.

@Klausmodious: No shade, man. Not all of us can sleep our way to the top. Some have to work for it.

@BigBird: Like getting favors from a buddy's job.

@Klausmodious: Richtig.

@BigBird: Anyway, it's Thursday. Nothing is going on there.

@Klausmodious: Brah. Did you not read? The mill is churning. The who's fucking who is coming out. It's gonna be a scene.

Chris left the one-on-one and returned to the group chat with a sigh. His thumbs hovered. He didn't want to disappoint the crew. He hadn't even lobbied to get into that spot in more than a year, not since Tresor had become a freak show.

@BigBird: 'Bout time you start pulling some weight, Fresh Meat. Tresor it is.

By the time Chris made it home, Isaac was eagerly awaiting his promised trip to the library.

"A cup of tea cures everything." His mom smiled as his oldest nephew bounded off the couch.

Chris knew from experience his mom's teas actually did cure most things.

After an extended visit to the library and a couple of hours cutting hair in the barbershop, Chris flopped onto his bed and passed out before dinner. The flat was quiet when he woke. He checked the clock. Eight. Time to start getting ready. And scoring something to eat.

In the kitchen was a plate of food covered in foil. Mom. Beside it was a shoebox.

He opened it to find Evie's hurried scrawl. PULLED A STRING OR TWO WITH A WHOLESALER.

A new pair of Nikes in his size.

Beneath the plate was an envelope. Barbara's writing was easier to read. SALE WENT BETTER THAN EXPECTED. CONSIDER IT HAZARD PAY.

Inside, a wad of cash promised him a very good night indeed.

Man, his brothers might be a pain in the ass, but their witches were the real deal. He had a very good feeling about tonight.

CHAPTER TWO

MIDWAY THROUGH CLOSING the store for the night, the bell over the door chimed. How naive of her to assume that flipping the sign to CLOSED would be enough to deter customers. Some people just didn't read.

Ofelia bit back a charm that would send them racing out the door—itching feet or a ghostly chill—she didn't need that kind of reputation. The store's popularity was still new enough to make turning anyone away seem risky even if tourists would only buy a few sample sizes that barely justified staying open the extra hour while they left fingerprints on everything. But she had been on her feet for twelve hours, and all she really wanted to do was slide onto her couch cushions with the next episode of *Buona Notte*. The badly dubbed witchy Italian soap opera would have to wait.

"Welcome to Charm Syndicate," she announced without looking up from tidying the counter, forcing an apologetic smile over her exhaustion.

A familiar gust of warm, salt-scented air blew in with her friend's voice, and Ofelia laughed in relief.

"Tell me how you really feel about it, sis?" Ayele Zafeiriou always looked the part of a goddess freshly emerged from the sea with a brief stop at Dolce & Gabbana for the proper outfitting of her luscious curves.

"What are you doing here?" Ofelia eyed the clock as Ayele sailed toward her, then glanced at the group of pedestrians gawking on the street outside, likely considering an approach.

Something about them made her pause. Not the group itself—they were clearly tourists, cameras and all. The tall, lean man in a long coat standing slightly apart caught her eye. For a moment she thought of Chris Vogel—how tall would he be now? Was he still in the city?—but the momentary flash of familiarity died quickly. This man was in his fifties, bearded with long, gray-streaked hair. Though she couldn't see his eyes, the fixed line of his lips was close enough to a sneer to guess at the rest of his expression.

Ayele bussed Ofelia's cheeks quickly, grabbed the shop keys, and returned to the door in time to lock it before the tourists could cross the street.

With a superior smile on her glossy red lips—Dior—Ayele pointed at the shop hours in gold-edged black script on the doorway in Czech and English and then gave a little wave. Below was a current list of upcoming events: classes, trunk shows, and pop-up collaborations.

When Ofelia looked for the man again, the space he'd occupied was empty.

Ayele spun and narrowed her eyes at Ofelia. "You got to start making them work for it. Ex-clu-sive."

Ofelia shook off vague unease. Hers wasn't the only shop in Prague offering humans the opportunity to flirt with the appeal of the supernatural. It might not be a garish tourist trap like the ones closest to the Prague castle grounds, the necromancer Azrael's seat, but some would always object to the shop's presence. Especially the older generations who knew the godswar as more than a history lesson in primary school.

She focused on the more pressing matter—Ayele's unexpected appearance. "I thought you had History of Modernism until seven?"

"Can't a girl get a night off once in a while?" Ayele feigned offense.

"You skipped class?" Ofelia frowned.

Ayele crooned at her reflection, fingers sliding over her smooth scalp approvingly before she met Ofelia's eyes in the glass. "You haven't seen the thread?"

Ofelia scanned the counter for her phone, adding "update social media" to her mental task list for the evening. "It was too busy in here today to be fussing with you all."

Ayele pressed a hand to her chest in horror before snapping her fingers excitedly. "Sis! I need some of that—"

Before Ayele could finish, Ofelia slipped the small glass bottle with the shop's label from the box of custom orders on the counter and handed it over.

"—serum," Ayele crowed, delighted. "You *are* a mind reader."

Ofelia widened her eyes theatrically. "Shh—don't let the word get out. I know my best friend's beauty regime by heart."

"Have your girl out here looking fresh twenty-four seven." Ayele preened.

Ayele did have the most beautiful dark brown skin. Ofelia loved knowing she'd been able to bring out her natural glow with the right combinations of oils and herbal essences, accentuating her gorgeous sea-cool undertones.

Ayele made the vial disappear into her oversized Birkin handbag and whipped out the latest issue of *Botanica Magazine*. She held it up like evidence. "Secret is out now. I see you out here like a big-time lady witch doctor."

The cover of the high-end lifestyle magazine caught the overhead lighting and shone.

Below the magazine title was a shot of the storefront, the window full of plants behind the curling black-and-gold script of the shop name, CHARM SYNDICATE. In the photo, Ofelia leaned in the open doorway, wearing her witchiest broom skirt and felt hat, ankle boots, and a peek-aboo mesh crop top that showed off her toned arms and bright brown skin. It had been a throwaway shot taken on the day of the profile, but the editorial team had loved it.

Seeing herself on the cover still thrilled and terrified her.

Agreeing to have the shop profiled in the magazine had been free advertising, and she'd tried to keep the writer and the photographer focused on the products.

She'd agreed let them use the photo on impulse, heady with the excitement of being valued for the thing she'd built herself. After all she'd lost, she'd managed to rebuild, start her new life in the only city that had ever felt like home.

The panic had come later. She'd done a good job of staying off the radar for almost two years. The fear that she'd once again ruined everything because she just couldn't keep her charm to herself had woken her every night since the magazine came out. The worst had been a reoccurring nightmare of the train station, watching helplessly as the thin boy disappeared under a rain of fists.

If she hadn't shown him his wolf, would they have run together that day?

Where was he now? Ofelia stared at the image of the successful shop owner with an exclusive line of beauty products and designer collaborations. Her image. *What kind of life did he lead, hiding a wolf in his heart?*

She pressed her hand to her lips as her eyes blurred and she forced a laugh. "I would have given you a copy."

"You muss that fine cat eye, Fifi." Ayele dragged a package of tissues from her bag and dabbed at Ofelia's cheeks as though each tear was a personal insult. "Oi, enough waterworks, my darling."

One thing Ayele lacked was sentimentality.

Ofelia's heart swelled with appreciation for the woman who'd come into her life a few weeks after she'd arrived in Prague just over a year ago with only a suitcase and hope for a future. She'd been one part fairy godmother, the other part kindred spirit.

"What am I supposed to spend Iye-mum and Mum's money on?" Ayele tutted as she went back to sampling the new products. "Oh, this smells like tiny little sugar cookies in an English garden."

"Write that down!" Ofelia demanded. Ayele came up with the best product descriptions. Ofelia grabbed the watering can as Ayele scribbled in the notebook kept by the register.

Ofelia had been collecting cast-off cuttings from neighbors and buying her more exotic starts from other hobbyists. Now the monstera nearly touched the ceiling, and the assortment of succulents in pots and hanging baskets of vines and creepers filled the south-facing windows overlooking a narrow cobblestone street. The leaves and greenery parted in the windows in strategic places, revealing displays of new product and limited-edition collaborations.

"You know that setting down roots is only a figure of speech." Ayele grinned.

Ofelia laughed, running her fingers along the edge of the alocasia's face-sized leaf. The plant shivered in greeting.

A knot of dread settled in her stomach, but she breathed it away. "Yele, what's up?"

"Finish putting your baby to bed." Ayele thumbed through her phone. "And then we need to talk." She cranked the music before Ofelia could reply.

Today had been the latest of a steadily increasing run of busy days. Her ability to mix scents and ingredients into homemade skin creams, perfumes, and beauty serums was a perfect cover to exercise her magic— the best lies contained more truth than deception. Custom orders were where she let her charm play. She was going to have to get help soon, at least for the store.

On her way back from locking the jewelry in the safe, she watched Ayele in the homewares corner, reorganizing as she danced to the latest hip-hop electronic DJ out of Lagos. Her friend's blissed-out expression changed with a glance at her phone. Annoyance and concern drew her brows together as she tapped a reply.

The uncomfortable sensation that Ofelia was missing something important needled her. She touched her fingertips together in sequence, asking for assistance. A tiny thread of awareness snapped taut, and she headed to the corner where she'd tucked her phone on a shelf during a fitting and forgotten it. She opened the group text, lost her courage and went back to restocking.

Ayele had introduced her to a few well-connected friends early on. Ofelia carried product from two of them in the store: a former Swedish model with a jewelry business and a Spanish designer. The four of them had hit it off, started going to shows and clubs.

She started restocking carefully curated clothes, sliding them onto the racks, and glanced at the screen, horrified by the number of messages since noon.

@Vikingbabe: Never guess who I ran into last night.

@Vikingbabe: Hint. He was out with that floozy Brigitte.

@Yelele: That's not a clue. She's a lamprey.

@Vikingbabe: Well now she's got a taste for Rat.

The Rat, their nickname for Kenneth.

When she looked up, Ayele was watching her, lower lip pinched between her teeth. "He's been turning up at Tresor."

While they were together, it had become their spot. By the time she opened Charm Syndicate, she knew the club's owners well enough to negotiate having products in the bathrooms, VIP suites, and the gift bags that went to their highest-end clients. She assumed Kenneth spent the time pursuing any number of potential partners, business or otherwise. That had been a failure of imagination on her part. What he'd been up to was so much worse.

She hadn't even been in love. Not like the movies made it out to be. But it turned out broken trust didn't hurt any less than a broken heart.

"Tresor was Kenneth's idea." She knew it sounded like an evasion. "I just wanted to dance. Now the shop is keeping me so busy— I don't have time—"

They'd met at the bar. After the first night, he seemed to be there whenever she turned up. The club did consistently have the best DJs in town.

"He's saying the shop is his—" Ayele began cautiously.

"*My* shop?" Ofelia looked up.

Ayele spared her the rest of the thread. "To keep you... busy."

Ofelia bit her lip hard and turned her attention back to the screen.

Ofelia didn't know whether to laugh or cry. How dare he—especially when he had downplayed the idea of her opening a store from go.

It shouldn't matter. It shouldn't *hurt*. Telling herself that didn't change the facts.

And that was *before* he'd started claiming Charm Syndicate as his idea.

She explored the ache and the anger until she was confident she could speak without screaming. "It doesn't matter. It's over. We're over."

Ayele focused on dusting, but her brows rose.

"What?" Ofelia fought the urge to stamp her foot. She was trying to be the bigger person here. To let it go.

"Given what he's been into these days," Ayele said meaningfully, "I'd think an association wouldn't be desirable."

Charm Syndicate was hers. Her idea. And Ayele was right. That kind of association could drag the things she loved the most—and her future in Prague—into the mud. She wasn't going to let him sully it by association.

She could call him, arrange a meeting. But she knew better than to assume a conversation between them would do it. She'd let being busy in the store sideline her from the social scene, and Kenneth had filled the void with his usual fast-talking nonsense. She needed to be seen. To put distance between them publicly enough to silence any talk. To make it clear to everyone that they were done.

Custom orders would have to wait. "I need to change… and shower."

"Come by my place—I'll order some food," Ayele suggested. "The car will arrive around ten. That gives us enough time to get ready."

"Us?" Ofelia juggled the box, her handbag, and her keys.

Ayele's other hand slipped out to catch the corner before she lost her grip. "I got you, sis."

CHAPTER THREE

As Ofelia took in the line at the door winding around the corner and into the night, a righteous warmth flooded her rib cage. The group-text explosion after she finally weighed in was the tip of the iceberg. No doubt even before she had acquiesced to going out that night, Ayele had been working her own kind of magic.

Like a game of telephone, the word spread.

Ofelia is calling in the squad for a run at that impostor holed up in Tresor would become a headline: *The Queen has Come to Reclaim Her Throne.*

Their car pulled into the loading zone just after midnight. Ofelia leaned toward the door, but Ayele held her back, gesturing for the others to go first.

The blast of camera flash made Ofelia's stomach swim in queasy uncertainty.

Ayele caught her eye and winked. She knew how much Ofelia hated that kind of attention. Maja and Diego loved the limelight—they'd draw off the bulk of the public speculation. After a moment, Ayele nodded and stepped out with one glance back at Ofelia.

"You've got this." She blew her a kiss.

Whatever cameras remained captured the rarely seen scion of one of the wealthiest shipping families in the world. Ayele didn't love notoriety, but she stepped into it, not for herself but to help cement Ofelia's status.

Ofelia counted to seven to settle the buzzing core of energy in her stomach. Letting any of her charm out of her control here would be a disaster.

The lure of Tresor was the potential for illicit encounters with supernatural creatures that the Allegiance publicly disavowed. The real thing would bring the necromancer's security team down on the club so fast no one would escape.

She swung her legs out first, the tall boots and chunky heels a stark contrast to the water-thin silk-and-sequins crop top and skirt combo that fell to mid-thigh and left the length of her shimmering brown legs bare. She'd been captured in glimpses in shadows in the background of photos that ran on the society pages many times over the years. A minor glamour helped, but the lack of connections to any great name or wealth did just as well to obscure her.

A hush had rocketed down the line. The paparazzi chased the big names of her ladies-in-waiting, as they jokingly called themselves, but the crowd knew who the real queen was.

Henny had the door open, his two flunkies holding back the queue that strained for a glimpse of Tresor's most notorious regulars. His stern mouth quirked.

"You've been missed, milady," he drawled.

"Good to be back, Henny." She rose on her toes in invitation. He lowered his chin to permit her to buss his cheeks.

The crowd buzzed with new energy, straining forward as if she'd somehow sedated the king of beasts.

Instead, he turned his stony glare back on them, and they withdrew just as quickly. Tresor's gargoyle, indeed.

The mingled hope and despair of the crowd rose when she slipped into the open door. It slammed shut behind her. It didn't matter when they'd lined up or how long they'd stood at the doors, no one got in without Henny's approval. And he knew how to build a good crowd.

After all, Heinrich "Henny" Graustein, the youngest son of one of the most storied gargoyle families in Bohemia, was the party boy of his clan.

She dropped off her light jacket and slid through the heated red darkness of the hallway, Persephone descending into the bass-soaked underworld.

Underground clubs had sprung up around Prague after the godswar, filling the city's dark nights with gritty, sweaty, euphoric beats. The best DJs from all over the world made Prague a stop on par with Berlin and Stockholm.

As the man responsible for booking acts worked his way down the hall toward them, Ayele bounded forward, pumping her fist to the hyper beats. "Geoff, you got PILA!"

She planted a big red kiss on his cheek before leaving them for the dance floor.

So much for what had brought them there, Ofelia thought. She would much rather be out there than doing all this stupid posturing.

Geoff took Ofelia's hands, bussing her cheeks. "We're so glad you could make it out. I'll have a table ready in a moment—"

"A table?" Diego angled his head. "*Her* table."

"None other." Geoff glanced over her shoulder and nodded to the house manager. "This way."

The VIP tables at Tresor were an entirely different world than the sweaty dance floor below. Here, cool air flowed down the passage, and the decor—the understated luxury of soft velvets—was embraced by metal and concrete dominating the dance floor.

An obscenely large bouquet and a bottle of champagne awaited them.

Ayele reappeared in time to pinch the card between her index and middle fingers with a little shriek. "This boy!"

Ofelia recognized the thick weight of the paper and the logo of the bar owned by Ayele's steady fling.

There'd been a gap in the liquor supply since the mobster Yan Petrov had lost a lieutenant. Rumor had it the lieutenant been caught in violation of the necromancer's codes. Whether at Azrael's hand or his boss's, that would be the last anyone heard of him. Was Sven Erling moving into supplying clubs, or was this just his way of flirting with Ayele?

She sipped to satisfy the toast. It was good champagne. Erling's best, likely. She plucked the card.

Welcome back, Your Majesty. Good seeing you on top again.
—The Earl.

"Optimistic of him." Ofelia sighed, giving in to a little smile.

Ayele reclined on the plush seat at Ofelia's right hand with the confident smirk of a woman who knew where she'd end the night. "When you see him, be a dear, let me know?"

The table afforded them a view of the entire dance floor. It worked both ways though. Ofelia, who had been raised to understand that she would always be watched in certain spaces, knew how to look without appearing to search.

She let the scene below her expand in her vision, the beat consolidating the movement into waves rising and sinking before swelling again. When the music spooled them up, tightening movements before a big drop turned them into a writhing mass of bodies, she cataloged faces and body language, following the range of emotions from chemical-induced ecstasy to ego-fueled confidence to the pure joy of movement. There were fewer and fewer of those these days, and she mourned her place in that change.

When she'd first returned to Prague, she knew the risks of setting up under the necromancer's nose. But the city was the first and last place she'd ever been truly happy. And it was full of supernatural creatures. The ones that could pass for human found creative ways to use their powers while staying within the letter of Azrael's codes. She wanted to build a place of her own among them.

Plus no one from her family would dare reach this far into another necromancer's territory to claim her.

Tresor was one of few places where supernaturals mingled freely with mortals. She'd met Sasha, the club's co-owner, on the dance floor that first night. They'd danced long and hard those first nights amid the sweaty press of thrashing bodies, driving the crowd into a frenzy suitable of the god of merrymaking himself.

"Witch," he accused with a grin during a break.

"Satyr." She returned the challenge.

He seemed pleased to have been found out, and they became fast friends. She was glad to have the company since Kenneth didn't dance. Over bottled water between sets, she learned Sasha was descended from a royal line of satyrs who were no longer physically distinguishable from humans.

"Horns and hooves are a thing of the past, Majesty."

"Does the necromancer know what you have here?" Ofelia grinned.

Sasha shrugged as if he didn't know or didn't care. Most likely the latter. The letter of the law was kept—no supernatural revealed their magic to the humans in their midst. They had enough bouncers on hand —gargoyles and their thralls—to enforce it.

On her second night, he escorted her to the club's finest booth.

Given how quickly Kenneth appeared behind her, he must have been keeping an eye on her after all. Sasha's husband, Geoff, made a rare appearance. In tennis shoes, scruffy jeans, and a polo shirt, he looked every bit the casual tourist he wasn't. Ofelia didn't doubt his blood carried some charm or other. He preferred the business and bookings to the dance floor, though she knew he often watched his husband from the one-way glass in the highest booth.

Near dawn, he walked them to the car he'd called to see them home. When Kenneth left them behind, she slipped an arm through her host's.

"Dwarf?" she asked, not deterred by the fact that he was over six foot tall. Their business acumen was known and feared.

"On my mother's side," he admitted.

Siren on the other, she suspected. But since he didn't volunteer, she let it stay a mystery between them.

"These have been some of the best nights of my life." She glanced back at the club. "I can't begin to tell you how grateful—"

As the car pulled up, he tugged her aside. "Sasha is an excellent judge of character. The table is yours, Majesty, whenever you grace us with your presence."

The words were so formal she understood the vow spoken. Her eyes widened. That table must be worth hundreds of crowns a night—and a powerful bargaining chip to get people in their door. "Why?"

"Reputation is more valuable than coin, as a powerful witchling like yourself surely knows"—he'd kissed her knuckles before winking—"plus it would break my husband's heart if you don't come dance with him often."

They'd given her the table and the crown. Kenneth had merely ridden her success as his own.

Though the music remained on point, the rough edges and inhibition of those original days had been eroded as Tresor rose to prominence. Even the supernaturals had begun to thin out as it became a place to be seen rather than just a safe place to dance. Eventually the good days at Tresor would become collective memory—stories told of the golden time when the scene was held by a queen and her court.

Prague was home again. That was all that mattered. It would be hers even when Tresor faded away.

Now they had to make sure Kenneth wouldn't take Charm Syndicate with it by association.

Scanning the crowd for him, her gaze tripped on a light so bright she squinted against the glare. It came from a man moving on the dance floor, pouring from his chest and flickering like sunlight on water. She sucked in a hard breath.

Heartlight was rare—even less common in these days of necromancers.

"Sis." Ayele's voice reached her as if from a great distance. From the concern in her tone, she'd been calling for a while.

Nodding, Ofelia forced herself to look away from the dance floor. Lingering halos traced the figures around her, but these rippled and glowed, extending out in ribbons of color and light. Auras.

None of the others seemed to notice.

She took advantage of the temporary benefit of secondhand Heartlight vision. Maja's warm ambers and deep orange, Diego's murky blue green. She froze at a glimpse of Ayele's colors—royal violet and golds. Colors she hadn't seen in years.

"You look like you've seen a ghost," Ayele said.

Ofelia wished for a moment she could tell her friend the truth. But none of her friends knew what she was—not even Kenneth. It seemed safest to keep it that way. "It's nothing."

When she cast a glance back over the dance floor, the man—and his Heartlight—had vanished into the crowd. If she focused, it would only take a minute to find him. But she'd have to try. The light that had blinded her a moment before was gone. Hiding Heartlight took magic almost as strong as the light itself.

Ofelia shook her head again, slower. It couldn't have been who she thought it was. Not after all this time.

Then her eye struck a familiar lanky body and bleached-blond, artificially tousled hair. Kenneth.

Ayele kept talking, knowing her words were rolling under Ofelia's awareness and would catch up eventually. "You found Kenneth?"

"This will be quick." Ofelia rose. "Stay here."

CHAPTER FOUR

Klaus, Luca, and Ondrej waited across the street from the club.

The youngest, pale and freckled Ondrej was still growing into his limbs and fairly vibrated in excitement. Luca slouched on the wall with a cigarette, looking out from under his overgrown hair as though revealing anything other than a general ennui might threaten his existence. Towering over the other two, Klaus bobbed to the subtle beat thumping out of the cement and stone walls. He clapped his massive brown hands together when he saw Chris and lunged forward for a hug. Klaus was a force of nature. Seeing him so happy made Chris glad he'd agreed.

They headed past the line winding around the building. It had once been secure government storage, or a bunker, or a detention center, depending on who you asked and what period you inquired about. It had fallen into decay on the edge of the city before being repurposed as one of the many illegal and potentially dangerous places to catch the bleeding edge of the techno scene, though the danger came mostly from the risk of tetanus on a rusty piece of metal or falling through a broken floorboard.

When threats to shut it down gained steam, a couple known for renovating clubs bought it and turned it into a legitimate underground music venue.

A year ago, a group of socialites had begun frequenting the club, bringing with them a gaggle of overdressed hangers-on. Suddenly Tresor was a known entity. Thanks to his mother's protections, Chris would pass for human to all but the most powerful eyes, his second nature dimmed to a faint ripple. But he didn't like knowing many of the nonsupernaturals were there to gawk at his kind. It was a good reminder that no matter how much he liked his friends, there would always be a part of him he had to keep hidden.

Plus with that reputation, it was only a matter of time before the place ran afoul of the necromancer and got shut down. Chris had quit turning up about a year ago.

But for Ondrej and his crew, he'd suffer through one night of outsiders eager to tangle with Prague's supernatural element.

At the door, Henny saw him coming. His big, gorgeous mouth turned down. "Can't do any favors tonight, Blondie—"

Ondrej stumbled to Chris's side, likely propelled by Klaus. "A-a-ahoj. Sir. Name is Kučera. I'm… I'm on the list."

The bouncer's look of surprise was priceless. He kept his long questioning stare on Chris.

Chris took distinct pleasure in lifting his hands innocently. "He's on the list."

Henny didn't check the list himself. He had a flunky—if another Garg topping six foot three and almost three hundred pounds of muscle could be considered a flunky—for that. The second nodded.

Henny crossed his arms over his chest and shifted his weight to let them pass. "Welcome to Tresor, Mr. Kučera."

His flunky handled the rope.

Chris went last, pursing his lips slightly as he passed. The curves of the bigger man's horns were just a suggestion in the salt-and-pepper hair. "Getting a little shaggy on the top, Henny. Come by my chair for a trim sometime. My treat." He left the bouncer behind them shaking his head in amusement.

Most thought Henny was a humorless slab of muscle—or stone, depending on what state he was in. Chris liked knowing he'd tapped into the Garg's lighter side. He was glad they'd parted on good terms. That was always his goal.

The club was in session. It was early—just after midnight—and there was barely standing room. His crew packed in tight formation at the opening to the main hall: Ondrej and Luca in front, Klaus and Chris on the outside, where they could keep an eye on the other two.

A light show drenched the dance floor and bar in stark, flickering colors. Klaus passed a hand over his bare skull, his amazed whistle lost in the din of music and the screaming crowd. But he caught Chris's gaze, and Chris knew what the bigger man was thinking at the sight of the shining rainbow of skin under glittering lights, moving as one to the beat.

The hostess—a muscular, olive-skinned Garg in a crop top and low-slung, faded jeans arrived to tag them.

"Left arms, boys." She favored Luca and Ondrej with a sexy smirk as she traced a finger along the sensitive skin below the heel of each hand and winked at Klaus.

Chris ignored the jostling from his crew as the thick gold bands appeared around their wrists. The bands seemed close enough to ink except for the shimmer and would fade the moment they stepped out of the club according to the letter of the necromancer's codes. But little shows of power like this gave legitimacy to the whispers that the club was more than just a hot spot for music.

"Show-off." Chris bussed her cheeks when she focused on him. "Looking good as always, Ange."

She stepped in closer. "It's been too long, handsome."

He settled his hands on her hips. Her fingertips curled around the curves of his ears in a familiar caress.

Chris knew he'd get shit from the other guys for his ease with her later. But casting a spell to protect his ears would cost her more than the bands. She'd saved him having to stuff dense foam plugs into his ears to make the volume tolerable to Woof. He never took the courtesy for granted, and he was happy to lend her strength.

When she stepped back, the throbbing din of music dimmed to thickened beats, though voices remained clear, relieving his sensitive ears.

"You're at table twelve. Have fun, boys."

She had barely faded into the crowd when Ondrej and Luca began bouncing, hollering like a couple of newbies. Klaus rolled his eyes at Chris, but he was grinning too. Ondrej was probably red as a tomato, but the lighting was shifting too fast to tell.

"Table! A table." An amateur boxer, Luca delivered a round of companionable body shots. "Look at this fucking kid."

Chris shook him off. "I'll catch up."

He moved into the press of bodies, unsurprised to find Klaus behind him. Chris could always count on Klaus to hit the floor first. One memorable road trip and seventy-two nearly sleepless hours in four Berlin clubs had cemented the friendship that was the heart of their little band.

Tonight he gave himself over to the beat without a shred of reserve. He rose with the snare-heavy buildup, and when the beat dropped again, he dissolved into the sound. His chest expanded, rib cage full of breath and sensation until it took everything in him to keep from throwing his head back and howling. In his chest, Woof threw up his head and sang for him.

The music lifted him, transporting him, removing the lingering annoyance with his brothers. The music carried him to a state of transcendence, alighting in his bones. He wondered if this was how his sister felt when she danced.

His skin prickled with recognition. Woof rose in his chest. He spun, searching for the source of that sensation in the crowd. There were a few witches out tonight. He recognized some from the gatherings at his mother's studio, but this was like hearing a song he'd forgotten he once knew by heart. He angled his head toward the edge of the floor. Klaus nodded.

"What's with you and the bouncer?" Klaus shouted when they were clear of the press.

He shook his head. "Henny?"

"No, the other one." Klaus laughed.

Chris shrugged. "Ange's cool, got to know her when Henny and I were on and off."

Garg society was particularly insular; even familial connections were rarely disclosed.

"Maybe you could put in a good word for me?" Klaus speculated as they approached the rope blocking off the tables.

Chris raised a brow. "She could break you in half."

Klaus grinned. "Exactly."

"Your funeral."

He paused at a familiar face moving through the crowd toward the bar.

A ghost.

Recognition punched the center of his chest. It couldn't be. Ghosts didn't age. And she had definitely grown up—the childish roundness in her face had given way to sleek angles and a small, determined chin. But her eyes were the same, and she still wore braids, now twisted into a complicated updo that resembled a crown.

"You coming?" Klaus punched his shoulder as a bouncer opened the rope for them.

"In a minute. I think I saw someone I know." A whiff of citrus and fennel reached him, confirming his suspicion.

"Why am I not surprised?" Klaus laughed and tossed Chris a water bottle from the cooler sitting inside the VIP area. "Happy hunting."

Chris washed the tightness out of his throat, then cut back through the crowd, chasing that scent. He'd never thought it possible to feel winded and amped up all at once. He ignored a couple of long, speculative glances as he passed.

Excitement thrummed beneath Chris's collarbones. He splayed a hand over his own chest as if he could keep the wolf in. He had her trail now, no mistaking it. After all this time.

A hand grabbed his arm. He was so focused he'd dragged the hand's owner a few steps before he realized he was towing a human like a coat thrown over his arm. He spun, frustrated to be dragged off his trail.

A familiar bleached-blond man about his height removed his hand. "Sorry, man, I called your name."

There were few former lovers Chris counted as mistakes. This jackass was at the top of the list.

The guy preened a little, trying to get his attention. "You block my number, precious?"

With every breath, she was moving away from him in the crowd. He didn't have time for this shit. "I don't know what you want, Kenneth. We're done."

The nearby onlookers had slowed to watch, rubberneckers at the scene of an accident.

"Oh, don't be a tease."

The man's phony British accent sent Chris over the edge, and he whirled on him, the low rumble in his chest becoming a wolf's snarl.

Kenneth recoiled. He wasn't the only one. Someone shrieked. The scent of fear filled Chris's nose, crowding out the fennel and citrus.

Fuck. Now he'd made a scene.

"Do I know you?" Just like that, the ghost appeared between them, her palm pressed against the center of his chest, her chin tilted up to give him a tiny conspiratorial smile.

The whole universe narrowed to that single point of contact. He took in everything about that hand—the long, blunt-tipped fingers adorned between the joints in a collection of delicate rings of hammered gold and twisted braids of silver, her nails filed to perfect crescent moons and shining with some sort of iridescence. An assortment of gold bangles danced at her wrist when he took in a big breath, confirming by scent what his mind told him was impossible.

I would know you anywhere, he wanted to say, but the words got stuck somewhere between his heart and his mouth.

That touch, warm and firm against cloth, rippled through him, claiming him. Woof rose against it, and for a split second her eyes widened. Even in the humid, packed room, she managed to be immaculate, dressed in some shimmering fabric that looked like it would disintegrate with a touch.

Around them, the crowd dispersed. The fennel built in her scent—magic. She was doing something to make them lose interest, he realized.

Before he could muster a response, Ange appeared through the lingering onlookers.

The gargoyle's gaze moved warily between the three of them before settling on Ofelia. "Everything okay here?"

Ofelia nodded, withdrawing her hand. She held it closed a moment too long, fingers curled into her palm as though trying to hold on to something. It took everything in him not to grab it and press it back to his chest to let his heartbeat tell her what he couldn't find the words to say. Nothing mattered, not the time or the distance or the club.

"Would you make sure my friend has a fresh drink?" Ofelia let her hand fall. "Please put it on my tab." Her eyes narrowed on the lanky blond. "We have some business to discuss."

Ange stepped into his line of sight, her smile too tight. "Let's go get that drink, Christof."

To gargoyles, names were sacred, which was why they gave everyone nicknames for common use. When a Garg dropped your name, you moved. Still took everything in him to obey—but he had enough sense left to heed her.

At the bar, Ange chased a guy nursing an empty off a stool, then whistled for the bartender. She crowded Chris into the stool, blocking his escape. "You out of your mind, kid?"

"Don't call me that."

"I'm old enough to be your great-grandmother." She shook her head, pushing the newly arrived beer at him. "Drink."

The gargoyle clans were tight-knit, their society closed to outsiders. Rumor had it Sasha had called in a centuries-old favor to get Henny and half of his family at the club. He also paid them a small fortune for the honor.

Ange had done Chris a favor by not throwing him out on his ass for riling up the crowd. A ban from Tresor might not matter to him in the long run, but his place in the larger community of supernaturals did.

Humbled, he rubbed his hand over his hair. "I wasn't gonna—"

"You sure can pick them. That guy is on Henny's shit list." She sighed, a wry twist at the corner of her mouth. "I don't even know how the fuck he got in here. Did he hurt you?"

"I don't need you to protect me." He scowled, sipping his beer petulantly.

"I know." She laughed. "But I also know that you don't have the sense not to mess with people you have no business messing with."

"That doesn't—"

"Not everybody is ready to fall in love with you at first sight." She smiled and tousled his already-ruined hair. "And some people don't deserve the chance."

"I don't give a shit about Kenny. That wi—" He caught himself. "Woman."

"How do you know Fifi?" Ange's expression held exasperated amusement, as if keeping up with human relationships was as complicated as he'd once found sorting gargoyle families. "The *three* of you—"

"Ofelia." He corrected her, purely being stubborn. "And no. I knew her when we were kids."

"Well, she did you a favor, calming down the crowd like that, so she must like you." She sighed, arms folded. "But if she has business with that jackass, it's none of yours."

He started off the barstool. No way he was leaving her to deal with that slime bag alone.

Ange planted a hand on his shoulder and involuntarily seated him.

"You just said Kenneth was no good." Chris flung out an arm in frustration.

"Listen close," Ange said. "Sasha and Geoff love Ofelia because she brings in her rich-ass party friends, which keeps the necromancer at bay until they're finished with this place. Kenneth will posture a bit, but he knows she's off-limits now that she gave him the boot. She'll take care of her business. Trust. She's a good kid, sort of like someone else I know. We keep an extra-close eye on the good ones."

He rolled his eyes at her, stuffing his annoyance under the knowledge that he should be flattered any member of a gargoyle clan gave a shit about him. "Why are you looking out for me? Did Henny—"

"My brother acts tough, but he's got a heart like a marshmallow." Her smile turned a little sad. "You let him down easy. I respect that. That practically makes you family."

"You've got a weird sense of family."

"You're one of ours now, handsome. Suck it up." She grinned, canines a bit too sharp for her otherwise human mouth. "I'm too busy tonight to babysit. Enjoy the beer, then go find the table I procured for you boys."

Again, the not insignificant sign of her favor struck him. He nodded obediently. But the tug to Ofelia was unbearable.

He started to rise once she'd faded back into the crowd. A triad of identical good-looking, exceptionally fit men in black collared shirts and slacks coalesced from the shadows. Garg thralls. Great. Undoubtedly they'd been assigned to him for the duration of his visit. Ange wasn't kidding. He sank back onto the stool and faced his beer, hoping Ofelia would leave enough scent behind to follow later.

She was in the city, and she had been for at least a year. Right under his nose. Now that he knew, there was no way he'd let her get away again.

CHAPTER FIVE

Ofelia wasn't the girl in the train station anymore. But even if the wolf hadn't risen in greeting when her palm settled over his heartbeat, she would have known the man.

The echo of that contact reverberated in her like a struck bell. Nothing mattered, not the club or the store or Kenneth finally in her sights. The slope of muscle pressing against her palm became her singular focus.

Chris Vogel had always been taller than the other kids their age. Back then, his gangling limbs and large head made him seem as substantial as a dandelion puff. Now he was a full head taller than she, but lean muscle slung along his long limbs and filled out the plain white T-shirt in ways that trapped her gaze. A face that had been an adorable mismatch of features had grown together in pleasingly angular ways like the rest of him, with piercing eyes and lips that begged contact with skin.

She'd kissed those lips impulsively fourteen years ago. It was all she could do not to tip herself up on her toes and find out if he still tasted like gummy bears and sunshine. Her body flushed pleasantly, and her mouth went dry at the sight of his throat bobbing just inches away. Threads of warmth radiated up through her palm with his inhale, boosting the calming charm she'd subtly woven through the crowd. She drew her hand away in shock at the confirmation of the light she'd seen across the dance floor.

Heartlight.

For the first time she regretted severing her connection to the ones who might know how a shifter had a *witch's* charm. He also clearly had history with Kenneth. Two guesses which that would be. Even without the Heartlight's clear brilliance, she could tell he was clean of any substances. That meant it was the other thing.

The universe had a sense of humor after all.

Then Ange cut through the crowd, and Ofelia focused on what she'd come for. Kenneth.

Still, she couldn't resist the temptation to see if the view was as nice going as coming.

"I know, he's fun to watch." Kenneth smirked and gazed around them at the packed club. "Is all this for me, dollface?"

Ofelia's molars ground together, but she kept her voice light. "Apparently I didn't make myself clear."

"Did you expect me to dig myself a hole and crawl in it?" The corner of his mouth dragged up, and he folded his arms over his chest.

The fitted, shiny blue shirt was one she hated. Ayele said it made him look like a gigolo. Part of her longed for her friend's presence. The other woman wouldn't have given him any quarter.

Ofelia was alarmed to find it was still a struggle to turn off the place in her that had once cared if he was eating and sleeping. No matter how much she tried, she couldn't forget that once she had slept in his arms, laughed herself breathless against his chest, and worst of all, shown him her tears.

"Banished by the queen?" He sneered, and when his eyes narrowed, she wondered if she'd just been one of his marks the whole time. "You forget who put your skinny ass on the throne."

She kept silent, hoping whatever poison he spewed would finally burn away the last of her sympathy.

"Consider it a parting gift." He spread his arms and bowed mockingly. "But make no mistake about whose kingdom this is, milady."

Oh, she was the biggest kind of fool. Ofelia let the realization of who he was—what he was—roll around so she would never forget this moment. Then she leaned in, lowering her voice. "Keep it. But if you don't stop trying to take credit for the store I built with my two hands, by closing, Geoff and Sasha will know what you've been doing here. You'll be lucky if they let you on the same side of the street after I tell them everything."

"How naive are you, sweetheart?" His lip lifted in disgust. "Do you think between the Gargs and the thralls, there's a second of what goes on in here that they don't know about?"

She refused to react. They'd been together for nine months, just long enough for his mask to slip and reveal what he really was. She knew his tells by heart.

His eyelid didn't twitch now. His gaze stayed locked on hers. Instead, his smirk grew. The one that came out when he had a winning hand. "You're good for business, dollface. Mine and theirs. Enjoy your little shop."

A slender brunette with bright green eyes materialized from the crowd and plastered herself to his side. Brigitte, of course.

"I'll be right with you, duchess." Kenneth never broke eye contact with Ofelia. "Just wrapping up some old business."

Ofelia's throat felt tight, hot. Outrage swelled in the space between her throat and her cheeks, strangling her attempts to respond. Her fingers twitched, longing to place the charm she'd prepared as backup in case talking to him came to nothing. She never used her magic to change people's minds if she could help it. But an exception to the rule might be in order.

"Unless, of course, you're having second thoughts." Kenneth peered at her. "I miss you, love. We were good together. It's not too late to come home. You can join us— What's the name again, duchess?"

"Brigitte." The brunette's feline gaze roamed Ofelia head to toe.

No, she decided. She wouldn't stoop so low. He wasn't worth wasting her charm on.

"He's all yours," she called airily before meeting Brigitte's eyes.

Ofelia didn't wait for her expression to change or for Kenneth's reply. She stalked away, taking the silence with her. She thought she heard Kenneth's chuckle, but it sounded weak. That wasn't nearly satisfying enough.

CHAPTER SIX

OFELIA DIDN'T REALIZE where her feet had taken her until she was admiring familiar shoulders doing obscenely pleasant things to a white T-shirt and the mess of curly waves on the back of Christof Vogel's head. He was subtly framed by thralls—Ange's version of a time-out—but he wasn't nursing his wounds. As the bartenders moved from order to order, more than one paused for glancing conversation. They all looked happy to see him. She knew the feeling.

She ignored the thralls and slid into the gap their presence had created between him and everyone else.

He looked over as she planted her elbows on the bar's surface. She realized her mistake a second too late. Too much time hanging out in the spotless VIP lounge. By this time of night, the main-floor bartenders had given up on the war against the inevitable stickiness.

His surprise turned to a wince when he glanced at her elbows. "Good luck detaching yourself from that."

Ofelia groaned, laughing. The corner of his mouth rose in answer. It was impossible to tell the color of his eyes in the shifting light of the bar. Were they the stormy North Sea she remembered?

"I got you." He leaned over the bar, plucking a towel.

Whoever he had become in the intervening years, he had the favor of bartenders as well as the bouncers. That was his second move of the night that would have gotten anyone else booted.

The nearest bartender waved a chastising finger at him and went back to his shaker.

Ofelia extracted herself from the bog and accepted the towel to clean her forearms. "What are you drinking?"

"Something this beautiful girl I used to know bought me before she gave me the brush-off to go fight with her ex."

Me, she thought, the flush rising again. He means me. It shouldn't have made that giddy hopeful feeling rise in her chest, should it? "Is it any good?"

"It's Belgian." He contemplated the label. "I don't hate it."

He angled the bottle her direction. The temptation was strong. But with her charm, drinking from his bottle would be as intimate as a kiss. She wasn't sure she was ready for that.

She was saved by the appearance of the bartender.

The bartender raised a brow, likely surprised to see her at the bar for more than a hello on her way coming or going.

"I'll have what he's having." Ofelia waved in the general direction of the bottle before looking at Chris. "Another one?"

Chris shook his head. "I'm good."

The bartender returned with a pint glass and a bottle. He poured and took the bottle away.

"Fancy." Chris raised a brow.

"Shut up." She laughed. "Thanks, Matz."

Chris tried to offer his seat, but she waved it off. He cleared his throat. "So that guy."

"Kenneth?"

"That one." Chris tilted the beer neck again, unable to meet her eyes.

Ofelia focused on her glass. "We had kind of an open arrangement."

His head snapped up, and his look was sharp. His nostrils flared, his anger on her behalf. "An open arrangement is where everyone knows what's up and is cool with it."

She took a long swallow of beer to distract herself from the twinge of self-pity. Mistake. She still hated beer. Its country of origin didn't change her opinion on the matter. She slid the glass aside. "If it helps, you weren't the first."

"It was just the once." He glared over the bar. "I was at his place. After, I saw all the stuff in the bathroom. Your stuff? He said what his girlfriend didn't know wouldn't hurt him. I blocked him."

"That's probably a good thing." He was just as determined as she remembered, bound by his own rules. It was surprisingly endearing. "How did you know it was mine?"

"I didn't know it was yours. It smelled a little like you." Now he looked a little embarrassed, his gaze skating away from her and back. "But your scent's changed. You've changed."

"You're a lot taller than I remembered." It sounded stupid, but how could she possibly do any better with him acting like he couldn't stop looking at her even if he wanted to?

"Fourteen years." He tipped his beer up.

He didn't mention the day at the train station. Or demand to know where she'd been all this time. No talking about the past. No fledgling witch. No wolf cub. Just two adults in a club who simultaneously discovered an unfortunate mutual connection.

He'd grown into something beautiful—wild in the middle of a city so old it had forgotten what wilderness was. His long limbs were too graceful to be purely human. It was completely mesmerizing. She bet he could dance. Arousal stirred under her breastbone for the first time since she'd walked away from Kenneth.

A flush of embarrassed hindsight hit her. He'd been *with* Kenneth. Just because she'd kissed him when they were kids didn't mean he was interested in her. She bit her lip.

Before she could write off her response as a potent combination of pheromones and nostalgia, his gazed hitched on her mouth long enough to make her skin tingle.

Oh. No need to worry about that then.

"Is he still watching us?" He set down his bottle and swung the stool away from the bar to face her. His legs were so long he had to drop his heels from the rail to avoid bumping her with his knee.

So he hadn't missed Kenneth and Brigitte on the other end of the long bar either.

She lowered her chin in a tiny nod and stepped between his thighs. He settled his massive feet on either side of hers.

"What do you want to do about it?" He canted his head like a curious pup. The light did incredible things to the line of his jaw, the arc of his cheekbone.

Hex him into next month was on the tip of her tongue. But she couldn't say that in public even if she was with the one person in the club who might find the thought as amusing as she did. An unexpected rush of relief washed over her. No need to hide what she was as she had with Kenneth. Did she imagine the answering relief in his gaze?

She shifted her weight to one leg until the outside of her calf pressed against the inside of his. The rough fabric of his pants—Canvas? Denim? —wasn't thick enough to mute the heat of his body or disguise of the flex of muscle in response to her touch. She leaned into his space, pursing her lips. "Throw this beer into his face?"

"Damn, girl." He narrowed his eyes like he was just beginning to suspect she was a little bit dangerous. And liked it.

"Ange would probably object." She mock frowned.

"She most definitely would." He closed the distance a little more. He'd been dancing and was damp at the hairline and under his lightly furred jaw. She wondered how he tasted. "Next option."

His eyes traveled down to where her bare leg met his jeans and then back up, slowly. Very slowly. The intensity in that stare seemed to burn the oxygen from the room. She was shocked every single person didn't drop to the floor unconscious. As it was, she felt far too lightheaded for having barely touched a beer. His gaze hitched on her hips, her breasts, her shoulders, her neck, her mouth, and settled on her eyes.

Certainly every bit of liquid in the air had been vaporized between them because her mouth was suddenly bone-dry.

He smiled slowly. "The suspense is killing me."

She finished her beer and set it on the bar beside his. Then she held out a hand. "Let's dance."

CHAPTER SEVEN

So this was how they were going to play it.

If she wanted to flirt like strangers and dance away the flicker of hurt that lingered in her eyes, he would do his best to keep up. And when she was done, he would be there.

The thralls reappeared, coalescing as if from the humid air itself. Ange bled from the crowd, focused on Ofelia. He couldn't see Ofelia's face, but something in it must have made the Garg back off, though she tossed him a warning glare as they passed.

He wanted to tell Ange he'd be just fine never setting foot in Tresor again if it meant Ofelia was back in his life. He settled on a wink and a smile.

With a twist of Ange's fingers, the thralls faded again. They weren't really people, but they functioned well enough as extensions of the Garg's eyes and ears. She raised a brow at him in an unmistakable plea. *Be careful, you idiot.*

Maybe. But what would be the fun in that?

Ofelia tossed a look over her shoulder as they stepped onto the dance floor. "Ange likes you."

"Gods only know why." He grinned.

With her gaze on him, Ofelia couldn't see the thrashing bodies bound for a collision. Chris did. His palm settled at the sliver of skin exposed at her waistline, tugging her backward into his chest. At the same time, he shifted his body into the gap so the dancer crashed into him instead. With his feet braced, he absorbed the impact easily.

The guy reeked of sweat and alcohol. He glared up at Chris as if wondering where the mountain had come from and deciding if it wanted a fight.

Chris gave him an oblivious grin. "Good night, yeah?"

The guy blinked a few times as the tension fled and he tried to figure out what came next.

"Bar's that way." Chris angled his head. "Cheers, mate."

The guy nodded and shuffled off.

Chris was not surprised to see a thrall fall into step with the drunken man. Ange would take care of that one in a minute.

When he returned his focus to Ofelia, she was staring up at him, eyes round with surprise. He smiled. "You good?"

Her gaze fell to his hand.

He belatedly registered the skin of her belly against his palm—warm and unbearably soft. His fingers flexed gently against the curve of her inhale. Wanting for her rocketed through him. He ached with it.

He won the war of self-control and started to withdraw.

She caught his hand, settling his palm at her side instead. "Thanks."

His fingers flared along her hip. The spangles of her dress were like barbed wire after that soft expanse of skin, but he'd be damned if he let go now.

"Onward." Her left cheek plumped in an enchanting half smile as she dropped his other hand to her opposite hip. "Stay close—don't want to lose you."

He had no intention of letting that happen. *Never again.*

She led the way through the wall of sound to the perfect spot in the center of the mass, close enough to see the DJ.

They moved together under the lights, bodies in charge as the beat dropped and rose again. He was proud of himself for ignoring the way her breasts heaved against his rib cage with every breath. Her attention was elsewhere.

He followed her gaze. Somehow she'd found Kenneth in the crowd. Irritation twitched at the edge of his consciousness. She still seemed to think he was worth giving a shit over.

Time to give her something else to focus on. His fingertips slid over the gap in her dress, and it was all too easy to imagine if there were no fabric in the way as he tugged her close and spun her around him.

She laughed, closed her eyes, and surrendered to the beat until he was pretty sure she wasn't conscious of anything but her own experience. Her hips matched each rhythmic chunk of beat, and falling in with her felt natural.

Soon he wasn't the only one moving with her—the dancers around them started to sync to her movements. He would have felt her intentionally casting, the way he did when Barbara twitched her fingers and came up with a lost book or paper. This was something instinctive. It spread outward in concentric rings with her at their center until they were all moving as one. The sync drew the energy in the room like the beat did for bodies, gathering it up and sending it back out over them all until the entire room surged and the crowd roared. There was no drug that could match this high. The DJ ate it up, sending back a mix worthy of the ecstasy before him.

Klaus and a beautiful dark-skinned girl drifted over. She gave Ofelia a hip bump.

She opened her eyes with a smile of pure pleasure. "Yele!"

While the girls were doing their thing, Klaus jerked his chin in Ofelia's direction. "You two need to get a room."

Chris laughed, brow raised as he scoped out Yele. "So should I not mention you to Ange?"

"Don't do me like that." Klaus shook his head. "I'm hedging my bets."

Ofelia slid back into the space between them, tossing a little smile at Klaus. "Can I borrow your friend for a bit?"

"You're doing me a favor, taking him off my hands." Klaus spread his palms and did a neat little spin, taking him back into the shorter woman's orbit.

Chris protested, but Ofelia settled an arm around his neck and the skin-to-skin contact captured his attention. She gazed up at him through dark lashes, and he saw none of the previous hurt lingering in her eyes. "Your friend?"

"We met in Berlin a couple of years ago." He scooped her close, hips swaying in time to the beat, legs in a tangle, her cheek against the damp collar of his T-shirt. "He's a good guy. He'll take care of her."

"I'm more worried about him." She looked up at him with an incredulous expression. Chris broke off, making like he was going for Klaus. Laughing, Ofelia hooked his waistband, dragging him back. "She won't hurt him."

"Good, 'cause I'm more worried about me right now anyway." He turned his break off into a dip, circling her into him, chest to back. Her bare shoulders were slick, and the curve of her neck smelled of tangerines.

"As you should be." A smile played at the full curves of her lips as she found his eyes again over her shoulder. "Wanna get out of here?"

His blood leaped, hammering in his veins, but he nodded. "Since you asked nicely."

"I did, didn't I?" She slipped a hand under his, lacing their fingers together.

It was better this way—they'd get out of this club, he could find out where she'd been hiding from him for so long. They could talk. He would tell her how much it meant to have her back.

She waved at Ayele. Her friend blew them a kiss.

Ofelia led him through the crowd, arrowing toward the red glow of the hall leading out of the underworld into the night above. She didn't look back, not once, trusting him to follow. He kept his eyes on the slim braid that had worked its way free of her crown and now bounced between her shoulder blades to the curve of her ass.

Ange smiled as they passed, shaking her head at him as if impressed. She tossed him a light length of fabric that carried Ofelia's scent. "Don't be a stranger."

On the street, the gold band faded from his wrist the minute they hit the cool, predawn air, along with Ange's spell. Night sounds returned to him—the dull bass thumping within the walls, distant traffic, and the ringing bell of the late tram. Even in the heart of the city where the sun still baked the pavement all day, the nights had gone crisp and shockingly chill. Especially after the heat of the club.

Chris was fine—he burned like a furnace most of the time. The wolf in his blood.

Ofelia shivered a bit in that scrap of an outfit. She grinned, rueful. "We had a car on the way over."

He lifted the fabric, shaking out to reveal a short jacket.

Ofelia's eyes lit. "I thought I'd forgotten that."

"Ange hung on to it for you." He helped her slide into it. "Better?"

She did a little twirl on the pavement, laughing, and for a moment he was a boy again and she was the first person who had ever made his heart lurch in his chest.

Chris took a deep breath, his heart hammering with anticipation of what came next. The moment he took Ofelia in his arms and told her how much she meant to him, that it didn't matter that time and life had driven them apart. He was her wolf, always had been, always would be.

When she stopped spinning, all he could do was stare. Saliva pooled in his mouth. His heart wasn't the only part of him that wanted her.

She took his hands, tugging. "Dance with me!"

It should have been ridiculous, dancing on the emptying street, late-night revelers leaving the club staring at the spectacle they made. He couldn't be bothered to care. He picked up the beat and swept her along with him. Her feet left the ground as they spun, and her arms wrapped around his neck. When his steps slowed, she slid down his chest until they were eye to eye again, her toes kicking above the pavement.

And instead of everything he wanted to say, he whispered the only thing he thought of. "Kiss me."

Her lips were soft and warm with surrender. He took his time because kissing her was his new favorite thing in the world. He'd never been much for alcohol or drugs—neither lasted long enough in his system to be worth it—but he was high on the feeling of her weight against him. Drunk on the taste of her in his mouth.

Hoots and catcalls on the street finally reached them.

She smiled, cheeks hot, but did not pull away. Chest to chest, she widened her eyes as if she could feel the wolf doing somersaults inside his ribs. "Come home with me?"

CHAPTER EIGHT

HOME WAS a one-bedroom flat above a storefront near the national theater. He didn't register much more than that as he followed her into the building and up the stairs, mostly because she had her hands all over him. Slim, nimble fingers under his shirt, in his hair, tugging at the loops of his jeans. He groaned, sliding her into the wall with a little thud and dragging a hand down the curve of her low back to cup her ass.

She snickered, a finger between them, pressed to her lips.

He angled his head. "Lead on."

Tangling her fingers in his, she dragged him down the hall, unlocking the door. She murmured something, and the prickly sensation of wards eased to a faint tingle at her command to recognize him.

Then she was on him again, fierce and demanding, yanking him into the darkened hallway.

He liked her all demanding like this. There was no question what she wanted—namely, him and clearly, naked. Both of those things were very high on his list of current needs as well. Really, he had zero complaints.

But there was something detached in her single-mindedness. He couldn't shake the feeling this was happening in a hurry, and he wasn't sure what the rush was for. She was too busy trying to get his shirt over his head while dragging him down the hall to what he presumed would be a room with some flat surfaces. He wasn't picky.

When she almost headbutted him trying to get to their shoes, he decided to put on the brakes. "Hey. Slow down."

He wanted this, but he also wanted that moment after the kiss on the street, when her breath had hitched and her eyes went a little crossed.

That response unleashed something powerful in him. He wasn't willing to sacrifice what it took to get her completely undone just to get in her pants as quickly as possible.

She kept tugging at him, still making demands. "Shh."

"Hang on." He hit the wall with a little oof when she jumped on him.

Enough of this already. He wasn't a pup anymore to be put in place. He lifted her off her feet, spinning to reverse their positions. Between the wall and his chest, she gasped, legs automatically going around his waist and hiking that dress up well beyond the point of decency. His arousal sprang to painful levels of intensity at the feel of her, already soaked through her underwear and pressed against his abs.

"Fi." Her name rumbled from his chest.

She ground against him, impatient.

A little gasp escaped her when he caught both her wrists and pinned them over her head. He growled and set his teeth to her neck below the jaw—not hard enough to mark but firm enough to get her attention. Reminding her he wasn't a human toy.

Her heartbeat raced against his tongue, and he felt her thick swallow. His free hand cupped her ass, holding her in place.

"Chris?" She whimpered.

He released his bite, licking softly until he reached her mouth again. Their eyes met. "Kiss me."

Kiss me.

Ofelia bristled, arched in challenge, but his grip was firm and stronger than she'd accounted for. That was the wolf. She'd let herself forget what he was even as she'd disarmed her wards to let him into her sanctuary. She'd never subscribed to the old enmity between their kinds—she'd seen how different it could be between shifters and witches—but she'd always known not to underestimate a shifter's strength and their resistance to magic.

She'd been thinking of him as a grown-up version of the boy in the train station. The boy who had taken a beating so that she could get away was gone. But this was a man who knew exactly what he was and how to use it to get what he wanted.

A little shiver raced up her spine as she met his eyes—no longer the bright gray of the Atlantic on a cloud-spattered day but something darker and far more intense. She recognized the searching.

"Don't make me ask again," he murmured, brushing her jaw with his lips just hard enough for her to feel teeth.

Another shiver. She had never been into dominance play, but this was definitely doing something for her. "That didn't sound like a request."

"Please," he demanded.

It was only a kiss. Warm slide of full lips against her own, slick tongue and the glance of teeth as it deepened. It shouldn't wreck her the way it did. She was almost convinced she wasn't affected until she heard the soft, needy little mewling noise that must have come from her own throat. She hadn't even realized he'd released her wrists and she'd locked her arms around his neck.

And the whole time his mouth moved over hers with the kind of uncrushable inevitability of the tide. She followed the angle his mouth led until she was completely open to his exploration, willfully defenseless. And the spiky desire that had been building up in her unraveled to something else, spreading and stretching, taffy-like, through her limbs and into her core.

When his lips settled over her jaw, moving toward her hairline, she sighed. An answering growl left him as he nipped her earlobe. "There."

The word, spoken without a drop of urgency, burned through her intensity. Stubbornness made her push back against him. There was no hesitation in the way he pressed her into the wall and sank his teeth gently into her lobe, pinning her again.

"What do you need?" he growled.

She coughed a laugh. He knew good and goddamn well what they were here for, what she wanted. And yet her breath caught on the words. He was good enough to bite down so she could tell herself her inability to speak was from being overwhelmed with sensation. He released, licking the spot he'd just bitten.

"I'll tell you what I want," he murmured into her gasping silence. "I want you to tell me what you like, and when, and how much of it. You can stop when I make you come so hard you don't remember how to speak."

The words left her shuddering and gasping. "Christof Vogel."

"You remember my name." He chuckled softly, breath rasping against the sensitive hairs at the base of her neck.

She snorted. "Of course I remember your—"

His teeth closed, just shy of a mark, and she squeaked.

"Yes!" she yelped.

"Like that?"

"That," she echoed dumbly, pressing back against him.

He groaned, then chuckled and buried his face against the curve of her neck so the words panted out against the slope beneath her collar. "Gods, you have the most amazing body. Watching you all night, feeling you up against me. I want to put my hands all over you. Can I?"

"Please," she whimpered as his fingers stroked the curve of her ass, kneading softly.

"What?"

"Clothes," she panted. "Off."

He hummed softly, a little victory for them both, and she pulled his chin up.

"Kiss me." She turned the tables on him saucily.

She expected him to resist, to challenge her. Instead, he crushed his mouth on hers, giving her everything without an ounce of restraint.

Distantly she felt the skirt work up over her hips, her shoulders pulling away from the wall just enough to drag it higher. The whole time he supported her easily. Her feet never touched the floor. That lean body was stronger than it looked.

When he made good on his promise, her skin came alive at each sweep of fingers and palms. It was as if only her mind had been in it before, and every touch stroked her body into the equation as he anchored her in sensation and connection. She realized too late this wasn't going to be a quick fuck where she could tune out her thoughts for a few minutes of the day.

"There," she keened softly.

"Mm-hmm. And?"

"More." The words didn't hurt. Didn't cost her anything. It felt good, and she liked it. She could give him that.

And then he got cheeky. "More what?"

"Touch," she said, a little testy.

"Where?"

"Where you were before." She growled.

He only laughed softly into the curve of her neck, leaving a trail of wet, toothy kisses that sent desire into her already slippery flesh. Seven, she must be dripping all over her hallway floor. She had to get them to bed.

His teeth closed, instantly bringing her back to sensation. How did he seem to sense when she was drifting away into her mind and anchor her again?

"What if I want to taste you now?" he asked, almost idly.

Her brain shut off entirely. But not until a bleated "yes!" escaped her.

Nice, Fifi, she chided herself. Very sexy, way to bring a man to his literal knees by sounding like a goat.

"I like that." His voice wasn't any better—hoarse and nearly airless. "I like hearing you wanting. Desperate for me."

Desperate. Was that what she was? She didn't feel like starting an argument she wasn't sure she could win. Especially when he ground his still-jean-clad cock into the damp center of her underwear—why was she still wearing those?—and the shock of sensation rendered her totally senseless.

That wordless moan belonged to her though. She buried her fingers in his hair, leaned her head against the curve of his neck, and surrendered. "Taste me."

The words didn't immediately bring him to his knees as she expected. Instead, he started at the inside of her shoulder, the bend of her elbow, the pulse at her wrist. She was only vaguely aware of being carried down the hall and settling onto the nearest flat surface—couch?—because by then he was sucking and nibbling at her breasts. She heard herself at a distance, words coming from her from someplace beyond her control, and his affirmative grunts.

And then his mouth was on the place she needed him most, and he made a sound like she would hear in her fantasies every time she got herself off for the rest of her life. *Devoured* was a good word to be, she decided. Also *unmoored* and *senseless* and *flushed* because they all paired well with *desire*.

When he rose between her thighs, his jeans were open, cock bared and straining. He had a condom in hand, and when he licked her earlobe, she turned her head to taste them together on his tongue. It was his turn to moan, a little more broken.

"Bed," she pleaded and hissed when his finger brushed the tender skin where his mouth had been, testing and finding her open and ready. He gave her a second finger, and her hips shimmied impatiently. "More."

Ofelia was not a talker during sex. Except somewhere along the way, she forgot to be self-conscious as she pleaded and answered. The words were there all along with urging and praise he responded to beautifully. The moment he slid inside her, she lost control of her voice entirely and he harried her into surrender.

CHAPTER NINE

OFELIA STIRRED UNDER THE DENSE, warm weight of an arm and a leg thrown over her in sleep. Light peeked around the edges of the dark curtains covering the windows. She inhaled the salty male scent, molding herself to the warm body beside her before she could stop herself. The crisp hair of a muscular thigh brushed her ass in a way that sent arousal jetting back into the pit of her belly. The arm reeled her in, drawing her up against the wall of a chest and a growing morning erection that made her shiver with delight at memories from the night before. There had been a repeat. At least one. The good ache rode her body with waking.

Oh no.

He was still here. The man from the club who had once been the boy from the lazy afternoons making magic in an old train station. Christof Vogel.

He'd been playing it cool all night, like it was no big deal running into her after all that time. Especially after that last day. But she'd caught him looking at her a couple of times on the tram ride back to her place with the kind of longing brought on by nostalgia and hope.

Nope. Nope. Nope.

This wasn't going to be no strings attached. Not for him. And certainly not after she'd let him stay the night. The last thing she remembered was laughing herself breathless over something while they were in a sweaty, sheet-twisted tangle. The next flash was breathing into the curve of his neck, breathing *him* in while he stroked her. Her muscles got loose, then her joints let go, and then, apparently, her damn brain turned off.

She worked a hand free to touch her hair. She hadn't bothered to wrap her braids or brush her teeth or shower. Her makeup was probably in a smear all over her face. She had to get out of this bed.

She could try to put a charm on him—something to push him deeper into sleep—but a full-grown shifter would be resistant to all but her strongest work.

In the end, she went the old-fashioned way, shifting her weight and limbs carefully until she was able to wiggle out without waking him. She expected a two-skinned creature to be more wary, more alert. But he was like a sack of boneless muscle.

For a moment she regretted the loss of warmth as she stepped into the cool air of the darkened room. It was early afternoon by her internal reckoning. They'd closed the door to the outside world just before dawn and let the blackout curtains keep it at bay. Her jaw popped with a yawn as she slipped into the bathroom and closed the door.

She locked it, sat on the edge of the tub, and put her face in her hands. It wasn't a mistake exactly. Not yet. Maybe he'd wake up in her absence, get a clue, and get gone.

She tied up her braids and took her time showering. Each time her fingers encountered a tender spot, she shivered at the memory from the night before. She turned up the hot water, but it had nothing on his touch.

By the time she'd finished applying selections from the row of pots of creams and skin treatments, she was sure he would have gotten the picture. He could even leave his number on the table, and they would pretend she intended to call him.

She slipped into a silk dressing gown, knotting the belt securely before opening the door.

The clothes were gone from the floor—not just his. Hers had been draped neatly over the chair in the corner. There was a suspicious amount of noise from the kitchen.

Oh no.

She hurried through the bedroom, down the hall. Music? No, he was singing. To himself. While rattling her pots and pans. Had he braved the refrigerator yet, or the pantry? Seven knew what he would make of the collected jars and tinctures in either. He hadn't run screaming.

Of course not. He *knew* what she was. The same as she did. Something in that certainty softened the knot of anxiety in her chest.

The sight in of him in the sun-drenched, plant-strewn kitchen wiped any thoughts from her mind. Barefoot in briefs and wearing her linen apron over his bare chest, he nearly shone as the light kissed every inch of fair, golden skin.

He moved as if he belonged in the space. He'd found strawberries—strawberries!—in her fridge and had turned them into little red-edged fans on a couple of plates. The sun tangled in disheveled strands of his too-long hair and the slight overgrowth on his cheeks. The rest of him was lightly furred, all pale brown and with a slight wave.

When he turned, she got the sense that he'd been aware of her the whole time.

He grinned. "Have a good shower?" He bent down and opened the stove, removing the most perfect—enormous—omelet she'd ever seen. "Hope you don't mind my helping myself to the fridge, but I figured by now you probably could also use something."

He sliced the omelet in half and split it between two plates.

"I don't usually eat before…" She still hadn't checked the time.

"Noon," he said. "Yeah, you told me when I asked if I could take you to breakfast. But I figured it's well past noon, so—"

Her phone pinged. She scanned the room, searching for the sound. He pointed at the kitchenette table in the bay window.

It was nearly… One. In the afternoon.

Shit.

She hadn't texted Ayele. The notifications at the text bubble were numbering in double digits. She ignored three from Kenneth and the group chat, opening Ayele's thread.

@Yelele: Well you certainly have a type. Can't fault it though.

@Yelele: I want details.

@Yelele: GM! Coffee? I need to run some errands, you should come with.

@Yelele: Brunch?

@Yelele: Halloo. Never thought you'd be the type to dump your best girl for a man.

@Yelele: You'd better be having that tall boy blow out your back six ways to Sunday.

@Yelele: That you are dead better be the only reason you haven't texted me back.

@Yelele: Okay I am kidding. Fifi, dearest?

@Yelele: Hey. Just. Hit me up.

> @Yelele: Okay, I'm coming to your apartment. I am
> armed. No one will find his body.

Ofelia fumbled the phone in her panic, spinning away from Chris to hunch over the phone as she pecked at the screen.

First: Stop the tsunami that would be a concerned Ayele.

Second: Get this man out of her house.

> @Fifiti: Sorry. I'm good. I promise. I just got out of the
> shower.

She read the long moment of bouncing circles as a sigh of relief.

> @Yelele: I'm going to kill you myself. My heart.

> @Fifiti: My fault. Bad friend. I'm just now moving
> around. Everything is fine. More than fine. Consider my
> back suitably blown out.

> @Yelele: ...

Ofelia imagined Yele's eyes rolling heavenward.

Chris was watching her expectantly, brows up, with two plated meals. "Everything okay?"

"My friend, Ayele. From last night." She waved her phone. "Just checking in to make sure... Uh."

"That you're okay." He nodded. "Good, smart. I tried to ask if you needed to call somebody earlier, but you were out cold."

Something about his casual acknowledgment and support made her eyes sting. Instead, she stepped aside so he could set the plates down on the counter.

He returned with a pot of tea and two cups. She sniffed. The silver-dragon oolong. He had good taste. Her phone buzzed.

> @Yelele: I am on the tram. Is he still there?

Ofelia saw a way out. Two birds.

> @Fifiti: Meet me for coffee in an hour?

"I'd forgotten we had plans to meet for coffee this afternoon," she called to Chris.

He nodded, making another trip for forks and cloth napkins. "You can have a bite first, right? I'm starving. I just thought we should talk."

Nope. Absolutely no talking.

"I really don't have—" She faltered when her stomach—the traitor—grumbled at the smell wafting from the plate. Where on earth had he found all that delicious food in her house?

He hooked her waist in one big palm, dragging her onto his lap. He shouldn't smell so intoxicating. He hadn't even showered yet. But whatever aftershave he'd been wearing had worn off, revealing his natural, subtle pine-and-salt scent.

"One bite." He angled his head, even more puppy-like with those absurd eyes. "Then I'll hop in the shower if that's good and get out of your hair."

It was beyond good. They were on the same page after all.

He poured tea, buttered bread, then obliterated half a slice in a single bite. She paused, fork in hand, staring. He swallowed, grinned shyly, and took a more modest bite.

Then the flavors exploding on her tongue caught up with her and she almost moaned. She hurried another two bites after the first.

"This is amazing," she managed around a mouthful.

"It'll do. What I wouldn't give for some feta. How do you feel about cheese? I noticed you don't keep a lot of dairy—"

"It doesn't sit well in my stomach—I mostly avoid it," she answered before she could check herself.

"Skip the cheese," he muttered, focused. "Capers. Artichoke hearts. Avocado. Do you like avocados?"

Ofelia felt the laugh burbling up in her chest. He was unflappable. The ordinariness was somehow reassuring, his lack of disappointment or surprise that this was going to end soon.

"I love avocados." Where had that come from? What kind of truth serum did he put in this omelet?

"Good." His thumb rubbed her hip, kneading the muscle below the bone. Her cheeks warmed—did he know she was sore there from their acrobatics?

He wolfed his half down, then sucked a bit of egg off the fork. The toast went down next and then the strawberries, including the leaves.

"I don't have a big appetite." She slid her plate toward him, unable to keep from smiling. "But it was amazing. It shouldn't go to waste."

He accepted that easily. As he seemed to do with most things. Could he truly be that guileless?

"Last night was incredible." He cleaned her plate in two solid bites and wiped his mouth primly. "But I need you to know something."

That sounded ominous.

"I never forgot you." He slid a hand over hers, squeezing softly. "And I know we have a lot of catching up to do. But it feels like I've been waiting for you my whole life. And I'm here. For you. Now. Forever. I'm yours."

No. This isn't happening. Ofelia jumped up, her hip bumping the counter hard enough to bruise. Panic wracked her.

He knew better. One didn't just let words like that loose in the presence of a witch. "You don't know what you're talking about."

Confusion flared in his eyes. "Fi—"

How had she been so stupid?

"This was fun, I mean, really great." She gathered plates and silverware. They rattled in her hands. "But I'm just getting out of a relationship, and I'm not looking for—"

She waved her hands, hoping he got the picture, and nearly lost the entire stack.

"Got you." He plucked the dishes from her hands and heading to the sink.

"Leave them," she said, momentarily distracted from the conversation when he peeled off the apron.

Then he had to go and ruin it. "I'm not asking you to marry me—"

Marriage? What the fuck?

"I can't," she barked, startled when it came out sharper than she'd meant. "This isn't… what you think it is. What you want it to be."

This wasn't happening. She'd just wanted to blow off a little steam with someone who felt safe. And it'd been so nice to see him again after all these years doing well. The *breathtakingly hot* part hadn't hurt either. But she wasn't trying to start a life with somebody. Not after she'd had everything she loved taken away from her over and over again.

He had to go. Right now.

She disappeared down the hall into the bedroom, scooping up his clothes. He remained where she'd left him, big eyes fixed on her.

"I'm late to see my friend, and you really, really have to go." She herded him to the door.

She flung it open and pushed him out. Across the hall, Mila was chatting to her oldest son on their way into the apartment, grocery bags in hand. Both paused, staring.

Ofelia flushed, and Mila hustled the boy inside.

"Thank you for breakfast." She shoved the clothes at Chris's chest. A sock dropped. They ignored it. "And last night. I will call you sometime. Goodbye."

She closed the door in his face. As she turned, she spotted a pair of monstrous sneakers next to the door. She winced, hooked them in her fingers, cracked the door, and without looking, dumped them beside where she approximated his feet to be.

Then she threw the locks, put her back to the door, and slid to her heels, spine bumping on the uneven metal surface. "Shit, shit, shit."

She pressed her fists to her eyes. What had come over her? Why did he have to say things like that to her?

It was absurd. It had been fourteen years since the train station. He didn't *know* her. Not really. He knew a foolish girl doing magic she should have known better than to try because she'd been so taken by him —and the wolf under his skin.

For a moment she regretted kicking him out so abruptly, but it was for his own good. Let him lick his wounds, resent her rejection. He'd forget her again soon enough. She'd seen the way people looked at him at the club, both the humans and charmed. She bet he would have chemistry with a mop head. He'd get over her.

The kind of love he was talking about would not be hers. Ever. That kind of love had cost her parents their lives. It had robbed a girl of a life in a city she loved with two people who had been her universe. She'd never take someone's world from them the way hers had been. Or try to replace it with one of duty that really meant control. That was the kind of shit that love did.

Her phone chimed. She staggered to her feet, wiping her eyes. When she read the text, she choked on a laugh and went to pick out an outfit for the day.

@Yelele: You have thirty minutes, hussy.

CHAPTER TEN

Chris almost laughed out loud. It was only a figure of speech.

The rising clatter of young voices reached Chris as he considered his response. He probably had a dopey-ass grin on his face. A big one, judging from the looks a couple of the moms were sneaking him. Well, if you couldn't tell your best friend…

@BigBird: I know how it sounds.

@Klausmodious: You never do anything halfway, do you?

@BigBird: Yeah, well, maybe I should have held back a bit.

@BigBird: She kicked me out.

@Klausmodious: After you confessed your undying love?

@BigBird: Guess I came on a little strong.

@Klausmodious: You think?

@Klausmodious: ...

He unfolded himself from the stone wall opposite the school and slipped his phone into his pocket as the doors opened.

One brave soul took that as her opening. "You are the nanny?"

He shook his head without looking away from the gaggle of kids emerging from the building. He wasn't even interested in having a flirt. Not today.

From the other side, a more familiar face closed in. "No, he's the uncle. Hi, Chris. How've you been?"

"Great, Laura. You?"

"Erik and I got back together, but we were thinking—"

"Sorry, I'm pretty busy these days. Have a good one, ladies." He certainly did not want to be anyone's third, not even before he'd found the love of his life was back in Prague.

"Uncle Chris!" Isaac, his oldest nephew, barreled down the steps.

Chris crouched and let the spindly, bespectacled kid hit him full force.

"Hiya, Zacky." He gave the boy a good sniff to see if he'd eaten all his lunch and how school had gone.

Isaac's hand slid into his as they started for the tram. "Picking up the monsters today?"

"The university is doing some work on your dad's new office, so he took the afternoon off," Chris said. "Took the monsters to the playground with Grandma. You and I have the afternoon to ourselves. Where to? Library? Bookstore?"

Isaac didn't perk up at the mention of his favorite places, which was unusual.

Chris leaned in, sniffed him again, searched for illness. Nope. But something was on his mind. "Let's grab a smoothie."

Sitting at the window overlooking the river in a nearly empty café, Isaac dropped his voice wolf-ear low. "I've been dreaming, you know. Of him. My wolf."

Tobias and Barbara had never hidden what they were from their son, as it had once been hidden from Mark, Tobias, and Chris. It should be too early to tell for sure, but Woof confirmed with another sniff. "Think you're right, Zacky. Welcome to the pack."

The boy looked even more miserable. "I mean, I thought I would be… like Mom."

A witch.

"I guess it was about a fifty-fifty shot," Chris said. "Maybe sixty-forty since Grandma… Anyway. How do you feel about that?"

Isaac looked his hands. "I'm not strong like Uncle Mark or you. Or even Papa."

Chris almost laughed. Up until a few years ago, their middle brother Tobias had lived his life in a cage, burying his instinct and strength under intellect and academia. He'd been miserable and unable to see it. But Isaac had only known the man who embraced himself fully. Chris's chest ached at the love and pride his nephew felt for his dad.

"You know, your papa wasn't always happy to be what we are." Chris took a long drink and let his nephew consider that for a moment.

Isaac pushed his glasses up his nose and gazed at Chris doubtfully.

"Hated it," Chris admitted. "Did everything he could to keep from having to let his wolf out."

Isaac gnawed his lower lip. "I'm scared."

"I think it scared him a little bit too. But he came around. Your mom helped with that. And now you have both of them to see you through it when it's time."

"And you?"

"Of freaking course you got me." Chris lifted a shoulder. "And Uncle Mark. *We* got you, little guy."

Isaac sucked down his smoothie and kicked his legs on the stool, equilibrium restored. "What was it like for you?"

"I was ready because I knew early, like you."

"You did?" Isaac grinned.

"I had this friend. She helped me see the wolf was my ally, my strength. Part of who I am."

On the way home, he thought about the gift Ofelia had given him on those long-ago afternoons in the train station. His mother told stories about wolves and witches being on opposite sides of an old conflict. A war, she'd called it.

Ofelia hadn't been concerned by what he was or shown any fear. The opposite, in fact: she'd been the one to encourage him to coax Woof out of the trees and into the dappled glade. Maybe it was because she was like him, generations removed from their past. But he sensed there was something else to it.

There was no universal craft—his mother had been adamant about that. There were as many ways to practice as there were cultures. Each had its own languages, rules, structures. The diversity was its strength, and as it turned out, its survival.

After the godswar, the necromancers had divided the world into territories, each controlling the behavior of other magical creatures with their rigid codes and squashing what they could not control. With communication between territories operating at the whim of the necromancers that controlled them, it was nearly impossible to connect with each other.

Necromancers could suppress what they could see. But there were others, like his own mother, whose practices were kept hidden.

And Ofelia's wards felt different than the ones his mother had impressed on their building, and she'd done the calming thing in the club. He'd never seen that before.

What did Ofelia know that they did not? His mom always said witches and wolves were alike in that they did better in a community. As far as he could tell, Ofelia was alone.

On the way home, Isaac pulled a book from his bag. Chris checked the thread on his phone.

@Klausmodious: You have a good heart. You're loyal to a fault.

@Klausmodious: This girl is lucky to have you. Remember that. Just cool it on the forever part, at least for the first few weeks, okay?

@BigBird: Yes, O wise one.

@Klausmodious: You're welcome. Also. I think her friend likes me, so don't fuck this up, okay?

@BigBird: Deal.

Maybe he'd come on too strong. He'd give her the weekend to show he wasn't a complete nutcase. If she really didn't want him, he'd figure out how to live with that—even if the thought carved a hollow under his breastbone. But he owed it to her to at least try to connect her to other witches in the city.

CHAPTER ELEVEN

THE COFFEE SHOP was slow this time of day. Ofelia found a seat at a table by the window with the remnants of the day's paper the staff had left for the next patron.

Ayele was late, of course. Ofelia ordered a croissant and a double espresso.

The headline drew her eye. BLOODLESS MAN FOUND IN CITY PARK.

She knew the papers were desperate for readership, but that felt over-the-top even for that. She scooted it out of the way in time for the server's return.

"Terrible news about that." The man spoke English, attempting to remove the paper after he'd set down the plate and saucer. "You should not let it affect your visit to our beautiful city."

Ayele snapped it out of his fingers as she worked her way to her chair, a tight smile on her face as she replied in Czech. "Perhaps. Or perhaps we should stay educated to stay safe. This is not the first one."

She gave her order, then settled in the seat opposite Ofelia, smiling mischievously.

"How many?" Ofelia hadn't been paying attention what with all of Kenneth's shenanigans. Even so, the bizarreness of the deaths should have stood out to her. Why hadn't she noticed?

"Two." Ayele folded the paper carefully. "The police are predictably clueless. No doubt the necromancer's Black Blade will have it wrapped up in a couple of days. Now"—she set the paper aside to focus on Ofelia—"about this new boyfriend of yours."

"It was a one-night stand."

"Well, when I thought you were murdered in your apartment, I made some calls," Ayele drawled. "He's a local kid, nobody of note." Meaning not connected to any of the elite families in the city. "The bouncers at Tresor vouched for him, though he's not a regular these days. Called Christof—"

"Vogel," Ofelia finished. "His mother is American and his father is German. He has two older brothers and a sister."

"You did a lot of talking for a one-night stand." Ayele's stare took on a new dimension.

"I knew him when we were kids," Ofelia confessed. "Before I left for boarding school."

"And here I was thinking you were replacing Kenneth." Ayele shook her head, sucking her teeth with a little smile. "Sounds like Kenneth was replacing this one."

She sipped her coffee, eyes averted. "We were twelve. Eleven? It was barely a crush. Anyway. We were in one grade together and not even for a full year."

"And now…"

Ofelia lifted her shoulders. "He was perfect because he wasn't a total stranger. But there's nothing there."

Ayele surveyed her, and Ofelia put on her best not-bothered-by-your-laser-eyes expression. "You didn't make a mistake, letting someone in, Fifiti. It just happened to be the wrong one. It happens to the best of us, love."

Ofelia clenched her jaw. She'd met Kenneth at a time in her life she was vulnerable. She could forgive herself for that. But staying with him, missing everything he'd been up to, was unforgivable.

She was her mother's daughter and her father's child: a keen observer and a powerful witch. She should have seen something, suspected it.

Now she didn't know if she would ever trust herself again.

"One night," Ofelia repeated intentionally, pretending Ayele had been talking about Chris.

"Well, you can pick them," Ayele acquiesced with a sigh. "Word on the street is your one-night is *the* most chaotic bisexual in town."

"I don't care who he does what with." Ofelia rolled her eyes. "It was one—admittedly very good—night. We're not moving in together."

"Good, eh?"

Good? Ofelia couldn't repress a grin. All her nerve endings fired at once at the sudden flood of memories. She almost giggled, tapping her feet on the floor in a little happy dance. When she looked up, Ayele was shaking her head.

"You are a damn fool." Ayele smiled. "It's a good thing I'm here to keep you out of trouble."

They sipped coffee in a moment of respectful silence for a good night out, then caught up on Ayele's university classes and the shop. On the way to Charm Syndicate, Ayele shared a few ideas about outreach to some of the local cafés.

"You are a natural businesswoman, Yele." Ofelia sighed as she unlocked the door.

"I know." Ayele sounded mournful. "Iye keeps the heat on me. This time she offered me an *internship*. Said I could even take Mum's family name. Like everyone there wouldn't know I was her kid too. I don't want to be just the boss's kid. Plus I am an artist."

Ofelia scoffed.

Ayele's eyes narrowed. "I have an artist's soul. So what—I cannot draw to save your life?"

"My life!" Ofelia cackled.

Ofelia kissed her best friend goodbye and locked the door behind her. She kept the lights off for a few more minutes, resting in the silence and the soft vibration of the plants welcoming her home.

At the altar, she lit an incense cone in the small dish atop the black-and-gold silk, the earthy, spicy aroma of frankincense base notes tickling her nose before the brighter citrus filled the space. The tiny charms dangling from the dried lunaria branch shivered, tinkling when they touched each other. Assorted trinkets were scattered around the base of the glass. She greeted her mother's ancestors all the way back to the first of the forty-two families. On her father's side she had only the battered image of a ruddy-skinned couple squinting into the camera on a clear mountain day—a holiday by the dirndl and lederhosen—hands proudly on the shoulders of a lanky boy standing between them, his front teeth missing. Her father had given her stories of her Grosi's craft, the healer. She'd bulked up that side of the altar with an art nouveau-style illustration of the three sisters—Prague's patron witches. When she'd first returned to the city, the eyes of the auburn-haired witch had seemed to lock on to her from the window of the tourist trap. KAZI, read the curling script below the woman, THE HEALER AND MISTRESS OF HERBS AND POTIONS. A fitting patron if Ofelia had ever seen one.

She bathed her head and hair in the thin, aromatic smoke, letting the repetitive movement and aroma steady her mind as she contemplated the state of her life.

She'd achieved her goal in coming back to Prague and found success in a business that would help her make the city home again. She'd gotten over Kenneth by getting under—on top of—someone else with great success.

But life in a necromancer's city could be a risky proposition even with one as relatively tolerant as Azrael. The confrontation at Tresor sat uneasily in her stomach. The headline also needled her. There was too much she'd let go by—signs she'd ignored—while she'd been so tightly focused on the shop.

She was going to have to start paying better attention to her home.

When she opened her eyes, the lights came up slowly until she was staring into her own reflection in the small gold-edged mirror. She thanked her ancestors and guardians and went to open the store.

Halfway to the door, something on the altar clattered discordantly. She froze, glancing at the clock. She should have opened ten minutes ago. She didn't have time for this.

She almost laughed at herself. Hadn't she just said she should be paying more attention?

She took a breath, steeling herself for whatever message had arrived. When she turned back, it took her a moment to notice what had changed. One of the charms had fallen off the lunaria branch. The wolf's head. She didn't even remember adding one, though she must have. She'd let her intuition guide her through the bowl of charms in the curiosity shop beside the river, owned by a medium with a knack for treasures. She hadn't even been thinking of Chris—only that wolves symbolized courage, strength, and loyalty. The charm had knocked down the photo of her parents and lay on the back, over the heart beside her mother's scrawl.

WEDDING DAY, PRAGUE, CZ

"Nope." She shook her head.

A couple of amber beads rattled from the pile of gemstones and rolled to a stop beside the wolf head.

"The amber is a bit heavy-handed, don't you think?" She sucked her teeth. She'd put them there for protection, forgetting they also symbolized romantic love.

Apparently her guardians had a sense of humor. While she was concerned with murder and drug dealers, they were more interested in her love life.

She set the photo firmly back in place, scooped the amber beads into a little velvet pouch, and tucked them away in the wooden box. In their place, she dropped a string of black tourmaline. A barrier, protection.

She ignored the sensation that she was being laughed at as she walked away.

♠

THREE TIMES A WEEK, Ofelia offered classes in the back room of the shop after hours. For a moderate fee, she provided the raw materials for custom lotions, perfumes, tinctures, or candles and allowed a glimpse into her process. She infused the lessons with a touch of the theatrical— atmospheric lighting and tribal lo-fi in the background gave the right amount of witchy vibe to intrigue her human students.

And most of her students were human: groups on a night out and executives looking to relax. For many of them, it was a chance to flirt with the supernatural without endangering themselves or to reconnect with family stories of wise folk in their own ancestry. It also gave them a in window into the meticulous care she brought to her work and a healthy appreciation of the complexity. After class she opened the shop for an hour of exclusive browsing. Most bought her product. A few became dedicated clients.

Classes were a business strategy and maybe a bit of a grotesque one at that. She couldn't fault Geoff and Sasha at Tresor for offering regular humans the chance to flirt with magic even if they would never know the peril involved in the day-to-day of being a magical creature.

At least she wasn't also hosting dealers.

She swallowed the bitter pill of pride and the realization that she'd played Friday night very wrong. She would deal with how much Geoff and Sasha knew about Kenneth. Neither had responded to her letter, which wasn't a great sign. Satyrs were generally lax about the legality of illicit substances, but she had a hard time buying Ange and the Garg clan's overlooking them. Gargoyles loved their rules and codes almost as much necromancers.

For now she had a class on tinctures for home and hearth to focus on. She lit a bit of incense—fresh, clean scent of cedarwood and infused with welcome—and opened a few bottles of wine for good measure. Then she breathed in her space, set her intention for the night, and unlocked the doors.

Her students came in small groups, chattering with excitement, fresh from an early dinner or at the beginning of a night out. Singles and men often turned up looking nervous, glancing around the shop and at Ofelia with big eyes. She assured them that they wouldn't be the night's sacrifice and helped them find a place among the others, forming small groups.

It wasn't that she'd set out to become a matchmaker. But if she'd somehow gotten a reputation for making good matches… that was just luck. Anyway, what self-respecting daughter of a spy would not know how to read people?

Getting a feel for her clients in a few minutes of conversation and steering complimentary personalities toward one another came as naturally as mixing a fragrance or the right ingredients for a custom cream. It was practically her birthright. She certainly didn't fuss with nonsense like love potions. Interfering with the will of others was a craft not to be taken lightly.

Occasionally something in the way one of her students moved, how they seemed guided from within, showed promise of more than just a distant ancestor's charm. Ofelia would drift over while the others browsed the store or chatted after class. She knew how to question them —unobtrusively—to find out how much they knew about their own powers.

Those she deemed ready were issued an invite to one of her real gatherings—an individual charm that could unlock the door to the shop at a specific date and time.

She hadn't given one of those out in a while, but she always had hope. Witches needed each other.

When she'd ushered the last student out, Ofelia tidied up the class materials and cleansed her space. She filled the kettle for tea and dimmed the shop lights. Then she turned on the charms.

The second group came individually or in pairs, drifting out of the darkness and bearing offerings—snacks and wine mostly. Most had always known what they were, their craft handed down through families long before the godswar and the necromancers forced them back underground. A few discovered themselves in Ofelia's public classes and became late initiates.

For both, it was often first time they'd had a chance to practice among other lineages. As power was bound to do, they grew and became more potent in the presence of others.

Her heart soared as the sound of their voices filled the space in greetings and catching up on the week's adventures. Seven regulars plus three others who had families or busy work schedules and came when they could.

"Mistress Ofelia." Cilka, found her pulling supplies for the evening.

"Just Fifi," Ofelia reminded her.

"Have you given any more thought to forming up…" she asked. "You know."

Ofelia sighed, focusing on her supply closet to hide her frown. Not the coven talk again.

"It's just we're a good number now—seven. Ten when the twins and Sandro show up," Cilka said. "The closing of cycles and the start of new."

Ofelia sighed. "The practice should be open. Each has his or her own relationship with their craft. Covens—"

"Provide structure." Cilka rarely lifted her voice and never interrupted. Ofelia blinked in surprise. The girl flushed bright red, lowering her voice. "It's guidance… and protection. And with you as high—"

"Don't even speak the words," Ofelia snapped, sharper than intended. "Enforcing rules and hierarchy is not what I started all this for."

Cilka recoiled, her eyes wide. "Then why did you gather us?"

"We need community—" That didn't mean she had to lead them. "I've lived among those who placed vows over people, where individual lives and even families could be sacrificed for 'the greater good of the Cadre'—the coven."

Ofelia heard the bitterness in her own tone even as she caught the slip.

Cilka's gaze softened. "Who better than you to know how to keep that from happening?"

The others were waiting, the buzz of conversation lowering. More than a few were probably listening in, waiting to see what the verdict would be. She wondered if they'd set Cilka up intentionally since she was one of the first to join the circle.

"It must be done intentionally and not taken lightly." Ofelia lifted her voice and her gaze to take them all in. "The circle we've formed lifts my heart. I love and value each of you. I'll think about it. That's all I can promise. Now, what's the topic tonight?"

Everyone wanted to talk about the murders—and the bodies drained of blood. There were rumors of something like this in Luxembourg and Norway. Some of the older witches recalled similar stories handed down from their elders outside the European territory. Communication between territories operated at the whim of the necromancers who controlled them and to varying degrees. Being supernaturals made sharing even more difficult.

"I heard the victims were all blooded." A tremor shook the voice of one of the elder witches.

It was an old way to refer to the supernatural beings that had existed among humankind for time immemorial. In the inevitable mixing, it was believed that those that could pass for human could only be distinguished by their blood.

Witches fell into that category. A few powerful or eccentric witches had returned to the largely abandoned countryside villages to reclaim their heritage away from the eye of the necromancer. But in his capital city, most existed among humanity in every range of regular jobs—executives or shop owners or service, labor, or care providers—unseen for what they truly were except in small gatherings like this one.

In truth, blood was a poor measure of power. Many humans carried a little supernatural—it showed up as luck or good instincts. Witches must be nurtured for their charm to fully develop. It was why she had started the circle to begin with. She wanted to give them the opportunity to know their power.

The others looked to the older witch who had spoken, and she felt more than a few add to a wave of comfort and reassurance sent his way. This was the strength of witches together. They didn't need her to lead them to do this for each other.

"Perhaps we should do something," Cilka suggested. "Scry? Try to see if we can find out anything about the one responsible."

"And who do we tell?" one of the youngest members of their group snapped. "Perhaps the Amazon will come to interview us? Or Azrael's Black Blade will make us all disappear."

"That's just fear talking."

"An anonymous tip—"

"He's a necromancer—he'll get a witness account soon enough from one of the victims—"

"—expose ourselves—"

"What should we do? Ignore it? Pretend—"

Ofelia let them go on for a few minutes. For many, they'd been holding tight to their fear all week with no outlet. She held the space, creating a bubble of quiet around the group that spread as their voices rose.

The voices became more resolute, sharper. When the conversation turned hard, she stood. Carrying on like this would end in broken relationships.

She rapped on the table twice.

All eyes shifted to her.

"We have given voice to our concerns. Now we talk solutions. The cauldron."

The glass bowl was retrieved. Everyone grabbed a notebook and pen. A few stalked away from the others. She gave them room to think. Time to process. One by one they returned, dropping slips of paper into the bowl. Ofelia slid her own in, smiling reassuringly at a few nervous glances.

When the last paper was included, she passed her hand over the glass, adding a drop or two of oil and a flame.

"The votes have been cast." She directed the resulting smoke at the blank wall, and they all watched words appear, identical lettering making each suggestion indistinguishable.

More than one for *Watch and wait.*

Scry for the killer.

Protect other witches.

Summon the victim was the boldest suggestion. And the riskiest.

Ofelia was relieved to see protection come up the winner. It was a moderate solution—better than nothing but little to no risk of exposure.

"But with no idea what the victims have in common, how can we protect any others?" Cilka protested weakly, confirming Ofelia's suspicion that she had voted for the more aggressive solutions.

"The circle has spoken." Ofelia kept an eye on her as she helped gather ingredients. She didn't like the set of Cilka's small mouth.

Nothing happened until they settled in to cast. Mid-spell, she felt Cilka's energy begin to drift. Without opening her eyes to take in the rest of the circle, Ofelia followed Cilka's attention.

Rather than laying the ground for protection, she was summoning.

Ofelia cast a barrier behind her to protect the others from any blowback and turned her focus to Cilka.

She and Cilka materialized in a version of the alley where the last body had been found.

Cilka whirled, eyes wide with shock. "Mistress—"

Ofelia let the title go. "Did you think I wouldn't figure out what you were up to?"

The alley was empty, just-past-midnight dark but still barricaded to keep intruders out. The smell of death clotted the air.

"I just wanted to know if I could see anything." Cilka's gaze was downcast. "I have the eye, you know."

"And if Azrael happened to be doing his postmortem with the victim?"

"What are the odds? At the exact minute."

"When magic is involved?" Anger flared hot and bright in her at the girl's shortsightedness. Now was not the time to give in to it. "No coincidences—you know that. You endanger everyone in that circle."

Ofelia knew how to escape a necromancer. She'd done it once, from a far more entrenched group than the necromancer Azrael's security. She'd lose her shop, yes, but she'd keep her skin and her magic and be able to start over. The others had jobs, lives, families.

But her new vow to pay attention took her gaze back to the alley.

They were here now, and she'd done her best to protect the others. They might as well finish what she started. "Well, little seer. What does your eye perceive?"

Cilka's exhale shook. Surprise? Relief? Victory? Ofelia would consider that later.

Ofelia turned her own senses to the alley to see what she could learn. She opened her mouth slightly and let the air wash over her tongue. Blood in that death scent, too much for the startling absence of it when the body was discovered.

"Not killed here," Cilka said sagely.

Ofelia nodded.

Cilka began to shiver. Ofelia followed her gaze. Okay, now they were getting somewhere.

The body had appeared, splayed out on the tarmac-patched cobble-stones. He had been middle-aged with a ruddy complexion, but his skin was now pale, bloodless in death.

Cilka stepped forward cautiously, ignoring Ofelia's cautioning sound.

The corpse turned its head, taking them in with sightless eyes.

Cilka screamed. Ofelia yanked the girl behind her, sketching a quick shield with her fingertips, which had the double benefit of obscuring the view. But she didn't miss the word its lips formed without a sound.

Hexenblut.

She hissed a dissolution, severing their connection to the dead.

In Charm Syndicate, she opened her eyes in the circle to see Cilka across from her, tears streaming down her cheeks. Somehow the girl found enough composure not to distract the others and break the circle by bolting.

A rush of pride filled Ofelia. As foolish as it had been, Cilka's curiosity and skill with the summoning spell showed how far she'd come from the whispering mouse who could barely light her cigarette with a thought. Ofelia had done a few stupid things herself as a young witch, feeling overconfident in her powers—like introducing a boy to his wolf in a train station long ago.

She'd hidden in the overgrowth that afternoon after escaping, trying desperately to invoke her spent charm as the wet sounds of fists on flesh echoed in the train station. The boys walked right by her at the end, winded and laughing, while she crouched still as a hare in the brambles. Chris had emerged later, limping and bloodied, dragging his backpack.

Shame filled her at the memory of being unable to unlock her limbs or even lift her voice to call out.

When muscle fatigue finally released her and he was long gone, she raced home as if pursued by an egbere from one of her mother's stories.

Her arrival had been greeted with shock at the sight of her torn dress and bloodied leg, and the whole story met with looks of horror and anger. Finally there had been single-minded focus and decisions made so quickly she barely had time to register what was happening. Their essential belongings were packed, and they fled just after dawn.

She turned away from those memories and the shame. What happened to Chris was her fault. She'd led him to believe he was strong enough to protect her and then abandoned him when the real monsters came that day.

Perhaps helping witches restore their lineage and step into their power was a kind of penance she would pay—gladly—for the rest of her life. But she'd never risk leading them into the kind of danger she had led Chris. Better to stay a lone witch in that regard. Never to lead anyone at all.

Ofelia turned her attention to the others, adding her intention to complete the protection.

After they had finished casting, they helped clean up and Ofelia walked them all to the door. She shut off the lights, closing the shop behind her. Only then did she allow herself to sag against the wall. Her knees shook.

She'd never seen the dead man before, but he didn't seem to be the type to frequent her store and he'd been found all the way across town, on the other side of the river.

Hexenblut. There was no mistaking that had been the word the unrested dead had spoken.

Kenneth's words from weeks ago rang in her mind: "It's moving fast. Can't get enough of the stuff."

Her stomach turned with the memory. She'd dropped by Kenneth's opulent apartment on a feeling. He'd been on the phone and waved her into the bedroom before slipping into his tiny office. Annoyed, she'd drifted around the kitchen instead. Maybe it was her parents' fault or her partial training, but she'd never been able to ignore a hushed voice.

He'd hissed the words into his phone. "It's not *really* blood, is it?"

She collected herself and locked the store doors. She knew she wouldn't let this go. But she had to make sure someone else did.

Cilka waited on the curb, looking small in her oversized peacoat with her hunched shoulders. She hadn't quit shaking all evening, tiny shudders that occasionally wracked her even now.

It was likely the first time she'd seen a dead body. And the speaking thing *was* disconcerting.

"Someone who wants a coven so badly should abide by the group decisions," Ofelia chided softly, joining her.

"I just wanted to know"—Cilka met her eyes, tears clinging to her lashes—"if there was anything that could help with the protection spell. Really."

"Take this for the nightmares." Ofelia sighed, slipping a small dropper out of her bag. "Summoning is not our work. The dead say all sorts of things, some as much nonsense as meaningful. This is why we let necromancers fuss with them. Keeps them busy chasing their tails. Go home. Get some rest. Two dropperfuls in some warm tea for dreamless sleep, okay?"

Cilka nodded, her chin wobbling, and then hurried off into the dark. Ofelia didn't worry about her. The string of random murders had shocked the city because it was so safe even at night. Ofelia's charm also granted them protection.

She was out of practice—defensive shielding and following spells took much more energy than potions and plant magic, which were her charm. The second two came naturally to her, a way to bleed off power that would build and become toxic if she didn't expend it. Active spells required stamina and energy—her own or someone else's.

The memory of Heartlight flashed briefly. That was the kind of power a witch could get drunk on if she weren't careful. Absolutely not. There were a thousand reasons why she would never call on Christof Vogel. With that stupid adoring expression in his eyes, he wouldn't even have the sense to turn her down.

Still, she would have to build up her stamina. Especially if Cilka was going to be the kind of witch who got herself into more trouble than she could get out of.

As for tracking down Kenneth, she didn't have the strength for a confrontation tonight. But she would have to, sooner rather than later.

Ofelia made her own way home, climbing the stairs to the apartment above the store. She was lucky to have been able to rent both spaces and grateful she didn't have to go far to collapse in bed.

Instead, she almost ran straight into Chris.

CHAPTER TWELVE

Ofelia gasped, wide-eyed, and reeled away from the man on her doorstep.

"Whoa, whoa, whoa." Chris stepped back, his shoulders a little hunched, as if that would somehow make all six foot whatever of him less imposing. When he lifted his hands, he seemed to forget about the enormous bouquet he was holding. It canted sideways and he almost lost his grip, fumbling to catch the stems and not crush the blossoms. Color sprang up on his cheeks, bright. "Shit, fuck. Sorry."

Ofelia pressed a hand to her chest. "What are you doing here?"

His sweeping gaze lingered in ways that made her bare limbs and hints of skin peeking out from fabric tingle. "You look… Wow."

"I had a class." Amusement fluttered beneath her collarbones, and she almost smiled. "I always dress the part."

"The part?"

"A little witchy."

He lowered his voice to match. "You got that down."

Again she resisted the feeling of relief that she didn't have to hide the truth.

But it was so late. What was he doing in the building—on her doorstep—at almost midnight?

He seemed to realize his appearance was suspect as well.

"I went to the shop first, but it looked busy and I didn't want to interrupt. I would have waited outside—I was waiting outside—but your neighbor had a lot of groceries, so I offered to help and she let me in and wouldn't let me leave without tea. Ludmilla?"

"Mila." The single mom of two who lived down the hall. She'd taken a shine to Ofelia when she moved in, invited her to dinner or a glass of wine. Ofelia had watched the boys a time or two when the woman had a late meeting or an infrequent date.

"She had a *lot* of groceries. And the kids were... being kids. It was late. I was gonna leave these and head out, but she kept serving me tea." His plain accounting, issued as an apology, was inexplicably charming. It didn't seem to occur to him that he could just... leave.

And he looked good in another snug T-shirt—a steely gray that made his eyes more striking—and jeans. The heat kindled in her core at the memory of clinging to his shoulders.

"These are for you." He extended the only-slightly-worse-for-wear bouquet in her direction. "The dahlias... reminded me of you."

She cleared her throat, gazed at the bright gold-and-yellow blossoms. "I am spiky and complicated?"

"You are vibrant and layered." The brush of his hand on hers as he handed it over sent little charges up her fingers.

Ofelia tugged hard on her lips to keep them from bouncing up, but her cheeks warmed. She hadn't been a secondary school girl for a long time. She wasn't going to swoon over a sweet word and a bouquet that must have cost him—Seven, it was a lot of flowers—a week's pay?

And she couldn't leave him on her doorstep either. Her neighbors were all nosy as hell. No doubt the gossip mill had started up as soon as Mila and her groceries had opened the door for him and persuaded him to stay. She'd likely extracted his entire life story over that bottomless cup of tea and would have shared it with the floor above by morning.

"I'm not trying to— I mean, we don't have to—" He broke off, ears sharper than hers picking up on a sound. He lowered his voice. "We have an audience."

Grist for the mill. They'd already seen him once, and in his underwear.

"Would you like to go for a walk?" Chris suggested. "Or late dinner if you're not too tired?"

Resisting his magnetism for an entire meal seemed like an impossible feat. And there was no way to explain that either. To call it charm felt wrong: no artifice, no sense that he was trying to win her or playing a game. He was so earnest—his expression open and wondering and obviously into her. She was already softening after two minutes on the doorstep.

"Just come in for a minute." She shuffled her keys. "We can decide later."

His brows rose and she realized her mistake.

"That's not what I meant." She turned to the door handle, her back to him. Memories of their night together, had clearly turned her into a complete rag doll, because the clever fingers that deftly portioned out fragrances and oils and cast spells failed her completely as she tried to insert the key.

"I'm not here for that." He stepped in so close the heat of him radiated against her skin and his voice was a low rumble over her shoulder. "I mean, not gonna lie, that was… really, really, great— Just—" His words careened off the curve where her neck met her shoulder, leaving her skin prickling in anticipation.

Air skimmed her shoulder blade in a long, slow draw. He was breathing her in. Well that was… something. He braced a forearm on the doorframe beside her as though it were *his* knees that had suddenly grown too soft.

She was done for. He hadn't even touched her, and she already teetered on the edge of a collision that was going to make her cry out his name.

He hovered a hand beside hers on the lock. "Can I help?"

No, you may not touch me again or I cannot be held responsible for what I do to you on this doorstep. Give the gossip mill something to talk about indeed. Trust.

She cleared her throat and banished that thought. "I've got it."

The lock gave way, and his hand settled on the door, propping it open so she could enter first.

It would be all too easy to blame him for her lack of alarm bells at what happened next. But that would do no justice to the skill and preparation of àjé trained from childhood in full command of their charms. It wasn't until she'd closed the door after Chris that she picked up on anything at all. And that was far too late.

She froze, staring down the hallway, and her charm prickled with awareness.

"What is it?" Chris murmured.

Everything in her screamed, *Run*. But it was too late for that. No doubt there were reinforcements on the streets. No point wondering how they'd found her. The *Botanica* article alone had been a signpost. She did marvel that they'd slipped into the heart of another necromancer's territory undetected, into her building with her just a floor below, silencing her wards. Of course, they'd been trained for this. They'd tried to train *her* for this once upon a time. Just like her mother.

A low growl came from behind her. Fine silver hair sprouted where

Chris had been clean-shaven, his brows growing dense as the pelt thickened on his arms. The wolf had been a shadow in the eyes of a boy fourteen years ago. Now his humanness faded to teeth too sharp, ears too pointed. His nose lengthened, taking his mouth with it.

"Join us, Fifi." She knew the voice coming from her living room.

"Of course she sent Baako." Ofelia stamped in irritation.

Chris's transition slowed as his look switched to confusion.

"Bring your friend."

She tried to plead with her gaze. *Go.*

"I'm not leaving you alone with a pack of witches."

"Don't let them hear you call them that," she muttered as she marched into the living room to greet her cousin. But it was the sight of the short, bareheaded woman in designer clothes standing in the front of the group that stopped her in her tracks. "Yele?"

"I'm sorry, Fifiti." At least she had the decency to meet Ofelia's eyes. "I didn't want you to find out this way."

Ofelia's voice broke. "You're *Cadre?*"

CHAPTER THIRTEEN

"Y-you lied to me," Ofelia stuttered.

Chris didn't understand who these people were or what they wanted from Ofelia, but anything that broke Ofelia's voice like that couldn't be good.

"Fifi, it's not what it seems." Ayele flinched, but she did not lower her gaze.

"I know a sycophant when I see one," she snapped, turning back to the newcomers.

How had he missed them? Moving through her building, having tea with her nosy neighbor, being shooed out at just the right moment with his bouquet in hand to stand on her doorstep. He should have scented them from the street. His hackles rose, and he made no attempt to check the low growl rumbling under his collarbones. Still, he kept Woof in check.

"She has done her duty." A taller woman stepped forward. She wore slacks and a suit jacket— like armor. The others were unarmed, but she carried a spear with a wicked curved blade. "Unlike some."

The words seemed to spark something in Ofelia. She made a small, desperate sound; then her fury supernovaed out. "My *duty*, Baako? Since when does the Cadre send àjé to spy on their own?"

"Oh, you're one of us now?" Baako snapped and then lifted her chin. "No self-respecting àjé runs like a child."

"What the hell do you want, Cousin?"

"Amanirenas requests an audience."

Ofelia froze, and Chris was sure that even outnumbered, trapped in her own home and reeling with betrayal, she was going to run. Try to at least.

Two of the *not*-witches stiffened minutely in anticipation.

He figured he could take two.

"Go." He hauled her behind him and unleashed Woof.

The scent of broken flowers filled the wolf's nose first. Sometime in the confusion, she'd dropped the bouquet, crushing it underfoot. He landed on four paws just long enough to spring for their leader.

"Woof, no!" Ofelia's shout came at a distance.

He wanted to wag his tail at her, pleased she'd remembered him after all this time. But the woman in a linen tunic beside Baako began to shift, her skin going tawny and sprouting furred ears lined with black as she transitioned.

A lioness. That was new.

"Don't hurt him!" Ofelia screamed.

"Call him off!" the witch demanded.

They collided in a tangle of fur and snarls. Furniture clattered against the wall. Something glass shattered.

The big cat got a good swipe to his nose and rolled him, kicking hard with back legs and sending him skidding across the floor. Woof twisted, launching himself back at the witch to be met with the blunt end of the staff.

Leaves fluttered as vines slithered across the floor. The vine wrapped around the second witch, yanking her to the floor.

"You have no business sneaking into my home," Ofelia shouted.

The shifter beside her hacked at the vine, but more kept coming as the monstera in the corner burst its pot and crawled for them.

"Enough." Baako locked her fingers, shook her fists left and right and released them, splayed her hands. Her companions all leaped away, avoiding the powerful force that knocked Ofelia and the wolf off their feet.

Ofelia tucked into a little ball on the floor, coughing.

The wolf's ears rang and the whole room wobbled. He scrambled to get his paws under him and failed. Instead, he pressed his body along the length of Ofelia's back, teeth bared at the approaching witches.

"Taking a concord outside the city?" Shock laced one of the voices. "It is against the law."

"See there is no vow between them." Another spoke. "What do we do with him?"

Before the wolf lost consciousness, Baako spoke again. "We take them both. You will clean up this mess, Ayele, and make the explanations to the neighbors and anyone else. Keep the shop open. No one must know she is gone."

CHAPTER FOURTEEN

Woof drove Chris to consciousness with a start much later. Scent flooded him, bright and floral, and for a long second he fixated on the memory of the crushed bouquet in Ofelia's apartment. But this was fuller, alive, and bound so fully with the scent of more witches than he had ever picked up on in one place. Including the one watching him. Not witch. What was the word Ofelia used? *Àjé*.

Tobias, who picked up a new language every other week, or his wife Barbara, who could interpret anything she read, would probably know what that meant. But Chris only had his nose, and if it smelled like a witch, it was a witch.

Chris opened his eyes. He lay face down on a couch of some kind, his mouth dry. The tatters of his T-shirt and favorite jeans clung to him. Shit. He'd wolfed out in front of strangers.

Woof whimpered pitifully in his chest.

A child of no more than fourteen, with a shaved head and round face, stood by the door in the relaxed posture of a bored guard. At the first sign of Chris stirring, the child went to attention, leaning out the doorway to call to someone. Then they returned a steady, fearless gaze to Chris. Their hands slid into the suggestion of a cradle as though making room for an invisible ball before their chest.

Power crackled off them, leashed and waiting.

Chris held up his palms in surrender.

The child lifted their chin once. "Wise."

Chris turned his head, taking in a room so expansive it had its own breeze. Colorful tapestries and images of animals hung from the big, earthen walls. Photographs, he realized. Whoever had taken them was a master artist—he felt as though he could touch the wrinkled, curving trunk of the elephant, the fly-speckled hide of grazing horses. Warm air, dense with the fragrance of plants and humid soil, moved through the room. The light was different here—brighter, warmer somehow. Sheer curtains waved from the windows, and he scented the presence of an enormous amount of water. He assessed the situation.

He clearly wasn't in Prague anymore.

Ofelia.

"Where is she?" The need to get to her drove him to push onto his hands, moving slowly so as not to startle his guard and wind up with a face full of whatever spell they were cooking up. He draped one of the light scraps of linen fabric beside him on the massive couch over his lap.

The breeze cooled the sweat that bloomed on his chest. More replaced it immediately. Wherever he was, it was hot. His tongue felt thick, sluggish.

Chris eyed the clay pot on the side table and the full glass beside it. He should probably wait to confirm it was safe. But that àjé, Baako, had knocked out a full-grown shifter like it was child's play and then left a kid to guard him. Undoubtedly if they hadn't wanted him to awake, he wouldn't have. No need to drug the water.

Still, he sniffed twice before drinking deep, and again.

When he set down his glass, he braced his elbows on his knees and rubbed his hands through his sweat-matted hair. "Hey. Thanks for the water."

The child's eyes narrowed.

"I'm not going anywhere." His head was foggy, disconnected. After a minute he lifted his head. "I don't even know where I am."

They didn't twitch, but something about the stance softened. They uttered a word, something that sounded like music and ended with a click. He nodded.

"Okay, so wherever *that* is, I'm officially farther from home than I've ever been in my entire life. I was born in Prague. You know it?"

The child's eyes widened.

He lifted his hand in greeting. Man, his muscles all felt fried. "Chris."

The kid nodded, like duh.

"Oh, you know everything, huh?" Chris laughed. That only made his ribs ache.

The kid smirked. Smug little turd.

"Well, what's the square root of 698 times twelve?" Chris grinned.

"Never mind, don't answer that. I can't even tie my shoes right most days."

The kid's upper body canted in that way that meant laughter was coming. "Three hundred and seventeen!"

"You forgot the decimal."

The kid looked at him, shrugged again.

"What do they call you?"

"You can call me Gir," the kid said imperiously.

It was a title of some kind. "Is that like boss or something? Head honcho? Little person in charge?"

The kid cracked up again. "Ayuh. Something like that."

The kid's accent was startlingly like Ofelia's or Ayele's without the posh globe-trotting veneer. He wished he was better at placing people. His dad would have known. Toby too, probably.

He felt around in what remained of his pockets. "Hey, Gir, can I get my phone? Need to update the group chat."

His guard sucked small teeth like little pearls, bright in the rich brown face.

Chris shrugged. "Answer's always no until you ask."

The kid's mouth canted. "My mama says something like that."

"So does mine."

Chris stretched, looked around. One way out. And that was guarded by a twelve-year-old. Great.

"Can you tell me if my… friend… Ofelia— Is she okay?" he asked. "Can I see her?"

"She asked me to stay with you." The kid's face shifted in a mix of emotions. Chris thought he picked out awe and a little frustration. "You are hungry?"

The one constant in Chris's life was hunger. It wasn't that he was underfed, just that he could always eat.

The kid cocked their head with a decided look of communication.

Telepathy. Great. He was up against telepathic kid witches. He wasn't going anywhere anytime soon. "I need to get word to my family that I'm okay. I won't tell them… anything."

The kid shook their head regretfully.

A few minutes later, trays of food arrived, carried by a bevy of youths in immaculate bright purple-and-green robes. A uniform of some kind. Fish cooked in big leaves, roast haunch of something that smelled close enough to boar to make Woof sit up at attention, stewed greens and tubers, and fruits: fresh, dried, soaked in liquor. Flatbreads and some kind of porridge that smelled like corn.

Chris thanked each of them as tray after tray was set down. They looked a little startled to even be acknowledged. One even winked at him. And then he realized they weren't breathing.

Undead. There was a necromancer close by.

A bowl of warm water and a towel came last. His hands. He washed obediently.

Chris's stomach growled audibly, but he looked up. "Hey, Gir. You gonna get in on this?"

The kid pointed a slim finger to their narrow chest, eyebrows up.

"Yeah, come on, even I can't eat everything." He gestured expansively at the massive table covered in food.

The kid watched him warily for a minute, probably assessing if this was a trick. "You won't get far, you know."

Chris plopped into a chair on the long end of the table farthest from the door. He grabbed what looked like the biggest drumstick he'd ever seen. "There's a necromancer around here, huh? Zombies gave it away. So you're like, not *exactly* a guard—maybe here to keep me company, right?"

The kid looked down, a little abashed.

Chris shrugged and set his molars to the bone of some animal's haunch. It surrendered with a resounding crack. He chomped the meat and connective tissues down, sucking the marrow with relish. Woof rumbled contentedly. He set the remnants aside.

The kid's eyes were like saucers. Chris ignored him. His strength returned with every bite, the aftereffects of the spell wearing away.

After a moment the kid joined him. They took the seat at the head of the table automatically, Chris noted. He filed that away. This kid was a powerful witch. Zombies bowed to them. Some kind of nobility. And Ofelia had asked them to babysit.

"What is this?" Chris asked of the stewed green paste that smelled like heaven, some sort of rich cream and spinach. "And how do I get it into my face as quickly as possible?"

The kid cackled. "Do as I do."

Chris followed, lifting bread and scooping, then adding little mounds of peppers and wedges of meat. When he had the perfect imitation of the kid's—albeit in larger portions—he stuffed the whole thing in his mouth. His eyes bulged. It was delicious and spicy as fuck.

The kid was laughing so hard the carefully tucked stuffing began to tumble out of the folded flatbread before they could manage a bite. Chris, choking down a mouthful, laughed until tears streamed.

The pitcher next to him was filled with beer, he realized when he took a big gulp.

When the meal was over, the zombies returned to clear plates and tidy what remained.

One escorted him to a small side chamber. "Toilet."

After a bath and following the pantomimed instructions on how to dress himself in the linen tunic that shifters seemed to prefer here, Chris found himself again in the main room. The kid had cleared a little space on the coffee table and had a small board with cups and shells.

"Game time?" The food had settled him and it was good being clean, but Ofelia was nowhere to be seen, and he had no way to get in touch with home.

The kid touched his arm. "You don't worry. All will be well. Please let's play."

"Did you read my mind, Gir?"

"Your face." The kid exaggerated an expression of concern: knit brows and downturned mouth.

Chris folded himself at the table, resigned.

Past dusk and after rounds of getting his ass kicked repeatedly by a preteen, Chris looked up at the faint scent of citrus and fennel.

"Tell me you aren't wagering with a child." Ofelia came into the room with a sigh.

The kid leaped to their feet, at attention, game forgotten.

Ofelia waved her hands in a soothing gesture. She looked— Well, she looked incredible. She was draped in some kind of a gold sheath of a dress, thin enough that the outline of her body was visible but modest for all that, revealing only bare arms and slits up either leg to the thighs. Soft sandals whispered across the floor. Her hair was freshly braided against her scalp in front, the back left loose and fluffy. Hammered-gold cuffs gilded the small arch of each ear, and the gold-and-lapis collar framing her throat below the chin to just over the shoulders looked like something out of an antiquities display.

"It's nothing." Ofelia shook her head, rolling her eyes at the youth and singsonging "tradition" in a way that made the kid chortle before she turned her attention back to Chris. "I'm sorry—you've been here all day. Are you well—"

"I'm fine," Chris choked out, feeling a little like he should bow or something. He cleared his throat, fought for composure. "I've had good company."

Ofelia put her hands on her hips, mock glaring at the kid standing between them. "You know he does not understand our money."

"Dates," the child mumbled. "We wager dates."

Ofelia met Chris's eyes, a smile tugging on her lips.

Chris lifted one shoulder. "I play better when I've got something on the line."

Her mouth fixed, a half smile flattening softly.

"What's wrong?"

Surprise flashed momentarily in her eyes. "So do I apparently."

He started to close the distance between them, but she looked back to the kid and opened her arms. The kid flung themself into her waist and hugged her tight. The smaller face turned up with such a look of affection Chris's chest caught.

They spoke softly in that lilting, clicking language, a glance or two passing his way making it clear he was the subject of the conversation. He heard a familiar word.

Ofelia choked, laughing as she switched to English for Chris's benefit. "You made him call you Gir?"

The kid looked embarrassed.

Ofelia sighed, facing Chris. "This upstart is Alam, my nibling."

"I thought you were an only child."

"They're my cousin's child." She shrugged. "I was here for some time when they were young. We were close. Are."

Chris understood. His nieces and nephews would all grow up like siblings. Big families could be like that.

"I've missed you," Ofelia said to the kid. "And I thank you for taking good care of my friend. Collect your winnings and tell your friends all about your day. I must talk with him now."

Alam looked skeptical and a bit envious but dutifully followed orders. They turned toward the door and looked back hopefully. "Can I come tomorrow? Just to visit."

So there would be tomorrow.

"You must ask our guest," Ofelia said.

Alam closed the distance expectant brown eyes on Chris.

Chris nodded and tried to smile.

The kid stretched out a slim, long-fingered hand studded with fat rings inlaid with designs between jewels, laid it gently on his wrist.

"You are under the protection of our family now," Alam said. "No harm will come to you. Do not be afraid."

The smile tugged Chris's lips before he could catch it. "I'm grateful for your protection. But I too have a family that will be missing me—worrying about me even."

Alam nodded solemnly, a censure in those brown eyes when they turned to Ofelia. To Chris's surprise, she looked away first.

"Good night, little boss." She laughed, but her voice shook around the edges. "Tell your fathers I said thank you and that you've done very well for your first day as a gir."

Alam grinned over a tiny, embarrassed shuffle of their sandals. They looked back at Chris. "No harm meant."

"None taken," Chris said. "I think."

And then Alam was gone, scampering away like more of a child than they'd seemed all day.

Ofelia sighed. She lifted a hand, unfurled her fingers, and the doorway that had been there a moment ago vanished. A shimmer rose up the walls, meeting at the center of the ceiling.

"There—we have some privacy," she said softly, moving past him to take a seat at the big table. She poured herself a drink from the pitcher, sniffed it, and put it aside again. "You must have questions. I'll answer as many as I can."

She seemed as though this was the first time all day she'd been able to fully exhale. The line of her shoulders sagged the tiniest bit even as her ribs expanded and released in long, slow breaths. Her fingers danced on the edge of a platter of fruit.

There would be time for answers.

He retrieved the water jug from the side table and slid a chair in close to her. She met his eyes and then lowered hers, sighing again. Her forehead rested lightly on the heel of one hand. "I had no idea—"

"Wait." He made a plate. She didn't smell like she ate a lot of meat, so he heaped up fruit and bread. The little pot of stewed greens was remarkably still warm. One he hadn't even gotten to contained some kind of squash in a savory curry-like sauce.

He slid it to her.

"I'd hoped to take you out to dinner." He bracketed her chair with his knees. "Feels shitty feeding you your own food, but—"

Ofelia stared at him as though she were seeing him for the first time. Her eyes shone before she blinked the moisture away. "This is—"

"Eat." The wolf made his voice gruff, an order. "We can talk later."

She did. Elegantly, but with a ravenous edge. He refilled the water. The peas and squash seemed to be her favorite.

Didn't they feed you, he wanted to ask, this family that gilded you like a queen after stealing you away from everything you'd built for yourself?

"Ayele spoke to your friend Klaus," she said between hasty bites. "He told your family you would be gone for a few days. Clubbing in Amsterdam, I think. I'll try to get you back as soon as I can, I promise, but they may insist on a vow."

"Thank you, I think?" His brows rose.

She looked away, miserable.

"Is this your place?" He changed the subject.

She stared at him.

"The photos." He gestured to the walls. "You took them? And the colors, it reminds me of your flat in Prague. Does your family own the building? Do they all live here?"

She blinked. "You aren't— This doesn't surprise you."

"The past few years have been *weird*. This is not the strangest thing that's happened to me. Believe."

Laugher bubbled up in her—he could see it in her eyes, the way her lips rippled like she was trying to contain it.

"My mom's a witch and my sisters-in-law," he said patiently. "My brothers are the most annoying assholes you've never met, who also happen to turn into wolves. It takes a lot to surprise me these days."

Her laughter broke. She looked like she'd needed it.

Her fingertips rested on his thigh, just above the knee. A little jolt raced through him, the want he'd been putting aside all day now sharper, more demanding. He rubbed his own fingertips across hers slowly.

"What are we up against here?" Again, her eyes widened in surprise. He had a feeling not much surprised her. After today, he thought he might understand why. "This is your family? Did you run away? Do you owe them something?"

Again the sigh as she pushed away from her plate.

They were together, they were safe, and her wearing whatever that excuse for a dress was stirred the heat in his groin that seemed to be a constant whenever she was near. His cock throbbed, pleasant memories of their night together taking precedence over everything. The way she'd surrendered to sleep at last like a light shutting off. Her body had draped over his chest, long limbs graceful even tangled up in his.

He was going to listen to this story, and then they would make a plan to get home, and then he was going to take her to bed and do whatever it took to make sure she got a good night's sleep.

"Come on." He tugged her to her feet. "I have a feeling this is going to be a long one. We might as well be comfortable."

CHAPTER FIFTEEN

SHE LED him to a chaise big enough for four. As he kicked his sandals off and his feet up, she tugged off the ear cuffs and rings. The bracelets came next, clattering onto the platter on the side table along with her belt. She laid it reverently aside, fingers tracing her family emblem, the thick leaves intertwining and vines forming the buckle and clasp. She'd seen it her entire childhood. Her mother surrounded her with it.

So you will always know to whom you belong, she'd said, her eyes bright.

The family?

To me and your father of course. She winked. *But mostly to me.*

Years later and thousands of miles away, Ofelia's heart strained at the binding of her rib cage. She'd thought she'd left this place behind forever. It was a complicated feeling. She'd missed and hated it for what it was— both the last connection to her mother and a cage to escape.

She had a palace full of aunts, uncles, cousins. They loved her, were eager to add her into the constellation of their family. They considered the bargain her parents had struck foolish. This was the life she was owed.

She tried to explain to Chris what it was to know she was wanted but also the expectation that she would fit a space meant for a woman born and raised to fill it. That a family she'd never known—one that welcomed her with open arms—loved the idea of a second chance with her mother. How it felt to have peers openly admire—and resent—her for the raw power of her charm as much as her lineage. How she'd let them all down in the end to take what her mother had wanted most for her—her freedom.

Sometime during her conversation, he'd leaned onto the cushions, opening one arm. She'd slipped her shoulder into the space he made for her between his biceps and rib cage without thinking.

"My parents left money in accounts all over the world." The hollow under his collarbone cradled her head perfectly. When his arm tightened around her, the breath that lifted her on his chest settled her more comfortably. "I waited for my opportunity, and I ran."

"They want you back." His fingertips rubbed the curve of her arm. "In general or for something specific?"

"Yes. Both maybe." She sighed. "I don't know. I'm waiting to be summoned."

"Summoned." His free hand came to the small of her back, encircling her. It was the safest she'd felt in her entire life. "By the… high priestess?"

"We are called àjé here. The First Àjé." She shook her head against his shoulder. "They don't even consider *witch* an acceptable translation because it means so much more to be àjé. It is creation and destruction. They protect and nurture. They serve as advisors, scientists, teachers, as well as defenders. *Mother* is a better interpretation. Alam's mum, my Aunt Serwaah, is First Àjé now. She had a few choice words about my abandonment of my duties. She *and* her concord."

"Concord?"

"It's a title, but it's also the word for a bond between an àjé and her shifter." Might as well break it to him now. "It's usually not a romantic bond, but in this case he's also her second husband."

"Of how many?"

"Four." She tensed.

"A good number." His thumb found the spot at the bridge between her shoulder and neck, light pressure coaxing release. "The directions."

Relief swept away surprise. She could add a desire not to have to defend this place and her family to the complex nest of her own feelings. Not to just anyone, but increasingly to him. She'd sort that out later.

"Families are big here—it's a way of unifying powers and protecting. Multiple husbands, sometimes wives. I have more cousins than I can count."

Chris accepted that like everything else, with a nod. "Ofelia, where *exactly* are we?"

It was the question she'd been dreading all day.

She pushed into a sitting position, planting her feet on the floor to ground herself. She would not run. Through the connection, she could feel the distant roots of the grandmother tree in the courtyard acknowledging her return with a tree's subtle joy.

"Tell me what you can." No demand for details. *An explanation.* "Start small. Is this your flat?"

"It was my mother's." She braced herself on her hands, squeezing the edge of the cushions as she looked around them. It wasn't that she was ashamed. She just liked the way he looked at her when he thought she was a girl in a run-down train station. The way he didn't hesitate to touch her, tease her. She didn't want to lose that. "It's mine now. This building belongs to my family."

Again he surprised her. "So you're a princess?"

She laughed. "You've spent too much time in Europe."

"Educate me, Your Highness."

She sucked her teeth, tossing a glance at him over her shoulder. He was smiling with that same open expression. Impressed but undaunted.

"My family is one of the oldest," she admitted. "One of the first."

"The first." His words were more prompts than questions, and she found it easier to explain when she just finished the sentences.

"Of the forty-two." The story she'd been told first as a bedtime tale and then as a history spilled out. "Forty-two tribes made a bargain to preserve our ways—unite our magic—long before the world became what it is now. In allegiance with a master of death, we chose a life apart, to protect and be protected. We have never known chains or the borders of the outside world." She understood her mother's pride in the words now. "My family and the others of the forty-two have upheld our bargain to hide this place from the rest of the world and, in doing so, have earned the right to continue to practice our magic openly."

"How long?"

"For nearly eighty generations."

"This city must be huge."

"Africa is an enormous continent." She sniffed, unable to keep a little bit of satisfied primness out of her voice. "It is not difficult to make much of its heart impassible with the right magic."

He laughed. Seven help her, she was going to fall in love with him if he kept doing that. Every time she thought he would just shut down—in disbelief or anger or overwhelm—he just grinned and rolled with it.

"And not everyone lives here." She found herself explaining. "After the godswar, the continent—the territory—was ours again. My family has many smaller cities and villages under our stewardship outside the hidden city. But this is our home."

"Mama Mummy closed the whole continent," he murmured softly, putting it together. "To hide the magic from the other necromancers."

Ofelia tried not to make a face in distaste at the nickname. Mama

Mummy—the necromancer who traveled with desiccated corpses as her escort. Illusions she'd given the world to distract them from the truth. "Except for a few strategic cities, mostly on the coast. Now it is mostly the old families who remain here in her true seat."

"Your necromancer knows what you are."

"Àjé have worked beside the necromancer to protect our society for two thousand years. Here we are... essential." She'd never spoken so much truth to anyone outside this place. Had never had to—everyone here understood their history. Let outsiders think a withered old crone controlled the continent, turning anyone who disobeyed into walking death. That she alone was powerful enough to rebuff any intruders into her territory.

Ofelia wanted Chris to understand. Even after she'd gotten him dragged halfway across the world, he'd thrown himself in with her—and trouble—without hesitation, just like when they were kids. The first outside her blood who'd stood up for her, defended her. Who loved her.

It was in his face. It had never left.

She looked away. "Who do you think had the idea for the Allegiance in the first place, based on what she'd done here?"

He was quiet for so long she risked a glance over her shoulder. Even the wolf was still, letting him navigate this terrain. And then the big eyes turned to her and she saw the animal's cunning and intelligence. She was wrong. The wolf was not quiescent. It was waiting. She'd never seen so little division between man and beast.

Was it because his mother was a witch? Such a thing was unheard of here. Her first uncle could never father a child of her aunt. Shifter and witch blood were too fragile, too different. Àjé scientists would salivate to get their hands on him.

The protective instinct rose in her, fierce and hot. The urge to keep him hidden, to keep him to herself, should have come with alarm bells. Instead, she bared her teeth. She had to get him out of here. Get him back to his home and his life and his remarkable family. No matter what it cost her.

You must know before you enter that room, Aunt Serwaah had reminded her, *what you are willing to offer and to sacrifice.*

She too had something of value on the board now. She was such a fool.

"Your aunt is the First Àjé and the head of one of the oldest magical families on what—the whole continent?" He placed each word carefully. "Your family's palace is the seat of the necromancer. You *are* royalty. Basically."

"That is your takeaway?" She looked back at him, eyes wide.

He grinned at her, all teeth, with eyes that were more gray than blue in the low light. His voice dropped, and his words rumbled through her, casting all her senses into disarray. "Oh please can I call you Princess?"

"You may *not.*" She snatched one of big pillows and swung hard.

His reflexes were fast, but she still caught him across the side of the head. He yelped in surprise, then grabbed another pillow and returned the volley. She threw up her hands, barely able to defend herself as her breath came in panting gasps of laughter.

He rolled off the chaise, searching for ammo. A square cushion hit her in the face. She fired back. He ducked and she realized he was headed for the bedroom. Smart wolf—he remembered her apartment in Prague. He'd teased her about the mountain of pillows on the bed… before he'd splayed her out on top of them and had his very wicked way with her.

No time for basking in those memories. She had a war to win.

She took the side route, through the tiled bathroom with the open skylights letting in the cool night breeze. She skidded around a tub big enough to fit a small army and into the bedroom. Just in time to get a pillow to the chest.

Chris stood to the side of the doorway, folded over at the waist and laughing so hard he was a dangerous shade of red. He managed to turn it into a mocking bow. "Milady."

She screeched, indignant, and launched herself at him. For a moment she was sure she'd surprised him, but he grabbed her around the waist and tossed her onto the bed like a child's doll. Oh, that would never get old.

She lay for a moment in shock at his casual, easy strength. A moment too long. His body slid over hers, all firm muscle through fine linen with his skin damp from exertion, pinning her to the mattress. He was a fire, burning the resistance out of her body.

There was no hope of catching her breath now even though he wasn't resting his full weight on her.

Nose to nose, they stilled as their laughter died together. His lips curved, full and inviting.

"May I kiss you?" His eyes were on hers, then her mouth and then back to her eyes again. "Your Highness."

He braced for an attack, but she grabbed his hair and tugged him close.

Kissing him felt like a continuation of their pillow fight, all play and levity. Until it wasn't and the thin material between them did nothing to hide the heat of their bodies. Her belly trembled against his arousal, her breasts heavy with longing. She yanked on his tunic and wiggled to get her thighs around his hips. His fingers slipped into the coils at the base of her neck, cupping her scalp with heart-aching tenderness, but she needed them to be elsewhere on her body right now.

He groaned into the side of her neck when she nipped at his ear. "What do you need, Princess?"

She was going to beg. And she couldn't find an ounce of shame to care. "Touch me."

He palmed her cheek, her throat, her breasts, one, then the other. She was breathless with longing for more—pressure, contact, sensation. All the while his mouth stayed on her face. Lips, cheeks, eyelids.

The heel of his hand settled against the curve below her belly button. She opened her eyes when he stilled.

"May I?" His mouth glittered with her eyeshadow, left him resembling some god of erogenous zones.

She relaxed her legs, letting him create space between them.

They'd been kidnapped—by her family—for an unknown reason. She had bigger things to worry about than getting her physical needs met. Her body was not conflicted at all. His fingers rubbed—no, slid—against her, and he planted his forehead against her collarbone, shuddering hard.

All the teasing was gone—he sounded as if he'd been running for his life. "Fuck. You're so wet—"

The wonder in his husky growl made her skin prickle with urgency. Tugging on his wrist was like trying to bend cold iron.

He looked up though, instantly a little wide around the eyes with his hair in disarray. "You want me to stop?"

"Yes." She panted. He began to withdraw, but she shook her head, gripping him desperately. "No. Not stop. I want *you* now—"

She kissed him, crooking her hips, hoping he got the message.

"No hurry." Again those little nibbles, this time down her jawline, her throat, the skin above her nipple. His head angled as his thumb taunted the most sensitive skin, Seven help her as madness threatened with each of those slow, wet sweeps.

"You don't have to—" She sucked in a breath over the sensation. "I don't need—"

Her senses returned briefly when he looked up at her again, puzzled.

His fingers slowed. He shook his head. "I want to give you… everything… if you let me. But I won't do anything you don't want me to do."

She gripped his wrist harder to keep him this time, her throat too full of unfamiliar warmth to speak.

His face took on a distant, listening expression, and his nostrils flared as he scented something. A beat later she heard it.

A polite throat clearing.

She looked up. They hadn't closed the door to the bedroom, though the angle of the doorway blocked the view.

Chris growled and slid smoothly off her.

Her playful lover was gone. He moved like a predator now, jaw beginning to jut and slide back, shoulders separating. It looked like it should have been a painful transformation. Only it happened with such liquid grace she wondered if it might feel like being set free instead. He didn't transform fully; instead, he lingered somewhere between wolf and man for a long moment, features blending into something truly ferocious. A low growl rumbled in his chest.

"Christof, wait!" Ofelia got to her senses and her feet, tugging her dress back into some semblance of order. She'd never seen anything like this half creature outside of a horror movie.

The man disappeared into the wolf and shook off the pile of clothing at his paws. She stooped to grab the linen as she passed, hurrying after him into the main room. "Woof!"

As a child, she had only glimpsed an echo of the wolf in Chris's eyes when he came back from the forest glade. A fleeting glance of a beast as pale and elusive as a unicorn. In her apartment, everything had happened so fast she hadn't had a chance to register what she'd seen.

Now, when she stepped out into the room behind him, her breath caught at the sight. He was enormous. The silvery, not quite white of his coat shadowed with threads of gray streaking behind his ears to the middle of his back made him seem otherworldly. His back rose nearly to her hip. Most of the shifters she'd known lost or gained mass going from human to animal, their animal skins true to living animals. If there were wolves of this size, they'd died out thousands of years ago.

He paced into the space between her and their visitors, ears up, tail stiff, the beginning of teeth showing under curled lips, and Ofelia felt a power that had nothing to do with her charm surge through her.

"Leash your dog, Cousin," Baako demanded.

"Mind your tongue, àjé," Ofelia said, reminding her of the basic respect all shifters were given here.

The wolf's growl made the hair rise on her neck. Six bladed spears dropped into readiness in answer. Pride arrowed through her at the sight of the Cadre's unease.

But in their eyes, an unbound shifter was a potential threat they wouldn't hesitate to neutralize. She couldn't let him get hurt again. Not for her.

As Ofelia closed the distance to him, one silver-lined ear flicked back. She had no idea how much of Chris remained, but she couldn't let them see that either. If they thought he was out of control, they would sanction him, remove him to shifter quarters. The hackles between his shoulders prickled her palms when she settled her hand with a confidence she didn't feel.

"This isn't the time or place," she murmured for his ear alone. "Though I appreciate the gesture, Woof."

He quit growling but didn't back down. Or shift back.

"You come unannounced and empty-handed." Ofelia focused on her abductor who was also her eldest cousin. "Again. What do you want this time?"

Baako's brows rose. "You try to insult *me*?"

Well, she had. But that wasn't going to get her questions answered either. Ofelia addressed another familiar face in the group. "Erandi, am I being summoned?"

"You are." The jaguar shifter had been on the edge of manhood the first time she'd been brought here. She'd stumbled on the golden-eyed cat hiding in the branches of Grandmother Tree. He, too, was an orphan. He understood what the others did not about what it was to be alone in the world. They'd spent long afternoons in the tree, becoming friends—and more for a time. A smile quirked his mouth. "Will you accept?"

He was the only shifter unaccompanied by his àjé. The concord scar on his arm was fresh. As powerful as they were, Alam was still too young to serve in an official capacity. Sending Erandi was a peace offering.

Ofelia put her back to the Cadre and crouched to cup the wolf's jowls in her hands. Sheer awe at the size of him cost her a moment of focus as she stared into his eyes. "I'll be back as soon as I can—"

"Both of you," Baako said.

Ofelia floundered, panic curling up her throat. He couldn't appear before the council. The risk of someone seeing what he was too great. She lurched to her feet, putting herself between the wolf and the room. "He has nothing to do with this."

"That's not your call." Baako's upper lip curled. "You'd best... clean yourself up. And get him back on two legs."

Ofelia was over having her cousin treat her—and Chris—like unwelcome guests. They hadn't asked to be brought here.

"He's not my familiar."

"Just a pet then?" Baako smirked.

Ofelia's fingers flared in invitation. Beneath her, the grandmother tree advised caution even as she responded to the call. A few of the shifters in her cousin's retinue twitched uneasily. They weren't in Prague anymore. Training might best blood when it came to finesse, but in terms of sheer power, she could tear this whole house down around them and they all knew it. And she wasn't untrained—just unrefined. She'd started formal training at seventeen, far too late for an àjé initiate by the hidden city's standards. But Ofelia had always been an exceptional student. In seven years in the place where being called "mother's daughter" was the greatest compliment, she exceeded every expectation and left no question of her lineage.

Their blades tipped up sharply, the other witches sliding back behind their shifters to craft a defensive charm.

"My orders are to deliver you, Fifiti." Only Baako didn't seek her concord's protection, shifting her short blade to her right hand as her left fingers twitched around an offensive charm. "The how was not specified."

Ofelia cycled through a dozen guards and a counter. Calling on Grandmother Tree was a bluff. She would not risk destroying her half of the palace in a fit of temper. But outnumbered and without her materials or a concord to draw on, she wouldn't be able to provide more than token resistance before they took her down. Again.

Woof placed one large paw on her foot, pressing lightly. His eyes were more blue than gray now, startling in the big lupine face. His brow crinkled in a question she understood without words.

"We must go," she admitted grudgingly. She knew some thought she'd made him her concord despite how publicly she'd railed against the bond in her time in training, so she spoke to clear their concerns. "But you choose your skin."

She ignored the sharp inhales from the àjé and the prickle of unease at their discomfort. What now—some obscure àjé rule prohibiting a shifter from appearing before the council in their animal skin?

Woof fixed the warriors in one more glance, and then his eyes returned to her face with another question. She gave the wolf her best smile, hoping she could convey her gratitude and respect for his showing up to defend her. They had once had a boy in common but had never had the chance to become friends.

"Yes, I will keep him safe," she promised.

Woof sat back on his haunches. Her hand slipped down fur and caught on bare skin. Chris stood up, and she strategically pressed the cloth to his hips. His glare didn't leave the warriors, and somehow even being naked with a face glittering with her eyeshadow didn't diminish the intensity of his expression.

"Come on." Tugging his arm was like trying to pull a block of granite. "They'll give us a few minutes."

That stormy dark glare flickered over her, and she shivered. Then, as if they were alone in the room, he turned his back to the doorway.

Someone whistled. One of the shifters purred.

Ofelia gave them the finger and followed Chris into the bedroom. Erandi's soft laugh followed them. Of course. She glared over her shoulder when she paused to scoop up her family's jewelry from the side table. He winked with a grin.

Inside, she raised a partition over the bedroom and bathroom doorways. While Chris struggled to get the tunic over his head again, she wet a washcloth and scrubbed at the lipstick on his face.

"I can't find the damn armholes."

She paused, located the openings in the fabric, then guided him through. She tried not to mourn the loss of that glorious bare skin, focusing on getting most of the glittery stuff off his cheekbones and lips.

His mouth looked as good as it had felt on her. Full lips plumped his poor cupid's bow out of shape. The broad curve of his nostrils and his dark, velvety lashes tipped with gold made him look like the X-rated version of a renaissance cherub.

To distract herself from jumping him right there, she asked, "How did you do that—hold a form between?"

"I watched this old French movie with my brothers as a kid," he muttered. "*Loup-Garou*? Anyway, that wolf man looked pretty scary. Sometimes going full wolf isn't ideal, so I thought Woof and I could try something like that. I just can't hold it long. My brother says it's a stupid party trick. This belt is—"

"Like so." She slipped it out of his hands, smoothing it expertly over his shoulder and then around his hips. She added the more complex folds and tidied the knot, ignoring the small voice inside that reminded her such details would be seen as her making her claim on him. "I think you're onto something, you and Woof. You should work on it."

He drew back, gaze wary. "You think so?"

"Absolutely." The intensity in his expression lit her up again. Warmth swamped her heart alarmingly. She bit her lip against a smile and nodded firmly. "I've never seen anything like it. It's incredible. And scary as hell. And having hands is… handy."

"Exactly."

Before she knew it, he'd harried her against the bathroom wall, his hands sliding under her ass to press her against his hardening cock. She squeaked in surprise but met him with teeth and tongue and desire.

This time the throat clearing from the other room wasn't so polite. And it was accompanied by the heavy thump of a spear butt on the floor that usually ended a sparring match.

"This is your family's color, the pattern too." His fingers traced her quick work with the knot, awe in his voice.

"The real trick was finding a tunic that fit. There's a bear—Ilya—his was the only thing that would come anywhere close." She stood back, admiring her handiwork. He looked presentable. Well, mostly. There was no hiding a hard-on in that garment.

His cheeks darkened as he noticed where her attention had gone. But instead of being embarrassed, he grinned. "Let's get through this in one piece and we'll pick up where we left off, yeah?"

Despite the anxiety brewing in the cauldron of her belly all day, Ofelia found herself smiling back. The effect he had on her… "Words are power, wolf."

"And you have my promise, àjé." He put his hand over his heart. "Now your turn."

He swiftly took the washcloth to her face with a gentle attentiveness she imagined might be necessary if he was used to doing this for smaller, less patient humans.

There was no time to reapply anything, but at least she wouldn't appear before the necromancer like a horny teenager caught mid make out session.

She poured a glass of water and murmured a few words over it until the water swirled and settled again. "Drink this."

He emptied the glass.

She took the glass back, startled. "You didn't even ask—"

"I trust you." He shrugged, then paused. "What was it?"

She shook her head. Unbelievable. "A charm for seeing. It will show you the truth of everyone you see. It's only temporary, and it may be distracting at first, but scents will be confusing in there."

"Where's there?"

"The council room." She forced herself to be calm, walking them both through what to expect. "Not every one of the forty-two will be represented. But the more there are, the bigger we know whatever they brought us here for is. Each is allowed a single guard. Maybe an àjé but often a shifter."

"Their familiar?"

"*Familiar* is an insult here—I shouldn't have used it, but sometimes Baako makes me so—" She threw up her hands.

When he caught them, she was startled to realize they had been trembling because of the contrast with how steady his were.

"Are you okay?"

Ofelia blinked against the sudden sting of tears. No one had asked her that in… how long? An automatic dismissal stuck in her throat. She most definitely was not fine.

He wrapped her in his arms, tugging her against his chest. "We get through this together."

Foolish, brave boy. How could he not see all of this was her fault? Guilt swamped her. She untangled herself hastily, tidying his tunic. "Let's just go see what she wants and get back home."

As they walked to the door, he slid his hand over hers and interlaced their fingers.

"Let me do the talking." She steadied her trembling breath. "Don't volunteer information. Just be… vague. I'll handle it."

She realized she had a death grip on his fingers, but when she tried to let go, he held firm.

"Words are power." He brought her knuckles to his lips. "Lips, zipped. Got it."

She shook her head without looking at him, unable to keep from smiling.

"Did I mention I know a few witches?" His lips brushed her ear.

"That's part of the problem." She took a step apart to clear her head but didn't let go of his hand.

The barriers slid out of the doorway with her nod.

"And don't just eat or drink anything anyone hands you," she added because apparently he needed to be told such things.

"Unless I trust them." He beamed.

She sighed, shaking her head. Incorrigible. She gave him a quick once-over. He puffed out his chest and made that tunic look like a linen caress. Again she wanted to smile. "It will have to do."

CHAPTER SIXTEEN

CHRIS TRIED. He really did. But his first glimpse of the world outside her apartment captivated him. They were escorted down a long, wide hall, open to the night air on all sides, and he glimpsed courtyards and people beyond—many more than he'd expected to be out at this hour. It had to be nearly midnight. The hum of electricity underlaid everything, and the passageways were well lit.

Murals covered the walls, old and new, depicting magic in all forms —àjé and shifters and others besides. The city being raised from the jungle, predators lying down with prey, the river alive with dancing craft, its waterways pulsing through the city like veins to a beating heart.

The questions stacked up in his throat. He puffed out his cheeks and sealed his lips shut.

"It's like I can feel the questions just begging to be let out," Ofelia murmured without even looking.

"Oh, am I still allowed to talk now?" Chris grinned. "When do I have to stop again?"

From somewhere behind him, one of the escorts laughed softly. The handsome shifter she'd spoken to, the one who smelled like some kind of big cat.

Ofelia scowled over her shoulder, but the smile lingered in her voice. "We've got time for one or two."

At the head of the escort, Baako—her cousin—glared at them.

Chris lowered his voice. "The people here—they're from all over the place. The world, I mean."

"You know the penalty for revealing yourself in other territories," Ofelia murmured.

Baako hissed in censure.

"You should have considered the ramifications before you dragged him here." Ofelia glared pointedly at Baako's back.

Chris reached out to cup her forearm in his fingertips and draw her attention back. He wondered briefly what their story was but figured now was not the time. Best to keep whatever was brewing between them to a minimum.

"The penalty in other territories. What is it?"

"Death," he answered automatically.

"Not exactly," she said.

Chris missed a step and had to hurry to keep up. "You're telling me people here were all sentenced to die in other territories?"

"Many."

"Walk with me, Cousin." Baako's words were not a request. "It is good for the people to see us united."

Ofelia gave him a complicated look of reluctance but lengthened her stride.

Before their escort re-formed seamlessly around them, she called over her shoulder, "Erandi?"

The shifter slipped to her other side and acknowledged him with a nod. "The price Amanirenas demanded for her part in the Allegiance was that necromancers must send the supernaturals who could not, or would not, hide themselves among human to her."

"Azrael agreed to this?" Chris said on a breath.

"Your Angel of Death was the first to accept," Erandi said. "Many others thought Amanirenas foolish, that it would be a liability collecting them in one place."

"Witches and shifters?"

"And others." Erandi nodded.

"But it's not a death sentence."

"There are some too dangerous—to themselves or the city—to be released." Erandi sighed. "It's not a perfect system, but many lives have been saved."

All his life his family had hidden under the threat of being revealed when the truth was a place like this existed. A sanctuary. For a moment his mind spun with the possibility they'd missed for another kind of life. One in which he and his brothers and mother could be who they were without fear. Where his nieces and nephews would never hesitate to claim their powers. His chest ached.

He reminded himself that her family had brought Ofelia here after her parents were killed and she had run. "You?"

"My family was killed when humans burned down our forest." Erandi gave him a half smile before his gaze lingered on Ofelia's set shoulders. "There was no life for me out there. For others, not so much."

Too soon, it seemed they passed out of Ofelia's family home—if a building so enormous could be called that—into a citadel that rose above a ring of compounds like hers that circled it. Here the walls and furnishings took on more of the desert, the jungle greens giving way to ochre and sandstone. The posted guards were no longer àjé and shifters but zombies.

None were the withered, wretched undead the necromancer known as Mama Mummy often appeared in public with. These had all been transitioned so expertly at death that only the scent gave them away.

Even Azrael's undead paled in comparison.

A quick glance from Ofelia told him the time for questions was over.

The lift rocketed them to the top of the citadel, and the doors opened into a single, enormous room with floors of interlocking stone slabs smoothed by time. The supports for walls rose around them—stone arches like the ribs of an ancient animal—but the walls themselves were transparent. Interlocking translucent symbols flared and vanished as his gaze passed over them, forming a shimmering dome overhead.

Unmarred by material walls, the room gave a 360-view of the city below.

It was like no city he'd ever seen, though the murals had represented it accurately. It was made up of a series of clustered settlements along interconnected channels of a broad river that curved through the densely populated center before disappearing into mountainous jungle. Lights ran along the streets and the canals, sharp blasts of color vibrant even in the night. The breeze blew freely through the room, cooler now than at midday but still humid and thick with the scent of forest and distantly cooking food.

Centuries of growth and decay stacked on each other without interruption—ruins amid the glass-walled high-rises and shining buildings. The distant sound of music and the bustle of cars and people reached them here under the sound of the night jungle.

The most startling thing of all was the land itself, aware, sensing *him*.

He tore his gaze from the view at the murmur rising from the center of the room.

The door they entered faced a gap in the circle of chairs. None were fixed, allowing the circle to be expanded or contracted to fit all assembled. Baako's escort stepped aside as they approached the gap, creating a chute through which Chris and Ofelia had no choice but to pass through into the center.

He kept his back straight and his face still, glancing at Ofelia for cues. Then he remembered the water she'd given him.

The eyes, she'd called it.

Inside the circle, he scanned the faces regarding them with curiosity and concern. There had to be at least thirty seated, each with a guard standing attentively at their shoulders.

His gaze revealed witches and shifters and minor necromancers among them. On shifters, the transparent overlay of animal skins shadowed human features.

Ofelia had said there were forty-two families. That meant most families were represented.

Shit. This was big.

They stopped before the only chair in the circle that could not be moved. It was built of stone and seemed to rise from the floor itself. It did not sit above the others, but there was no questioning it was a seat of command.

A muscular, dark-skinned woman with kinky hair cropped to her skull sat with one ankle propped on her opposite knee, assessing them with the indifference of a sated lioness. She wore her sleeveless tunic and simple pleated skirt like a warrior. If he had to guess, she was probably middle-aged, but time had left no marks on her.

It never would. Her irises shone copper instead of any human shade.

Mama Mummy, one of the immortals who made up the Allegiance of Necromancers, claimed the entire continent after the war, bordered only by Kadjiah's lands in the east. He expected the aged, kindly-looking grandmother flanked by wasted undead from the feeds. Again the questions piled up behind his lips, but he knew better than to ask now.

At her right sat a woman with a startling resemblance to both Ofelia and Alam. She must be Ofelia's aunt, Serwaah, the First Àjé. To the necromancer's left was an extra space between her chair and the next. Chris blinked, but all he could see was the seated woman's shadow. Something about it struck him as odd.

Ofelia swept her arms up, hands coming together between her chin and her breastbone, fingers and thumbs not quite touching as though she cradled an enormous ball between them. The àjé in her Prague apartment had done something similar before they cast whatever spell had knocked Chris and Ofelia out cold.

Here, no one reacted defensively. Instead, when she bent one leg, sweeping it below her and lowering herself into a graceful curtsy, the assembled host nodded as one.

The necromancer's greeting balanced amusement with the faintest hint of a rebuke. "You are a difficult one to get ahold of, my child."

"You could have just called," Ofelia said, the touch of exasperation in her voice making a few of the gathered circle gasp and shake their heads. Ofelia lowered her head and her voice. "Nana."

It sounded like a title rather than a name.

"Some say I shouldn't have had to." The necromancer's cheek twitched.

Ofelia's gaze rose, sharp and steady again. "You promised I would never have to stay beyond my will."

"You may leave at any time," the necromancer agreed, her eyes solemn. "But first, introduce me to your—"

"Friend, ma'am," Chris interjected. "Someone who cares about Ofelia."

He ignored the glare Ofelia leveled at him. The room was quiet enough to hear a grain of sand scrape across the floor.

Should he offer his name, or was that a more sacred exchange?

From her left, the necromancer's shadow shifted with no corresponding change of lighting, leaning toward her shoulder. Even Chris's altered vision wavered, trying to make sense of what it registered. The shadow wasn't alive or even a person perhaps. But it took a shape human enough to trick the mind. He couldn't determine features or age—it was too much strain to try to understand what he saw. It bent a head shaped like a bull and the necromancer stilled, her gaze fixed on Chris.

The message communicated, the shadow's head lifted, now hawklike.

"Wolf shifter." Amanirenas lowered her chin once, satisfied. "Something else."

Ofelia met the necromancer's eyes briefly, undaunted by the shine in the inhuman depths.

"Does he have a name?" the necromancer asked finally.

"Christof Douglass Vogel. Chris, ma'am." He could almost hear Ofelia's eyes rolling in exasperation. What had she said? Oh, offer as little as possible. Don't volunteer. Right.

But based on the state of his clothes, they had his wallet and his phone. He wasn't giving them anything more than they could have learned from a facial scan. And from what he saw out the window, he was sure they had that kind of tech. The city might have been built on and protected by magic, but it was just as modern as any of Azrael's.

"We have come at your bidding." Ofelia drew her attention. "We would hear what you say."

Wise, Chris considered. The words expressed willingness to listen but no obligation.

"Something is hunting in the city you have chosen," the necromancer began. "Taking blood from the dead."

"Witches." The First Àjé sniffed.

He'd caught glimpses on the news. Of course the reports had said nothing about the victims being witches. Nor had he recognized any of them from his mother's gatherings. She and his sisters were strong enough to defend themselves, but there were plenty of lesser-trained witches who would be vulnerable.

"We believe whoever is responsible is working with, or for, a powerful entity," the First Àjé added. "The one your parents were tracking when they were murdered."

Ofelia went so still beside him Chris glanced at her in concern. She'd said her parents had died in a car accident. If the news surprised her, her face gave away nothing.

"We believe he seeks to refine an element found in the blood. One that would give him power. We don't know exactly how he plans to use it—"

"This is how you bring me back into the fold?" The vitriol in Ofelia's voice shocked Chris.

He wasn't the only one. An unhappy susurrus went up among the assembled leaders.

"Fi," Chris whispered, reading the room.

She ignored him.

He faced the necromancer instead and spoke into the silence left by her rage. "How do you know it's the same person?"

The necromancer's gaze settled on him with what he hoped that was approval, not annoyance. Someone in the circle cleared their throat, and as one, the attention in the room shifted to Chris. He caught more than one of the guards beginning to arm themselves.

"I'll take your vow." He wasn't going to get himself kicked out and leave Ofelia facing this alone.

Ofelia stared at him as if trying to decide if she would mute him herself.

He flashed a smile at her, and before she could summon a spell, he finished the offer. "Silence, right? Everything I see and hear stays with me. As long as I live?"

The First Àjé rocked back in her chair. "You're *offering*—"

"The one you're looking for is in our—in Azrael's—territory. Right?" Chris faced the stately woman and tried not to focus on how much he'd like to see if that was what Ofelia would look like in a couple of decades. "That's why you want Ofelia. She does know the territory. I grew up in the city. A vow is the only way you can trust me enough to let me help, so I'll take it."

The First Àjé stared at him. Finally her gaze drifted back to the necromancer. Her brow arched.

The necromancer inclined her head. "Accepted."

Chris waited for the bolt of lightning or the painful twisting of his tongue and throat. A little writhing around on the floor perhaps. Some sort of sorcerous agony had to be involved for all the reservations they seemed to have. Nothing came.

Something else occurred to him. "Why haven't you talked to Azrael?"

Beside him, Ofelia exhaled a long breath through her clenched teeth that might have been his name.

"You know, necro to necro?" He went on. "He has this enforcer— they call him the Black Blade—he's probably all over this."

The First Àjé and the necromancer exchanged a look.

The necromancer's mouth angled. "You've chosen well, Fifiti."

"I've chosen nothing," Ofelia snapped. "Your bonds are barbaric and predatory." She turned to Chris, her eyes alight with fevered intensity. "You want to know why they won't just go to Azrael, warn him there's a witch killer on the loose in his territory?"

Chris swallowed, glancing at the glowering faces circling them. "Fi—"

"Their Allegiance is a sham," she snapped. "It's a détente between a bunch of apex predators who would rip each other apart as soon as look at each other. What is it they say? Keep your friends close and your enemies closer."

The First Àjé had the same look his mother did when his siblings fought at the dinner table and she wanted more than anything to down her entire glass of wine and begin rubbing her temples. Of course, she was too composed to let any of that slip, but he recognized the signs. "Daughter."

"I am not *your* daughter," Ofelia snapped. She turned to the circle, including them in her accusation. "If they tell Azrael they know about the hunter, it gives Azrael something to use against them. So instead, they let foreign witches die. They're not àjé, what do they matter? Until it's a threat to them. Now they hope they can clean up this mess without exposing their weakness. I left, so I am expendable."

"Do not attempt to justify your cowardice." Baako stepped to the First Àjé's side. Side by side, the resemblance was obvious. "The Cadre serves the people through the will of the council, our First Àjé, and the Nana. If we are to die, we do so willingly, that our families may live. We protect ourselves, our tribes, our people. Your mother knew that."

The words of a girl who still had her mother to one who did not seemed extra cruel.

"Do you have your own thoughts, Cousin?" Ofelia asked. "Or is it easier to be brainwashed?"

"I think you are a deserter." Baako bared her teeth, hand clenched on her spear.

"Enough." With the single word from the necromancer, the àjé stopped in her tracks and Ofelia's mouth clamped shut on a retort.

Ofelia sucked in a hard breath through her nose, blinking. Tears hovered on the edges of her lashes.

The necromancer spared neither of the young women her glare, but her words were for Ofelia. "If we fall, who will protect this thing we have built? The people we have sheltered? The many who don't have the luxury of running away?"

Ofelia's expression was a mask, but he felt the power building in her, as wild and green as the land around the citadel. Instinct told him using it here would be the worst possible place. Willfulness, the necromancer might tolerate. A complete magical meltdown? Probably not. But whatever the necromancer had done to her had frozen her in place. She had nothing left to lose but her control.

Taking a breath, he put himself between Ofelia and the necromancer. The council gasped.

He ignored them. Having his back to the necromancer made the hairs on his neck stand up. He ignored that too. "Look at me."

Her eyes flew to his. The pain in them was a nest of razor blades exploding in his chest. The hair on his arms was growing long and pale, bristling. Color leached from his vision. He welcomed Woof.

You want to fight, we'll fight them. He left the words he couldn't speak out loud in the wolf's gaze. She'd read him in the apartment, surprising them both. *We'll fight till we're free or we're dead.*

Her eyes widened a fraction in question.

For you? His gaze fixed. *Yes.*

She closed her eyes and her fingertips found his chest, palm to the thumping heart beneath bone. He settled something only passably resembling a hand over hers. Even through thickening layers of fur, the heat of her body raced into him, and her scent drowned out everything else.

When she opened her eyes, rage gave way to grief that knit man and wolf to her for life. *That is a gift too big for me to ever claim.*

Her power subsided. As Woof retreated, the rest of the room came back to him in sound first. Worried gasps and a cry of outrage.

A force stronger and more complicated than any other in the room prickled the air. The comfortable humidity vanished, and each inhale was like sucking sandpaper into his lungs. Chris coughed. His skin protested, sweat blossoming, then disappearing immediately. The lights in the room wavered as if they, too, were uncertain of the wisdom of continuing to illuminate the room.

"I apologize, Nana." Ofelia gasped, yanking him to her side again, placing her shoulder in front of him as if to protect him now. He didn't like the terrified uncertainty in her eyes at all. She didn't understand what was happening either. "I failed to advise him. The responsibility is mine—"

The necromancer lifted a hand, and Ofelia let the sentence go. The necromancer's shadow shifted, rippling, but she kept her eyes fixed on Chris in a long stare that threatened to curdle his blood in his veins.

"If you show your skin again in this room, I will take it from you, boy."

Chris lowered his head, repentant. No wolfing out in front of the necromancer either then.

The necromancer sat back in her chair with a disgusted exhale, and the humidity of the room returned to normal.

The electricity steadied, and the counselors resumed their low-level side conversations.

"Daughter Zafeiriou has made the proper excuses and arrangements," one of the councilors confirmed.

At the sound of the name, Ofelia's head snapped to attention. "Why Ayele?"

"When you chose to settle in the seat of another's territory," the necromancer said, "it was decided that keeping our eye on you was a good idea."

"You planted a spy in my heart." Ofelia's voice cracked. "Now you dangle the suggestion that my parents were murdered. And you expect me to *want* to help you?"

"You have a chance to avenge your motherline." The First Àjé's voice was even, but Chris sensed a plea in the words. "This is what daughters do."

"Then send yours," Ofelia snapped.

Baako's fist tightened on her staff, and she shot the First Àjé a look.

Chris thought the warrior àjé might like that very much and wondered how much of her anger with Ofelia's refusal was that she herself had been denied the chance.

"It is not so easy to sneak in and out of another's territory," the necromancer said. "It will be several days before we can arrange your return. You have time to consider this opportunity."

"Vengeance won't bring my mother back," Ofelia said, the fight gone out of her voice. "We take our leave."

Halfway to the door, the necromancer spoke. "The two-skin must remain. He has a vow to make."

Ofelia paused, heaving a breath. She glanced at him and then the circle, torn. The strain of the confrontation was beginning to show in the corners of her mouth, the little crease pulling her brows together. He recognized the look of a witch about to come apart at the seams.

"Get outside, stick your toes in the dirt, ground yourself." He hoped he looked more confident than he felt. "I'll catch up."

"It may hurt a little, but she won't harm you." Her endless brown gaze sloped toward his from under her lashes, and the quickening of his heart had nothing to do with fear of the necromancer.

Her eyes shone too brightly. It gutted him. Even with his wolf, he wasn't strong enough to protect her.

"This is the most exciting night I've had in a long time." He forced a grin as he stepped backward toward the circle and winked. "Wait up. I made you a promise."

Her cheeks bunched a little, the smile not quite meeting her eyes, but a step in the right direction. "Erandi will see you home—back to the apartment."

When she was gone, he faced the necromancer… and froze in shock. The entire room had emptied soundlessly.

Only the First Àjé remained, exchanging meaningful glances with the necromancer. The shadow was more solid now, and Chis got the distinct impression its attention did not waver from him.

"I can handle a little vow, Serwaah." The necromancer chuckled. "It's good for me to do a basic charm occasionally. What do you tell the children—simplicity is the foundation of a great practice?"

The First Àjé fixed her with a measured look but departed.

"So, Christof Douglass Vogel." The necromancer faced him, resting her elbows on her knees to study him as though he were the most fascinating thing in the room. Or prey.

"Ma'am."

"You know who I am."

It seemed too obvious to warrant a reply. But she was silent, so he cleared his throat. "Yes, ma'am."

It was old superstition that led people to give the most powerful necromancers nicknames, as if saying their given names aloud could somehow invoke their presence. They were instead referred to in a reverent hush as the Angel of Death, the Red Death, Silver Tongue, the Nightfeather, Mama Mummy, and so on.

The image of the old woman, stout and spry, who often appeared publicly with her desiccated zombies, was the only one anyone had ever seen. He made himself focus on her mature, if unlined, face. "It's the eyes. Not just the color, the shine. Your eyes don't change."

Her mouth lifted. "You are a very observant boy, Mr. Vogel."

"Just Chris." He shrugged. "Mr. Vogel's my dad."

She exhaled softly. "He is like you?"

Chris felt the squeeze of Ofelia's caution. But the necromancer had seen something different about him before and had not revealed it to the council. Still, he honored Ofelia's demand. "I don't really understand much about how it all works and why we are the way we are."

"It is wise of you not to tell me a lie." She sat back and rolled her fingertips over the armrest of her chair. "You know magical creatures."

He lifted one shoulder. "I protect my family the way you protect yours."

Her eyes widened, and for a moment he thought her shock was mocking, but this time the smile did curl her mouth. "Clever. You honor your mother."

"Yeah, she's pretty amazing." He cleared his throat. Time to change the subject. "This witch hunter. Is there a pattern, anything else about the way he does what he does?"

She remained silent, watching him.

The sweat bloomed under his arms and along his back.

"Every decade or so, he slaughters a handful of witches and disappears before we can hunt him down," she said finally.

"Something is different about this time, isn't it?" Different and worrisome, he guessed, because they'd pinned their hopes on someone who despised everything they stood for even if she loved it with all the pieces of her broken heart.

"He's made a mistake," the necromancer admitted. "He's struck again. Soon and too close to his last appearance. He is either overconfident or desperate."

"Or he's close to whatever he's planning to use the blood for," Chris offered sensibly.

The shadow shifted beside her, but the necromancer didn't twitch, considering Chris in her flat metallic stare. "It is unusual at my age," she said, and he had the feeling the words weren't aimed at him, "to be surprised by one so young. The last one to do such a thing was you."

A sound rolled through the shadow like a distant thunderstorm, but Chris thought it was amusement.

"You suit her very well." The necromancer returned her focus to Chris. "Trained, you would have made a fine concord for an àjé of her potential. But you are not, and she has chosen another path. I thought, perhaps, she would come to her senses, but time has not been our ally. It might be an easier road to forget this altogether. You could wake up tomorrow in your own bed and this will all be scraps of a dream."

Chis started, his heart racing. "But you said—"

"It could be as if you'd never met at all." The necromancer ignored him. "It might be better for you. Once the others find out what you really are, there will be interest in you that even I cannot avert."

"What I really am?" He swallowed, his throat suddenly dry.

"A wolf-skinned witch child," the necromancer murmured. "Startling. Some will want to push to see what you are capable of. Others would prefer to take you apart to find out. A little forgetting would solve the problem."

She lifted her hand, and with a sudden leaden sinking in his stomach, Chris knew the decision had been made for him. He was going to lose Ofelia again, and this time they'd take her from his memory. His tongue dried to the roof of his mouth; his throat tightened.

He sucked in a hard breath. "No."

The necromancer splayed her fingers and words formed on her tongue that he would never be able to recall later.

His limbs felt heavy, his senses dragging. He shook his head, knowing his heart would always yearn for what he had lost even if he no longer remembered her face. "Please."

A hand of shadow settled on the necromancer's shoulder. The necromancer cast a glance at what he assumed passed for the nebulous face.

"Prague is my city." Chris caught himself on his forearms as his knees buckled. "My home. Don't I get to fight for it?"

Did he imagine the look in her eyes softened? Maybe it was his brain losing consciousness making his sight ripple, but he swore the shadowed figure nodded.

The necromancer continued in that low, droning language, something older than human.

In his dreams, he ran through Prague, only it had decayed into a massive forest and the calls of the birds were ones he no longer recognized. He had to get home. If he could just make it back to the building in the shadow of the ancient fortress turned city park… Home. But when he rounded the last bend, those ruins had succumbed to the trees and the brush, and the shadows of big cats hovered in the branches. He fell to his knees, tasted dirt and leaves and blood, and howled.

CHAPTER SEVENTEEN

CHRIS WOKE to voices arguing in hushed tones. His body was heavy and sore, as if he'd detoured for a marathon. He lay still, letting the voices wash over him.

"She has forbidden it." Alam's youthful voice was firm.

"She has forbidden *you*."

"And you are *my* concord."

"Don't you dare." The big-cat hiss gave Erandi away. "You weren't there last night."

"I can't believe I'm agreeing with Ofelia on this." Alam sighed, less confident but resigned. Relief washed through Chris at the sound of her name. He still had his memories: sunlit afternoons in the dilapidated train station, the taste of gummy bears on her lips, her scent on his skin, the weight of her body on his. Her scent was old though. She'd been gone for a while.

"Of anyone, you should understand. It is not fair to *him*—"

"Quiet. He's awake."

Alam made a frustrated sound not unlike the jaguar.

Chris filled a glass and drank it down, then another for good measure. He shrugged on the tunic near the bed and did a hasty job with the belt. Nothing as nice as Ofelia had done the night before, but it would do.

The jaguar shifter leaned into the doorway. "We woke you?"

"Nah." Chris rubbed his hair and lifted his voice. "Hi, Alam."

The small àjé appeared around Erandi's elbow. They brightened at the sight of Chris in one piece, their long-fingered hands clasped in eager delight. "You heal fast! I am told your other skin is a magnificent wolf. Big as a lion. Moonlight on snow."

Erandi cleared his throat, cheeks darkening, and seemed to have difficulty finding someplace to settle his gaze.

"I wish I could have seen such a thing." Alam plowed on, oblivious. "Alas, no, I am too young to be present at the council meetings. And yet *you*"—a pointed look at the jaguar—"got to attend because you and Ofelia—"

"How do you feel, wolf?" Erandi interrupted, nudging the àjé.

Alam straightened up, all business. Small hands darted in a complex pattern before them and a shimmering image appeared over Chris's chest. "Heart is good. No vision problems? Headache?"

Chris squinted but his vision was clear. He felt around his mind, but there were no obvious blocks. Whatever had been done to him was more subtle than that. His head did throb faintly. "A little."

"I can do something for that." Alam knotted slim fingers.

Chris held up his hand. "I'm good. Thanks."

"I'm a good healer." Alam looked disappointed but shrugged. "It's not my specialty. but I am very good."

"I'm sure you are," Chris said gently. "But I'm good on spells for a while."

"Charms," the young àjé said. "Your loss."

"Ofelia wanted us to give you this." Erandi offered him a woven basket. Inside were his phone, keys, and wallet.

Chris turned the device on. Fully charged. The group text was out of control. There were a couple of messages from his mom but nothing from his brothers. He exhaled, not sure why that bothered him.

"Where is she?" Chris tried not to look at the door.

"She's gone to her aunt," Erandi said. "The other one. She'll be back by sundown."

He met the jaguar's golden-brown eyes. "I can—"

"She waded through a lot of bullshit from Baako to get that for you. Call your family."

Chris exhaled. He had no idea how necromancers' vows worked, but he imagined an attempt to break them, even inadvertently, would be painful. "What can I say?"

"You won't be able to say anything to compromise the city." Erandi gave a lopsided smile. "I suggest you keep it simple. Leave a message if you can. We'll go."

"Wait." Chris didn't want to be left alone all day in the dark again. And the shifter wanted to tell him something, but Alam refused. If he could just persuade them he could be trusted, maybe they would let him in on whatever it was. "I mean, this will just take me a minute."

Erandi started to smile as Alam frowned and said, "We have duties—"

"I was wondering if maybe there was someplace I could run… you know… the wolf," Chris suggested, and the young àjé's expression changed to interest. "It would help me clear my head, and I got the vibe that shifting anywhere near the necromancer is a no-no."

"It is discouraged." Erandi's brow rose.

"You could show me someplace where it's cool," Chris said lightly. "I'd be okay if you wanted to hang out. Woof likes ki— young people."

Erandi and Alam exchanged a look. The kid fairly vibrated with anticipation.

"We'll be outside." Erandi nodded.

Thankfully Chris's mom didn't pick up, so he wound up attempting a message three times until what came out didn't sound like he had a mouthful of peanut butter or he'd lost his train of thought mid-sentence. *Back in a couple of days.*

Erandi and Alum waited patiently for him in the hall.

The shifter smiled wryly. "She's had a thousand years to perfect that charm. You didn't stand a chance."

As they moved away from the citadel, the buildings in the outer circles became less grand. Solid but less sizable residences and apartments over shops seemed to be the more common buildings through the rest of the residential area. A modern city center began on the other side of the market, sloping down the hill out of the jungle and along the broad river delta. They turned away from the main flow of traffic heading toward the market, instead following the road to where the birdsong and animal calls were louder than the music of transports and voices.

When they reached the line of trees, Erandi shifted, spotted coat as perfectly suited in the cover of brush as in his native rainforest.

Seeing the shifter roused Woof in his chest, and Chris surrendered. Alam's disappointment at having to carry both tunics seemed outweighed by delight judging by the little gasp they gave when the big wolf leaped easy circles around them, shaking out his coat and wagging his long tail in greeting.

Woof tracked the jaguar by scent but got taken by surprise when the big cat dropped from above. They rolled, battling without claws or teeth. If Chris had been a natural wolf, he thought he probably wouldn't have had a chance.

They regained human skins near a series of pools formed by cascading waterfalls where Alam had set up a blanket for a picnic.

Chris ran his hand through his sweaty hair, picked the leaves and detritus off his skin, and grinned. It was probably stupid to feel so happy. He should be worried about… everything. But it was the first time in his life he didn't need to hide what he was and he wasn't in the shadow of his brothers. Prague felt so far away. It was easy to forget—for a little while— that witches were in danger.

And to protect those witches, he needed to be at full strength, help Ofelia make peace with the necromancer so they could get home, and get whatever information he could while they were here to take back home. He took a deep breath. His muscles felt warm and loose again, the necromancer's magic fully lifted. It was a start.

"Swim?" Erandi waded in without waiting for an answer.

The water was startlingly clear, and Chris swam deep before his lungs ached with the need to breathe. He surfaced, gasping and treading water.

"You fight well for a dog." Erandi's bronze skin shone, dappled with water, his dark hair clinging to his head and shoulders.

"My sister-in-law's cat would kick your ass." Chris grinned.

Erandi laughed, drifting closer with a look in his eyes that Chris recognized. He couldn't lie and say he hadn't felt some of that attraction. But the urgency wasn't there, the sense of need that had driven him into arms and beds since he was old enough to seek its fulfillment.

"Another lifetime then." Erandi's easy grin returned.

"Thank you."

Erandi shrugged, shaking water out of his ears. "Come. I smell lunch."

When they returned, the blanket was full of food. Alam's clasped hands and innocent eyes greeted them. "You truly are magnificent, Christof Vogel."

"It's too late for you to jump ship, mage—you're stuck with me." Erandi narrowed his eyes, chuckling. "Did you portal from the kitchen?"

Alam shrugged, a little guilty now. "I got antelope, your favorite."

Erandi flopped onto the blanket.

"Portal?" Chis settled next to the flatbreads and dips. If stuck on a deserted island, he could live on that forever.

"Alam makes little doorways." Erandi mimicked brushing aside a curtain. "It is their charm. But sometimes they don't always end up where they intend."

"The volcano field was an accident." Alam's shoulders crawled toward their ears. "We were testing to see how far I could go. Not far, it turns out. The connection is unstable and the result unpredictable."

Erandi flung an arm companionably around their narrow shoulders. "I'd trust you to portal us anywhere."

"Especially when there's food involved." Alam shoved him off. "You lot eat like it will get up and run away if you don't devour it first." Their gaze found Chris. "And I can't send you back to Prague if you're wondering."

"Nah, not leaving without Fi." Chris closed his mouth around a bite that consumed the entirety of his attention.

Shifter and àjé traded another one of those long looks. Chris tried not to be too eager, but if he could get one of them talking… Maybe circle the problem rather than coming straight at it. "Why does Amanrey—the necromancer—hate shifters?"

"It's not hate," Alam said, then pronounced carefully: "Amanirenas."

"The shadow is her son." Erandi exhaled sharply. "He was murdered by a team of mercenary shifters hired to infiltrate her camp while Rome waged war against her for control of her homelands."

"Though in her attempt to save him, turning him into what he is now was how she came into her power," Alam said.

"We're lucky she didn't bar us from the sanctuary forever." Erandi smiled wryly. "It's certainly why she didn't care if shifters were tapped out to protect it in the beginning."

"Those days are done," Alam said, fierce. "No àjé can bond a shifter by force. And I would never…"

That piqued Chris's interest. There was no war between wolves—or any shifters—and witches here. They were more than allies. Ofelia had mentioned some kind of bond between them. He needed to understand how it worked and if he could use it to help her out of whatever this was.

"I know you wouldn't want to." Erandi bumped their shoulder. "But if you need to, to protect us, you must."

The àjé and shifter exchanged a glance. Alam folded skinny arms over their chest. "Fine. You've got your way. Now he's curious. Are you happy?"

Erandi and Alam looked to Chris.

"I'm going to do whatever I can to help her." He shrugged, meeting both sets of eyes with utmost solemnity. "Whatever you tell me will be used for that purpose alone."

The air seemed to go still, motes of dust sparkling in place for a long moment before releasing again.

Erandi looked at him strangely. "Amanirenas was right—you are not like other shifters."

Chris shrugged. He liked both of them and wanted more than anything to trust them. But after the previous night in the council, he realized that Ofelia might be right about keeping some things to themselves, at least for now. They were outnumbered and overpowered and had something the necromancer and the council wanted.

"Great goddess." Alam sighed wearily. "It's not a love bond."

"Sometimes it is," Erandi chirped and dove into his haunch. "Your mother—"

"Do not bring her into this." Alam rested their forehead against a palm, then reached for a piece of flatbread. "It's not her we're going to have to worry about—" They tore off a chunk with their teeth to avoid finishing the sentence.

"What?" Chris said, amused.

"Ofelia forbade them to talk to you about the concord bond," Erandi said.

"And she forgot you?" Chris's brows rose.

"I happened to be out." The jaguar looked pleased with himself. "And we cannot be compelled through our concord."

"This concord thing, it's not just a vow, is it?"

Erandi shrugged. Alam waved the hand not holding the bread in a "go on" gesture.

"It binds us, allowing us to share our strengths to protect each other and our home for as long as we live," Erandi said simply.

"In principle, it's akin to facultative symbiosis," Alam chimed in. When both shifters stared, they tried again. "A sacred pact based on mutual benefit?"

Erandi laughed and rubbed a palm over the kid's hair. "The scholar."

"Someone has to be the brains," Alam grumbled. "Anyway, she said I couldn't tell Chris about it; she didn't say I couldn't correct you when you're telling Chris about it."

Chris had to admire the kid's skill at getting around words. They would have fit in well among his siblings.

"It gives us many advantages," Erandi went on. "For one, bonded shifters heal faster."

"Most shifters heal fast," Chris said.

"Double it." Erandi lifted his brows. "And our lifespans parallel theirs, so we live longer."

"Shifters also have full citizen privileges, including serving on the council in concord," Alam added.

Chris struggled to see why Ofelia was so opposed. Maybe it was the lifetime thing that spooked her.

"And what do you get out of it?" Chris asked the àjé.

"Protection for one." Erandi laughed when Alam hesitated. "Most àjé aren't warriors, even trained. They mostly get self-defense, some immobilization, that kind of thing. Baako and Fi are exceptions, though it's mostly out of rivalry. She spent five years training for a shot at kicking Baako's ass."

"Did she?"

Erandi winced. "She did her best. Baako has been training since she was a kid. Ofelia has… gaps… in her education."

"But you have no chance of getting Ofelia to agree to concord," Alam said with certainty. "She thinks it's a loss of autonomy. Calls it shackles if you get her really worked up."

Erandi rolled his eyes skyward, whistling.

Chris borrowed a note from his nieces and nephews. "Why?"

"Shifting takes an amount of energy." Erandi shrugged.

"It's why you're always eating," Alam said brightly. "Caloric intake is one way to meet the energy demands."

Erandi lowered his brows, and Alam slid the rest of the antelope his direction.

"Our àjé can draw from us," Erandi said. "It's how they achieve the most powerful magic. It's not damaging usually."

"Unless we take too much." Alam lowered their voice.

"Does that happen?" Chris stopped chewing.

"In the old days, all the time." Erandi shrugged. "The charm wasn't so generous to us. Ultimately, burning out a shifter was seen as a necessary sacrifice."

"It was a very bad time in our history." Alam's lower lip stuck out. Still child enough but already so powerful that they'd undertaken a lifetime bond. One that involved a potentially deadly power exchange. "Many àjé worked to refine the binding over time. Now it is better for both of us."

"They got attached to us, and it hurt when we die," Erandi elaborated. "The bond itself is different now. Àjé do not control, for one. The shifter must invite the àjé, and the council must hear and recognize the response to ensure free will is honored."

Chris looked at Erandi. "Ofelia turned you down."

Erandi shrugged.

"When he first arrived, he lived with us and he and Ofelia were like…" Alam laughed, then grew quiet at Erandi's stern look.

"It's okay—I already figured that out," Chris said. It would have been decent of Ofelia to warn him that this was her former lover, but he'd picked up on the vibe. And he couldn't say that he didn't get it. "How did you two decide to… concord?"

"My training was complete," Erandi said. "I wanted to serve my home. My family."

"Usually it's someone closer in age, but Mum approved because I'm really powerful and no shifters my age are ready to concord." There was no boast in their voice, no sense of rank or privilege. Chris liked the kid too much already—he was going to be fond in a minute. "Plus Erandi's been like one of my older siblings my whole life, so it feels natural to have him try to boss me around all the time."

"Someone has to keep you in line, little mage." Erandi gave his àjé a lopsided smile, beautiful with affection and admiration. "It is a gift, this bond."

They might see it that way, but Chris understood why Ofelia might reject the idea. In a few days he'd seen how fiercely independent she was. She'd been on her own for so long, and perhaps because her mother and father had chosen to raise her outside the city, the condition of the rest of the world tarnished her ability to see what good had been built here. There wasn't enough time for him to convince her that relying on someone, asking for help—him or her own family—wasn't a weakness.

Returning through the rings of the council-family compounds to the palace at their center, he paused at the mural just inside the main gate. In it stood three nearly identical figures robed in purple and gold with elaborate hair. Identical and familiar.

"Triplets are a rare thing." Erandi stepped to his shoulder, a quiet strength beneath the warmth of his skin as he leaned in to explain. "And these were fated for greatness. The First of the First."

He gestured to the right-hand figure. She stared past the viewer with a spear in one hand and a ball of light glowing over her opposite fingertips. "Serwaah leads the àjé."

The one on the left beamed benevolently, offering the viewer a plant and a flowing river in her cupped palms. "Their sister, Ejo, is a bit of recluse—"

"She is devoted to her task," Alam said.

Erandi's gaze swept the forest around them. "You felt it in the council room last night."

Chris nodded, recalling the sense that the land was as aware of him.

"Here the last-born is considered the eldest and the wisest," Erandi said. "Ejo figured out a way to bind herself to the land itself and everything it grows."

The central figure stared directly into the viewer's eyes, and Chris recognized that knowing half smile. "And Ofelia's mother?"

"The spy." Erandi sighed in admiration. "Nyhira."

"The finest covert operator the Cadre has ever trained." Alam's eyes shone.

"We have operatives in the other territories," Erandi explained. "They are called Spiders. They are our early-warning system. If the Allegiance falls, we will be ready to protect the territory."

"And they are in place if we need to extend our claws," Alam said.

"It's a great honor and sacrifice," Erandi said. "Because of the risk to shifters in other territories, Spiders do not take a concord. We set them up with permanent covers once they complete their training. They live abroad, prepared to be activated if needed, and they rarely—if ever—come home."

"Nyhira was the most powerful of the sisters and the bravest," Alam said. "She was our spear and our shield. There were dozens who would have given everything to be her concord regardless of the risk. Even my mother wanted an exception to be made. Nyhira refused. She met another witch assigned by his coven to track the hunter. He was working undercover as a Swiss diplomat. After the hunter eluded them the first time, they stayed together. They settled in Prague, and she asked to be deactivated. Years later, she alerted us to the hunter's reappearance and that they were in pursuit. That was the last we heard from her. The operative sent to collect the bodies went through their things and found a letter from Ofelia's boarding school. It was the first we knew of her. Of course we brought her home. What else could we do? She was alone in the world."

"Nobody counted on Ofelia being—" Erandi's hands flared in a helpless gesture.

"Ofelia," Chris said.

Erandi exhaled a laugh.

"Why does she not want this?" Alam looked bewildered. "She has a family that loves her, and a legacy."

"Both of which expect her to be something she never prepared for," Erandi said sagely.

"The thing that got her parents killed," Chris finished.

Alam huffed and faced the mural again. Erandi met Chris's eyes over his concord's head. Chris felt the plea in his gaze, and he lowered his chin in acceptance. He might never convince her to take him as her concord, but he would use what he'd learned here to protect her, as he promised. He could stay by her side and if she needed power, he would be there to give it to her.

The apartment was empty when Alam and Erandi dropped him off. Chris watched the sunlight fade through the big tree in the courtyard, the last orange-gold rays flickering off green and brown before softening to a sleepy lavender.

The city was coming alive, the heat of the day fading and bringing people out into the streets. He wanted to explore the city with her. But knowing how much pain this place had bought her and how much loss she'd suffered, what beauty could she possibly find in any of it now?

Dragged back again, this time with the expectation that she would fight for them. A fight that wasn't hers. No matter how they shaped it.

Prague was his city. His mom had taken on the witches of the city as her responsibility, including his sisters-in-law. His nieces and nephews could be in danger. All his life he'd been searching for his place, his role in things. Maybe he'd finally found it. And a way to get Ofelia off the hook.

Now he just had to convince a necromancer.

CHAPTER EIGHTEEN

ON HER WAY out of the city, Ofelia reminded herself again that Chris was safe and recovering from the necromancer's vow in the palace. He had come back from the council room on his own two feet, but he hadn't been awake, not exactly. When she'd guided him to bed, he'd gone in without a sound or protest and promptly fallen asleep. There had been no sleep for her in the chair beside the bed, watching his every snuffle and woof for a sign that some permanent damage had been done. Dawn came and went with him sleeping so soundly she could have set off a bomb and he wouldn't have stirred. But she couldn't sit still any longer.

Asking Alam to check in on him had been a stroke of genius. It had ended her cousin's ceaseless demands for a recounting of the council meeting, and the young àjé was had already surpassed her healing abilities. If anything went wrong, Chris would be in good hands. She'd extracted a promise Alam would not fill Chris's head with nonsense about the concord. She didn't want him getting any ideas. Correction—any *more* ideas.

After fourteen years apart, the first thing she'd done was walk him into this mess of necromancers and killers. Chris was already too willing to fight for her. Wait on her. Feed her. She was going to have to protect him from himself.

Alam agreed to the first happily and the second with foot-dragging reluctance. Ofelia knew growing hero worship when she saw it. Thankfully Erandi was nowhere to be found. He wouldn't be so easy to compel.

In the busy morning streets of the city, she lost herself in the vendors and delivery vans, the stream of bodies carrying her far from the inner rings. The contributions of each of the forty-two families could be seen in every part of the city, from the colorful walls of the artisans to the information screens embedded at every corner that flickered to life as someone approached and dimmed promptly after use. On one, a well-dressed couple referenced a map of the city; on another, a vendor took a call; and on another, a group of teenagers listened to music. From building design and street layout to the shops, and the wares in them, there was nothing at least one of the forty-two families hadn't given.

Here, magic and technology were sisters that shared the same womb of need and possibility. When faced with a challenge, they looked to the other, saying, "Shall I take this?" And sometimes they tackled it hand in hand, like the solar-powered automatons trundling by with passengers in their brightly colored, capsule-shaped cabs.

The air was thick with the scent of cooking food. She'd forgotten the early heat of the day, humidity that put Prague's summer to shame, and the way the air felt more alive. There was music everywhere, not just in the voices calling out to each other but the cowbells and bird sounds, the rattle of a cup of beans poured from a sack, the clank of a machine shop operator making repairs, the cries of an impromptu game of football being played as she passed.

And amid all of it—magic. Little charms used to keep the insects at bay, the sight of cloven hooves amid the footballers—a faun youth among human and àjé children—the way a particularly ingenious baker broadcast the scent of her wares far enough to make Ofelia's stomach rumble across the street. When she looked, the middle-aged woman smiled toothily and held up a roll of roasted plantain wrapped in fresh bread that lured Ofelia like a fish on a hook.

The woman refused to take any payment, lifting her cupped hands and bowing in gratitude. "A blessing from the first of the first."

Having her mother's old title bestowed on her made Ofelia's heart ache, but she laid a little charm for a prosperous day on the woman's fingertips and hurried off before tears could get the best of her.

She'd been barely seventeen the first time she'd walked these streets, fresh from the loss of her parents and overwhelmed by what their death had gained. Even before boarding school, it had been just the three of them. Here she had aunts, uncles, cousins, a rich history, a lineage. She'd been taken away from the cold, vicious society of wealthy human kids and into a warm, open culture of magic. It hurt to admit how good it felt to be here, how natural.

She reminded herself they didn't even want her here. They'd be willing to let her sacrifice herself as her mother had so they could continue to live openly while others like them around the world were forced to hide.

She boarded a riverboat leaving the city. Though she wore a simple tunic and pants under her scarf, news of her return traveled fast. More than one nodded respect to her family as she passed. One offered her a seat on the crowded boat. Ashamed of the regard she hadn't earned, she refused and gave small charms freely until she was exhausted.

She disembarked at a mostly abandoned stop cut into the edge of the jungle. Here the plants and trees formed a wall of dense green broken in places with a colorful burst of flower petals or a glimpse of sky high above. The sound here was just as lively as the busy marketplace—the hum of insects underlying the call of birds and the too-humanlike cries of mammals, the distant crashing of brush and wood that could have been just a tree falling or a family of forest elephants cutting new trails.

Ofelia slipped off her sandals and flexed her toes in the loamy dirt. She was prepared to make the rest of the journey on foot. Part of her penance perhaps, but also her aunt's doing. Ejo didn't love visitors, so she saw no point in making it easy for them.

Ofelia breathed in the dense, verdant air and lifted her fingertips, letting her charm flow freely beyond their reach. A tendril of vine unfurled and slid around her pinkie, crawling up to her wrist. A root pushed up against her feet. She sent energy back, repaying them for the expenditure this little inspection took. The vine squeezed her once before releasing.

And the forest parted.

Ofelia let the roots pushing beneath her feet indicate her path and found the house faster than most would have. Inside was cool and dark. She sensed her aunt's presence at a distance. She must be occupied in some other part of the territory. Ofelia wandered through the round, mud-walled house, climbed the steps to the second floor. A bed had been prepared with a bouquet of lilies and orchids beside it.

Ofelia lay down and let the scent wash over her. Her eyes drifted shut faster than she expected.

When she opened them again, the woman at the window turned to face her.

"Welcome home, Daughter."

The room hadn't changed, but the light felt different. For a moment Ofelia's breath caught at the sight of that face. She could almost believe it was her mother. And then sightless eyes moved past her, and the light shifted to reveal an unlined brow and a mouth too young.

At first it had been startling to see two faces so much like the one she'd lost. The three sisters had shared a womb and features but were so different in personality. She'd tried to imagine where the mother she'd known fit between the First Àjé's sternness and the guardian's placid calm.

Impish, they said. Always bucking tradition but too brilliant to be considered trouble. The first time Nyhira saw a Spider deployed, she'd looked to their mother and proclaimed, "I, too, will protect and defend our home from far away." At least that's what they told Ofelia.

"You didn't have to make the journey." Ejo's lips did not move. Instead, her voice was the whisper of the leaves, the creak of tree branches. "Grandmother Tree and I have finally reached an accord."

Ofelia picked flowers and leaves out of her hair until the bed was strewn with them. "Is all this necessary?"

"I am not the only one who missed you." A smile twitched the soft, full lips. "Let me feed you."

Ofelia followed, pressing a jasmine blossom to her nose briefly. Her aunt moved in the house as gracefully as if all her senses were intact.

The kettle whistled in the kitchen. On the table an assortment of fresh fruits had been laid out with root curry and rice. A simple meal but not basic. The flavors and seasonings exploded on her tongue, warm and familiar.

Her aunt sat patiently, pleased.

Ofelia ate like she hadn't in days. "Will you join me?"

Ejo shook her head, smiling. "I get my nutrients from above and below these days. Food just complicates things."

The room shifted, and Ofelia realized she was in a dream. For a moment she almost lost her place in it by waking. Then she took a breath and focused her gaze on the teapot. The more she concentrated, the more the room around her steadied until it was still again.

"Impressive," Ejo said. "Your mother could never stop herself from breaking a dream once she realized she was in one."

Ofelia's heart ached. "She taught me to focus on one thing."

"Good."

Ofelia was too preoccupied with concern to let the praise settle. Surely Aunt Ejo hadn't given up her body. Ofelia remembered her strong hugs, the grip of her fingers, the long twists of her locs pressing against Ofelia's cheek. "You're gone?"

"I have finally succeeded in the task of my lifetime," Ejo said. "I am in every leaf and stem and blade of grass, stone and hillock of ant dirt. I've scared the shit out of the termites, let me tell you." She laughed softly. "I have found immortality—don't weep for me. Being in your presence is a joy, niece." Her pause gave Ofelia time to blink away her tears. "Though I am sorry for what brought you back."

"You're the only one who doesn't call it home." Ofelia studied her carefully, memorizing her face and her hands and the twists of her long gray hair. She wondered if it was the last time she would see them. If, after this, her aunt would only be a voice and then a whisper of wind in the trees. It seemed the youngest sister hadn't been the only one who found another way to give up everything in service of her home.

"This isn't home," Ejo said, settling on the stool across from Ofelia. "Not for you. Perhaps in another lifetime it will be. But home is other for you. Though not a place. And each of us has many lifetimes in one."

Ofelia frowned. Too much time being one with the trees had made her aunt even more cryptic. "What does that mean?"

Her aunt beamed suddenly. "You are very much like your mother at this age, all logic. You have her charm. Even my guards like you. I bet you could grow anything with a smile and a wink."

"Are you lonely?"

Her aunt cackled, gleefully this time. "My dear. I am never alone anymore. It's the happiest I've been in my whole life."

"But a family," Ofelia said, feeling her cheeks heat. "Connection."

"Sex?" Ejo grinned. "That's what you're going to ask about next, right? If you think sex is good, imagine surfing the roof of the canopy at sunset with the macaques. Thrill of a lifetime. I can do it every day if I like. Dusk and dawn. I'm fine. Babies and a mate have never been my desire, Ofelia. What is yours?"

"Freedom," Ofelia said, musing as she picked at her food. "The ability to choose my own life, my own fate. Not to be bound to duty and responsibility like everyone here, like Mama was."

Ejo's face lost all humor. "Don't you dare, girl."

Ofelia froze, shocked.

"To assume everything your mother did wasn't from her own heart, her desire, because you don't understand it is to be willingly obtuse," Ejo said. "Perhaps you wouldn't make the same choices. But you didn't live in her skin."

Ofelia's breath caught as tears threatened again. "Tell me what happened. The truth."

Her aunt took her hands. "Are you sure?"

Ofelia swallowed.

"We believe the hunter took your father first. Perhaps thinking he was the more powerful of the two and it would leave her defenseless. We think when she found his body, she summoned something powerful. An elemental. A blood rite, perhaps. We are less sure about that part. It should have stopped him. Perhaps with another it would have. But she burned herself out before the spell completed. And the hunter slipped away."

"The accident?"

"Staged," Ejo admitted. "The Spiders saw to that. We couldn't risk Azrael discovering what they were. Summoning them."

"Protecting yourselves," Ofelia said, but the old bitterness tasted sour even to her. "My mother died for a life she never got to live."

"Think bigger, little bee." Ejo softened. "If I know my sister at all, there was only one thing worth sacrificing everything for."

The first years at boarding school, her parents came for her at every holiday, taking her for little getaways to beaches and old cities and museums. She'd tried to ignore the conversations they had around her, the meaningful glances exchanged when they thought she wasn't paying attention. In a fit of teenage pique, she accused them of wanting her out of the way. It was the first time she saw her mother weep.

They didn't visit the final year. There were cards and presents and a credit card she spent to the limit to have it paid without notice or complaint. It didn't fill the void they left.

And then one raining night, the MFP arrived in their crisp uniforms and faces long with regret. For one shocking moment, she was glad her parents were gone, thought they'd gotten what they deserved for abandoning her. It was easier to hate them than to live with the alternative. That hadn't lasted.

Ofelia rested her forehead in her palms, her appetite gone. "I don't know what to do."

"I know, dear heart." The older woman rested a hand on her back. Even in the dream it was warm, though it lacked the weight a hand should have.

For one long moment Ofelia wondered what her life would have been like if she'd fallen for all their talk about legacy and duty. How much time she could have spent at this table with the woman, laughing and talking and remembering her mother. She would have taken Erandi in concord if he offered. Maybe made him her mate too. Her aunt wasn't the only one who could buck tradition and take her concord as a husband. She would have had children by another witch of course. Perhaps someone they could have both loved.

It would have almost been worth it.

Instead, Erandi had helped her get away. She'd never even asked him what price he paid for that or thanked him. Amanirenas had never barred her from leaving, but that didn't mean she made it easy.

"This thing they ask of you." Her aunt spoke softly. "If there was another option—"

"I know."

"But no one can force you."

"Can you remind Aunt Serwaah?" Ofelia scowled.

Her aunt chortled. "My dear sister is used to giving orders. But she never could tell your mother what to do. *That* is your inheritance."

Inheritance. Vengeance. She often wondered why her mother had kept it from her. She could blame not wanting to make a child keep secrets too big for her. But maybe it was setting her free from the expectation it would come with.

"Is it selfish not to want to die for a life that's never been mine?"

"There is nothing inherently noble in martyrdom," Ejo said. "But who said anything about death?"

"My mother was one of the most powerful witches in her generation and she fell." Ofelia sighed. "The only thing we have in common is not taking a concord."

"But you could," her aunt said as if binding a perfect stranger to her was the most reasonable thing in the world. As if he would agree to such a horrible fate.

Most alarming was the quiet voice inside her that warned he just might. Chris had leaped into the necromancer's silence vow so easily. Why not this? She shut down the dawning awareness that some part of her might want a lasting connection to him. It didn't have to be love. And she wouldn't be alone.

Her aunt hummed. Her eyes, ever distant, seemed farther away. Even when she still had physical form, she would have moments like this where she would send her consciousness to some other place in the city. She traveled fastest along the networks of roots—trees had already perfected such connections—but the tangle of waterways, or even animals, would do in a pinch.

Having once been hidden in the jungle's heart near the equator, the protected zone was now hundreds of thousands of acres.

Her aunt's role as guardian and eyes in the forest was more important now than ever. No wonder she had surrendered her body to the task. Still, Ofelia mourned for her loss. Sacrifice.

First her mother, now her beloved aunt. How much more would this place take?

That was why she had to get out of here while she still could.

Her aunt sat up, all ease gone. "The choice may no longer be yours to make."

"What?"

"Go now."

"What do you see?"

"To the palace." Her aunt shook her head. "Quickly."

Ofelia rose, torn.

Her aunt took her hands, the warm flesh almost real enough to make tears sting her eyes. "There is a reason our family sits at the right hand of Amanirenas. You carry that too. When the time comes, you will know what is needed. We are always with you. Now go."

Ofelia sat up in the bed. The light through the trees now matched the light in her dream. She'd been gone an hour, maybe less. The rustle of branches and leaves buffeted the silent house, urging her on.

She followed the sound of trumpeting outside. A family of forest elephants kicked up dust in the clearing before the house. The matriarch curled one foreleg, lowering her head and trunk. Of course Aunt Ejo would be on favored terms with the most elusive animals in the jungle.

Ofelia bowed in respect and accepted the ride.

Forest elephants made paths through the densest parts of the jungle. She shouldn't have been surprised that they managed the trip in half the time it had taken her to get there and then some. Still, she did enjoy the surprise she made showing up at the palace with such an escort. The gathering crowed parted and bowed in waves to the matriarch and her family, their eyes going to Ofelia with awe.

Before Ofelia could suffer from pride, a prehensile trunk slipped around her waist and deftly deposited her on her own two feet. She stumbled a bit but managed a bow of gratitude. The family turned to greet well-wishers bearing baskets of fruits and wreaths of flowers.

The distraction was enough to allow her to pass through the halls relatively unimpeded. Erandi and Alam stood outside the closed doors to her flat, looking wildly uncomfortable.

"No one is to enter," Alam said warily as she approached.

Ofelia's heart quickened. "Then they shouldn't have picked my rooms."

She'd been gone for half a day—what had Chris gotten himself into now? *Seven, help me get him out of it.*

Erandi rested a hand on her shoulder. It was the first time he'd touched her since her return, and the surprise drew her up. "He *asked*—"

"He is a stubborn fool who doesn't know how to keep his head down and his mouth shut." Ofelia tried to shake him off, but his grip was firm, gentle.

"You tend to have that effect," Erandi murmured, "on the ones who love you."

There was no accusation or regret in his words. Instead, he smiled, so faint she might have missed it if she didn't know his face so well.

"Step aside," Ofelia demanded, ignoring her aching heart.

Erandi met Alam's eyes. The young àjé nodded.

Ofelia slipped into the room in time to hear Chris's voice, confident even if it shook at the edges. "I know the city. I have good connections with the… supernaturals that live there. If they're in any danger at all—"

"You mean your kin." The necromancer had taken the simplest seat at the oversized dining table, the armless, backless chair little more than a solid version of a soldier's campstool. It looked like a throne beneath her. "Witches."

He sealed his lips shut, his eyes too bright.

"I have seen many things in my time," the necromancer said. "But you are something unusual in all that. Witch-born, wolf-blooded. Last I heard, they were still fighting their foolish war. Turning the fear and rage of their oppressors on each other. What a terrible waste."

"You've been out of the loop for a while then," Chris said through gritted teeth.

The necromancer waved off his protest. "The proof stands before me, doesn't it? I'd like to meet this witch who bore you. She and I would have much to discuss, I'd think."

Ofelia saw his hackles go up as he misunderstood the necromancer's words as a threat.

The necromancer's escort coalesced from the shadows in the corner of the room. It took a shape approximating human but with the head of something older, wilder.

Ofelia stepped in quickly, clearing her throat. "Your pardon, Nana. To what do we owe the pleasure of your visit?"

Amanirenas didn't laugh, though her lips curled in something like amusement. "Your *friend* has set forth a proposal that I find interesting. He believes he has information and contacts that can help identify and find the witch hunter. And he has offered to lead the effort."

Chris wouldn't quite look at her, his gaze locked on Amanirenas. He'd learned that much at least. Never take your eyes off the biggest set of teeth in the room.

"You offered what?" Ofelia hissed, unable to stop herself. "You have no business—"

"Careful, Daughter," Amanirenas chided. "Presuming to tell others something you would never stand for."

"This isn't his fight," Ofelia said.

"Isn't it?" The necromancer cocked her head. "As he says, he was born in the city. It is his home."

"It's really more mine than yours when it comes down to it." Chris nodded, looking almost apologetic. "This hunter may have… ties… to your mother, but he's working in my territory."

"Ties?" Ofelia gasped. "He killed her. And my father. Whatever ties he has are not to Prague."

"There are vulnerable witches in the city. Who knows what he intends to do with the blood? Witches everywhere could be in danger."

"Things between Azrael and I have been *tense* for some time." Amanirenas gazed at her folded hands.

"I'm sure they have," Ofelia muttered. When it came to necromancers, *some time* could be a few decades or a century. And when things between them got *tense,* cities might be melted to glass or reduced to rubble. "What does this have to do—"

"You have chosen not to avenge your mother's death, as is your right." The necromancer met her eyes, and Ofelia clamped down on the urge look away. "However, my obligation to your motherline requires vengeance."

Ofelia lowered her eyes first, unable to hide the secondhand sting of the necromancer's words. In the silence, she wondered at the bond between her family and this necromancer.

In the chaos following the godswar, Amanirenas had revealed herself and taken control of the continent with merciless swiftness. Those who did not come into line still worked as zombies, rebuilding cities after the war.

Yet she had always been an indulgent—if stern—benefactor during Ofelia's stays in the hidden city. She had treated the rebellious, grieving teenager like a favored grandchild. Ofelia's tantrums had been ignored, her running away overlooked. What had her mother been to this being that such benevolence had been transferred thoughtlessly to her?

"In any case, this is a local matter," Amanirenas finished. "It is best cleaned up without his knowledge."

"You send him alone, with no àjé to protect him." Ofelia spun on the necromancer. "You might as well kill him here."

"That's a vote of confidence," Chris said wryly.

Her voice broke. "You have no idea what you're doing."

"The hunter has shown no interest in other supernatural creatures."

Amanirenas cocked her head again, considering him. "Your wolf is to make contact and apply a charm that the Cadre can track. We will do the rest. I believe you underestimate him greatly."

"Thank you." Chris's laugh was strained. He ignored Ofelia. "So do we have a deal?"

"Deal?" Ofelia said.

"Your service for her freedom?" Amanirenas considered.

As understanding clattered into place in Ofelia's mind, the words rushed up her throat. Whatever the past was, Ofelia wasn't going to be shamed into letting Chris put himself in danger for her again. "I will do it! I will find the witch killer. I will… avenge my motherline."

"You're sure?" Amanirenas mused.

"Fi—" Chris began.

"I am willing." Ofelia spoke over whatever Chris was trying to say now. Why wouldn't he just shut up? "I've had a change of heart. I will do it."

"A change of heart indeed." The necromancer studied her face before letting her gaze settle on Chris. When she did smile, it held no humor at all. "Then you will take a concord. That's where your mother failed. If she'd had a concord to draw on, we might not be in this mess now."

Ofelia's ears rang with the words. She'd been backed into a corner. Aunt Ejo was wrong. There was never a choice. Or perhaps there might have been if not for—

Chris looked just as surprised as she did. Then his expression hardened in resolve. "I'll do it."

"No." Heat raced up her chest and into her neck.

Something boomed, and when Chris jumped, she realized it wasn't just in her head. The building shuddered. A heartbeat later, the floor split and a root twisted up through the ragged tear. It sought her out first, snaking around her ankle like a hound called to heel.

Ofelia repeated the protest with her whole chest, and the leaves on every tree rattled for a mile in every direction around her.

A commotion started outside the room. Raised voices shouted in alarm, demanding entrance.

"Be careful, àjé." Amanirenas lowered her voice. "As the child of my favorite Daughter, you have always had my esteem. But others do not love the freedom you enjoy. Especially when you unleash your temper like a brat."

Chris crossed to Ofelia's side, unperturbed by the roots snaking up out of the floor and along the walls that sealed the room in a woody, earth-scented cocoon.

"I know what I'm doing." He touched her arm, his voice urgent. "I talked to Erandi and Alam."

Oh, she was such a fool for sending them all out together. How irresponsible she'd been, thinking the worst that could happen was an awkward conversation between a current and former lover. Scratch that—two ex-lovers after this bullshit.

Instead, all he'd seen was the way a shifter could be bonded to a witch, to provide protection and his own life if needed for *the witch's* survival. Since the moment they'd reconnected, he'd been feeding her and looking after her and pledging himself to her. Of course he'd gotten swept up in the romantic potential of such a bond.

He was a lovestruck moron, but she was an idiot.

She almost groaned aloud with their predicament. But Amanirenas was right about one thing. She was her mother's daughter. She could behave with dignity.

She could try at least.

She collected her power, coiling it inside her until it once again fit. The trees left off their rattling. The roots slithered off the walls, leaving trails of damp soil and a few displaced bugs as they retreated into the floor.

Amanirenas nodded. Her shadow disappeared, presumably to reappear on the other side of the door, because a moment later the din of the Cadre fighters and àjé preparing spells faded. Baako's voice, strident, and the First Àjé's, wary, countering it.

Ofelia shut them out. She swallowed her pride and her fury and ignored the sensation of the trap closing around her.

"Forgive me, great one." She pushed her shoulders back, as though she were truly making a choice, and did not look at anyone in the room directly. "I have been a frightened child instead of the woman I was raised to be. It is my honor to take on this responsibility for my mother, for my family, for our home."

"And the concord?"

Ofelia gritted her teeth. Of course she would have to answer that. "Without the proper training—for both of us—I fear that bond would do more harm than good. I will accept his help. He does know the city and those in it better than I do. And he is loyal to me. As you have witnessed by his vow to protect our people."

"Our people," Amanirenas mused.

Ofelia's molars ached from clenching her teeth.

"You agree to this, Christof Douglass Vogel?" The necromancer's gaze finally swung to him.

"Whatever she needs," Chris said. "I'm your wolf—hers—the job's."

As Amanirenas rose, her shadow re-formed by her side. "I will speak to the First Àjé. Whatever support the Cadre can lend, you will accept."

Ofelia fought the urge to say she wanted nothing from either, but she sensed Amanirenas knew it because her smile became a warning.

"This is a chance we may not meet again in your lifetime," Amanirenas said. "We cannot fail."

"I obey." Ofelia bowed.

When the necromancer was gone, Ofelia exhaled, bracing her hands on the back of the nearest chair in case her knees buckled.

Chris made a sound, and she looked up. Was he *laughing*?

"Well, that was fucking hair-raising." He grinned at her with all the enthusiasm of a pup wagging its tail.

Rage swelled in her. For a moment she imagined that giant root dragging him by the heel out into the courtyard and thrashing him against a few walls.

His expression shifted with understanding—maybe not of what he had done but what she had been driven to. He rubbed his face, and his smile faded. "I'm sorry, Fi. I thought—"

She was too exhausted to shout. "You thought you would do this alone?"

"Not alone," he said petulantly. "I do know *most* of the supernaturals in the city. I have friends, allies. The gargoyles, a couple of trolls. Worst case, my brothers—"

"You would drag your family into this mess?" she asked.

His brows rose.

Ofelia shook her head, dismissing the urge to be embarrassed.

"I didn't count on your finding out until it was done." He closed the distance between them, resting his hands on her shoulders. "I may not have come from the witch motherland, but my family and I have fought our way out of a couple of tight corners. I can handle myself, Fi. At least we're in it together now. You need someone to have your back."

She shrugged out of his grip. "I needed you to keep your mouth shut. That's all I've asked you to do since the moment we got here."

"I'm not a dog." He ground out.

"No, you're a harebrained wolf cub with a savior complex," she snapped, the satisfied heat of a good comeback flushing her skin.

For the first time she saw a flash of something other than that boundless devotion in his eyes. The sight roused something fierce in the pit of her belly.

A low growl sounded in his chest.

She took a step into his space, answering his challenge with her own. Good, let him get angry at her. Stop seeing her through his rose-colored memory glasses.

He took a deep breath and shook, too much like his lupine half. Then he rubbed his hand through his hair and stared at her. "I'm not gonna do this with you now. We're both amped up, and adrenaline sweat is doing nothing for me right now. Plus you smell like— I don't even know what all that is."

Ofelia stared. She wanted him to be pissed at her, to wolf out and go for her throat so she could bash him over the head with the nearest hard object and then hex his ass into last week. Or fuck him senseless. She was startled to find she didn't know which.

"I smell?"

He sniffed delicately. "Is that elephant? Whoo. Yep. Are they still here? I've never actually met one, and Rand says there hasn't been an elephant shifter in generations."

Seven, give me strength. I'm going to murder Rand *with my bare hands.*

"Why don't you take the first shower? I'll see about getting us some food." He stepped around her as though she were a chair someone had left pushed out of place. "And then we'll figure something out."

And then he was gone. Ofelia stood for a moment longer before tilting her head back and roaring so hard the leaves rattled again. Then she headed to the bath.

CHAPTER NINETEEN

WELL, he'd survived round two with a necromancer—and Ofelia's fury. That called for celebration. Ofelia still looked like she wanted to strangle him bare-handed, but maybe after a shower and a hot meal, she'd calm down. It always worked for him.

Still, she'd pushed him closer to an edge he hadn't been against in years. That was going to take a moment to come down from. He hated feeling that kind of anger—rage. It left him anxious, unhappy. He did his best to avoid ever getting to that place, swallowing it when it came.

And that *she* could push him into it was deeply unsettling. She was his match, his person. She wasn't supposed to get to him like that, was she?

The commotion outside the door had dissipated, and with it, most of the hangers-on. Erandi and Alam were still standing guard, trying unsuccessfully to look like they weren't eager for some news.

"Everything's fine," Chris said.

Alam waved a hand. "Will you concord?"

"Lost that fight." Chris shook his head.

Erandi exhaled sharply. "You want me to try—"

"Not if you want to keep your claws." Chris grimaced.

Alam snorted.

"I need to get some food in her, maybe a little wine. What does she like—can we talk to the kitchen, or can you just portal something up?"

But when he finished rounding up a meal and returned to the apartment, she was gone again. She'd showered, left a mess of dirty clothes strewn across the bathroom floor, and disappeared. Birds were all over the place, pecking at the bugs and the worms that had been deposited by the roots. And shitting everywhere.

He growled and asked for rags and buckets. Alam sent in a crew of undead and tried to convince Chris to come out and see the night market. Stubbornly, Chris grabbed a brush and a bucket and went to work with the zombies. He didn't want to fall more in love with this place when they were bound to leave soon and he'd never see it again. When the work was done, he flopped into a bath. When he woke up an hour later in tepid water, she still hadn't returned.

When was she going to stop ditching him?

In the morning, Erandi found him asleep at the dining room table and took pity on him. "Try the tree."

"The tree?"

"They call her Grandmother. The courtyard tree." Erandi angled his head out the window. "She's fond of Ofelia."

Chris nodded resolutely.

"But you might want to just wait till she comes back," Erandi called after him, nibbling at the platter of fruit. "We can spar if you want to burn off some energy."

Chris thanked him but headed outside. He must be getting used to the climate; the morning air felt cool on his skin. He followed the glimpses of daylight into a central courtyard around a massive tree. It made sense, he thought. Ofelia's family was one in which plant magic ran strong. It was in everything from the murals to the crest sewn into fabrics and twisted into the jewelry they wore.

He had no idea what kind of tree it was—it had to have been hundreds of years old, its canopy reaching so far overhead Chris could only make out green and the spots of light that filtered through. Huge vines draped from its branches, each the thickness of a small sapling and still looking like toothpicks compared to its main trunk.

He stared up into the branches and leaves, shading his eyes with one hand and sniffing again to confirm his suspicion. Seriously?

He grabbed a promising-looking divot in the trunk only to have it ripple from under his hand. He stared at the tree. He took a running start and tried to scramble up to one of the low branches. The bark that had been like sandpaper a moment before refused to give his fingers purchase. He skidded to the ground.

Hands on hips, he stared up at it, growling softly. "What fucking kind of tree—"

The kind that had come up through the floor when Ofelia was angry.

That rattled all its leaves like an army's shields and swords before a battle. What had Erandi said? *She's fond of Ofelia.*

Chris closed the distance, stepping over roots bigger than his chest, and rested his palm against the rough bark. He lowered his chin. He didn't bother with words. Instead, he slowed his breathing and closed his eyes. His pulse quieted in his ears, the sounds of the palace full of people fading away from him.

His senses expanded, stretching out over the roof of the palace and high up, where the sun was brighter and hotter than the ground. The slow, patient transformation of sunlight to nutrients, water coming up from deep within the maze of roots that spread for miles, connecting with other trees to form a network. The city spread around him, belling out like the view of a wide-angle lens until he could see it all, feel it all.

A woman's voice, laughing, welcoming him. *You* are *a wonder, little wolf.*

He raced—or was pulled—along the network, an invisible presence beside him that felt like someone he should know. Coming back into his body was like stepping off the most intense roller coaster he'd ever been on. He would have fallen, but the roots were bracing him, and his hands… they were *in* the tree. Vines snaked around his wrists to his shoulders. It took everything in him not to struggle. They slid back until the air tickled the skin of his fingers again.

He didn't open his eyes to begin climbing. Everywhere his fingers touched was a hold, every spot his toes settled a purchase. He followed his nose until at last he opened his eyes to find himself crouching on a branch as wide as a compact car, hundreds of feet above the ground. Where the branch met the trunk, a shallow bowl formed. Overhead, leaves shaded it from sun and weather, and it had been stocked with blankets and books. Curled up in a ball, fast asleep, Ofelia looked like the girl he remembered.

He slid into a space at the back of the hollow, resting his shoulders against the branch. He was sweaty again, and his muscles ached, finger-tips to legs. He flexed his hands, which were bark brown and red with effort. Insect bites itched at his shoulder.

Ofelia opened her eyes. She blinked at him a few times, then looked accusingly at the tree. Leaves rattled overhead, and Ofelia looked away. "She doesn't usually let people up here."

He angled his head. "I asked nicely."

"I had no idea it was possible to charm a tree." She narrowed her eyes at him, then sighed. "I'm sorry I yelled at you. And called you names."

"I accept your apology."

She waited, staring at him expectantly.

He reached up, grabbed one of the branches overhead, and hung from it for a minute, letting the pleasant twinge of the sore muscles in his back stretching occupy his attention. The welts on his shoulder were on fire.

When he looked back, she was still staring. "What?"

"Aren't you going to—" She waved a hand.

"Apologize? No."

The fire flared in her eyes again.

"I get why you don't want to have anything to do with it," he said. "I do. I tried to get you out of it. Thanks for nothing, by the way."

She sputtered.

"This isn't just about you, Ofelia," he said, exhaling. "My *family* is in danger as long as that killer is loose in Prague. And I *will* do anything to protect them."

He knit his fingers together to keep from reaching for his shoulder. Itching only made it worse. He rubbed his back on the trunk.

"You're right," she said after a long breath. "I got so focused on my own loss, I forgot the bigger picture."

He lifted a shoulder. "It didn't help that they came at you with that whole familial-obligation-vengeance thing. I think if they'd have just asked for your help, you probably would have said yes, huh?"

She stared at him. It was a look of such wonder, surprise, that he smiled.

"We don't have to do it by their rules. You don't want to concord, we don't. Just let me help. I promise I won't offer to die for you again if you don't want me to."

She smiled and buried her face in her hands.

He slid closer, brushing aside old leaves and her blankets. "But can I tell you something, between you and me?"

She looked up, curious and wary.

"The way you stood up to the necromancer," he murmured. "The thing with the roots. And how your eyes got all flinty. That was hot."

The laugh burst from her like summer rain. She shook her head as if she couldn't believe her own amusement. He grinned—it was a good look on her.

She looked up at him out of one eye, the little smile still tugging on her mouth. "How hot?"

"Want me to show you exactly?"

Again that amused little head shake but a full smile. His chest filled. She deserved this—lightness, joy, adoration—for the hell she'd been dragged through the past few days. Family could be hard—he knew it. Even when you loved them.

He stretched out a hand, palm up. She set hers in it. He tugged her forward, gently so she had time to unfold and refold again, this time in the cradle formed between his thighs and along his chest. He tugged a bit of bark free from her hair, which was braided again, swept the braids back over her shoulder to expose the curve of her neck and collarbone. When his lips settled there, she sighed and softened.

Each kiss rewarded him with a new ease, a sense of her melding into him. He could get used to the way her fingertips slipped up and down his arm, his chest. The soft puff of her breath on his cheek warmed his core. She'd breathed like that after their night together, sated and at ease.

Despite the climb and stress of the past few days, his strength came surging back. He hauled her onto his lap, and her mouth found his. Her fingers in his hair were strong, her lips demanding, and he gave back teeth and tongue and lips like a promise. She could never ask too much.

When he hiked her shift up her thighs, they parted and he hitched her up high, grinding into her to let her know exactly how hot that scene with the necromancer had made him. She rolled her hips against his erection, and he gripped her thighs hard enough to leave marks.

"We have to get out of this tree," she panted, fingers biting into his arms.

He glanced around—they were above most of the rooftop. No windows in sight.

"My aunt is in the tree." She clambered off him but didn't let go of his hand.

"I thought it was your grandmother." He dusted the bits of bark off her dress, straightening her clothes.

"We call her Grandmother Tree out of respect because she's so old. My aunt is the forest. In the forest." She shook her head once again, amused and delighted. Then her expression turned grim as she stared at his shoulder. "Those are poisonous spider bites, Chris!"

"The tree's your aunt?" He did feel a little woozy.

Ofelia nodded, distracted. "Hold still."

She leaned forward until her lips touched the nearest welt. He shivered. The bites stung for a minute, bright and hot as sparks. Then they simply went away. No more itch, no more swelling, his senses returning.

"What did you do?" He craned his head to peer at his own shoulder.

"Neutralized the poison." She shrugged.

He stared at her.

"Once I know it, I can counter it."

"What do you mean, know?"

She looked confused by the question or maybe how to answer. Something distinctly witchy was coming. "I can figure out what's in things by taste. Sometimes scent, but taste is more accurate. If it's poison, my charm creates an antidote. So far at least."

"So far," he echoed.

Ofelia blinked at him in that way he recognized very well from a witch who knew that something she found reasonable was incredibly dangerous.

"My gods, no wonder she wanted you to have a concord."

"You're not going to tell me it's crazy?"

He glanced down the tree, buying himself some time by trying to figure out how the hell they were going to get down.

"You know what you're capable of. I'm just going to be there if you put something in your mouth your charm can't handle."

Her face brightened, concern melting away. "Was that— did you just make a dick joke?"

"If that's how you want to take it." He winked.

"*You* don't take anything seriously, do you?"

He thought she was teasing after what they'd just been through. But when she continued to stare at him, then shook her head, he realized there was a strong chance she meant it.

Like, just because he'd found a way to laugh despite it all, he didn't realize what a mess they were in.

"What's wrong?" Her brows furrowed.

"Nothing."

"You are… surprising." Her smile went uneven, then fell away.

He lifted a shoulder. He'd been hearing that his whole life. *Surprising* was just more of the same. *Different. Strange.*

He hadn't realized he'd built a shrine around her in his heart until it began to crumble under the weight of realization. He'd thought she saw him. The real him. Thought maybe she'd been the only one who ever had. That she was home. But she was like the others.

No one seemed to get him, not really, for whatever he was beyond their attraction to him. The rest of him was an oddity no one could quite manage.

"Wait." She touched his hand. "Chris, I—"

"Come on, get me out of this spider-infested tree."

She paused for a long moment, her eyes round and fixed on him and too shiny for his comfort. He wished they were still making out. He knew how to make both of them feel good… physically.

She shook herself free of whatever thought had put that soft, pitying look in her eyes. "Hang on. I've got another way."

She led him down the branch to a spot where a clump of climbing vines hung from a crossing branch overhead. She spoke two loops into the vines, and they wrapped around each other securely.

She knelt, holding up a loop. "Step here." She rose, put her foot in the other loop, and grabbed the vine. "Okay, arm around me."

That was easy. Holding her made that pleasant ache bloom in his chest that banished his unhappiness.

"Hold the vine too." She grinned, sliding an arm around his neck. He squeezed her as he began to get an inkling of what came next. She met his eyes. "Ready?"

"For what?"

"To step off the branch," she said.

He shook his head firmly. "Oh hell no."

"Close your eyes," she ordered.

He obeyed.

"Kiss me," she murmured.

That came easy. Even with his eyes closed, his mouth couldn't help but find hers. Her arm tightened around him. She deepened the kiss, stealing his breath. Her breasts pressed into him, giving him her weight. He softened his knees to catch her. And then she shoved him. He staggered back a step, right off the branch beneath their feet.

For a moment everything hovered. And then their weight tugged the vine. But instead of a snap and a long fall, the vine slid with them, slowing their descent from a tumble to a graceful swoop. His stomach protested and he clamped onto her, and the vine, with all his strength.

They glided to the ground with the swish of vines and leaves. He stumbled a half step, but she caught him, her knees flexed in landing.

He opened his eyes. "Are you serious?"

"It seemed better than trying to talk you into jumping." She untangled the vine from them and released it. It slid back up the tree.

"Fuck that." He stood up, growling. He was done getting pushed around by this àjé.

Her eyes widened. "I'm sorry?"

"You're sorry?" He grabbed her around the waist, tossing her over his shoulder. He started to spin.

She shrieked laughter, pounding his shoulder blades. "I'm gonna throw up!"

"I thought we were gonna *die*," he choked out.

He stopped spinning, setting her on her feet. They both wobbled.

When she reached out, he grabbed her, drawing her close again.

She beamed up at him, dizzy and flushed.

"And as soon as I can walk straight… we're going upstairs." He lowered his mouth, hovering over hers. Want rose in him so hard it ached beneath his breastbone. He should know better. He was going to get his heart broken again. She couldn't see him. Not really. But he couldn't resist her.

Ofelia purred like a big cat, and he was very suddenly hard as a rock. He took her mouth again, her sweet salty lips and warm tongue as eager for him as he was for her. Her belly pressed against him, and her eyes got that hazy sheen. Her fingers slid against the hair at the back of his head, and the contact lit his bones on fire.

A throat cleared behind them.

"Busy," Chris barked.

"I see that," Erandi said. "Which is why I sent Alam ahead to let them know Ofelia is on her way. Though I can do nothing for the rest of the courtyard you are currently scandalizing."

Words slid against his brain and bounced off.

Ofelia recovered faster. She peered around Chris's shoulder, glaring. "What are you talking about?"

Erandi stood a few feet back, as though attempting to give them privacy. "The window to take you back to the city opens soon. Until then, you train. Both of you. First Àjé's orders."

"Whatever help the Cadre can provide." Chris echoed the necromancer's words. "I thought she meant telling us whatever you knew about the witch hunter."

"That too," Erandi said. "Later. Training starts now."

Ofelia snarled. Chris put a hand on her arm. They had agreed.

The fight went out of her with a sigh. She yanked her arm free and stormed away.

Erandi looked at him, brows raised in approval. "Let's go."

"You couldn't have waited an hour?" Chris huffed and started after her.

Erandi cleared his throat again and jerked his head in the opposite direction with a barely concealed laugh. "I had my orders. And you're with me. We train separately. Unless you've got a few spells up your sleeve?"

CHAPTER TWENTY

SERWAAH DIDN'T SEEM to have gotten the memo that they were being sent in to identify and track the hunter. She supervised Ofelia's training herself with Alam or Baako as Ofelia's charm partner.

Ofelia's hands ached from learning to build charms it took most trainees months to master. Her tongue bled from cants that took years for most to learn to speak. Sunup to sundown—a break to eat—and then to midnight.

Chris fared no better. The intensity of sparring and conditioning in both skins all day had pushed him beyond exhaustion. And though the opponents held their worst blows, serious injuries were always possible.

Chris came to bed hours after her the first night with his chest bandaged. When she pressed, he peeled it aside to show the four slashes. Cat claws. They were already healing, edges sealing to thin, pale lines that stood out against his golden skin. He flopped onto his back, arm over his eyes as she peered at them in consternation.

"Erandi?"

He lifted his arm, opened one eye with a sideways grin. There was no beating the joy in him. Even with him weary, it clung to the essence of who he was. "I did get him by the jugular."

She bared her teeth, a little pleased. "Good."

He was asleep before she could curl into his side. They could survive this.

The following day, Serwaah began on poisons and her surety left her.

Ofelia ingested more of them than she had in years, preparing her charm to counter anything that might be used against her. None of them truly harmed her, but they could still make her sick. When she finally collapsed into bed, she rose only to stagger to the bathroom to vomit up whatever she had managed to eat.

On the fourth morning the training room was empty, quiet. Serwaah and Baako arrived with the senior àjé class a moment later. "Come."

Ofelia was too tired to ask.

The mud-walled arena where shifters trained sat outside the city's central rings and canals. Red earth turned the sun into a hard glare over everything. It had to be twenty degrees hotter here, and Ofelia pitied Woof in his full coat.

The First Àjé held up a hand in the shade of the tunnel leading into the arena. The àjé halted as one. Ofelia shuffled to a stop to realize she was surrounded.

"Conduct yourself with honor, Cousin," Baako muttered from just behind her shoulder. "The eyes of the city are on our house today."

Ofelia bristled, but her reply died at the sight in the arena before them. Two shifters sparred in the center ring. She hoped it was sparring. It looked too real for her comfort. They were overseen by a mountain of a man, ruddy from the sun and densely muscled with a shock of bleached strawberry blonde hair and one missing hand. He was Ilya the bear, who had shared his extra tunics with Chris, she realized. She didn't know this shifter, but Commander Mahari must hold him in high regard if he supervised training.

A few other pairings traded practice blows in smaller rings around the main combatants, but most of the trainees stood or crouched in a big circle around the match as the bear called out commentary on the fight for the rest.

A tall, pale, furred creature was in the center, facing off against a familiar sleek, spotted cat. A burst of pride filled her when she finally made sense of what skin she was seeing. Chris held a single, unique form. Wolf-headed, he towered over his opponent with his powerful lupine hind legs but the deeply furred chest and long-armed reach of the man. He'd merged the two into a massive, terrifying shape with the animal's power and the man's dexterity. He used his shield and the short staff but also, in one truly electrifying moment, his teeth to keep the jaguar at bay.

The First Àjé glared into the heat waves between the audience and the combatants. "What is this?"

"He calls it his tall wolf." Commander Mahari joined them so silently Ofelia jumped. The gray-haired woman chuckled. "I've never seen anything like it."

Erandi was circling, head low and tail whipping in frustration, but his ribs heaved. Ilya kicked a shield off the ground and hooked it on his fore-arm, tightening the straps with his teeth. He snagged a club on his way into the arena.

The general angled her head. "Combined with what Ilya's been teaching him, another week and I'd have him with the advanced cadets."

Chris bared his teeth and flattened his ears to his head as he paced a circle to keep both attackers in his sight. Ilya lunged. Chris blocked but struck the jaguar, who had made a move for his off side. Then he went after the bigger man.

Ofelia almost couldn't watch. She clenched her fists at her sides, willing someone to step in, to stop this.

But Chris held his own.

Pride filled the back of Ofelia's throat. She wanted to pump her fist with glee, bare her teeth at them all for doubting Chris. *See who he is. What he is. Even without your training and your duty.*

The First Àjé snorted softly as though she'd heard anyway, and Ofelia didn't dare lift her eyes. "Let's go."

Mahari loosed a piercing whistle, and the mountainous man ended the match. "Circle up."

As one, the trainees moved toward the center. Ofelia lost sight of them for a moment as the students formed a half circle around the combatants.

When she spotted them again, someone had tossed Chris and Erandi towels and tunics. Chris was fully human again, bare-chested and breath heaving. A fresh set of lines crisscrossed his chest and his shoulder. As fair as he was, his skin took the sun well except in a few places gone an angry shade of strawberry. Erandi's neck bore a few teeth marks, and the towel came away stained red. But they were goofing off with the other shifters, slapping each other's backs and passing water back and forth like old comrades-in-arms.

"We have guests." Their commander strode across the sand.

Erandi stood at alert, hands folded in front of him and face still. Chris tried to imitate him but couldn't stop grinning.

"You fought well, wolf." The commander clapped him on the unmarked shoulder.

"Commander." He bowed his head, unable to keep from looking at Ofelia. *Do you see me?*

Had he ever been among so many like him who weren't his family? Her heart ached at the sight of his pride. Even being pushed to his limit, he was happy.

She lost the battle to keep an answering smile off her face. *I see you.*

The First Àjé cleared her throat.

Ofelia blinked, heat flaring in her neck and her cheeks under her aunt's censure.

"Your desire to serve the city as defense is honorable and true." Serwaah addressed witches and shifters. "For those of you who wish to serve as concords, it is important to understand what your bond entails. Today we will demonstrate what it is to bond with your àjé."

Ofelia's heart sped up. Not this, not again. She opened her mouth to protest. Nothing came out. She glared, unable to do more than shake her head minutely. A charm bound her voice and her ability to move.

The other shifters tensed. The bear—Ilya—began to speak, but a slim brown hand reached out and covered his wrist. Ofelia recognized the àjé from the infirmary as Violet, a retired spy. They had bonded briefly over time in Prague. Ofelia liked the àjé, but Violet was not a trainee anymore. Why had they brought a healer? Sudden cold raced through her limbs to her extremities, and the trapped shiver wracked her body painfully. What did they expect to go wrong?

"All help the Cadre can provide," her aunt reminded her with a pointed look. Without breaking the stare, she called over her shoulder. "Christof."

He came, but his smile faltered at Ofelia's expression.

"Acceptable progress has been made," the First Àjé said. "But the enemy you face is an old one and powerful. A concord would make sharing energy *easier*, but it is not impossible to do so without."

Chris nodded, his jaw set. He had known this was coming.

"Break it." Serwaah challenged, fingers locking to strengthen the charm she'd used to bind Ofelia.

Ofelia blinked hard, feeling the tears of frustration on her lashes. She heard a hiss from an àjé that must have been Baako.

Ofelia closed her eyes, searching for the binding. Every charm was like a marble, smooth and round. But usually each had a dissonance, something she thought of as a rough edge that could be penetrated. This one contained her voice, held her still when she wanted to run. The First Àjé's craft had been honed over decades. Ofelia found no suggestion for a point of entry. Ofelia hated to admit her aunt was right. Perhaps she could have been stronger if she had stayed to complete her training and she might have done this alone.

It was her own damn fault that she had to draw on Chris now.

Rage splintered the joy in her chest.

"Look at me. Just me." Chris crowded into her space, blocking out everyone around them. This close the heat of his body put the sun to shame. It chipped at the ice forming over her heart. "I get it, I do. But where better to try it out than here, where we have help if it goes wrong?"

Her eyes popped open in surprise. His skin shone with exertion, the hint of stubble doing nothing to soften the angles of his jaw. She breathed him in, the sweat and sand and wolf.

Chris smiled so sweetly it sealed the pieces of her fractured heart back together. "Can you do it just once? For me?"

He didn't know what he was asking.

"Before the concord ritual, this was the method of energy transfer," Commander Mahari explained to the trainees, both àjé and shifter. "It is highly imperfect. Energy is lost in the transfer, and the process takes too much of the àjé's attention to maintain and risks incapacitating the shifter entirely. If she were to lose focus, or consciousness, the transfer would be broken, unlike the concord bond, in which her shifter's strength becomes part of her natural defenses."

The circle grew around them, and everyone took a step back. Chris's eyes stayed locked on hers, and now she saw Woof's fierce glare in them. He nodded.

She *could* do this. And she would protect him through it.

When she closed her eyes again and sought him out, the Heartlight she had once seen in a dark club days ago pulsed brightly. She touched it with her own. They were right—with the concord bond, it would have been easier. She wouldn't have had to search for it. It would have been linked to her own. She could have tapped him without conscious thought. She hated it.

She grasped it now and pulled hard. Heartlight flooded her until all she knew was glowing waves of power. It surged up the charm, and now she saw the fine line of dissonance she hadn't perceived on her own. She directed the power at that imperfection. After a moment of steady pulsing, the whole thing shattered like glass.

Her voice was her own again. She let the sound of her rage fill her up, and when there was no more room, she sent it out. Overhead, lightning crackled in a sky that had been a flawless, sunbaked blue a moment before. The wind picked up; the temperature dropped. The forest around them began to whip in the gale.

Without opening her eyes, she could see all of it, the gathering clouds, the tossing leaves and branches, dust flying. She wasn't done.

The first drops hit hard and fat and became a deluge. Over the downpour came the shocked cries of the trainees.

Ofelia turned her face up to the sky and roared. Thunder laughed back, lightning snapping down and sparking off posts and walls.

Enough, Fifi. Once, she'd heard her mother's voice all the time. Over the years it had faded. Hearing it now as though they stood side by side made her rage waver.

The rain tapered off, the clouds drew back inside themselves, and the thunder faded.

Joy replaced the anger. *I've missed you, Mama.*

The sun shone bright and hot again. *You've grown, Daughter.*

Ofelia sucked in a breath. She could finally show her how much. What she was capable of.

She tapped the living network of the jungle. Fresh runners shot up around the arena walls, sliding up like snakes, rooting and sending out profusions of leaves and flowers. She could taste *everything,* her senses brighter and more sensitive. She knew what her aunt must feel like, being part of the land itself.

Now you're just showing off. Ofelia's heart ached at the sound of that familiar, wry laugh. *Look to your mate.*

Shifters were strong, they recovered faster, but they were as mortal as àjé. And this one—the Heartlight was intoxicating. The power seemed endless and all hers. She couldn't feel its end. All she had to do was keep taking.

You don't want that.

Ofelia gasped. *Chris.*

She peeled herself away from the Heartlight and her mother's clear voice, ignoring the longing that followed. She snapped back into her body, eyes open. "No more."

The world returned to her, the air lushly perfumed by with fresh rain and new flowers.

Chris had gone to one knee at her feet, free hand braced on the ground. His head hung low, shoulders slumped. He swayed. She dropped to her knees.

"Oh, Seven help me," she whispered, taking his face in her hands. "Chris. Please look at me."

It seemed to take him an enormous effort to lift his head. He was still smiling, but the expression was strained. The vitality in his skin had been washed away, leaving it the shade and texture of old linen. Heartlight pulsed fainter now.

"I took too much." The panic rose in her throat. She started to call for help, but his fingers gripped hers.

"I'll be okay. We've got this."

She bowed her head until their foreheads touched.

She'd been a teenager when she learned growing plants energized her

—though that seemed paltry compared to what she had taken from him. Still, she scanned the lush greenery around them. They'd made this together. Surely the exchange could work both ways. She bound that new strength up and brought his knuckles to her lips, sending it back to him.

"It gets easier after a time or two, to control the flow." Relief filled his voice.

She shook her head. "Never."

He snorted softly. "Yeah, okay. Sounds good."

Commander Mahari crowed with victory. "See how she is giving back to him!"

"Well done," Serwaah admitted grudgingly.

Around them the buzz of conversation held awe and maybe a little bit of fear. Ofelia wondered whether this had shown some of the idiots who intended to volunteer as concords how dangerous it could be, how stupid this whole business was. But she couldn't worry about that now. She couldn't take her eyes off Chris. She sent more energy toward him, through their locked fingers.

"You can stop now," he muttered, drawing them both to their feet.

"This deserves a celebration." Erandi clapped a hand on their shoulders.

"Ofelia, to the training room," Serwaah ordered. "There is much work to be done today."

Erandi squeezed Ofelia's shoulder, lowering his voice. "I'll look after him. Bring him back in one piece."

She surrendered Chris reluctantly and returned to the palace with the àjé.

In the training room, she paused at her station. She placed her shaking hands on the wood table, amid the vials and implements and dried samples, and fought the urge to weep.

The rest of the àjé in training filed in, more than a few giving her long glances as they passed. She ignored them, kept her eyes on her station. Perhaps they thought her shameful for balking at something they would have done eagerly. Or a coward for not being eager to avenge her mother. She no longer cared. She bent her head to her assigned tasks and did not look up until the end-of-the-day bell chimed.

The others filed out, but Ofelia remained at her station. She felt Serwaah's approach but didn't look up.

"I know that was hard," the First Àjé murmured. "But you needed to know how it felt to take, and even to take too much, so that you would not do it again unless all options had been expended."

Ofelia looked up, knowing the hollowness in her chest was visible in her eyes. She had neither the strength nor desire to hide it. She was beyond playing untouchable. This pain was too raw. "I'll never do it again."

"I'll make offerings to all Seven in the prayer that you never have to."

"Are we done here?" Ofelia stared past her shoulder.

Serwaah sighed deeply. "There is so much more I would have given you with more time. I have prepared you the best I can given the circumstances. You should rest. Soak if you can. Water will help rebalance you."

Ofelia was at the door when her aunt spoke again.

"I would give anything—" The words carried through her voice was low with confession. "Hate me if you will. But you have a shifter willing —even without the protections he's owed—and I won't lose my niece the same way I lost my sister."

In her rooms, Ofelia soaked until her fingers were as wrinkled as raisins. Then she waited up. Her memory of concord ceremonies and the following celebrations was sketchy at best. She hadn't been here long enough to see more than one or two. And theirs wasn't a true concord. There had been no vow; the connection was not permanent. It was a disadvantage, not having that power instantaneously, but Ofelia decided it was worth it. That way she wouldn't be tempted to tap it again. She shut down the part of her that howled with longing for that connection. Never again. The one that echoed her aunt's words, *the protections he is owed*, was harder to quiet.

Erandi brought Chris back earlier—and more drunk—than she'd expected. Or maybe his staggering step was the result of having his life force drained out of him in a single afternoon.

Erandi grinned when she opened the door, more than a little tipsy himself. "Where do you want this lump?"

"Bed," Chris slurred. "So tired."

"You know we fly in the morning." She hurried after them, pausing to grab a pitcher of water and a cup for the table. She muttered a spell over the water to help rehydrate him.

"He'll sleep it off," Erandi said. "Shifter metabolism."

"Shifter metabolism!" Chris echoed in what had likely been a drinking cry for the past few hours before mumbling unintelligibly.

Ofelia rolled her eyes.

They got him into the bed in an easy, companionable silence. Erandi propped Chris up enough for her to get a glass of water into him.

Chris sank into the pillows with a low groan, forearm over his face, and was silent for long enough she thought he might have passed out.

"Remember when Baako had to come get us from the constable's office in Dola?" Ofelia hissed a laugh through her teeth.

Erandi rubbed his forehead, a smile in his voice. "Do *you* remember it?"

"We picked a fight we couldn't win. They detained us to keep us from getting the shit kicked out of us by three Cadre teams."

"Beer courage."

She made a face.

"Sweet wine courage for you then." He snorted. "Your mouth always gets away from you when you've had one too many."

"You weren't exactly the voice of reason." She glared, then sniffed. "They would've had to work for that beating."

"The constable detained us to protect the Cadre from Serwaah's wrath if they had," he chided affectionately.

She drew a long breath, rolling her memory of the bitter, prickly words around in her mouth for a moment before whispering them like a curse. Or a confession. "They called her weak because she chose my father instead of coming home to raise me here."

"I'd hoped you didn't remember that part." Backlit by the dim lamps she'd left burning in the living room, his face was shadow. Maybe she just imagined the echo of the pain she felt. The isolation. It had drawn them together in the first place.

His eyes flashed, animal shine reflecting the low light, making it easier to read his expression. It was a gesture that made her chest ache with familiarity. Just like the new gratitude that came of his concord with Alam.

There was no one she trusted to protect her cousin more. "Are they right? Am I repeating her mistake?"

He hissed, so catlike she would have laughed if everything didn't hurt so much. "You know that's bullshit they said to rile you up?"

She hung her head.

"I've never seen anything like what you did today," he murmured, his eyes on the man stirring on the bed. "The two of you."

Chris groaned softly back to awareness. "My mouth tastes like weeds."

"Be thankful," Ofelia snapped at him without any fire. "That charm will be the only reason you don't wish your head had fallen off your shoulders by tomorrow morning."

He blinked up at her with a smile still potent for all its drowsy inebriation.

Seven, she thought, he was something to behold even like this.

He closed his eyes again. It seemed reckless of the gods to put so much charm in one exceedingly handsome form. If there'd been an ounce less sweetness, more guile, he would have been a nightmare.

Erandi hummed softly, lowering his voice. "Seems like more than luck that brought you together again—"

"If the word *fate* leaves your mouth, I'm going to deck you," Ofelia muttered. "You've been spending too much time with àjé."

"Occupational hazard, I guess." He laughed under his breath, caught her hand, and brought her knuckles to his lips. "Good night, Princess."

Ofelia stomped, but he'd slid backward before she could smash his toes.

When he was gone, Ofelia resumed her perch on the edge of the bed, resting her elbows on her knees.

Behind her, Chris groaned. Maybe now he was realizing what he'd gotten himself into. How vulnerable he truly was with her unable, or unwilling, to take the bond. Poor wolf.

She slid the glass toward him on the nightstand. "Drink more water."

"You did something to the water." He sounded wary.

"Now you ask questions?" She laughed. "Drink."

He rolled onto one elbow to take the glass obediently. "Àjé."

When he'd drained the glass, she took a moment to refill it in case he woke, thirsty again. When she looked back, his eyes were on her with a clarity that made her think there was something to these claims of shifter metabolism.

"What?" She fought a smile.

"Consolation prize?" He rolled onto his back, offering himself with wide arms.

She rolled her eyes, flopping down, half on his chest. "You are nobody's consolation, Christof Vogel. You are the prize."

"I like when you say things like that." He snugged his arms around her, burying his face against her temple with an absurdly long breath. "They make me feel good."

She sighed, readjusting her expectations again. He *was* going to pass out soon. She stroked his back, adjusting her position so she could get her arms around him fully. It brought them eye to eye. He tucked his face against her cheek and nuzzled. His nose was cool, and she sealed her eyes shut against a startling fondness for him.

His grip on her didn't exactly release, but a few moments later he inhaled with a hitching snore.

"Thank you for not running." She ran her fingers through his hair. "I'm glad you're here."

CHAPTER TWENTY-ONE

OFELIA STEPPED down the narrow stairs of the private jet into the sun. Salty air whipped over the runway of the small Mediterranean island. She glanced back once, meeting Baako's gaze in farewell. Behind her, Alam stood poised beside Erandi, who had managed to talk them both into the escort that accompanied Chris and Fifi out of the territory.

Alam had spent most the flight—their first—glued to the window. Erandi had stayed close, listening to the briefing.

Considering the àjé had been tracking the witch hunter for three hundred years, they had shockingly few details. The certainty that he was some kind of supernatural seemed to have taken over as the most popular theory after the death of her parents. A less supported argument was made for a human cult that knew of witches and trained a killer in each generation.

The blood was a puzzle. Due to the enormous power generated, a blood spell in use would have been a beacon—especially if it had gone wrong. Instead, the blood had been taken, but then nothing. According to intelligence from the network of spies, Azrael's investigation was stalled.

Chris and Ofelia's orders were to lie low until the Cadre could give them any relevant information and then try to make a positive ID. Officially, she was to cast the tracking charm for Baako's team to finish the job. Privately, she doubted any entity powerful enough to kill her parents would give them that chance.

Ofelia had absorbed everything with the diligence brought on by years of being top of her class. Once, she'd planned on medical school, or chemistry, where she could hide her charm in a mundane occupation. That had ended the night she'd been awoken by the head of her dorm and taken to the officials waiting to inform her that her parents were dead.

A week later, she'd been pulled from staring into space in her chemistry class with more news. A family she had never known had arrived to take her home. Any doubt she'd had had died the moment she'd met the woman with her mother's face. Her aunt. Only home hadn't been hers, and they tried to turn her into one of their weapons.

As Ofelia reached the last step, Baako called her name. "Walk in light. Seven protect you."

Her problem wasn't Baako, not really. If anything, she might have envied the cousin who had been raised with no question of her place.

"Take care of our mothers." Ofelia turned her face to the sun and took the final step. Leaving the hidden city behind was harder this time. Seeing it through Chris's eyes, she finally understood what a miracle it seemed to those who could not hide what they were as easily she could.

She shaded her eyes. Ahead of her on the single runway of the small airfield, Chris was laughing and clasping hands with three familiar men— his friends from the club. She exhaled. Maybe she was making too much of it. He seemed fine wherever he was. And what did she know of people anyway? She'd judged Kenneth poorly, and Ayele—

"Fifi." Ayele waited apart from the others, flanked by uniformed staff and dressed in all white, her bare skull shining in the bright sun. The woman she'd thought she knew well.

"My gratitude to your family for coordinating our return," Ofelia said, her voice tight, "at a considerable risk, I'm sure. You will be rewarded."

Ayele's face tightened, pain streaking across it before she smoothed her expression. She bowed. "We are grateful to serve."

Ofelia's throat clenched, but she kept her face impassive. Or so she thought.

When she looked up, Chris was already watching her from his circle of friends, his gaze focused across the distance. She read the question in his eyes: *You okay?*

She wondered at how easy it had become with them, this kind of communication.

Ofelia lowered her chin once. He didn't look convinced, but he returned to his conversation seamlessly.

In the house, Ayele led the way, all her old playfulness gone. The ache of missing their old banter tangled up in the fury of having been deceived.

Ofelia stared at the pristine white furniture and full set of luggage waiting in the big suite overlooking the sea. Her favorite products had been laid out in the bathroom, even the ones from her store. Her store. What about her plants and her custom orders? Seven. She supposed she'd have to close the store for a while. If she failed, it would never open again.

Brooding, she stepped out onto the balcony.

A moment later the door opened and a second set of luggage arrived. Chris trailed it, looking wonderstruck. "Did you see how big this place is?"

"The island has been on Ayele's mum's side for generations." Ofelia nodded grimacing at how blind she'd been. Ayele's cover story had been a twist from the truth: she *was* the daughter of a Nigerian shipping magnate and a Greek heiress, all right. Only the former was àjé and the latter a weather witch who used their connections in both territories to get extra leeway with their various properties on both sides of the border and proved a useful go-between for the Cadre.

"How are things with you two?" His expression focused.

"Now I know who she is—*what* she is." She shrugged, surprised he cared, surprised she wanted to tell him the truth. "She is an ally of my house. And the mission. That's all that matters."

He didn't look as if he bought it. But he nodded. He took a breath. "How about a nap before dinner? I don't know about you, but I could use some sleep."

He waggled his eyebrows.

"Tempting." She laughed. "But I have some things to take care of. You should rest though. We head out early in the morning. Again. Drink more water."

In the doorway she paused. It was that or run into him.

"Fi." His chest heaved as if he'd lost his breath. "About Erandi."

They had cornered her on the plane as she took one last look at the report after briefing.

Ofelia's traitorous body keened at the thought of the two predators closing in on her. Chris, taller and lean, Erandi, broad-chested and absurdly graceful. She faced them, wondering if the climate control on the jet had suddenly failed. Heat pooled in her hips, and she bit her lip to keep from sighing in anticipation. It shouldn't have been as intimate as it was. She squeezed her thighs together, as if that was going to help stop the mental images that left her feeling overheated and a bit faint.

But it turned out to be an ambush, not a seduction. Disappointment surprised her.

"You didn't tell them something." Erandi braced an arm over her head, his voice pitched low.

Chris folded his arms over his chest in a way that made her mouth water, blocking them off from the rest of the escort. "Something about the witch hunter."

"Are you going to snitch on me?" Ofelia dared a challenge.

Erandi's thick dark brow rose. Chris's mouth quirked in response.

"You are going to let him stay with you, in your Prague," Erandi ordered. "For your protection and my peace of mind. Or I will suggest Baako ask you a few more questions."

Ofelia gritted her teeth and tried to ignore the little thrill of knowing that her apartment was a one-bedroom. Sharing a bed for a little longer wouldn't be the worst thing. Their detour had been a series of frustrations. "Fine."

They exchanged a glance.

"That was too easy." Chris laughed.

"She's going to try to give you the slip the first chance she gets," Erandi noted.

Ofelia sucked her teeth with a glare big enough for both. She'd been alone far too long to need two overprotective shifters in her business.

But her throat pricked with unexpected emotion as they said good-bye. It was impossible to look away from two powerful, lethal shifters clasping hands before a laughing embrace and worrisome to think she was somehow depriving Chris of the opportunity to live a life without hiding.

Erandi opened one golden eye to take her in. "You too, Princess."

"Beast," she muttered but went.

Two strong arms closed around her, scents mingling, breath in her hair and on her shoulder. Pressed between two heartbeats, Ofelia felt her anxiety ease. She slid her arms around them, locking them together.

"Stay alive," Erandi muttered, hoarse. "And come home. Both of you."

"I promise," Chris said, and the words crackled between them.

Ofelia gasped at the snap of a vow against her skin, reminding her that he might not be a witch, but he was much more than just a wolf.

Alam whined and they made room, laughing before the captain's voice announced descent. Chris buckled in next to her and took her hand in his.

Based on the arrival of his luggage in the suite, he wasn't waiting for Prague to insert himself into her living space. It would probably do no good to remind him they were on an island thousands of miles away from the witch hunter.

She took him in. Days in the sun and training had turned his skin a ruddy light brown that made his eyes more striking. His lean strength had gotten more solid, grounded. He still dressed like a party boy—white T-shirt over khakis and a fresh pair of white Adidas—but his face held an intensity now. He had purpose, she realized. It was sexy enough on its own. Knowing it was somehow connected to her rekindled the fire in her hips.

"Don't have to apologize or explain," she said. "I probably should though. It was a long time ago, but still."

"You don't have to." He shook his head. "I have eyes."

Unable to keep from laughing, she planted her hands on hips, stared up at him.

"He cares about you," Chris said, suddenly serious. "And so do I. We have that in common."

"That's not the only thing you have in common." Ofelia raised a brow. Did he think she was an idiot? There was so much chemistry between them she got second-degree burns being in the room when they were together.

He flushed, a rosy color under the glorious golden brown. "I like him. A lot. But I would never... go there if you weren't okay with it. I meant what I said. I'm yours."

Oh, not this again. Ofelia didn't think she could handle any more feelings right now. She patted his arm. "And I care about you both. So there. We're all even. And now he's going back to the hidden city, and we're off to hunt a witch hunter. So. Let's focus on the job ahead, okay?"

He bobbed his head, though he looked like he wanted to say more. She looked pointedly at the door. He stepped aside.

"Ofelia," he called as she stepped into the hall.

She paused. "Yes, Christof."

"We're not going to stop until the witch hunter is dead, are we?"

A chill raced through her. She thought about lying. But he'd come through so much with her. She owed him one truth. "No. I'm not."

"Good."

CHAPTER TWENTY-TWO

CHRIS HAD NEVER FELT LESS like a party in his whole life.

Ayele had filled the house with socialites, musicians, and hangers-on. She'd hired three well-known DJs. They'd been going strong the week Chris and Ofelia had spent in the hidden city.

The official story was Ofelia had been so smitten with Chris she'd taken him with her to the island the morning after they'd met. Ayele invited his bunch later. That way when they returned to Prague, they would be just one of the group of socialites and no one would be the wiser.

Ofelia barely returned in time for dinner, but she was flirty and possessive enough to leave no question they were intimate. She drifted away to talk to her Swedish-heiress friend, and he found himself circled by his crew. As above their usual standards as this was, they were adjusting well.

When the music started up again, they found lounge chairs by the infinity pool.

"Can't believe you and Ofelia Adjei are actually a unit." Klaus lifted his beer in cheers.

"I give it two weeks tops," Luca shouted.

"Man. You are such a fucking downer." Klaus rolled his eyes. "Maybe this time it'll stick."

"You know these chicks. She's just in it for the good time." Luca frowned, exhaling sharply. "Hey! They're perfect for each other. Bets on who quits who first."

"Fuck you, man." Chris set his beer down harder than he needed to. "You don't even know her."

Luca rolled his eyes, palms up. "Please, can you quit acting like this is some kind of true love? Like people like this are even capable of it. Look at them. Silly gits never worked a day in their lives for any of this. Their families got rich off the godswar."

Ondrej looked between them, concern brewing in his face.

Chris ground his teeth, feeling that uncomfortable anger getting harder to ignore.

Klaus set a hand on his shoulder. "Come get another drink with me. I got twenty says skinny-dipping is bound to start any minute now."

Chris sat a moment longer, focused on Luca, who stared back belligerently.

"Let's go," Klaus muttered, squeezing hard.

They headed back to the poolside bar. Klaus ordered another beer. Chris snagged a bottle of water.

"He never learned to pace himself. He's been out in the sun and drinking too much for days. And he's jealous."

Chris grumbled. "He's gonna get his ass tossed in the pool."

"Would serve him right." Klaus grinned before he sobered. "So you gonna tell me where the hell you've been the past couple of days? I covered with your fam, man. But I don't buy that shit about you two running off for a lovers' extra-long-assed weekend."

Chris raised a brow. He felt the words coming up his throat. But before he could swallow them, they simply disappeared as though they had never been.

"I can't," he said simply. Honestly.

Klaus seemed to accept that, though he had to take another swig of beer to wash it down. "This girl, Ofelia. You're good?"

Chris drank his entire bottle in a series of long swallows. He was not good. He was in love with her, and now they were pretending to be dating while trying to find a possibly immortal witch hunter in his home city. He was fucked.

"Good gods, man. You're sure." Klaus exhaled, grinning.

"She's only ever been it for me. I just didn't know it until she turned up." It was the only part Chris could say, but he was certain.

"I know one of your thousand brothers probably has dibs on best man," Klaus said, slapping his shoulder, "but I at least want an invite to the wedding."

Chris's laughter died far too quickly.

"Was I wrong then?" Klaus demanded.

"Luca is right." Chris scraped at the label of his bottle as though it had personally offended him. "This is her world—and that store she owns. It's the real deal. I can't even finish my apartment. What the fuck business do I have even trying?"

Klaus set his beer down on the table and gestured to the bartender. "Another water, here, yeah?"

The man disappeared. Alone, Klaus stared into his face.

"Listen, brother," Klaus muttered. "I'm only gonna tell you this once because that bony head of yours is big enough already. You're the glue that holds our merry little band together. Like I'd put up with Luca's shit and bug-eyed Ondrej without you? Gaping like a fucking carp, that one." He glanced over his shoulder where the youngest member of their crew was, indeed, gaping at a beautiful Spanish girl who was drunk and dancing with her friend on the other side of the pool. Klaus sighed. "You are a good man. You're loyal—to a fault—and you have a good heart. Plus you're good with kids. And chicks love dudes who are good with kids, amirite?"

Chris shook his head, his laugh coming easier. "Right."

"This girl," he said. "Whoever she comes from, however much money she has, better earn the right to have the kind of love and loyalty you've got to offer her. That shit is priceless. Make sure she's worthy of it. You deserve the good stuff too."

Chris rubbed the heel of his hand against his brow. "Thanks, man."

The bartender returned with another icy cold bottle.

"Perfect timing, my good man." Klaus clapped Chris on the shoulder and let him go. "Now I gotta go collect my money, 'cause if the skinny-dipping hasn't started by the time we get back, I may kick it off myself."

"I'll catch up." Chris lingered, waving down the bartender again.

The house was L-shaped with an interior courtyard, pool, and entertaining areas facing the Mediterranean. Miles of sea and sky in hyperreal shades of blue stretched out in front of them, the distant shores soft shadows on the horizon. Ayele stood at the end of the farthest vista where she could face the sea but also keep an eye on the goings-on. The glass of rosé in her hand was no longer sweating.

"Brought you a fresh one." He passed her the glass.

Ayele smiled faintly, eyeing him. "Do you know how many people have ever done that for me at a party like this?"

"I imagine they're too focused on their own good time to worry about the host." He leaned against the opposite wall. "I hope my friends haven't been too much trouble this week."

She barked a laugh. "They're delightful. Especially that little angry one. The Italian?"

"Luca."

She took a sip. "That's the one."

"I'm sorry about him."

"Klaus and Ondrej have been on their best behavior," she admitted. "Even if that poor boy never closes his mouth."

"He's new to all this." Chris's gaze swept the revelry. "I mean, we all are."

"*You're* handling it well."

"I'm doing my best to keep up." He thought they might not be talking about the party anymore. If they were telling the truth, it was time for his own. "She still loves you or it wouldn't hurt so much."

"I knew what I was doing when I took the assignment. Keeping an eye on her seemed easiest if I was close to her." She sucked in a hard breath, eyes fixed on a distant point on the sea. "I don't have siblings. Or even a real friend probably. I knew the truth would come out. I didn't know what it would cost."

"Now that the truth *is* out, you can get past it."

"That easy, huh?"

Chris laughed. "Probably not. But worth it, don't you think?"

"You're not what I expected." Ayele half smiled, taking him in again.

He scented Ofelia. She was close, and he was like iron filings to a magnet. "I'll work on her, okay?"

Ayele's eyes shone. She brought the glass of wine to her lips. "I'm going to wind up liking you, aren't I, Christof Vogel?"

"I hope so." He pushed off the wall and followed his nose.

Ofelia was inside one of the open-air alcoves framing the courtyard with the rest of her crew. They were talking, mostly over and around her. She had the thousand-yard stare he recognized as a witch plotting.

"May I borrow Fi for a minute?" He extended a hand, relieved when Ofelia took it without protest.

The blonde glared up at him covetously. "Haven't you had her all to yourself for long enough?"

"Young love, Maja." The shorter man rolled his eyes but moved his knees aside for Ofelia to pass. "Be patient."

Ofelia let him draw her away to an empty balcony with a couch. She sank into it with a sigh and accepted the water bottle. "Thank you."

"You looked like you would rather be anywhere else," he said lightly.

A smile lifted the corner of her mouth.

"Are you going to tell me what you didn't tell the others?"

She didn't let her glance settle on him. "I'm thinking about whether to close the shop while we sort this out."

Ah, so it was to be a distraction then. Make him think she was including him on an important decision that had nothing to do with what he'd really asked.

"I mean, you have classes, right. People coming through. Maybe you'll get some information."

She smiled as if he'd said something brilliant. He decided to play along for now. And maybe help Ayele.

"Maybe Ayele could help you out." He kept his expression innocent but held her gaze steady. "I mean, she's àjé too, right? She was at the store all the time with you. And it would be weird if you ditched her."

"I'm not going to fall for that, you know." Her eyes narrowed. "You trying to fix things with that àjé spy."

He ignored the bitter tone in her voice. That was hurt talking. And anyway, she wasn't the one to call him out. "Well, I'm not going to fall for your bullshit about the store being the thing you're worried about."

She stared. He showed his teeth.

"And I'm not going to let you out of my sight." He offered his hand. "Now one night of party left, and then we're on the job. Can I have this dance?"

CHAPTER TWENTY-THREE

BACK IN PRAGUE thirty-six hours later, Ofelia laughed at the sight of Chris sprawled on the oversized love seat in her living room.

After they landed, he'd taken off for his parents' place. He returned, glowering like a thunderhead with a duffel bag of stuff. When she asked, he claimed nothing was wrong, then took her to bed with the kind of intensity she definitely benefited from.

But it wasn't just sex.

Ofelia from a week ago would have never recognized the eagerness to slide into bed and curl up around six foot plus of shifter who managed to smell divine—even with whatever that appalling aftershave he wore. She blamed it on the stress of the past week, then added coming up with something for him that wouldn't hide his natural pine-and-wild-roses scent to her mental task list.

But when she came out of the bathroom, hair wrapped and wearing the T-shirt he'd abandoned, her wrecked bed was empty.

She found him wrestling a fuzzy throw blanket into covering a laughable amount of his long body. "What are you doing?"

"Going to sleep." He punched the cushion under his head.

"On the *couch*?"

He pointed at the door. "I'm closest."

"What does that have to do with sharing a bed?"

"Anything that gets through the wards has to deal with me."

She marched back to bed. He'd figure out how dumb his plan was when he couldn't get any sleep. And anyway, she could protect herself.

She spent the night tossing and turning until she finally fell asleep and woke up to an empty apartment.

Ayele was downstairs in the shop, so she spent the day in her apartment working on custom orders.

When her wards chimed hours later, Ofelia blinked, bleary-eyed, and shifted her safety goggles to her forehead. She glanced around as the front door opened and closed. Chris called a greeting.

The kitchen table was covered in vials and tubes, jars of oils, and dried herbs. She'd found an old antelope skull at a flea market and kept it as her memento mori for charm work. It sat on a stack of vintage biology and chemistry books beside the creeping fig—also flea market finds. The fig had been in a terrible state when she returned home, but bathed in charm work all day, it was lush and full, nearly covering the skull so that only the horns and sockets could be seen. Desert blues drifted up from the speaker she'd lost somewhere under the fresh herbs, and a column of pink smoke rose from the love charm brewing on the Bunsen burner.

All in all, she looked the proper storybook witch.

On his way into the kitchen, Chris shifted a bag of groceries to his opposite hip and stepped carefully around the consecrated space without asking a single question. "Dinner in an hour."

For a moment the sight of him sliding a fabric apron over his head and moving about her kitchen like he owned it robbed her of any other coherent thought.

He grinned. "Nice apron."

She glanced down at the heavier leather model she used. Sometimes a charm went a little sideways, and she hated losing clothes to stains or burns. "You too."

"Heard anything from our friends?" He lowered his voice with a wink.

"Is that your attempt at code?" Ofelia's brow wrinkled. "You know the wards block sound. You can just say the Cadre."

"Where's the fun in that?" He tossed a packet of noodles on the counter.

"No, I haven't heard anything from my aunt, the First Àjé to the necromancer Amanirenas," she shouted at the top of her lungs. When Azrael's cronies didn't charge through the door, she shrugged.

He stared at her until heat crept up her neck.

"Nothing." She pinched her lips to keep from smiling.

He popped open a container of deli olives, the big fancy kind that glistened in the late afternoon light. "It doesn't smell like you've eaten all day, so I'm gonna let your hangry slide."

He wafted the olives under her nose and held out the container. She held up her dirty hands, and he obliged by popping a particularly juicy stuffed green olive across her lips. If she sucked his fingertips lightly, it was only to keep stray oil from dripping into her charm work and ruining anything.

His pupils expanded and his nostrils flared as his fingertip slid over her lower lip. "Finish up so we can eat while it's hot."

"Bossy."

"You didn't argue last night." He turned back to the pile of ingredients being assembled on her counter.

She didn't look up again until the smells coming from the kitchen distracted her from the career-success serum she was building for a young executive. Her stomach threatened mutiny. Ofelia tried to focus but gave up quickly, letting the charm dissipate before she accidentally botched the serum. She wanted the woman to get a promotion, not be appointed CEO. Not before she was ready. That could be a curse, not a charm.

"Wash up." He didn't seem to care that there wasn't any room at the table to eat. He set plates on the kitchen's bar counter, poured two glasses of a hibiscus-strawberry iced tea, and set out silverware.

She stared at the steaming plate of pasta, fresh basil, and tomatoes in a light oil. "Where did you learn to cook like this?"

"My mom cooks to keep us alive, but she doesn't love it. My dad would eat the same three things for the rest of his life." He lifted one shoulder, diving into his plate. "My brothers eat anything you put in front of them. My little sister's the only one that's got any taste at all. I got curious about what else was out there. Guten appetit."

Ofelia ate. Every forkful made her feel more solid, brought her back into her body. She rolled ingredients around her tongue in slow, thoughtful bites, but if there was a charm in this, it wasn't in the ingredients.

"This is magic, you know." She pointed her fork at her nearly bare plate.

He speared a sauce-drenched baby tomato on his own plate and offered it up to her. "What did you expect from a wolf-skinned witch child?"

"Is that what Amanirenas called you?" She took the tomato and the flush of heat that came with him watching her eat it.

"Several times. Witch-born, wolf-blooded was my favorite."

By the end of the meal they were laughing, conversation going easily back and forth as wine replaced tea. She clapped when a fluffy sponge cake pocked with fruit emerged from the oven.

"Dessert too?"

He rolled his eyes. "Dessert always. I don't make the rules."

They cleaned the kitchen together. She went back to her custom orders while he made what sounded like dozens of phone calls. When she got to the repeat orders, the ones that were mostly skin care and good luck and no danger of accidentally hexing someone due to inattention, she turned her ear to his conversations. The jovial chatter that had become her background over the past hour resolved to questions, answers, listening. He was working, she realized, talking to everyone he knew in the city that had any connection to the supernatural.

By the time she'd finished packaging orders, he was asleep on his makeshift bed on the love seat. Leaning against the counter, she watched him for a long time. He was only snoring because the couch was putting his neck at a weird angle.

She slipped into bed. He was just a wall away. Not even her normal nest of pillows could comfort her. She groaned and resumed the now familiar round of tossing. This had to end. She really had to talk sense into him about getting back in the bed.

In the morning Chris left early to run one or more of his innumerable nieces and nephews to or from school. Being an unpaid nanny seemed to occupy most of his day aside from the times he went into the shop to barber. She wondered if that was by choice. He was young, unattached, and lived at home. Maybe his siblings simply dumped the responsibility on the nearest warm body.

It was his life and none of her business. Just because she'd dragged him into her family drama didn't mean she'd gotten an automatic pass into his. But she didn't miss the set of his jaw when he came back from picking the kids up after school.

"I'm lucky to have not one but two asshole brothers." He dumped groceries on the counter. He paused with apron in hand and leaned back to give her an approving head to toe. "Naughty shopkeeper?"

She flushed at his scrutiny, tugging at the silky bow tie. She had been doing the books for the shop, a task she loathed and was woefully behind on. So she'd procrastinated a bit by playing around in her wardrobe beforehand.

"I like it," he pronounced grimly, then went back to slamming pots and pans in the kitchen.

Aside from that moment during their final meeting with the necromancer, she'd never seen him angry. And he'd clamped that down that so quickly. Anger was like every other emotion—it had a use. Getting upset occasionally was healthy, if only to access whatever information it brought. If he was denying himself that out of familial obligation—

She didn't exactly manage her anger well. She had no plans to give lessons.

In the short term, she knew what would help him let off a little steam. She released the bow tie from her puff-sleeve blouse and sashayed into the kitchen, knowing her stride set the pleated wool miniskirt swinging. He slowed down unpacking groceries, trying not to watch her. When he almost dropped an onion, she smirked.

She hopped up onto the counter and crossed her legs. "No news from *you know who* today."

His gaze traveled up her stockinged calves to the little bows where they ended mid-thigh and the fire it lit continued up her thighs to her belly. "The secret witch council in the hidden city in the middle of the African continent?"

"That one." She braced her palms on the counter and leaned forward to give him a view down her shirt.

His nostrils flared. "I don't think you want to tease me today, Princess."

"Who's teasing?" She uncrossed her legs.

He stalked across the kitchen, then braced his hands on either side of her. "You'd better hold on to something."

She silently thanked his asshole brothers as she gripped his shoulders and held on for dear life.

"Hey, can you come to the shop tomorrow?" she asked afterward, sliding off the counter on wobbly knees.

His eyes lit as he licked his upper lip, and a little thrill raced through her at the thought that he was tasting her. "Yeah, why?"

"I need to reset the wards so they recognize you." She shouldn't feel so excited to see the joy that brought him.

As Chris settled onto the love seat later, she thought maybe he was right about not letting himself get too comfortable. She should be focused on getting him out of her place altogether, not making him more welcome. It was easy to be like this with him, but she shouldn't let it be a distraction.

Just because they were in a holding pattern until the àjé found out what Azrael's investigation determined didn't mean she couldn't do a little investigating of her own.

Before she went down to the store the next morning, she sent Kenneth a message.

@Fifiti: I need to see you.

CHAPTER TWENTY-FOUR

AYELE HAD JUMPED at the opportunity to help in the shop. And she was good at it. People loved talking to her, and she knew all the products as well as Ofelia did, so sales were up. Which Ofelia shouldn't complain about, but now she was on her way to selling out of some items, presenting a new problem—when was she going to have time to replace them? She was barely caught up on custom orders.

Without comment, Ayele left a portfolio of beauty-care formulators and contacts on her desk in the corner of the stockroom. The thought of outsourcing even her nonmagical products tied her stomach in knots. Realistically, she knew custom orders alone would be technically enough to soothe the need to use her charm—which was why she had opened the store in the first place. She hated being grateful to Ayele even if she longed to hug her.

Ofelia told herself that she wasn't nervous about her first day working in the store together with Ayele, who had pretended to be her friend, a confidante, and then turned out to be a minder charged with keeping an eye on her. She told herself none of that mattered. They were on the same side. And keeping Ayele busy in the shop was one less person she'd have to shake when she finally got a lead on Hexenblut.

But with no news from the Cadre or a response from Kenneth, she had no excuse to avoid the shop. She was saved when Ayele was called in to make a report, leaving Ofelia alone in the shop by herself all morning.

Chris came in around lunchtime with a takeout order from the doner kebab stand.

"You're early." Ofelia sniffed. "Is that falafel?"

He grinned. "Your nose is almost as good as mine."

"Why don't you leave it in the back? I have to finish this before I close for lunch. We can eat and I'll do the wards."

When he returned, his hands settled around her waist from behind, over the thick corset belt she'd paired with a silk slip dress and chunky heels. The heat of him penetrated the leather, and a little thrill raced up her spine when he tugged her back into his chest.

"How's the morning been?" He pressed his mouth to the curve of her neck as he tugged the silk up her thighs until his fingers connected with bare skin.

"Quiet." She glanced up self-consciously. They *were* behind the counter. The shop was empty with no one to see them except the plants and her ancestors. She tugged away. They already had enough ideas. "Did you fight with your brothers?"

His face wrinkled. "Huh?"

"The grumpy one—Mark, is it?" she asked. "Or is the professor giving you the silent treatment?"

He still looked blank.

She exhaled sharply, gestured at her own body and then his hands, which were still creeping around her hips. "You're always extra… horny… when you've had a fight with your brothers."

He shook his head, grimacing. "I'm not—"

She raised a brow.

"*Extra* horny?" He leaned against the opposite counter, frowning.

She mourned the loss of his touch briefly, but she'd already lost count twice and she *was* starving since she'd been too anxious to eat breakfast.

"That's not why I come on to you—"

"Isn't it?" she said without considering her words. "They come down on you and you pretend it doesn't bother you, and then you come in here and take it out on me."

"Take it out—"

"In a good way." She didn't look up from her tally. "I'm *not* complaining. The past couple of days have been off the charts. Trust. But just… It might be good for you to stand up for yourself occasionally with them. Healthy. We can have perfectly good sex, *and* you can set some good boundaries with your family. Win-win."

Silence.

She finished her count, updated the stock in her point-of-sale system, and clapped gratefully. "Okay, let's eat! I'm ravenous."

Chris stared through the windows out into the empty street, scowling.

She replayed her words and winced. *Fuck*.

"It's really none of my business." She slid her hands up his chest over the pleasantly snug T-shirt beneath a retro letterman jacket.

Up close she could appreciate the detail and the workmanship of the jacket. This wasn't something he'd gotten off a rack. Not this quality satin in carmine, with striped cuffs and patches of giant embroidered peony blossoms sewn on the chest and shoulder. She craned her neck to see the back, where the eyes of an embroidered tiger were barely visible surrounded by blossoms and leaves. It was busier than something she'd usually consider stocking in her store, but she was into the botanical vibe. "I like this."

He made a noncommittal sound. "Yeah, it's one of Evie's."

"Evie?"

"My sister-in-law." He stepped away. "She's a designer. Acaz?"

"Evelia Acaz is your sister-in-law?" She froze, considering the jacket again. "Seriously?"

"She and Mark didn't do anything official, but neither one of them are going anywhere." His eyes glanced over her. "Anyway, she was playing with a retro collection. And flowers. I had the idea for the jacket, and she made it. It didn't wind up fitting in the collection, so she let me keep it."

Ofelia gnawed her lip. She'd reached out to the Acaz studio without much expectation when she opened the shop. There was no way one of Prague's up-and-coming designers would bother with a pop-up or even selling pieces out of her store. Now that Charm Syndicate was more established, she'd made some inroads. But the Acaz studio was still out of reach.

"I can put you in touch if you want." Chris shrugged. "She'd like this store a lot. She's... like you."

Evelia Acaz, the designer, was a witch? Ofelia wanted to shriek.

He pulled out his phone. "Hey, we gonna eat or what?"

"Yeah." Ofelia noted the tension in his face and squeezed his hand. "Hey. I wasn't thinking earlier. All that stuff I said."

"No big deal." He let her go. "Sorry that's the way it feels. Probably pretty weird."

She bit the inside of her cheek. The tightness had come back to her chest, and she didn't know what to do to make it go away. She'd gone too far. Said something wrong. Lunch first, and then maybe she could tease him into a quickie in the back of the shop and convince him she really wasn't bothered. Sex with him was fun, playful, and even when he was intense, she knew she was safe, taken care of. She watched his shoulders walking ahead of her and tried to come up with something to say to make this right.

The shop doorbell rang.

"I forgot to lock—"

And then her wards armed all at once.

Chris's head went up. Before she could catch the next breath, he'd wheeled around, palming her middle to draw her behind him. Surprise at his reaction delayed her own. Most supernatural creatures weren't aware of her wards. Only other witches or powerful necromancers would pick up on them. Somehow he'd not only sensed them but understood their warning.

Maybe Amanirenas was on to something with that wolf-skinned-witch-child business.

"Can we help you?" Chris kept his voice light, she gave him that.

"I'm looking for the proprietor," a rich baritone announced. "Ms. Ofelia Adjei, I understand?"

"That's me," Ofelia said, stepping around Chris. He edged in close to her side as she returned to the counter. She took a half step sideways, and he followed. It took all her self-control not to glare at him. "And you are?"

"Mr. Socrates Altair Manhammer, warlock," he announced, sweeping forward in a bow. "At your service."

Ofelia sealed her lips shut for a moment, praying for composure. What the hell kind of overdone name was that? "Manhammer. That's unusual."

"It is a name of my own divining, representing the power which I command."

"That's…" It was no use trying to keep her brows in place. "Is it spelled—"

"As it sounds." He stared at her strangely.

"And warlock, that is… a title?" Ofelia was dangerously close to squeaking with the threat of laughter.

Chris grunted. She spared him a glance. His nose had gotten a bit pointy. She checked his fingers—those had gone first in the council room. They were hairy. But his expression made the hair on her neck stand up. All the softness and distraction had given way to an iron focus. She wondered how the warlock didn't turn tail and run.

"You should remember your place, handmaiden." Manhammer's voice rang with outrage.

Her humor evaporated. "What can I do for you today, Mr. Manhammer?"

"Interesting shop you have here." His flat lips tightened on a smile. She wondered if they had come that way or if they had been shaped by a lifetime of disapproval. "Though whoring your gifts as mortal fripperies is a disgraceful use of the abilities you've been granted, child."

Chris started forward, a flush in his neck, but Ofelia took his wrist, squeezing. "I like to think of it as sharing my talents with those in need, but that is another way to look at it."

She sent out a tendril of her charm, trying to get a sense of him. His struck back like a raptor's beak. She jumped, and Chris's hand settled at her waist, steadying her. She noted the way Manhammer's nostrils flared when they touched, his lip curling in quickly mastered disgust.

"It is a time to restore the great lineage of our craft," the warlock said. "The path of our True One."

When Ofelia didn't respond, he spread his palms as if giving them a gift. "I am not surprised you haven't heard of his teachings, our kind scattered and smashed as they are. Many of my flock have spoken of you, Handmaid Adjei. I come to extend an offer to you to join us. We are too few not to welcome all no matter their origin of their power."

"How open-minded of you," she said evenly. A subsonic growl emanated from Chris. It vibrated into her chest, and her charm flared in response.

Manhammer folded his arms behind his back, rocking. "In this strange world, some walls must come down, with the proper guidance of course." His gaze settled on the wolfish hand still splayed below her waist. "While others should never be allowed to waver. The prohibition on consorting with lesser beings for one."

"And you are the one to guide us?"

"I am the shepherd who has been called." He inclined his head as though it were a burden he had assumed. "We live in a dangerous time. There are those who would see us wiped from the earth and others who would prey on us for pleasure and profit. They turn our blood into street drugs to the uninitiated as you offer your potions to the weak. Our survival is in unity. I would welcome you into the service of our True One, to receive the safety of his presence."

The hair prickled on the back of Ofelia's neck as the words replayed again in her head.

Kenneth's words from weeks ago rang in her mind. *It's moving fast. Can't get enough of the stuff. And it's not really blood, is it?*

"And who speaks for this True One of yours?" Ofelia crossed her arms over her chest, refusing to give her uncertainty away. "You, I presume?"

"I am his ears and his voice." Manhammer nodded. "All who heed will be blessed. Those who don't shall perish."

Tension solidified in Ofelia's shoulders. Empty threats of the faithful or the something far more sinister? One of the less popular theories about the witch hunter claimed it was a mortal from some kind of secret society. A fundamentalist witch hadn't occurred to her. But where else would Manhammer have acquired so much power and such bent beliefs about his one true whatever? What if the targeted witches were ones who turned down Manhammer's "generous" offer?

"All who heed *him* or *you*?" She sent a surge of strength into her wards and watched him begin to understand he was no longer in a friendly space.

They held nothing that would hurt him—those were too risky to use this close to the necromancer—but a few might make him exceptionally uncomfortable. Nausea, vertigo, the itches. He swallowed hard, and she suspected he was beginning to feel the effects.

Ofelia had heard enough. "So generous of you to stop in, but we're about to close for lunch—"

"The arrogant shall perish alone!" he thundered.

The door chimed again. This time Ayele entered with her purse over her shoulder and the mail under one arm. "I see we have a visitor."

Her eyes widened theatrically at the sight of the red-faced man in the store, but Ofelia saw her fingers begin to twitch. Knowing Ayele, it might well be a tornado she was brewing.

Manhammer must have recognized her for what she was because his air of casual superiority faltered. He blustered, outnumbered but still feeling his righteous anger. "Forsaken women without guidance and fraternizing with animals."

Chris's growl was no longer subsonic.

"A visitor who was just leaving." Ofelia held up a hand. She'd spent all morning organizing the store. The last thing anyone needed was to have to start again. "Be blessed, Mr. Manhammer."

He stared them all down as if considering his options. Ayele's smile was a threat. Chris's teeth were no longer human. Ofelia extended a hand toward the door, indicating an escape.

He stalked out.

Ayele crossed her arms over her chest and stepped not quite enough aside, and he was forced to contort around her to get to the door without touching her.

Ofelia flicked her fingers as he passed through the doorway and the door closed too quickly behind him, hitting him in the backside. The leaves closest to the door rattled. She twisted her thumb and index fingers, and the lock engaged.

Ayele flipped the sign.

"Well, that was exciting." Ayele spun on them both, hands on hips. "And I was worried about walking in on you two making out." Heat rose in Ofelia's neck, but Ayele had already moved on. "Put away the teeth, wolf boy."

Chris gave a lupine-like shake and his wolf retreated. "What a creep."

"He's all bluster." Ofelia splayed a hand on the center of his chest just because she could, and the contact was strangely reassuring. "Don't let him get to you. There are a few like that."

"You've seen guys like that before?" Chris exhaled sharply as if clearing a foul smell from his nose.

"They come down out of whatever backwater bred them every few years"—Ayele slapped the mail on the counter—"where they've been communing with old gods." She waved a hand, conjuring the foolishness. "And somehow they've determined that the problem with the craft is lack of purity—and male guidance. Now they're too good to be *witches*. Men!" Ayele huffed, bull-like. "Present company excluded."

Both Chris and Ofelia stared. Against her will, Ofelia's lips twitched. It was so hard to stay mad at Ayele. She was so cute when she was worked up.

"Manhammer was a definite choice." Chris laughed.

"The warlock thing was new," Ofelia agreed, still trying to shake the uneasy feeling the visit had left behind. "You'd think he'd at least have done a little research before calling himself an oath breaker."

"What's the likelihood that his threats are not empty ones?" Ayele's eyes watched the door like a hawk.

"He doesn't seem strong enough," Ofelia mused. "But if he had help…"

"Believers?" Ayele harrumphed in agreement.

"Something like that." Ofelia liked how quickly their minds worked in concert. "Will you—"

"I can—" Ayele fell silent as they began at once. When Ofelia nodded, she continued. "I'll follow up with the Cadre. See what information they have on any packs of mouth-breathing fundamentalists in the area, if the name Manhammer is known."

"Thanks." Ofelia exhaled.

"I've got his scent," Chris added. "I can give you the last few places he's been today if that would help."

Ayele eyed him speculatively. "You come in handy."

For a moment the three of them stood in an awkward triangle of dissipating tension.

"Are you hungry, Ye?" Chris asked lightly. "We were just going to eat. I bought some extra kebobs."

Ofelia's gaze narrowed, but Chris maintained a guileless expression. Suspicion crept in when the silence lengthened. Just how spontaneous was this lunch?

Ofelia let the remainders of the fantasy of a lunchtime quickie fade. The appearance of Manhammer had dampened her enthusiasm for sex anyway. Pity.

Ayele pointedly avoided direct eye contact, but when Ofelia lowered her chin, she smiled. "I suppose I could have a nibble."

Ofelia lingered for a moment after they went down the hall to the office. Ayele was right—jerks like Manhammer were increasingly common. But there were no coincidences, and his appearance in a city beleaguered by a witch hunter bothered her.

"Falafel's getting cold, Princess," Chris called from the office.

"Oh my god, you call her what now?" Ayele's laugh rose behind him. "She's going to put out your eye if you keep that up."

CHAPTER TWENTY-FIVE

Twenty-four hours later, Kenneth deigned to respond to her message.

> @KenDoll: Get together at my place tonight. Come by.

Ofelia grimaced. A party was not the place she wanted to confront him. Maybe he knew that. He was as human as they came, but he wasn't stupid. His charm was his oil slick of a personality. Nothing more.

She debated her options. Confrontation would be useless. She didn't even need him to tell the truth, not really, and she wouldn't trust any explanations he gave her.

She reconsidered the viability of the party. Plenty of distractions to cover her snooping. She needed to find out for herself—a single taste would tell her everything she needed to know about the drug and its components.

She sent Chris a message.

> @Fifiti: Event for the store. Don't wait up.

She dressed the part of their usual revelers, in a tunic-and-leggings combo she'd gotten to sell in the store, fallen in love with, and taken home instead. Occupational hazard. The tunic was a thin, gauzy material with an iridescent shine to the bronze thread that made it look a bit like elegant chain mail. The thin, open weave showed off the strappy bra she'd picked. The high-waisted leggings hugged the curve of her waist with wide panels flowing over her hips leaving her plenty of room to move. She rubbed a bit of one of her new body oils on her shoulders and upper arms.

It felt a bit like armoring up if she was honest.

A short tram ride later, she stood before a sparkling high-rise building. She took a breath and stepped inside.

At the security desk, Cyril the night guard smiled warmly. "Miss Ofelia, it's good to see you again. I hoped you two would work things out."

"I'm just here for the party," Ofelia said, watching as a well-dressed group of three strode to the main elevator bank. "Listen, is there any way I could use his private elevator? For old time's sake."

His face shifted. Ofelia made her expression even—hopeful but not desperate.

"Come on." He waved her in.

A few of the more prestigious units had private elevators. Of course Kenneth had wanted one. He had to have the most, the best of everything. She understood it now. He'd been crafting the image he needed to gain himself access to the people he wanted. Not because he had hopes of building relationships but so that when they came looking for a good time in the form of a pill or powder, they could do so without feeling the taint of the streets. And he could charge a premium.

When she confronted him, he'd been proud of himself.

"It's like a convenience fee," he'd crowed. "So they can keep their noses clean."

When she hadn't celebrated his brilliant business sense, his face had taken on a petulant, calculating glare, and she realized she too had been part of his game. She shook the bad taste out of her mouth as the closet-sized elevator chimed and the doors slid open behind the narrow secondary door next to the kitchen. The guests would enter through the more impressive foyer, the one with the view of the city sparkling in the west.

She listened to the din of voices under music from the great room and headed to the kitchen. The proper thing to do would be to greet the host. But they were well beyond that. She poured herself a flute of champagne.

To satisfy her hope for a quick resolution, she prowled through the office, bathroom, and bedroom.

She rested on the edge of the unmade bed and focused.

The brunette from the club rounded the corner and let out a little cry of alarm. "What are you doing in our bedroom?"

"I was invited." Ofelia smiled coldly, tilting her head. "Run along. Let him know I've arrived, would you?"

Brigitte's lips tightened with impotent fury. She vanished in a huff of cheap, overpowering perfume and stiff hair.

Ofelia prepared for a wait as some sort of power play, but he came faster than she'd anticipated. Showing up unexpectedly in the bedroom probably hadn't hurt. Maybe his stash was in here after all. He waved Brigitte off. She stalked away, seething.

"Security let you up?" he said by way of greeting.

"I have my ways." Ofelia tipped her glass at him, careful not to spill on the Icelandic wool rug she had picked out. "How have you been, Kenneth?"

"Like you care." He pouted. Of course he was the victim. He'd lied to her, destroyed her trust, and moved on with a plastic bimbo within days, but *he* was the one who'd been wronged.

"Can we not do whatever this is?" She sighed. "I'm not trying to get you back."

"Then why did you come?" he snapped, throwing a quick glance over his shoulder.

She was done with subterfuge. "What do you know about Hexenblut?"

He blanched, his already-sun-deprived face going the color of old fish, and he broke eye contact. A fine sheen of sweat appeared over his upper lip. His pulse jackhammered against the skin of his throat. "No idea. Is it something for one of your silly little potions?"

He always mocked when he felt threatened. Good. She was on to something.

"One of my clients is asking about it." She smiled serenely. "She heard about it from a friend of a friend, that kind of thing."

She marked the moment his gaze switched from unease to avarice, and her heart sank. Having the faintest hope she'd overestimated his involvement or that she'd been something more than a tool to him was delusional. She *knew* that. And yet. Hope died last, after all.

"I might be able to find something like that for you," he said with another quick glance. "But not now. Let's set something up. Who's the mark?"

"She's discreet; she'd prefer me to act as an intermediary."

"She?" He licked his lips.

"Bored with Brigitte already?" She feigned a sip. The bubbles burst lightly on her closed lips. Without even getting her tongue involved, she could tell where the grapes were grown, the kind of season they'd had, and the mineral content of the soil. If she'd licked her lips, she would have known the yeast strain.

"I just like to know the customer, you know." He shifted uneasily. "For my own protection."

"You're selling to me."

"And half the city knows you're connected to me." He snorted, reading her expression better than she liked to admit. "Like it or not, doll."

It was his endearment for her, and it had grown from sparking minor annoyance to blinding rage. She set her glass down carefully on the side table and rose.

"Your choice." As she slipped past him in the doorway and into the hall, she paused. "Professional courtesy. We were something to each other once. But I'm sure I can find someone else."

She turned her back. His grip on her arm came as a surprise. She imagined it probably wasn't as shocking as the jolt he got in exchange.

"Bitch." He hissed, letting her go. His skin was faintly red but otherwise unmarked. He'd feel that sting for hours though.

"Oh, I made up a new little 'potion.'" She smiled in mock apology. "I forgot to tell you how popular this is with young women. It's flattering on all skin types, and it deters unwanted advances."

"You need to leave," he muttered between clenched teeth.

"I'm on my way out—just need to use the loo." She mocked his fake accent with a flat smile and ducked into the hall washroom, locking the door behind her.

The heavy tread of his footsteps paused outside, and she jumped at the light thump of something—his fist?—on the wall. He muttered something muffled by the door and then strode away.

Ofelia opened her clutch.

When she'd packed, she hadn't imagined needing to use everything inside. She'd hoped, perhaps beyond reason, that she was wrong and Kenneth wasn't connected to this. Even if it meant her only remaining lead was Manhammer. She needed to figure out who his supplier was. She had a hard time imagining the creature she was after had spent three hundred years hunting witches to make an illicit drug, but maybe she was missing something.

She wouldn't get another shot. After this, Kenneth would have her removed from the building safe list—worse, he would have the night guard fired for letting her up the private elevator. She would have to check in on Cyril, make sure he came out of this all right.

Time to take more advanced measures. She slipped three fingernail-sized bronze honeybees from her purse into her palm.

"Silence, listen, watch," she whispered. Tiny antenna twitched in response.

In the hall, she gave the woman waiting for her turn an apologetic smile.

In the empty bedroom, she slid one bee from her palm to her fingertip. The tiniest pressure against the paint was enough to start it wiggling. When she let go, it began to dance in a zigzagging pattern along the wall before disappearing into the texture and paint.

Kenneth "worked" in the office, usually playing video games but often taking calls as well. She set one bee loose on the desk.

She hesitated with the final bee.

The expansive chef's kitchen was underused. The foyer didn't encourage one to linger.

The only other place he took calls made her groan internally.

The corner window of the great room, overlooking the city and the distant silhouette of the Prague castle, was currently the most occupied spot in the entire flat during parties like this. People always flocked to that view.

One thing was certain—Ofelia couldn't slink about the edges of the room. She sucked in a breath, assumed her most serene expression, and headed into the fray.

The party was in full swing now as the final rays of sunset cast hazy blades of light. She knew most everyone there from the circles they had frequented. She ignored the looks of surprise and curiosity at her presence. No doubt word of her appearance would make the rounds; speculation on a possible reconciliation would keep her name on everyone's lips. As much as she hated the attention, it was useful being known. Especially if Hexenblut was beginning to circulate in this crowd. She just needed a single hit. If she couldn't get it from Kenneth, one of them would be greedy—or sloppy—enough for her to get her hands on it.

Brigitte held court by the grand piano. Marking her territory. She'd have better luck lifting her leg on the couch. The opulent gift had been one Ofelia left behind without a second glance. She never played anymore if she could help it.

Ofelia kept moving toward the corner view. The crowd parted in waves. She greeted everyone she passed with a nod and the touch of a too-knowing smile, as if letting them in on a secret. Brigitte's voice cracked, the pitch becoming more than a little desperate as Ofelia's trajectory seemed bound for a face-to-face confrontation. When Ofelia walked by the piano, she gave Brigitte a wink.

Once, Ofelia would have felt bad for showing Brigitte up in such an excruciating fashion. But she had no time or interest in subtlety. Witches were dying on the streets below. Possessiveness swept over her. She'd chosen this city. That meant they were her witches. Chris was right. This wasn't just about her.

At her destination, she gazed out the window with her back to the room, as though anything outside had to be more interesting than all of what went on within. Eventually the gazes fell away and the din of the party continued around her.

She palmed the last bee and feigned dropping something. As she crouched, she let her fingers open. The last bee settled in the carpet.

Before she could activate it, a dark-skinned hand glided into her line of sight, palm empty, palm flaring to reveal empty fingers. "You seem to have lost this."

A rectangle of expensive black card stock appeared between his slim fingers as if by magic. She appreciated it even if she knew better. Sleight of hand took skill. "Clever trick."

He was her age, average height, and lean as an arrow. A pale little scar marred one corner of his full upper lip. It gave his mouth a rakish look when he grinned at her. His eyes were ancient as dunes and the same dusky gold color.

"I'm sure you've seen much better." He winked lazily.

"Have we been introduced?" Ofelia let her curiosity show though her mind was still on the deactivated bee barely visible in the thick carpet.

Before she could slide her toe over the bee, his foot found it. The brittle crunch came a second before the sharp snap on the inside of her wrist. The price for the destruction of one of her creations.

"Such a clever creature deserved a better end." He winced as if he felt it in his own bones. His voice held the languorous French once spoken in the southern North American territory, and his broad-featured, dark-skinned face reminded her of home. "But you will forgive my desire for discretion."

She looked at him directly this time, longing briefly for the second-hand effects of Chris's Heartlight. Seeing power had never been her strength. But he was neither witch nor necromancer, of that she was sure.

He seemed to be leaning in, though he closed no distance. "I think you are looking for me."

She flipped the card over. The opposite side was a crisp white, unmarked except for where a single rusty blot of ink had been spilled. It was covered in a tiny bit of cellophane.

Not ink.

The hairs rose on her arms and neck, her body's response clear and potent. She wanted suddenly to be very far away. She forced herself to hold still.

"How—" The question died on her lips with awareness of the crowd.

He gestured to the spot on the inside of her arm that was welting as if stung. "Perhaps something cold will help?"

And give her a chance to get in some of her questions. This was what she had come for.

Ofelia rolled her shoulders back and led the way to the kitchen. "Follow me."

Once there, she put as much distance between them as possible, watching him return from the freezer with a cloth wrapped around a bundle of ice to put against her outstretched wrist.

He offered it with his name, as careful not to touch her as she was him. "You can call me Legs."

Her brows rose.

"Irony." He gestured to the length of his lower body and almost pulled off chagrined and amused. "You must be the Ofelia I've heard so much about."

She schooled her face to a skeptical mask. "Kenneth?"

"He talks," Legs confessed. "Quite a bit."

Ofelia focused her gaze on pressing the ice to her wrist as if that was the only thing that mattered.

"Kenneth has done an admirable job of connecting my product with the right people," he said. "But my supply has increased. I understand your store deals in the unusual and your clientele is quite exclusive."

Ofelia blinked. He wanted her dealing this shit out of her *shop*?

"Highest grade." The thinnest echo of his grin played around his lips. "I assure you. Only a carrier material and a proprietary delivery agent. Clean experience, no aftereffects, no messy side effects."

He gestured at her handbag, where she had made the card disappear on their way into the kitchen. "Consider it a free sample. Like a perfume, yes? If any of your clientele requires it, you should reach out. The card will assist."

Kenneth appeared in the doorway, his gaze bouncing between them. "I see you two have met."

"I had an incident with the stove." Ofelia pasted on a smile, offering up her ice-covered wrist as evidence, oddly relieved to see him.

"The stove?" His laugh vibrated with tension. "You can't even boil water, Fi. I tell you, this girl."

"I should get something on it to prevent scarring." She tucked her handbag to her chest.

"If you'll excuse us." Kenneth gripped her elbow, gritting his teeth with the effort of ignoring the sting.

Legs nodded. "At your pleasure."

Kenneth all but pushed her down the hall toward the private elevator. "You have no idea who you're dealing with. Come to me—I'll give you the wholesale price." He punched the button hard enough to make her wince. "I promise. Mark it up however you like. But that guy—"

"Who is he?" Ofelia dug her heels in as the door opened. It wasn't anger but fear in his voice.

"You don't ask that." Kenneth's pale face was nearly bloodless in the low light. "Tresor is yours, okay. I'll keep my mouth shut about the fucking shop. Whatever. Stay out of this."

A sick feeling surged in Ofelia's gut as irritation gave way to concern. "Are you in trouble, Kenneth?"

"You don't care about me anymore, remember? I'm the bad guy you don't want any part of. So back off." He pushed her inside before she could respond. "I've got everything under control."

Which meant he was absolutely in over his head. "The necro—"

"Not here." He punched the door closed. "Now go."

It sounded like *run*.

CHAPTER TWENTY-SIX

OFELIA GLANCED over her shoulder as she stepped off the tram and again as she hurried down the winding streets toward Charm Syndicate. No one was following her. She contemplated the card in her purse. Her fingers twitched with eagerness to handle it again as her stomach rolled with revulsion.

In front of her building, she paused at the door to the upstairs apartments, an uneasy flutter in her chest. The lights were on. Chris. No way was he going to sign off on her using her charm on an unknown blot that might be a murdered witch's blood served up as a drug.

Still. She had to know.

The shop. She had consecrated the space; she would be protected.

Inside, she locked the doors and pulled the blinds, unable to shake the feeling that she was being watched. But her wards had not activated when she entered, so nothing rode her. And the street was still empty.

The altar was unchanged. She lit incense and invoked her ancestors' presence. In the back room of the shop she cleansed the space, using charm as well as sigil. She cleared furniture and activated the floor, inviting the Seven to bar the space from outside interference.

Not gods, her mother had told her once. *They walked among us, and we mistook interest for favor. Think of them like comets. The remnants they left in us—elemental things—are what we call on when we exercise our power.*

Our charms, Ofelia had murmured.

Her mother had smiled benignly. *That is one way of calling it.*

It sounded so innocent that way, so harmless. The space prepared, she lowered herself cross-legged in the center of the room and pulled the card out of her bag.

Only when she had stilled her own breathing and solidified her personal wards did Ofelia lift the card to her lips. One taste would tell her what it was made of and where it came from. Like alcohol, the recreational experience would move through her system too fast to affect her for long. Based on what Legs had said, it seemed harmless enough in that regard.

The smell hit her first—it always did—subtle as perfume and potent as decay. Base notes of rotted leaves and loam, top notes of salt and the tang of iron. The middle—bloomed orange peels and cacao, an invitation.

Her nostrils flared, in instinctive response to clear that scent from her even as she brought it closer.

The notes swelled on her tongue. Her charm activated with the intensity of a dozen iron needles, splintering each note into component parts. Blood.

Unexpectedly, the vision overtook her.

It was so real that for a moment she forgot where she was, who she was. Inside it, she ran through a humid darkness in a body that was not her own. The soft ground gave under her feet, and tall reeds slapped her calves and thighs as she passed, slowing her. The occasional prick of a thorn or sharp blade sliced her skin.

She must not stop running. She did not look back. It was coming. It was always coming. If she could just make it— Where would she be she safe? It would never let up.

She stumbled to a stop, heaving with exertion. Her eyes caught on her hands when they braced on her knees. The strong, broad palms; long, dark fingers; dirt under broken nails weren't hers. Who's body was she in? He was wearing some kind of cargo pants, a functional print—camo— but no shoes or socks. The broad, weathered feet dark as the soil beneath knew this ground. This was home.

Run.

This time her feet found firmer ground, places where she could get good push-off, build speed. Spiderweb-like moss from low-hanging branches slapped her face; a twig tore her cheek. She tasted blood. Had that thing chasing her turned the bayou against her?

Bayou.

Or it was just reckless hurry that made the witch whose body she rode clumsy in his own home. She broke into a clearing, and her heart surged with relief.

A second later her chest clenched, her insides solid as a rock, then liquid with panic. A tall shape rose from his comfortable crouch in the mangrove glade—her sacred place. It had discernible features, no face, but she sensed it smiling at her. Pleased.

Ofelia recalled Amanirenas's shadow, but this was no guardian or companion. This creature had its own agenda.

Shock flung her out of the body she'd been riding, and she caught a glimpse of her host. A man, medium height, solidly built with a broad brow and sturdy features. Late middle age had left the first hint of wrinkles on his dark face, streaks of gray in his short, cropped hair. Hands thick and scarred had worked his craft on the land his whole life, knew the rock and the soil and the roots and the water.

Those hands spread now as he shunted the burst of despair in favor of resistance. He would not run, not anymore. He would fight. His fingers worked the conjure, vibrations rising in his throat that she could not hear.

But he was tired, and the shape that was not human was too fast. It wrapped around his throat, lifting him off his feet and binding his fingers and wrists with sharp, guttural sounds in a language Ofelia had never heard.

"A good chase, little one." Recognizable words formed, but the sound made her stomach clench. "But the time has come for you to give up the secrets in your veins."

Everything went dark.

For a moment Ofelia thought she had been blinded, but that was the end of the vision. Awareness of her shop came back at the edges of her senses. The room had gone dark, candles snuffed with an oppressive energy that deadened the air. Her body sagged as if feeling every mile the witch had run, and the faint trace of river mud and rotting loam lingered in her nose. The witch whose blood had been turned into a drug.

Then the sickness hit. Ofelia doubled over, gasping, as her insides cramped and her heart leaped into an all-out gallop. Surprise left her scrambling to understand what was happening as her charm reacted to a poison hidden within the drug.

The sample had been tainted. Her charm cracked through her veins like lightning as it raced to counter.

Her stomach heaved, constricting her breath. She had just enough time to roll onto her knees. She didn't make it to the trash can. Instead, she wiggled as far away from the mess as she could and wrapped her arms around herself.

Her extremities went cold, then hot. Pins and needles gave way to extreme numbness. She was probably sweating profusely though she couldn't feel it. She wondered what color her lips were, her skin. Her body shook hard, convulsing—seizure?—and then went back to trembling. Whatever it was, it should have killed her by now.

Later she would be grateful for the hundreds of poisons Baako had supervised her tasting the week before. Now she just prayed her charm would be enough to exhaust whatever this was. She dragged herself under what she hoped was one of the tables and drew her knees and her arms into herself.

Her heart slowed, each beat stretching and leaving a long gap before the next. Even without vision, dark spots bloomed and spun in her eyes. Her charm was an autonomous response—she didn't try to direct it or waste the energy she'd need to calm herself by panicking.

Now it was a race, the poison to kill, her charm to evade. She had no control of either, and she'd never been more scared in her entire life.

Her airway closed. She prayed.

It wasn't the Seven she called out to. Not now.

Mama. Her aunts. Her cousin. Her necromancer. Her family. Chris.

The wards shivered, tingling awareness. Someone was trying to get in the shop. Ofelia would have gasped if there was any part of her not currently fighting for her life.

How stupid she had been. She was alone, vulnerable, and she'd led him to her.

She curled her hands in as best she could, trying to draw on anything for defense. Her wards would deter the most casual of intruders, but she no longer made the mistake of thinking the witch hunter was anything human.

A familiar voice, a word she could not recognize. Her name?

Hope flared with the memory of the arena.

But the words she needed to draw on the Heartlight fell away from her.

CHAPTER TWENTY-SEVEN

MAYBE PACING the window like a wolf in a cage wasn't going to bring Ofelia back any sooner, but it was giving Chris something to do.

Event for the store, don't wait up was the most bullshit excuse he'd ever seen. Erandi had warned him, but after they'd dealt with Manhammer together in the store the other day, he'd assumed they were on the same page.

By the time he made it back to her place, she'd already left.

The apartment smelled like her perfume and something peppery. He followed his nose to the jar on the bathroom sink among makeup and brushes. He inspected the bottle. GlArmour was written in her careful handwriting. Awkward, but whatever. Ayele was the mastermind behind branding. Ofelia was product development. He sniffed it—pleasant—and some kind of light oil base—maybe almond—dribbled on his fingertip. It glittered faintly. Then the stinging began.

What kind of event was she headed to that she felt the need to coat herself in this? He looked at the name again. Glamour. Armor.

Damn it, Fi.

She just did whatever she was going to do and left him catching up. Again. He was sick of it. They were supposed to be working together. Instead, she was keeping secrets. She didn't respond to his texts. So he paced.

Hours after sunset, she still hadn't returned.

Event for the store, don't wait up.

The store was dark.

He grabbed the spare keys and flung himself down the stairs. Lucky for him, no one happened to be on the way up or out, because aside from not giving anyone a heart attack, he wasn't going to stop and explain himself.

Not when Ofelia was most definitely in trouble. The entrance to her shop was separate from the apartments, so he blasted through the front doors onto the street.

Outside, his skin prickled warning. He froze. The adjacent street corner was empty, but it hadn't been a moment before. He picked up the scent—witchlike but something darker, headier, undefinable. Necromancer?

The scent led away from the door of the shop. He shifted his weight from foot to foot, torn between following his nose and his heart.

Fuck the scent. He went to the shop door, keeping his body angled toward the street as he unlatched it. Inside, he flicked the lock and scanned the empty street again.

"Fi," he called into the darkness just in case. Couldn't have her charging around the corner, ready to hex him into next year. "It's me, Chris."

Silence. The store was dark still. Her wards flexed against his skin as though they were activated but with nowhere to strike. Something was wrong.

He followed his nose. Her scent was knit into the fabric of the place, under fading whiffs of people who passed through every day and the rich confluence of her products, each managing to be distinct without becoming overpowering in concert. He marveled again at her craft.

Woof stirred under his solar plexus, roused and alert. Chris obeyed the desire to scent again. This time his nose shifted and lengthened, taking his jaw with it. The wolf's presence deepened his sense of smell, but there was only so much human physiology could manage. He needed the longer nasal passages and more nuanced scent organs.

The result unfurled inside his skull like a map, the locations and proximity and strength of various scents imaging the room in a way his eyes would never manage. Ofelia's scent was freshest on a clear trail to the back room she used for classes and the group of witches she refused to call her coven. And it was recent, stronger by the door. She'd shown it to him but refused his request to attend the coven meetings. She'd probably seen through his flimsy excuse that he wanted to scent the witches in attendance and make sure no one was up to no good.

Apparently a wolf lying at her feet all night as protection was out of the question.

He charged through the shop, sniffed, then let more of the wolf rise to his skin and body as protection in case Ofelia wasn't alone. Outside the classroom door, he hesitated—what if she was casting and he was disturbing her? He'd learned the hard way not to interrupt a witch mid-spell.

But something about her scent was wrong. He'd apologize later, clean up the mess, and maybe make it up to her with eggplant parmesan and a bublanina for dessert. She liked that one.

He turned the doorknob. "It's just me—"

The only lighting inside the room was from the final two candles guttering out in pools of wax. Her scent was overpowering, sweat and fear but no panic. How long had she been down here in the darkness?

She'd thrown up at least once, and the acid tang almost blocked the final, more insidious aroma. Metallic and old. Blood imbued with magic too complex for easy discernment. Familiar though. And the flash of memory of the street corner made his hackles stand on end.

Ofelia was lying with her back against the counter—a position she'd clearly dragged herself into—and she wasn't quite unconscious because she lifted her hands, palms out.

He dodged the attack, considered himself lucky it was poorly aimed, and dropped into a slide to get to her. "What was it?"

At her silence, he took her face in his hands. Her eyes were filmy white, a patina of sweat coating her skin. Her skin was an unhealthy shade of gray beneath the brown. Dried blood cracked at the corners of her mouth and nose; flakes stuck to his fingers where they cracked off her cheeks from her ears.

"Christof?" Shaking fingers wrapped around his wrists, surprisingly strong.

"I'm here." He dragged her against his chest, cradling her between his legs.

She stiffened, then went soft. A card fluttered to the ground beside him, and he reached for it but her grip held firm.

"Don't touch," she wheezed. "Poison."

Her breath came in whistling gasps now. He forgot all about the card.

She'd explained to him how her charm worked, in detail, one night after they'd collapsed into bed in her family's compound. The more poisons she ingested the faster and more effective her charm became at forming the antidote. Her version of training then had been exposure. Dozens, she'd said in response to how many she'd had that day. Maybe a hundred during her crash course. As if they knew that given the chance to test the drug herself, she wouldn't be able to resist.

"Can you become immune eventually?" He'd never been so grateful that her aunt knew how to protect her better than he did.

"I'm sure there's something out there that could kill me." She'd lifted a shoulder against him in the dark, a yawn making her jaw pop. "Haven't met it yet though."

The downside was she suffered the symptoms for as long as it took for her charm to form the antidote.

It looked like she'd been here for hours.

"What's different about this one?" he murmured as tiny waves shook her body.

"Changing. Keeps changing." Her voice stuttered. "Can't get ahead of it for long enough."

"Fuck." He banged his head against the cabinet behind them, wincing at the bright clarity pain brought. "What can I do?"

"Nothing." She went still.

"Fi?" Chris howled. "Fuck!"

If he got her to his mother—and his sisters—could they help? Barbara might be able to find something in one of her books, couldn't she?

No time. No time.

Ofelia's pulse fluttered against his fingertips. He settled a hand under her breast, confirming the sluggish beat of her heart. Her mouth was turning blue.

He curled around her, pouring the words into her ears. "Ofelia, I want you to draw from me."

Ofelia grunted, twisted her face away.

"Stubborn."

If they had taken the concord, the bond would have kicked in already to protect her by tapping him. But she had refused. And he'd been stupid enough not to fight her.

And now.

He remembered what Commander Mahari had said. There were many spells before the concord bond was developed. Some took from the shifter without need of their consent. Ofelia had used one of those in the arena, her eyes shining with tears the entire time. But she'd surprised them all by turning it back to him, reversing what should have been a one-way transfer. He dredged the words she'd spoken up from his memory to his lips. He stumbled—it was magic not meant for him, and it hurt to speak.

Each sound held barbs, sharp and reluctant to leave his mouth. He focused on his intention. They raced out of his chest, twisting through the air and into Ofelia's skin. But when the last tore ragged claws across his lips on its way, he knew he'd done it.

Her charm tugged his rib cage like an unfurled sail, the words forming lines that strained at the bindings. He exhaled hard and let the blazing flow at the center of his chest flood her until her breath returned to normal and her pulse quickened.

At last they lay in the darkness, folded around each other. He was probably holding her too tight, but he couldn't make himself let go.

"I had it." Ofelia's eyes opened, a little bloodshot but mostly clear. Her lips had returned to their velvety rose brown, her breathing regular if heavy. Her voice wavered. "I *had* it."

"The hell you did." He didn't know if it was the spell or the sight of her lifeless that had taken the years off his life. "You stopped breathing."

"I died twice in the training room." She tried to support herself on her shaking arms and failed. "I always come back."

"Fuck that." He shoved his back against the counter, pushing them both into a sitting position. "You don't get to do that in front of me ever again, understood?"

She pushed her legs underneath herself, tried to stand and would have fallen if he hadn't reached up to brace her. "It *is* why I came to the store."

"Fuck that too." He levered himself to his feet and took her with him. "You don't ever do that alone, understood?"

"Can't have it both ways."

Was she laughing? Relief and annoyance tangled in his snarl. "Try me."

"You're so bossy." She wrapped her arms around his waist, fingers clutching his T-shirt. "Like somebody's babushka."

"Fuck all the way off." A chuckle escaped him, and he let relief win. He tucked her in his arms, squeezed her so hard she had to fight for breath. His chest felt tight. "You're alive."

"Not if you suffocate me on your rock-hard pectorals," she protested. "What is that smell?"

He decided not to answer that. "You like my pecs, huh?"

She pinched him. Cleaning up the shop was going to be first on his list in the morning. "Shower. Now."

On the way to the door, propping each other up, her whisper reached his ear. "You came for me."

"Of course I did," he snapped, and the wolf surged in his chest in agreement. "You belong to no one, and still you're mine. I'll come for you no matter what. Always will."

The street was dark and clear, the scent of necromancer and witch washed away by a fresh rain that had cooled off the pavement and cobblestones.

To anyone in the halls upstairs, they might have looked to be returning from a hard night of partying. At the door her legs gave. He had to carry her inside.

He managed to get her out of her soiled clothes and into bed but little more, praying her wards would warn them if the owner of that scent came back.

"Thank you." Her voice drifted toward him.

He was probably dreaming the words, but he squeezed her tight and answered anyway. "Anytime, Princess."

CHAPTER TWENTY-EIGHT

OFELIA MUST HAVE MISSED her alarm and slept too long. Except when she tried to sit up, her entire body shrieked in protest and her stomach lurched. Unlike most mornings, her charm was somnolent to the point of silence.

Her mouth was dry and hot; she tasted old blood. The sweet scent of poison coated her nose. Memories came back in hard, hot flashes. Fighting, failing, dying—to be brought back from the edge repeatedly. Oh Seven, she'd been so bad off she'd prayed.

A soft groan rolled through her chest.

"You're back." The ragged voice sounded so different from Chris's usual tone her eyes bucked open.

He was splayed on her blanket on the floor between the bed and the door, hair in wild disarray and face softly furred with several days' growth.

She sat up sharply, and the room spun. She was clean, in one of the fuzzy button-down nightshirts she kept in the back of the closet.

"Slow down." He flowed to his feet, all wily grace despite the exhaustion making his shoulders slump. Dark circles dulled the bright stars of his eyes. He seemed hollowed out, as if he'd burned through extra flesh and into muscle.

When he propped a hand against her spine, she almost protested, but the room tilted and she slumped into him. "How long?"

"Not long enough apparently." He grunted. His chest was not as comfortable as it had been, the line of his collarbone hard against her cheek. "Take it easy."

His fingers absently stroked the back of her neck, soothing.

"How long?" The quaver in her own voice startled her.

He exhaled. "Three days."

His hands continued to steady her. She hated them and her own weakness in turns. He was still talking even as she tried fruitlessly to hold herself up, fight her way free of the stupor clinging to her consciousness.

"—cleaned things up and has been keeping the store open."

"Ayele?"

"We agreed it was best not to close. Wanted to see if anyone came sniffing around to see where you were."

He and Ayele were working together now, orchestrating her life?

"—outside the shop that night." His voice sounded like a question though he hadn't phrased it as one. Almost as if he didn't know how. Or was afraid to ask.

"Legs," she muttered and then slipped back into unconsciousness.

The next time she woke up, the room was dim. There were voices in the kitchen. Chris and one she didn't know. The remnants of her wards were flaring in warning. Another witch. The kettle hummed softly, but someone shut it off before it could whistle. Teacups rattled. Ofelia drifted, losing track of time and the conversation.

A woman's voice, muffled. "… should call Beryl in on this one, you know."

"Can't do that." Chris. Weary. "Too much I can't say, and if Mom tries to undo it—which she will—"

"What do you mean, you can't…" The voice dropped off before rising again. "Oh, Baby Wolf, what have you done? Who bound your voice?"

"Shh!"

A shuffling of feet and cloth and then the voices retreated.

"… have to promise…" Chris, from closer to the door, urgent. "I shouldn't have even called you, but—"

A long female sigh. "… glad you did. I don't know much about her grace—charm, you call it?" The sound of a coat and shoes. The angle of the hall made the voices clearer for a moment. "But from everything you say, it did what it was supposed to. This reminds me of what someone leveled by a terrible virus looks like. Her system must just have to clear the residual. It's like a flu—lingers for a bit."

A long pause.

"Good gods, don't tell me you boys never got the flu." The witch sighed.

"We got them, good for our immune systems." Chris laughed. "But you know Mom."

"I know your mom, yes." More cloth shuffling. "She never let it last this long, did she? Speaking of. She's watching the monsters. I have to get back before Toby does. He's been in a mood since he's been on drop-off all week."

Chris groaned softly.

"Don't worry—it's good for him." Soft laughter. "You've been spoiling us."

"Mark."

Sucked teeth, words that sounded strained by tight lips. "Being Mark. We'll all survive a few days. Zacky misses you though."

"I'm sorry." Chris couldn't sound any more tired than he did now.

"Don't you dare." Words squeezed out softly, as if around a hug. "She needs you. We'll survive. But eat something, okay? Many somethings. And call me if you need more groceries."

"Love you, Bebe."

"Love you too, sweetheart."

Ofelia lay awake, staring into the dark of the ceiling. She hurried to wipe the last of the wetness from her eyes as the door creaked open a half hour later.

"Think you can eat something?"

"How long?"

He exhaled slowly. "Just a day this time."

She choked out a sob. She remembered nothing. The only thing she hated more than feeling helpless was the fear that came with that much lost time. If she had been alone, would she still be on the floor in the shop right now?

He switched on the lamp beside the bed, and she winced at herself. Fresh sheets, new shirt, a T-shirt this time. One of his.

"Haven't had a chance to do laundry." The small light sank deep shadows into the hollows under his eyes. The bowl in his hands smelled like broth. "You had the sweats pretty bad."

Her stomach felt sour, and her throat burned. Not just the sweats then.

Shame filled her. She closed her eyes.

"Let's just"—he sighed—"get something in you. Maybe this time—"

She could keep it down. The words were unspoken. The worry in them lingered. She could only imagine what the past few days had been like for him. He hadn't signed up to be her nursemaid.

"I should be good now." She hoped.

She had to get out of this bed. To take her life back and her shop and stop that murderous bastard selling tainted witch blood as some kind of drug.

"Let's just give it a spoonful or two and see."

"Ayele—" She wouldn't have been alone. He hadn't needed to stay.

"She asked to help." He offered a spoonful. "But you kinda freaked out when you woke up for the first time and she was here."

Oh Seven.

She let him feed her, and then they waited.

"Who was here just now?" Hearing how easily he expressed love had made tears burn in her eyes, as much as the worry in the voice responding.

"Barbara," he said, rubbing his face. "My other sister-in-law. She's the closest thing I could think of to a doctor for whatever this is. And I was afraid to leave you to go the store just in case."

When the broth didn't come up, Ofelia took the bowl even though her hands shook. "I can do this. You should—"

He nodded, searching her face. She couldn't decipher his expression.

"I promise I won't make a mess you have to clean up later." She tried on a smile.

He rubbed at the back of his neck with one hand like he was trying to work out all the knots worrying about her had put there. But when his eyes settled on her again, there was no blame, no judgment. She looked away first.

"I'm gonna start a load of clothes." He braced his palms on his knees with an exhale and rose. "I'll be in the other room if you need anything."

And then he was gone.

The blankness of the past few days terrified her. She had no recollection of even seeing Ayele, never mind saying words she couldn't take back. Guilt squeezed her chest, and she closed her eyes against the sudden pressure of tears. She had to get her shit together. Had to quit being a burden.

She took as much soup as she could—precious little before her stomach ached with warning. She breathed deep until the feeling passed and then levered herself up. Shower.

The bathroom mirror nearly shocked her out of consciousness again. Her skin was sloughing in places, her hair matted where it had come undone from her braids. She ran a warm shower.

"Are you sure you don't want a bath?" Chris asked from the other side of the door, trying to sound casual.

"I'm fine." She ignored her shaking hands.

She was leaning on the walls by the time she finished. She wrapped her hair towel with shaking arms. There was no way she was going to be able to do anything with it. She shuffled into her fluffiest robe.

Out in the kitchen, Chris was trying to look like he hadn't been pacing. The edge of his thumbnail was a freshly gnawed red.

"Didn't break my skull." The attempt to sound light fell flat when her voice shook.

His brows rose.

Defensive, she muttered, "You look like shit."

His chin lowered.

"I know, takes one to know one." She sighed. "Hey. I could use some help."

He moved too fast. She jumped and would have lost her balance, but he caught her elbows, keeping her steady. "Yeah. What. Sorry. Anything."

Her throat tightened. Why was he so fucking kind? If he had just looked even minorly inconvenienced, she could have found the strength to do this herself.

"My skin," she said. "It was like snake venom at first, no bite. Anyway, there's some peeling… I have a cream that will help."

"Of course you do." His smile was pure sunshine for all the weary clouds it rose behind. He scooped her up. "Let's go."

Standing between his thighs in the bathroom, she thought she'd never felt less sexual as she leaned hard on the counter while he smoothed soothing cream over the healing blisters and fresh skin.

He touched her gently, in a way she imagined he helped his nieces and nephews into coats and shoes. She was dangerously close to crying again. She thought she hid it until he slid a hand towel next to her on the counter.

Without looking, he murmured, "It's okay—I won't tell anybody the most badass witch in all of Prague shed a few tears because she felt like shit."

"I'm not—" She coughed a laugh.

"The most badass witch in Prague?" he finished. "Agree to disagree."

He helped her back into the robe. Their eyes met in the mirror. If she were a weaker woman, she might have sagged into his chest, closed her eyes, and leaned her head against his collar. Oh, but then there was still her hair to take care of. Prague's most badass witch wouldn't even be able to lift her arms in a few moments.

"I can help." He hesitated. "If you want."

Exhaustion made it impossible to catch the dubious expression before it slipped free.

He whipped his phone out of his back pocket. "O ye of little faith, prepare to be wowed."

He offered the phone. A little girl spun in the video preview, sending the beaded tail end of her twists flying, the joy on her face obvious. "You did that?"

A gust of breath in the affirmative left him, too much like the wolf's chuffing for her not to smile. Woof. Something about the fact that he'd kept calling a two-hundred-pound predator the nickname she'd given it as a child made her love him most.

Love.

Her vision blurred. This was gratitude. She owed him for taking care of her. Giving up so much time and energy worrying over her.

"Okay, back to bed." He rose abruptly, pocketing the phone. "If you pass out and hit your head, we'll be back to day one. Bonnet will help keep out the worst of the tangles, and maybe tomorrow—"

"The oil and the combs are on the shelf, by the towels," she said. "I can sit without passing out. Promise."

She might pass out if he smiled at her like that every time she did something halfway decent. Before she could change her mind, he grabbed the basket and a couple of towels and herded her toward the living room.

A half hour later she sat between his knees on a pile of cushions before the couch with a giant bowl of popcorn, the opening credits to some action movie she'd never heard of flickering over dramatic music.

The moment he'd made his first part, the tension went out of her. At the end of a handful of two strand twists, his stomach rumbled. She picked up a few kernels and offered them blindly. Tingles raced down her fingertips as he nibbled them out of her hand. When the last was gone, he laid a kiss on her palm.

They went on like that until the bowl was empty, and then she turned her focus to the movie. Or she planned to. She woke to the end credits, her cheek pillowed on a cushion braced against his knee. Her scalp was cool, his hands still. She looked back to see him reclined against the cushions, fast asleep. His mouth was open, and his exhaustion was so complete he didn't even stir when she levered herself up off the floor.

The rest had helped. Her head felt clear, her limbs lighter. She pulled the throw blanket over him.

In the kitchen, she surveyed groceries he'd hurriedly unpacked but left scattered on the counter. The pot on the stove was cooling soup, the broth of which she'd already had. It wasn't going to be enough. She'd watched him devour an entire baguette full of meat and cheese while he danced around her kitchen, preparing exquisite dishes in epic proportions, most of which he'd eat.

"Shifter metabolism." She shook her head, laughing to herself.

She reached out and found the remains of her wards. Remnants clung to the walls, the door, and floor. That too was to be expected. She could lay no permanent wards here. That meant smaller, less stable wards, which required regular reinforcement. But she'd been too weak over the past few days. No wonder the witch had been able to come in without discomfort.

She forced a deep breath into her tight lungs and pulled down a plate.

Her hands shook a little, but if she moved slowly, it had the added benefit of being quiet. Good, because she didn't think she had the strength to draw a silence bubble around her own kitchen yet. Her charm was a tattered flag in a weak wind.

When she set the plate on the counter and surveyed her work, a little exhale of relief left her. It wasn't pretty, but it would do. She went to the refrigerator for the mammoth jar of pickles she'd seen tucked in the back. He really had a problem.

"Is this for me?"

She jumped in shock and dropped the jar. One big hand snaked out and caught it.

Seven, he was fast. And quiet. She hadn't heard him move from the couch.

"Sorry, didn't mean to startle you." He winced, straightening, and set the jar on the counter beside the plate.

"Well, you saved the pickles from disaster." She tried on a smile. "Do you want one? Or a few? Maybe let's just leave the jar out. Sit. Eat. Something. Everything."

When she faced him, he was grinning.

"What?"

His shoulders lifted in a shrug.

Heat sprang into her cheeks. "It's nothing. Just eat, okay?"

She started to turn as he sat down, but he caught her wrist.

"Come here." The low rumble of his voice reeled her in. He tucked her between his legs and tugged her against his chest. He was so warm. His arm tightened, and she rested on his thigh, not quite seated.

"This is the nicest thing anybody's ever done for me," he murmured against her temple. "Thank you."

"It's a sandwich," she muttered, willing her heart to stop tumbling around her chest like a happy puppy. "And a poorly made one at that."

"I beg to differ."

He palmed the whole assemblage of bread and meat and cheese in his free hand. A ragged slice of lettuce hung out one side, and a tomato almost slid free entirely. She poked it back into place. Mostly.

He laughed. "*This* is a work of art. Bite?"

She shook her head. "Too much meat."

He set it down and opened the jar of pickles, sliding it toward her. When she'd grabbed a spear and nibbled, he scooped up his sandwich and took a bite. He moaned, sparking desire in her core despite her exhaustion.

When he swallowed, he kissed her temple. "Best sandwich ever."

"You must be very hungry," she drawled, blinking fiercely.

"Starving," he admitted. "But this is tasty. You used the good mustard."

"I wasn't using that bright yellow abomination you bought," she muttered. "Where did you even find that American garbage?"

"Hey, don't knock it till you try it," he said. "A friend of a friend gets it. One of my dad's. He used to bring a bottle home whenever Mom got homesick. We grew up on that stuff."

Embarrassment shuttered her lungs again. "I didn't mean—"

"S'okay," he said around a mouthful. "Sentimental value only gets you so far. This stuff is way better."

"That was rude," she said anyway.

"You say what's on your mind," he said, laughing. She stiffened, but he held tight. "I like that about you. You talk back—to everyone, including a necromancer—and you never let anyone talk down to you or tell you who to be. Look at everything you've built. That store is all anybody is talking about now. There's no mystery about what you feel or what you want. You say it, you make it happen. It's sexy."

Warmth bloomed in her chest.

He sucked a blob of mustard off his pinky and nudged the jar at her. "Pickle, please."

She handed him a spear. He waited until she'd grabbed one. For a moment, the silent crunching was the only sound between them. She watched him—one elbow up on the counter, munching contentedly, a little smile on his face. How had this world produced a creature like this —how had he stayed that way with a face like that? A fierce, leonine protectiveness rose in her, and she almost laughed. She could barely stand upright, but she would fight anyone who hurt him.

He'd been exactly who he was with her, open, compassionate, unapologetically generous. Kind.

All she'd done was prickle and try to escape his attempts to help her. She was so determined to deter him, to convince him he was wrong about her. But he'd seen her at her worst and still liked her. Thought she was sexy.

She gnawed on her lip. Would it hurt to give him something back? "You're pretty sexy yourself."

"Me and my rock-hard pecs, huh?" His brows rose and his eyes darted to her but didn't linger.

She wanted them to. Those big soft eyes—an impossible shade so gray they were nearly blue—saw her as no one had. She wanted to be seen, to see herself in them. She laughed, face warm and heart light. "Well, you were squishing my face into them."

"I'm bad at people I care about getting hurt." He shrugged. "Write me up."

The warmth hung between them. She cleared her throat. *Say something.*

"I'm bad at being grateful. Since my parents left me at that school… I've been the one who's taken care of me. If someone does something for me, I feel like it means I failed somehow." She took a breath, willing herself not to lose courage now. "I know it's messed up. I'm just afraid that if I start letting other people take care of me, I'll forget how to do it for myself. I'll need them. And then one day they won't be there and I'll fall."

He held very still for so long, waiting. Letting her breathe until her heartbeat was no longer racing.

"Thank you for sticking with me," she said, proud that her voice didn't shake. "Not just this. But since we've… since everything started."

She was rewarded by the softness in his eyes turned entirely on her. She felt light enough to float right off the floor. Only his arm around her kept them grounded. He held her gaze in that same steady stillness until the last resistance went out of her and she could count the small dark freckles in his irises that complicated the color so beautifully. A flush heated her skin from head to toe, hot between her legs and at her neck. Her eyes darted to his mouth and back.

A smile quirked his lips. "That didn't kill you, did it?"

She hissed, eyes narrowing, but before she could push herself away, he tugged her close. The fight went out of her. Her arms slid around his waist, and tension she hadn't known he'd been holding left him.

Stubble rasped her cheek as his chin lowered until his mouth brushed her ear. "You're welcome, Princess."

A tremor raced up her spine and her knees got wobbly even as her breath stuttered in outrage. "Oh you!"

His arms held firm, and it turned out she didn't really want to fight herself free. The heat of him through the thin T-shirt softened her muscles and soothed the ache around her heart. And that felt like something magical all on its own.

"I'm not trying to take your job," he murmured. "You're always going to know what you need first. We can take care of you together. We make a good team, right? Talk to me—I'll do anything I can for you."

Her stomach rumbled.

He laughed. "Is that a yes?"

"Yes."

Despite the demands of the pulse between her thighs, after another bowl of soup—this time with veggies and a bit of pearled grains of couscous—she could barely keep her eyes open. When she yawned so hard her jaw popped, he laughed and scooped her up.

"Dishes?"

"Morning." He laughed. "Later morning."

They brushed their teeth side by side. He helped tie her hair scarf when her arms shook again. Between cool, clean sheets, she sighed happily and patted the mattress. "I don't want to be alone. Please."

In the darkness, his sigh was surrender. In the bed he tried to spoon her, but she would have none of it. She glued herself to his back, legs around his waist, arms tangled under his.

"Octopus," he muttered, threading his fingers through hers and holding tight. His voice was muzzy, halfway to sleep. "In the morning— later today—we're going to talk about what happened. And you're going to tell me what you've been hiding these past few weeks."

"Making demands now?" She squeezed him tight.

"Taking a lesson from you," he murmured. "Asking for what I want and expecting to get it."

CHAPTER TWENTY-NINE

WAKING FIRST GAVE Chris the distinct pleasure of seeing Ofelia's face unguarded, soft with sleep. Sometime during the last nap, they'd gotten even more tangled up. Now he was facing her, watching her eyelashes flutter against her cheeks as her eyes moved in a dream. His cock throbbed when her nipples brushed his chest through her thin T-shirt. He ignored it.

Soon she'd wake up, the mask would go on, and she'd be back to eluding him at every turn. She'd opened up a bit last night, but old habits die hard. For the millionth time, he regretted the lost time between the train station and now. What would it have been like if she had stayed in Prague? If they had gone to secondary school together? She probably would have gone away to university anyway. She was too brilliant to be stuck here. They would have dated other people for a while—that was okay too. But eventually they would have found their way back to each other, and it would have been like no time had passed at all.

The train station had been his stupid idea. If he'd taken her home after school instead, ignored his meddling brother and his prying mother, and made her part his life, she might have been safe. Even at the park, where they would have been surrounded by people, the boys wouldn't have dared to take things so far.

But in either case, she would have never been able to guide him to his wolf. To reveal her magic to him. Maybe one afternoon, in the shower of shining dust, she wouldn't have sealed his fate with a single, innocent kiss.

Nothing would have been the same without the train station and her disappearance and the years between. They were exactly who and where they were meant to be.

He knew she wasn't the same kid anymore. The feelings he had for her weren't little-kid-crush feelings. Believe. He'd been trying to show her but so far seemed to be failing miserably. The taking-the-couch-on-principle shit had gotten old. It meant he was walking around semihard almost all the time. It was probably a bad sign that he'd gotten used to his balls aching.

"It's too early to be thinking big thoughts." Ofelia yawned, and her thumb rubbed at the line forming between his brows. "You're going to give yourself a very sexy wrinkle in twenty years if you keep that up."

He laughed, molding himself to her. He'd been too tired to do anything but shuck out of his jeans and sweatshirt the night before. His skin was hot and a little sweaty from being wound up with hers. Her T-shirt—his—had ridden up to bunch under her perfect breasts, an alluring contrast of texture to the silky underwear that had been the last clean pair in her drawer.

The loads of laundry would be endless.

Later.

For now he lifted the blanket to catch a glimpse and check his memory. She shivered a little in the cooler air and pressed closer to him. Yep. Aegean blue, brilliant against her dark skin. And a deeper blue between the thighs. He sniffed lightly and almost groaned. Arousal rendered him incapable of more than a dazed "Wow."

"See something you like?" Her voice rasped, slow and inviting.

He met her eyes, palms finding her hips and gripping. "Everything."

Her hips shifted impatiently against his hands.

The primitive creature in the back of his head wanted to tear fabric and pound them both into oblivion. He reminded himself she'd been terribly sick, they were both weak, and that particular pair of underwear looked way too expensive to shred anyway.

In any case, as much as he liked having her lay her own desire out so plainly, *somebody* needed to be taught a lesson about always needing to be in charge. And it wasn't him.

"We need to talk first."

She coughed a disbelieving laugh. "Are you—"

"Serious?" He rolled until she was on her back beneath him. "Deadly serious."

Did he sound like he was gasping for air? Maybe. It also did not help that her thighs were now fully parted and cradling his chest so that he could feel exactly how aroused she was.

"What did you taste the other night?" His mouth hovered over one nipple. Experimentally he brushed his stubbly cheek along it through the overwashed cotton.

Her pupils widened. "An interrogation?"

He ignored the question, bracing on his elbows and pretending they had all the time in the world.

She huffed, lip between her teeth. "Something that was given to me."

"On the black card?"

She nodded and then eyed him expectantly.

He mouthed her nipple through the fabric until she shivered again. "Was that so hard?"

Her eyes narrowed. Her fingers sank into his hair, tightening at the root. He almost groaned, grinding his molars together to resist the urge to lose himself in her body.

He let her nipple go, pushed his fingers under the cloth and kneaded the tight bud. "You didn't want me to touch it—why?"

"I didn't know if the poison would transfer to you." She panted. "Was it there?"

"The card?"

She nodded.

"Gone. Yele didn't find it." He hovered, watching the brief look of calculation that passed over her face. He'd deal with that later. He squeezed. "What was on it?"

She groaned. "Christof."

He removed his hand.

"Something Kenneth got himself into dealing." The words escaped like a plea. "He called it Hexenblut. I heard him talking about it a couple of weeks ago. And I found his stash. It's why I left him. He was using me to draw people."

Witch blood, his brain translated automatically. Now they were getting somewhere. He rewarded her by pushing the shirt up altogether so there was nothing between his mouth and her skin. Godsdamn, she tasted good. "And was it—"

"Blood?" She shuddered and her focus turned inward.

He listened to the vision, soothing her with long slow strokes when her skin prickled and her eyes grew wet. Her shoulders trembled and she started to curl, but instead of into herself, she reached for him. Good. He took her in his arms, letting the heat between them cool as he rocked her. "You're safe. It's over. I've got you. So not just a name then."

Her voice steadied on her next inhale. "It's the real thing."

They lay in stillness for a long time. Chris hoped that unnamed witch would find peace.

"But why a make a drug? And humans aren't dying of it"—she turned her face to his again, pressed a tentative kiss to the corner of his mouth—"so my sample must have been tainted."

"You got it at Kenneth's."

"He was throwing a party. I thought I could sneak around, find a bit." She shrugged helplessly. "It seemed a good place to start."

Start? She'd thrown herself into the eye of the hurricane, armed with some prickly body oil. He didn't know whether to be impressed or terrified at her willingness to put herself at risk. No wonder where she came from, they paired witches with battled-trained shifters.

But that wasn't where she had come from. She had been raised outside the borders of the hidden city by a witch who served as a spy and an external arm of her people. She wasn't used to having someone to rely on. To protect her.

Well, that was about to change.

She wriggled impatiently, trying to get out of the T-shirt, he realized. He helped with the last bit. One glimpse of her—naked, her brown skin flushed with heat—nearly undid him. She squirmed, curling her hips against him.

"Seems like a terrible business model." He frowned, gripping her hips firmly. "Poisoning people with samples. Kenneth—"

"Doesn't know what I am." She growled impatiently. "He's as mundane as they come. Not so much as good parking mojo. But Legs—"

"I'll get there."

She laughed. "No. Listen. There was a guy there *named* Legs—he's the one who gave me the sample." She recounted the whole exchange. "Who knows who he is—what he is."

He ran his fingertips up the back of her knee to her hamstring, thinking while she shivered. "So Kenneth is working with this—Legs?— to deal some new drug. And they poisoned you because you came around asking for it."

"Kenneth was freaked out. Thought he was afraid of me undercutting him, but he was just… afraid."

He traced the line where her underwear curved over her ass cheek. Her hands tightened in his hair. It was all he could to do stay focused with one tiny, thoroughly soaked, silky scrap of fabric between them.

Chris sighed. He didn't want to think about that guy at all, especially right now. But he'd started this. Time to finish it.

"Is that what you hid from Baako and the others?" He slid his fingers over the center of that silk-clad heat. "That Kenneth was connected to this?"

She nodded. "Kenneth is greedy, but he's an idiot. He's not part of this. I just wanted to leave him out of it if I could."

"Is that all?" He pressed a little, nudging swollen flesh with his knuckle until she moaned.

Another nod, harder this time.

"Good."

He rewarded her with a slow circle that made her hips levitate off the bed. Her breath stuttered.

"Look at me." He stopped abruptly, catching her hips again when she tried to follow his fingers.

Big dark eyes met his, wide with desire and pleading. He liked having her needy like this, clinging to him. He couldn't resist. He tapped his index finger on her center, once, twice, to make sure he had her attention.

"You're done," he said. "Running around on your own, hiding things from me, playing detective. Putting yourself in danger... alone. We're in this together from here on out."

Her nostrils flared. He stroked his finger up and down. Her eyes glazed satisfyingly.

"You did too." Her gasp hitched. "You talked to Henny."

"I have an in with the Gargs." He laughed. "Henny and I went out a couple of times. And Ange treats me like a little brother. I couldn't tell if she was protective of you because of her interest or the club's, and I didn't want to risk it. I'd have happily told you everything I'd learned if you'd bothered to ask."

"Ask?"

"Yes, a question." He nipped at the skin on her belly. "Whatever pieces we have are no good if we don't put them together."

She set her lips, but he could see he had her.

"Together," he repeated and nudged at that tantalizing scrap of fabric. Maybe he'd leave it on. That could be fun.

She nodded. "Now can we please—"

Her voice trailed off into a whimper when he tasted her... through the cloth.

If he'd known this was what it took to get her to see things his way, he could have been off that couch a week ago.

No. That had nothing to do with this. Not really. That was about what came after this. The life they were going to have—together—if she wanted it. If she wanted him. That wasn't just going to be about the sex.

Maybe giving in now was a mistake. He'd have to start proving that he wasn't just here for the good times all over again. But he couldn't help himself. She was nearly naked and making soft, needy sounds in the back of her throat that eroded his willpower.

She tugged his scalp, delicious pinpricks of sensation pulling him out of his head and into his body.

"What do you want, Fi?" he rasped. When he met her eyes, she smiled like a siren and he was lost.

"You," she said, "inside me."

It had only taken dragging her back from death to get her to open up to him. But she had. Beggars couldn't be choosy. It was a start.

He'd deal with forever later.

CHAPTER THIRTY

RELEASE SHUDDERED through her as he rode the last of her orgasm, leaving her thighs shaking and her breath coming in hard, desperate gasps. She squirmed on the sheets as he slowed down, drew out the last of her pleasure with lazy precision. Her fingers slipped down the sweat-slicked slope of his back to the dimples above his perfect ass. She didn't know how much more she could take, but if he stopped now, it would certainly end her.

"Still with me?" His voice eddied against her ear, the tiniest rasp of teeth against sensitive skin pulling her back into her body.

She hoped someone never figured out how to bottle Christof Vogel. He was a potion her charm had no defense against. She licked her lips, tried to come up with something clever. Failed and blew a raspberry instead.

Chuffing laughter, he flopped down beside her on the bed. If she expected any urgency in his face, any focus on meeting his own need throbbing between them, he hid it well, or he simply had none. Knowing him, all guileless curiosity, it was the latter. Propped up on his elbow, staring at her with amusement brightening his eyes and a flush on his damp cheeks and his fingers—

Oh Seven, he was still stroking her, wasn't he? Firm, lazy strokes, easy on her sensitive skin, sending little tremors through her.

"You don't have t-to—" she began, stuttering as her body started up again.

"Is it okay?" He blinked at her, wide-eyed. "I just like touching you. Watching you while I touch you."

She had no argument for that.

So serious, that face, watching her for cues. "I can stop."

"No!" she gasped out, then laughed softly. "It's good, it's nice, I just don't think I'm gonna get there again so soon."

"That's okay—it's not about getting anywhere, is it?" Kisses on her forehead, her cheek, her chin. She tilted her head, and he found her lips too. When he pulled back, she chased his lips. Flushed and grinning at her, he paused. "If it stops being nice, you'll say something, right?"

She nodded obediently.

Again that smile. "Good."

She sighed out raggedly when his breath ghosted over her throat, her ear, the side of her jaw.

She let herself drift. Flares of sensation poured down her legs and up into her belly and settled in her chest, molten and tender. Without conscious effort, she found herself leaning into him, angling herself to give him better access, to put them closer.

Against all reason, pressure built in her again, slow and aching in her hips and thighs. She whispered some nonsense about not expecting anything.

"Hush," he said. "No rushing. Let's see what happens."

What happened was she was going to lose her mind with wanting that sensation hovering just out of reach. If she could just get him to go a little faster, a little harder. She whimpered, unable to find words.

"I've got you."

This time the orgasm gradually washed over her, warm and salty sweet. Oh, those were her tears, sliding down her cheek into her open mouth. And why on earth was she crying when she had never felt so light, so happy, in her whole life? Poor Chris—she was probably scaring him. When she looked for him, he was still watching her, smiling that open smile like all he'd ever wanted was just to be right here, right now.

When he rolled, sliding between her thighs again and reaching for the oil she kept on the bedside table, his brows drew together in question. For the first time there was intensity behind that openness, want. Her. He wanted her.

He'd seen her at her most damaged, weak, failing, and he wanted her anyway. No, he'd brought her back—to herself, to him, to this singular place they'd created between them.

"Yes," she gasped.

The pressure of him against her, inside her, was exquisite coming on the tail end of such effortless release. Again she rocked, urging him on, deeper. Again he slowed her.

"Look at me," he murmured so softly she almost missed the plea in the words. The question.

She let her gaze be her answer. Let him rest in it, anchored. And when the world fell away, there was only blue and brown, the deep dark earth and the hazy spring sky, turning endlessly together, meeting and parting and meeting again. And then she drew herself tight around him.

His hips stuttered hard. She held his cheeks when he would have tucked his chin, kept his gaze fixed on hers. Smiled. Stroked his back, his shoulders, the curve of his spine arching and flexing, the ridges of his ass. Pressed a careful finger to the soft place between.

"Fuck." The word burst from him, his once bright eyes on her, dark with lust. "Yes."

"Yes." She smiled.

Her third orgasm trailed his. It took her by surprise, leaving them both gasping and clawing and whimpering to stillness again.

Ofelia sighed, cradling as much of him she could hold. His arms banded around her.

"Octopus." She laughed.

He chuckled into her neck. "Takes one to know one."

Sleep took him first. She watched the rise and fall of his shoulder blades in the afternoon light slanting through the half-open curtains. She should wake him, or at least roll him off her and go wash up and drink some water. For now there was nowhere else she would rather be than breathing him in.

Her charm thrummed beneath her sternum, a familiar energy begging for release. She extended her awareness to her wards. No time like the present. This time, instead of restoring existing wards, she dipped into the stones and rebar, seeking the presence of the building itself and the earth beneath. In her time away from the àjé, she'd forgotten how they scoffed at wards, believing instead in calling on the spirit of a place. Wasn't that part of the reason she'd chosen Prague to begin with—the way the ground itself thrummed with presence? Each time a building was raised, it tapped that energy through the builder's intention, unconscious as it often was.

A skilled àjé would invoke that spirit the moment the first stakes were set. But it was never too late to acknowledge their connection.

Hello. Her charm beckoned to the building. Would you like to help me protect those who've chosen your walls as shelter, as you were meant to do?

The building sighed softly, as if waking from a long slumber. Glasses rattled softly as the walls gave a little shiver of recognition.

She fed it her charm and knowledge of everyone who called the building home. She knew how to recognize the àjé now. There would be no more sneaking up on her. And then there was Chris. She'd added him on hastily when they'd returned. Sloppy work. There was nothing like coming home at the end of a long day to feel the building itself warm and chiming softly in welcome. This time she built him into the building's awareness—it would recognize and welcome him as it did her.

When she was finished, her charm hummed contentedly, pleased to be exercised and calling her attention to something else.

She and Chris were still connected. Now that her charm was active again, it chimed awareness of the tethers. She felt the origins of it in words like lines, tying them together, tapping his strength for her. It wasn't a true concord bond, and it left him vulnerable to overuse. He'd done it the night of the poisoning and never called it back. He'd left himself open, and she'd been drawing on him for days. It explained his new exhaustion, the hollows in his face.

"Christof Vogel." Tears stung her eyes. "What am I going to do with you?"

One by one she slipped the tethers free, tiny knots of power cool in her awareness. They dissolved, and she pressed her lips to his brow, imbuing it with a charm for strength, speed, restoration of health.

His Heartlight flared. Her charm sang in answer like struck crystal. His heartbeat slid into time with hers. The curious scratchy tension was back in her throat at the thought of how consistently he'd shown up for her, in every way since they'd crashed into each other's lives again.

Seven. What *was* she going to do—with not just him but her own heart colluding against her?

Self-delusion hurt more than any spell ever could. But it wasn't safe to want, not when she had to be willing to do whatever it took to stop the witch hunter—and now Legs was on her list after that stunt with the drug. He was higher up than Kenneth, and she was certain he would bring her one step closer to the witch hunter. Holding back anything in reserve, even hope for her own future, might be the thing that got her killed.

CHAPTER THIRTY-ONE

Chris was in the kitchen on a mission. His stomach was going to gnaw a hole through his intestines if he didn't put something in it.

"Anything from the bees?" He looked up as Ofelia emerged from the shower, unable to keep from staring.

"Nothing." A shy little smile twitched her lips as she perched on a stool at the counter before eying her silent phone.

Food. He needed to focus. He cleaned out the fridge and the pantry and considered his options. "And Kenneth?"

"Not picking up." She fiddled with the ties of her robe. "Unsurprisingly. What did Henny and Ange say?"

"They've been hearing rumors." A plan began to form in his mind. He switched on the oven. Thank the gods she had a cast-iron pan. "Ange's gonna keep an eye out for anything new. Sasha keeps most of that shit out of Tresor. No matter what Kenneth said."

That seemed to satisfy her, though she started poking at her phone, responding to text bubbles that appeared. He concentrated on their next meal.

"What about that scent I picked up outside the store?" He slid the pan into the oven, then leaned on the counter across from her. "Really think that was Legs?"

She lifted a shoulder. "Maybe. Or someone who knew what was on that card and wanted to make sure I was down. There's one way to find out."

"Fi."

"The card is gone." She lifted her gaze and widened her eyes dramatically. "I couldn't try it again even if I wanted to."

It was a good thing that card had disappeared. She might be just brave or nuts enough to do it.

"I wasn't thinking that anyway." She sniffed the air, and her stomach grumbled in demand. "What are you making?"

"Shakshouka." He checked the temperature and the timing. "Eggs and tomatoes are all we have left. Some bread. Gotta get groceries. Later today. What time is it anyway?"

"If you give me a list, I'll go." She didn't look up from her phone. "I need to get out. And it's dinnertime."

"Good, 'cause it's dinner food. Tired of people turning everything with eggs into breakfast." When she was silent, he looked up. She was grinning at him in the way that relit the flame in his belly. Gods, had he ever seen a more beautiful person in his whole life? He'd never get tired of that look on her face—surprise, pleasure.

She flushed at his attention and went back to poking at her phone. He tried not to laugh. He'd never seen anyone text with their index fingers. All the while, the phone rattled away from her on the counter, forcing her to stop every few words and retrieve it.

He grabbed a clean kitchen towel and set her phone on it. "At least it won't slide."

He'd already turned to retrieve plates when she launched herself around the counter and into the kitchen at him, her arms around his waist. He laughed, moving carefully. "What's that for?"

"Taking care of me." Her warm breath wobbled on his spine. "Again."

He appreciated the gratitude, but tears made her clam up and try to put distance between them and he couldn't have that. He liked this Ofelia —grinning at him, talking to him. Not keeping him at arm's length.

"Watching you text is painful." He navigated the small space carefully, holding the plates up with her clinging like a barnacle. "Like a little chicken trying to get a piece of grain on a sheet of ice."

She groaned but was laughing again when she let go and took the plates.

He dragged the pan out of the oven. He served up the food, pleased he got the portions right when she cleaned her plate.

"What are you over there pecking at anyway?" He jabbed his fork at her phone.

"Rallying the crew," she said, then admitted, "Asking Ayele to rally the crew."

"You guys talking again."

She met his eyes. "I'm trying."

"Good."

She surprised him. "Think you could identify that scent again?"

"Of course."

"Think your boys are up for a night out?"

"Always." He laughed, then frowned. "Ofelia, you aren't serious."

"I'm tired of waiting." She set down her fork. "Aren't you? Your nose. My charm. I say we track it down. We're wasting time waiting for the àjé to tell us what to do. What if he slips away?"

She had a point.

He grabbed his phone. "Let me show you how it's done."

"Do mine too." She slid hers at him. "I need to start getting ready."

She scooped up their plates and went to the sink. While she did dishes, he managed two text threads. She disappeared into the bedroom, humming.

Chris watched her briefly between replies. If she'd shown the slightest sign of illness, he would have barred the door himself.

But there was no question her charm was back, and she'd done something to the wards—he couldn't really say they were wards anymore. More like the building itself was aware of him, as the jungle had been. He'd ask her about that later. She'd done something to him too—the tethers between them were gone, but the flow had been reversed.

In the bathroom, he just stared at himself in the mirror in search of the signs of the weariness that had become his companion the past few days, only to find it gone.

Ofelia caught him flexing and laughed as she eased back into the mirror to apply her makeup.

"I didn't know sex could do that." He tried not to gawk at the sparkly postage stamp of a skirt.

She blew him a kiss. "Sounds like someone hasn't been fucking the right witches."

"Any." The flick of the brush and powders that seemed to go on effortlessly only increased her glow and mesmerized him. "Witches."

Deciphering the look that crossed her face—surprise? Alarm? Longing?—when her eyes locked on him was impossible. It vanished quickly, replaced with a smirk. "Did I mention I'm out of underwear?"

Part of that was undoubtedly since just about every pair she owned was now hanging to dry in her bathroom.

But it also meant…

He eyed the skirt. She winked. Then her gaze switched to the mirror as she went to work with mascara. "You gonna get ready or what?"

He exhaled sharply. "Girl, I'm always ready."

She stared at him. He laughed and went to pick out something from his dwindling supply of clothes.

Klaus, Ondrej, and Luca met them at the first club. They danced for a bit, but Chris picked up nothing familiar.

Ayele was waiting for them at the next stop—a converted warehouse south of old town.

Chris crossed the divide to buss Ayele's cheeks. "You look like a goddess."

"You let him flirt like this?" Ayele glared at Ofelia.

Finally Ofelia shrugged. "He's not wrong."

"You know how it is." Ayele preened, then threaded her arm through Ofelia's. "Come, let's get a table."

Chris hesitated. Something tauntingly familiar touched his nose. He took distinct pleasure in Ofelia's shiver when he pressed a palm against the bare skin of the small of her back and leaned in to murmur, "Make nice, I'm on something."

Her eyes narrowed, and she hooked the back of his neck with one hand. Collared, he let her drag his ear close. "Don't be good."

"I'll try." He winked. "Hey Klaus, wanna grab a drink?"

Klaus hadn't looked away from Ayele since they arrived. Now he pouted as if he'd been dragged out of heaven by one heel, but he nodded. "You're buying."

"Deal." Chris used their slow circuit of the dance floor to narrow in on that scent. At the bar he ordered for both of them and paid. After a toast, he set his down with only a sip. "Watch these—gotta take a piss."

Klaus grunted. "Gonna ditch me?"

"If I'm not back in five minutes, you have permission to go back to trying to get Yele to notice you." Chris laughed. "You can keep my beer too. Fair?"

Klaus grunted again. "You and Ofelia good?"

"Very," Chris said. "Why?"

"'Cause the girl's looking at you with the googly eyes," Klaus said. "And you'd better not break her heart and ruin my shot with her girl."

Chris's chest ached with something like hope. "Wouldn't dream of it."

The long hall to the toilets was poorly lit. Perfect for illicit exchanges of all kinds. Chris let his nose lead him. In the shadow outside the door, a couple of guys stood too close, heads bent together.

Chris recognized the stringy-haired kid. He was all over the scene, a sweaty little rat making money mostly off tourists.

"Hey, nice to see you." Chris clapped a hand with one of Ofelia's bees tucked in his palm on the kid's shoulder. She'd warned him about the sting when it was activated, but it was like an electrified rubber band hitting his skin.

"The fuck!" The kid must have felt it too, spinning under Chris's grip. He stared before recognition hit. "Luca's friend? Squeaky Clean."

Was that what Luca called him? Chris gritted his teeth. "Need a minute of your time."

"You mind?" the kid's customer snapped, nervous.

"Sorry." Chris stepped past them into the toilet.

A few minutes later, the kid sidled in, washing his hands and glancing at Chris, warily. "You need something?"

"Can't a guy have a good time once in a while?" Chris tried to look awkward.

The kid's brow wrinkled. "Luca said—"

"Luca doesn't know shit." What business did Luca have bringing him up with a dealer? "Got that new stuff? Hexe…"

The guy blinked. "Eight hundred."

Chris tried not to look outraged.

"It's pure. Nicest high of your life."

Chris fought the urge to roll his eyes. "Gimme two."

"You with that girl, the pretty one?"

"They're all fine here, man." Chris reached for his wallet.

"The dark one, legs up to here." The kid lifted his palm to eye level. "Is it true what they say—"

"Don't"—Chris slapped cash into his hand with enough force to send the kid into the wall—"repeat every shitty thing you hear."

"Sorry, man. Enjoy." The kid skittered away.

Little cockroach.

Chris only knew the brief rundown Henny had given him of the drug scene. It was tiered. Guys like that were at the bottom, last to get the best stuff. Theirs was as likely to be cut with cheap stimulant as something more dangerous.

Chris glared at the little plastic-coated squares the guy had palmed him, its rough-edged dark blot shining in the low light. He didn't like the thought of this Legs person slipping her a tainted sample on purpose. Not at all. He pocketed it and headed for the door.

CHRIS LET his nose guide him to Ofelia on the dance floor. Her eyes lit when her gaze settled on him, an invitation curling her lips. He swung her close, cradling her hips against his as they let the bass take over.

She pressed her cheek into his neck. "You found something."

He slid her hand to his back pocket.

She raised her brows. "Really?"

"Can you blame a guy for wanting a little reward for his hard work?" He huffed and slid the packet free.

She rolled her eyes but hooked her elbow over his shoulder. Chest to chest they swayed and rolled with the long, steady beat drop. She glanced between them, palming the packet. He was vaguely aware of the crowd around them coming into sync. Did she know what she was doing or was it just a side effect of her charm?

She brushed her lips on his collar. "You got it."

He nodded, keeping his mouth close to her ear and his gaze scanning the room. "Same thing?"

She passed it under her nose before tucking it into some unseen pocket. "Yeah, maybe."

Chris didn't like the sound of that. He locked her hips in, holding her close. "You're not going to—"

"Try it? No way." She threaded a hand in the hair at his nape. "At least not here."

He growled.

"At home, with my guardian ready to lend me his strength?" she sang sweetly. He glared. She glared back. Then she kissed him. He liked that she sounded a little breathless when they parted. "You handed off the bee?"

"Of course." Low-level guy like that probably wouldn't bring them much. "I need to talk to Ange. Think you can get us into Tresor?"

She smirked.

"That's what I thought." He snatched her up for another kiss, just to wipe that smug look off her face.

It was too bad they hadn't reconnected a couple of years ago when he was desperate to get into a place like Tresor. Now all he wanted to do was to get her home, curled up on the couch in one of his T-shirts, and watch that poorly dubbed Italian soapy drama about witches she was so hooked on.

Breathless, they returned to the table to find Ayele rolling her eyes. "They're going to kick us out if you two keep making babies on the dance floor."

"We'd make cute babies." Chris shrugged.

Ofelia stared at him, but a smile tugged the corner of her mouth.

Ondrej joined Klaus in hooting obnoxiously. Good to see the kid fitting in.

Ayele snapped her fingers in delight. "He's not wrong."

"Enough, all of you," Ofelia said over the heat in her chest. She surveyed them all skeptically. "You lot want to close the night at Tresor?"

Her friends perked up. They'd had fun slumming it in common places for a while, but they knew where they belonged. Even Luca brightened up.

Ofelia was at home anywhere she was, and she moved crowds the same way. Chris liked that about her. He liked everything about her.

Including that skirt. And what was—or wasn't—underneath it.

At Tresor, Henny's brows crawled north at the sight of them even as he gestured to have the rope withdrawn. "Be careful, Lancelot."

"New nickname?" Chris grinned on his way past. "I must be in big trouble."

Ange found him. As he steadied her while she applied his mutes, he ducked close to her ear to murmur, "Need to talk."

"Working," she drawled against his neck.

He tilted his head into the hollow of her throat, inhaling the clean scent of moonlit granite. "Wouldn't ask if it wasn't urgent."

She sighed and bumped her forehead against his jaw. "Give me ten."

When he pulled back, half his crew and most of Ofelia's was giving him side-eye. Until Ange opened her arms and Ofelia slid into them. "Welcome home, Highness."

They exchanged a not-entirely-chaste kiss that made his night.

Ange glared at Klaus, Luca, and Ondrej. "You boys be good."

"Ma'am." Poor Ondrej's face was red as a fresh-roasted beet. He might have looked a little faint.

"Get this one something cold, yes." Ange patted his cheek. "He's overheating."

Klaus hooked Ondrej by the neck, trailing Ayele.

Luca stared at Chris, Ofelia, and Ange for a moment, then shook his head and wandered away, scowling.

"That one gives very bad vibes." Ange's gaze followed him before returning to Chris. "Watch him."

"I am," Ofelia said first.

Ange jerked her head. "Come on, lovebirds."

Chris faltered, self-conscious. "We're not—"

Ofelia squeezed his hand. Right. And after everything they'd been through the past few days, it should have been even easier—effortless.

So why was it all so jumbled up in his head?

Because he was in love with her, and as far as she was concerned, they were friends with benefits. That was why. Shit was messy.

Ange left them at one of the back tables. Each little booth tucked away from the action was warded for silence but also to keep passersby from even noticing they existed.

The booth was spacious, but Ofelia tucked in close to him. Her brows squeezed together.

He rubbed the skin on the back of her knuckles. "What's wrong?"

"I should have thought about your hearing at the other clubs," she said. "I could have done something like that for you. Why didn't you say anything?"

"I've been fucking up my ears since I was a teenager in places like this." It wasn't even worth a discussion. He kept his eyes on the crowd and his nose working. "Earplugs work well enough. And Woof heals fast."

"I'm supposed to be looking out for you."

Something promising drifted by, and he sucked in a little breath. Without being able to let the wolf surface, his ability to pinpoint the scent was frustratingly absent.

"Chris."

Nope. Distracted, he muttered, "I'm not your concord."

Did the temperature in the room drop ten degrees? Chris shook off the sudden chill and returned his focus to her. Ofelia looked like she'd been slapped.

"You're not the only one who's used to taking care of themselves." He hadn't meant it as a rebuke. He rubbed her fingers between his own. They didn't soften or wrap back around his. "I don't expect—"

"But you should," she said, voice low and angry. "After everything. You should expect... *more*."

Was she mad at him? Where the hell was Ange? He shrugged. "I don't do shit for you to get some kind of leverage."

Even the concord bond wasn't about that. He'd watched Erandi and Alam; Ilya the bear and Violet, the spy turned healer; even Baako and her concord. He'd spoken to the other shifters in training. He wanted to know what he was getting into before he'd offered to take that bond with Ofelia.

Just like every relationship, at any given moment someone always gave more. The trick was in the end, when it was right, it always balanced out. If he and Ofelia hadn't reached that equilibrium yet it was because they were still figuring things out. But they could. If she would just give them a chance. He knew they could.

He angled his body to her and searched desperately for the right words to say. "I only meant you don't owe me anything. Right now you need to focus on the job. I'm okay with that."

"Well, I'm not." She tugged her hand free. She stared into the club, unseeing. "I'm not okay with you suffering in silence when I could help you."

Returning, Ange took one look at them and frowned. "Did somebody die in the ten minutes it took me to get back here?"

"Just a little difference of opinion." Chris forced a smile.

Ofelia's gaze snapped to him, then pinned Ange. "How did you do that, with the sound?"

Ange's brows shot up and she grinned, sliding into the booth on Ofelia's other side. "Come here—I'll show you."

Ofelia leaned in. Ange cupped her face gently with one hand, stroked her ear with the other. Ofelia sat back, eyes wide. But he recognized the calculation in her expression.

"You don't really have to touch them," Ange murmured conspiratorially with a wink at Chris. "But with that one, it's a nice bonus."

Ofelia's face didn't lighten. "Okay, take his off."

"You sure?" Ange looked between them.

"It's okay," Chris said. He wouldn't turn down the chance to have Ofelia's hands on him. "Do it."

Ange sighed but sketched something out on the table before her. Suddenly the club was a cacophony of sound. He tried not to wince. The tension headache that had been building at the base of his neck all night came back with a vengeance.

Ange, the empath, saw it. Her own face tensed.

He held up a hand. Turned to Ofelia. If she needed this, he would let his head explode with pain until she figured it out.

Ofelia slid in closer to him. Her hands, cool and dry, slid around either ear. He leaned in unconsciously. Her touch alone was a balm. And then the soft tingle, like warm rain, coated his skin. As it settled against the curves of his ear, the music changed. He felt it move through his chest, sliding over his skin and around him like a wave.

It took him a minute to understand what she'd done. Instead of blocking the music, she'd changed his perception of it, drawing in his other senses to take the pressure off his hearing. He experienced it with his whole body now, sparing his ears the intensity.

"How is that?" Her voice was clear and warm, as though they were in bed again, mouth to ear. She tucked a wave of hair back into place.

"Perfect." His chest tightened and his throat went fuzzy with emotion, and he was unable to keep from reaching for her, dragging her even closer.

"Good." This smile was his favorite—the secret one that was just theirs.

Her fingers kneaded the base of his skull. Every bit of pressure eased the strain in the muscles.

"Save the couple's massage for later." Ange sighed, but a tiny smile eased her expression.

Ange hadn't seen Kenneth in days, but a couple of his guys had been at the club. She'd thrown one out for dealing but the others had known better and stuck to the streets and the alleys outside. But she had asked around a bit about the new drug. More people were talking about it.

She slipped something from her pocket, pushed it to Chris. "I grabbed it off the guy I tossed."

Another small, plastic-wrapped square.

"That's it." His nostrils flared.

Ange's eyes went from startling bright green to the gray of ancient, time-worn stone, the division between whites, irises and pupils disappearing. Her fingertips left little dimples in the soft wood. She swore and tucked her fingers into her palms.

Ofelia made the sample disappear to the same place the one from the other club had gone. "I need to talk to Kenneth. If you see him—"

"And why are you two playing junior detectives?"

Ofelia lifted a shoulder in a familiar gesture that brought a rush of heat to Chris's chest. "They're calling it Hexenblut—witch blood. Can't have the necromancer's Black Blade showing up looking for us, can we?" She folded her hands on the table and met the Garg's eyes. "I'm protecting my people."

Ange's gaze, green again, swung to Chris.

"Looking after her." He lifted a shoulder.

"Gargoyles are prohibited from interfering without our liege's leave," Ange said slowly, then translated in case they didn't get it. "I can't help you beyond these doors. Be careful, you two. I don't like how this feels."

As they rejoined the others, Ange sent them off with a little grin. "Shifters protecting witches. Now I've seen it all."

CHAPTER THIRTY-TWO

FRUSTRATED by the lack of progress in the club, Ofelia turned her attention to the next gathering of witches. She was already starting to think of them as hers. She was ready to have the coven conversation too.

Unfortunately, though her public classes were still fully booked, attendance at the witches' gathering disappointed. Only three charms activated. She tried not to let her concern show.

As she walked them out, one of her oldest students lingered, waiting until the others were gone before speaking. The stooped-back, silver-haired man looked like a retired laborer and had the most precise and nuanced sound charm she'd ever heard. "They're concerned about the murders."

"But there hasn't been another." A fact that was making her somewhat desperate. Legs was still out there. She was no closer to finding him, and he was her best lead to the witch hunter.

He fanned his sturdy, callused hands. "Yes, but fear is fear. And there is safety in numbers."

"You aren't afraid?" Ofelia met his eyes.

"I'm an old man—I've been practicing alone most of my life. I value my independence these days more than my fear. And I like what you teach here."

The next morning she called Cilka. The younger woman sounded distracted. After a little small talk, Ofelia broached her attendance. "Missed you last night—did something come up?"

On the other end, Cilka's soft breathing paused for a long moment. "I'm grateful to you for everything. But you know how I've always wanted more. And it turns out there's a good reason for that. Mr. Manhammer says—"

Cold settled in Ofelia's chest. "You met Socrates Manhammer?"

"Did he stop by the shop?" Cilka chirped. "I told him all about you. That you were powerful. We've been gathering at the old shipping yard. We meet again in a few days for the new moon spell."

Ofelia's mind spun. "The guy who calls himself a warlock?"

The unchecked mockery in her voice sliced between them.

"He's a great man," Cilka said tightly.

Ofelia took a breath. "Cilka, I'm sorry. I'm not judging you... or Manhammer. I just think—"

"He's read all the old texts and communed with the spirits of the powerful witches." The hope had left Cilka's voice. "*Our* witches." She took a hard breath. "You wouldn't understand."

That stung.

"We come from the same source"—Ofelia felt herself losing an argument she hadn't even known she was in—"even if our practices are different. Manhammer seeks hierarchy and sows division where there should be none."

Silence.

"I know you're scared." Desperation crept into her voice. "But turning off your discernment—"

"Witches aren't safe in this city." Cilka's voice hardened. "You heard that man in the alley. Witch blood. Socrates—Mr. Manhammer—wants to protect us." *Unlike you.* The quiet condemnation in the unspoken words hung between them. A flinty certainty Ofelia had never heard entered Cilka's tone. "And we're going to do something about it."

Ofelia's alarms went off all at once. "I'd like to give him another chance. Maybe I could come with you."

Cilka barked a laugh. "Manhammer warned us about false prophets. People who would try to lead us away from him. I never thought that would be you."

Ofelia pressed a hand to her eyes. This was going nowhere. "Just be careful, please. And if you need anything, you have my charm. Don't hesitate—"

The line disconnected.

Ofelia stared at her phone. She opened a text to Chris.

@Fifiti: remember that douchebag from the store?

She deleted it.

@Fifiti: we have a problem…

But *they* didn't have a problem. She was sure that Legs had been behind the poisoned sample, cementing him in her mind as the connection to the witch hunter. Manhammer, as repugnant as he was, thought he was protecting witches—and their blood—by aligning him under his leadership.

That meant it wasn't Chris's problem at all. She deleted it and pocketed the phone. With a sigh, she grabbed the grocery list he'd left behind that morning and the shopping totes. Her own self-righteousness had left her coven open to this. She'd fix this herself.

CHAPTER THIRTY-THREE

To the relief of his brothers, Chris got the kids off to school before putting in a few hours at the barbershop. Mark *almost* thanked him before getting in one dig about needing a haircut if he wasn't too busy.

On his way back to Charm Syndicate, he caught a familiar scent on a passing tram. Woof leaped in his chest, urging him into a jog to catch it at the next stop.

He pushed through the packed tram, ignoring looks of interest on his way. Pleasure settled in his chest when she saw him and her face transformed from a distantly focused stare to a smile of recognition. It was like someone had turned on a light, and everyone around her sat up a little straighter, seemed to grow a little taller. He knew the feeling.

Ofelia was, as always, the most beautiful person in a hundred-mile radius. It always felt like a new discovery.

He'd left in a hurry that morning, before she was out of her silk headscarf and the T-shirt he was pretty sure he was never getting back. Which was okay, 'cause the sight of her bare legs and lace-covered bottom peeking out when she reached up onto a shelf for something was his new favorite thing.

Now she wore loose-fitting pants in a bright, multicolored print of mostly greens and blues over sandals. She sat up a little, revealing a fitted bandeau in the same material. The wedge of warm brown skin over her collarbones and below her rib cage glittered faintly with her breath. Her hair was up in two little twists on either side of her head, her makeup on point, sunglasses tucked into her top. Her smile turned mischievous as he closed in.

The seat on either side of her was full, so he grabbed the bar overhead and hung on as the tram hit a curve, leaning into her space to breathe her in. Arousal soaked him, the brief memory of finally getting his hands under her skirt the night after coming back from Tresor almost making him shake.

"Hey, Princess." He took in the cloth tote bag bulging between her feet and two more balanced on her lap. "What happened to the list?"

She'd insisted on doing the shopping. It was cute how suddenly determined she was to pull her weight in their fake relationship. He'd tried to keep the list light, just essentials for their next few meals. But she was loaded like a pack mule.

"I got a little carried away." She tilted her chin up at him, all merry defiance in those plump, kissable lips.

"Woman." He tried to sound chiding, but the grin made it hard.

They were a couple, right? When she didn't pull back, he leaned in, sucked her lips against his.

The uptight babushka to Ofelia's left clicked her teeth disapprovingly. The old dude on the right winked at him when he broke the kiss. Ofelia looked a little dazed, a little flushed, and even prettier than a moment before.

She hooked her fingers in the front pocket of his jeans and hummed. As the tram slowed to a stop in front of the national theater, he grabbed all the bags, ignored her protests, and hurried her off before the incoming passengers could push them back. He squeezed close behind her in the press of people—tourists, commuters, locals—and took another deep whiff of citrus and fennel.

When she slipped her arm around his waist while they waited to cross the street and asked him about his morning, the rest of his life played out before him. A couple thousand days like this one, gods willing, a couple of stupid little fights so they could make up, and hopefully a trip back to her home.

They should probably talk about the likelihood of that first.

For now he told her about his clients as they walked. Even when the crowds thinned out, she stayed tucked under his arm.

"You know, you ought to do a pop-up in the shop sometime," she mused.

"You'd be good with that?"

"I mean, it would be extra good"—she laughed—"if you could use some store product. You like that pomade I made you, right?"

He loved it. He was used to having the unruly hair of the family. His mother's tight curls met his father's unruly waves and some throwback ancestor in thick strands that curled when they were damp or wet and hung looser in the front than the back and sides.

Ofelia had concocted something that kept them in line without weighing them down plus smelled amazing.

Speaking of smells. He sniffed, nose wrinkling.

"What is all that noise?" Ofelia coughed. "And smoke."

Now that Woof wasn't tuning everything out but citrus and fennel and the barest hint of a floral top note that hovered around the tips of her ears, it finally reached him. Something was on fire. A horrible flashback of pulling Tobias out of their burning cabin froze him for a moment.

Ofelia started running. It was a good thing his legs were longer, because he could manage a loping jog loaded with groceries and almost keep up. He skidded around the corner a few paces behind her.

A crowd gathered across the street from her shop, rising conversation punctuated by sharp cries of alarm. The street was blocked off, and the emergency workers moved around the smoking door.

A low moan tore out of Ofelia's chest.

The plateglass window of the storefront shattered in a blast of heat. Shards of gold and black glass danced in sunlight as they rained onto the sidewalk, and clouds of black smoke poured out.

Thank goodness for shock. She faltered for a moment before her fingers started twitching.

The hairs on his arms and neck rose in awareness. Chris dropped the bags, and glass cracked at his feet. He ignored the soft thump and roll of fruit across the sunbaked cobblestones.

"Fi, you can't." He wrapped his arms around her, pinning hers to her side as Charm Syndicate went up in flames. "Not here."

"Maybe I can stop it." Her fingers, parted mid-spell, curled, twitching against her sides.

When he didn't let go, her scream was pure anguish and rage. "No!"

"You can't." He pressed his mouth to her ear so she would hear him over the blare of fire engines and chatter of the crowd. "Too many people."

For a second he thought she would turn on him. Woof would have handled it better, but the only thing more shocking than a witch trying to put out a building fire would have been a two-hundred-pound wolf in tattered jeans and a track jacket trying to stop her. So he sucked in a breath and braced for the pain.

Instead, her voice fractured on a strangled cry. "Please."

"I'm sorry, Princess." He ignored the needles of pain and held her tight.

She thrust herself into his chest as if she could claw her way into his rib cage, gripping his jacket, the T-shirt beneath, and probably a little skin with fingers still sparking with magic.

The wind changed. Acrid, dark smoke blew out onto the street from the broken door. Even though they were a safe distance from the heat and the worst of the smoke, Chris spun, shielding her with his body. Gouts of smoke poured from the ruins of the Charm Syndicate windows.

Her shop. Her apartment might be where she slept, ate and kept her outrageous wardrobe, but her shop was home.

Oh gods, how he hated that look in her eyes. Furious. Broken.

"Don't look." He tucked her head into his shoulder. The hunger for violence rose in his chest. "I'll find out who did this. I'll find them and I'll—"

She jerked her head back, red-rimmed eyes meeting his, wide with shock. Her expression was a rictus of grief. It broke through his anger. She needed him here now.

He turned slightly so that he could better see over her head, but there wasn't much more than smoke. Emergency personnel clustered, pushing everyone across the street and redirecting traffic.

"Can you do something small to slow it down, help them get ahead of it?" he murmured.

Ofelia went very still in his arms. He could feel her thinking. Good. She breathed out softly, a sound like relief, and said something that made no sense at all. "The building can."

She slipped her hands between them, and he gave her a little space, letting the open panels of his jacket form a little mini tent to shield her hands.

The hand movements didn't always seem necessary. He'd seen his mother and sisters-in-law use magic without them often enough. They did seem to help with focus. He imagined Ofelia could use every bit of that now. He swept the crowd with his gaze, alert for anyone who might be sensitive to magic. It was too early for the necromancer to have sent his people, but one never knew when they might be lurking.

But whatever she was doing didn't belong to her. The usual strengthening of the citrus in her scent when she practiced didn't come. Ofelia seemed to be channeling her magic into the ground beneath their feet. Across the street, the building itself seemed to ripple in his gaze. Whatever awareness he'd sensed in it the other day had been roused.

The smoke thinned. Sweat beaded on her brow. He listened hard for the crackle of the emergency radios. He heard "offensive," immediately followed by a team of fully outfitted firefighters clearing the glass of the window and going in. He didn't want to think about the ruins of her beautiful plant collection.

He kissed a drop of sweat away before it rolled into her eyes. Tiny mutterings escaped her. The voices on the radio carried an edge of relief.

He repeated the words into her ear. "They're going in."

Ofelia rested her palms on his abs when she was done. The skin of her forehead against his collar was hot and crackled slightly with the strength of a good blast of static electricity.

"Christof? Ofelia?" someone called from the crowd. He recognized her neighbor, Mila, the nosy one who had made him tea while he waited for her the first day and then pushed him out of the apartment at just the right moment to catch Ofelia on her way into hers. "They're here! Thank the gods. Laurence, they're all right!"

She pushed her way through to them, taking in the spilled groceries and Ofelia's tearstained face. "We were so worried."

Chris let her go so the other woman could hug her. Other neighbors from the building emerged from the crowd, relief on their faces.

"They evacuated us, but we didn't see you," Mila panted. "And when we saw it was the shop. Well, I know you work sometimes even when the store is closed. You're okay, both of you?"

He thought of how many people he knew lived in buildings where they barely saw, never mind knew, their neighbors. How they might have blamed her shop for causing the blaze. These people cared for her like their own.

"I was at work." He spoke when Ofelia couldn't, gesturing at the bags around them. "Fi was doing the shopping."

Someone crouched beside them, beginning to gather anything salvageable and repack it into the canvas bags.

"Do they know how it started?" He stooped down to help.

The woman shook her head, but she bit her lip.

"They want to talk to you." The tall man, Laurence, approached. "Can one of us go with you?"

The solidarity touched him, but he waited for Ofelia to decide. "Yes, please."

"I'll go." Mila took Ofelia's other arm.

"Do you think they'll let me upstairs?" Ofelia's eyes darted to Chris, panicked.

Chris took a breath for them both, squeezed her fingers. "We'll ask. Not everything has to be done today, Fi. Let's just get through this."

She nodded, unusually docile.

The incident officer was waiting for them at the cordon. A woman in her mid-forties looked Ofelia up and down and sighed.

She started in Czech, her words directed at Ofelia's neighbor. "I need her full name and identification for the report."

Ofelia responded. It took twice more before she stopped addressing Mila and instead faced Ofelia directly.

Chris caught Mila's gaze. "Your boys. They're okay?"

"They're in school." She sighed. "I have to figure out where to stay tonight… until they let us back in."

Chris hummed, scanning the other neighbors all clustered in the street. The hand squeezing his brought his attention back.

"Sir," the officer repeated impatiently.

"Yo," he murmured, still thinking.

Ofelia squeezed again.

"Sorry." He cleared his throat. "Yes, ma'am."

"And you are?" Her brow rose as she scanned them again.

"Ofelia's boyfriend. It's been a couple of weeks, yeah."

"Your name, sir," the officer said dryly.

Chris handed over his ID.

"Vogel, eh?" the officer asked, glancing at him again. "Any relation to—"

Chris sighed. "My sister."

The officer took some notes.

"You think this has something to do with the academy?" He supposed it was better than what he was thinking. He couldn't get that warlock's disgusted expression out of his mind. He'd hated seeing Chris and Ofelia together. Enough to commit arson?

"The fact that your sister is one of the most notorious godsdancers in the territory may have some bearing," she said flatly.

Ofelia frowned, uncertain.

"Lots of people don't like what she does—call it magic." The woman didn't look up from her notes or bother to disguise the mocking in her voice. "And this is—was—one of those 'magical' shops, wasn't it? Potions and whatnot? Tourist trap. Worse than all that alchemist nonsense."

"That's ridiculous." Heat rose in Chris's chest. "These people need occupant services and to know the status of their ability to get back into their homes."

The woman quit writing and stared at him. She wasn't the only one. Ofelia's eyes were round and bright. Mila's fingers pressed the tiny smile on her lips.

A second officer jogged over. He took in the scene, and something in Chris's face made him stop a half step back. "Investigator is on-site."

"We would like to speak to them," Chris snapped, "as soon as possible. Would you let them know we'll wait here until they're ready for us?"

The younger officer swallowed and returned to the front line. Clearly annoyed, the first snapped her portfolio shut, glaring at them, and stalked away without a word.

The rush of heat dissipated, leaving Chris feeling alarmed and more than a little embarrassed.

"Good for you, boy." A couple of the neighbors clustered in, patting his shoulder, grinning.

Chris hung his head, unable to look at any of them, full of shame for how he'd raised his voice.

Ofelia squeezed his fingers again, hard. Her eyes were still big, still too wet, but they held something else. A weak smile lifted her cheeks. She bumped his shoulder with hers. "You were pretty brilliant."

Discomfort lurched under his breastbone at the tang anger left in his throat. It was like he'd left his body for a moment. Their admiration only made him feel worse.

"I'll be right back." He grabbed his phone and exchanged a glance with Mila. "Come get me if that one comes back?"

She nodded and stepped into the space he'd vacated to put an arm around Ofelia, and he told himself the hurt look in Ofelia's eyes was for her shop.

CHAPTER THIRTY-FOUR

By the time she'd finished speaking to the police and the investigator, all the energy Ofelia had rebuilt over the past few days had been drained away with the smoke. All the while, Chris stood apart from the crowd, on his phone. Her eyes stung from smoke and emotion. Couldn't he just stay focused for a minute?

He was probably chatting to those idiot friends of his. Or the gargoyles.

But she heard the tinny voice on the other end of the line replying to his question that the apartment was available and his as long as they needed it. Unintended side effect of the spell from the club—she could pick up on whatever he was hearing. That was what she got for dabbling —trying on a spell without fully understanding how it worked.

Guilt swamped her. All she could do was stand around amid the groceries spoiling in the sun. That too was her fault. So much food, wasted. She couldn't even summon the energy to undo the spell as he made arrangements, his voice urgent and decisive as she rarely heard him.

If she'd just stuck to the fucking list. If he hadn't stopped her from killing the blaze. If. If. If.

Ofelia was staring into gutted remains of her shop when Chris finally wandered over. The scream was building again.

Chris's shoulder brushed hers, and she spun on him.

He held out a bottle of water and a wan smile. "Drink something— we've been standing out in the sun for hours. You're probably dehydrated."

Ofelia's fury sputtered. If she took the water bottle with more force than needed, he didn't say anything. Her throat was bone-dry and scratchy. She rummaged through her purse for some blotting paper, sure she looked frightful.

When she got control of herself, Chris was focused on a conversation with her neighbor Mila. His eyes held the same single-minded intensity that always made her feel seen. An ugly twinge of uncertainty tightened her throat at the sight of it aimed at someone else.

As if sensing her mood, Chris smoothed his fingers down her shoulder, thumb pressing into the tightness building in the side of her neck. Without a word, his touch reassured her that he was there.

"—a miracle. The fire stopped—that's how they were able to get it contained easily. The upstairs apartments are mostly undamaged. The first floor has some smoke and possible water damage." Mila pushed frazzled blond hair out of her face with a frown. "You and I will be out the longest, Fi. And they won't even let us in tonight."

Another thing that was her fault.

"They arranged housing?" Chris's hand settled on Ofelia's spine, fingers rubbing the muscles on either side of bone.

"I'm not sure how I'm going to get the boys to school." Mila nodded unhappily. "And a hotel, no kitchen. We'll have to eat out. Some of the others have family to stay with… Or I just take him out of school for a while and go to my mother's house in Okoř."

Guilt fisted in Ofelia's chest. She blinked hard.

"Would Vyšehrad be better?" Chris asked cheerily.

Ofelia joined her neighbor in staring at him.

"I know a place." Chris lifted his phone. "I explained what happened, and they're happy to have you. It's a good building—clean, safe—and the unit is furnished. Small, but it's yours as long as you need it."

She nodded slowly.

"Great, settled. Let's go."

◆

"Hey, Princess. This is our stop."

When Chris rocked her awake, Ofelia realized that sometime after slumping into the seat on the tram beside him, she'd fallen asleep. Immediately she regretted opening her eyes. Waking brought memories of black smoke pouring out of Charm Syndicate's shattered window.

Memories brought a tide of emotions she couldn't control. Anger, sadness, fear. Rogue waves. She couldn't turn her back on them or she'd lose herself completely.

What had the fire inspector said? Arson. She closed her eyes.

Shock, she knew. This was some kind of shock. The same kind that had settled on her after the news of her parents' death. For days she'd simply been *not there*. She was sure she'd talked to administrators, teachers, and fellow students, but she couldn't remember a single conversation. A few days later when the family she had never met arrived to take her home, she'd left everything without protest and gone with them.

It had taken her almost two years before she'd come to her senses and realized that her mother's home wasn't where she was meant to be.

But this was different.

"Just a little bit farther; then we're home," Chris murmured like he was reading her mind again.

Every time she'd drifted into a hazy zone of functioning on autopilot, he'd gotten more solid and immovable. His fingers locked with hers at every opportunity. His regular squeezes became like a pulse. The rhythm drew her back into herself.

Now she let herself be herded along with Mila and the boys toward the hulking mass of Vyšehrad.

On the neighborhood street across from the park, he paused, considering something as he stared up at the top floor of a beautiful old building. He muttered under his breath.

"What's wrong?" Ofelia hesitated.

He shook his head, a wan smile creasing his mouth, and she realized he must be exhausted too. "It's Sunday."

Before she could ask why that mattered, the building door opened.

Ofelia's body rang with awareness as a trio of the most powerful women she had ever seen outside her mother's homeland stepped onto the porch. The threads of a bond ran between them, their powers attuned to each other by their practice.

She recognized the tallest of the trio immediately. How Evelia Acaz, the hottest young designer in Prague, managed to look elegant in a maxidress of some stretchy, summer-friendly material and slides on her feet was a thing Ofelia would take notes on later.

The smallest of the three witches, round and shapely with a crown of inky curls, hurried down to meet them. "What an awful day—we're so glad you are all right."

Ofelia missed a step, and Chris slowed automatically. She shook her head once, unable to explain but knowing she had to find the words because that worried crease was forming between his brows.

"Give us a minute, Bebe," he told the petite woman. It had to be a nickname—there was no way a woman whose magic tasted as expansive as sunshine over a field of lavender had such a tiny, perky name. So this was the witch who had come to check in on her.

"Of course." She paused before them, hands clasped in front of her so tightly the knuckles of her doe-brown skin had turned white, as if she were trying very hard not to reach out and pull all of them into her arms.

The witch snuck one more glance at Ofelia before turning her big smile on the older of Mila's boys. "You're taller than I thought you would be! I'll bet you're a very fast runner. Do you like trains?"

It was exactly the kind of random, innocent ramble that brought a shy smile from the bewildered older boy and his brother. She looked up at their mother. "I'm Barbara. I can show you to a place you can wash up, rest."

Chris nodded and Mila went, a grateful smile finally lifting her face as she herded her boys ahead.

That left Chris and Ofelia to face the remaining witches.

Evelia's gaze swept over them, then the street they had come down. Ofelia recognized the watchfulness of her expression. But when a hand just beginning to show the faintest signs of age in the walnut skin touched her shoulder, Evelia stepped aside.

"Hey, Mom," Chris murmured softly, and Ofelia was embarrassed by her surprise. Of course this was his mother. Though her skin was darker and she was dwarfed by the giant young man, the same threads of Heartlight ran through her chest.

"Let my home be your sanctuary." She spoke with as much regalness as any First Àjé, inclining a head crowned with a mass of locs bound in colorful cloth.

Ofelia released Chris, knowing she must stand on her own two feet. She pressed a fist to her heart, lowered her head.

"I am empty-handed and unattended." The words burned her throat. She swallowed her pride. "But for the time of my sanctuary, my power is yours, mistress."

The corner of Evelia's mouth quirked—approval or surprise—buckling the faded scar on her cheek.

"You remain sovereign, and your practice is safe here." The witch tutted softly and closed the distance, clasping Ofelia's shoulders with a little squeeze. "Call me Beryl. You're just in time for dinner."

When she looked back, Chris watched them, his face a mix of concern and something warmer. It felt like home. Just another something to lose.

CHAPTER THIRTY-FIVE

"I've got it," Chris protested. Ignoring him, Evie took one of the bags from his shoulder.

He held the heavy outer door to the building for her to pass first.

They started up the building stairs. Ofelia and his mother were already a flight ahead.

Evie dodged his attempt to take the tote back, her voice pitched low. "Are you sure you don't want to stay upstairs?"

"In my old bedroom?" he muttered. "With Mom and Dad down the hall?"

Evie flashed the suggestion of a smile. "You could always double up with Mark and the girls and me."

Chris groaned softly. "Where is he?"

"At your parents', minding his offspring as he should be." Evie chuckled. "And trying to keep your sister from telling too many stories of you boys as kids."

Chris tried to swallow the worry sticking like a bone in his throat. "Issy's here too?"

Today of all days.

He'd started to lose Ofelia on the tram. She was back, but he didn't know for how long. She needed to shut down completely. She always did better after a solid bout of sleep.

"We put an air mattress in what we thought was the bedroom, and I grabbed some extra clothes from the studio that should fit her. Bebe stocked the fridge with a few essentials," Evie said.

On the second-floor landing, Bebe was handing off the keys to Mila with a warning about the sticky door.

Chris paused, meeting the tired woman's eyes. "You're all right here?"

"It's just perfect." Tears nudged at the corners of her lashes. "Good night, and bless you, all of you."

The boys' voices came from inside, calling her attention to the plates of food in the kitchen. She nodded at them all again before closing the door.

"I gave her my number if she needed anything." Bebe fell into step on Chris's other side as they continued up the stairs. Her gaze traveled up the stairs. "So this is your Ofelia."

His eyes sought Ofelia automatically, a whole floor ahead of them and deeply in conversation with his mother. The anxiety he'd expected to feel was absent.

"She's... a friend"—Chris smiled at the sight of their heads bent in toward one another—"who needs help."

Bebe and Evie hummed in unison.

At the third floor, Chris stared at the propped-open door, hesitating. The whole family. On a normal day, the entire Vogel-Gilman-Svoboda-Acaz clan was a circus. Maybe he could grab plates for him and Ofelia, make their excuses, and head downstairs.

He lifted his voice. "Hey, Fi, maybe you should turn in early—it's been a long day. I can run up and grab us some food."

Ofelia and his mother halted on the step, turning to him with identical expressions.

Oh great, she was part of the family already. That hadn't taken long.

"We were just about to eat," his mother said. "You can leave early if you need to... rest."

Evie huffed a laugh. Bebe tucked her chin into her chest.

Chris fought the warmth soaking into his chest to a draw. "Whatever you're up for."

He should probably prepare her for the condition of his apartment anyway. He'd hoped to be further along, but getting kidnapped and charged with finding a witch hunter hadn't left him a lot of energy for work. "But we should probably just get this stuff in the fridge first. Whatever's left of it."

"I've got it." Barbara slipped the remaining tote from him before he could stop her, and Evie handed off hers. "I meant to make the bed earlier anyway."

"Dinner—" He faltered.

"Your brother can handle the barbarians." Barbara grinned. "Having to step up has been good for him—he's got a few new tricks now."

Chris started to argue, but Evie slipped an arm around his. His elbow cocked automatically to give hers somewhere to rest before he registered surprise at the contact.

On anyone else, her expression would have barely been a smile. On Evie, it was as close to a grin he suspected anyone but Mark and her children ever saw. It dazzled him into obedience.

Elbows linked, they went up the stairs together.

At the top, a cacophony of voices came from deep in the flat. Chris took a deep breath.

"Hold your ground, wolf." Evie patted his arm and let him go.

Chris snagged Ofelia's hand before she could follow his mother and sister-in-law inside. A question formed on her brow.

"I wasn't thinking." He glared briefly over her shoulder and into the din. "I just thought this would be safe—Mom's wards are rock-solid."

Ofelia's smile faltered. "I can tell. The walls are embedded with them. It's very kind of her to open her home, and the apartment for Mila."

"That's Mom. You don't even need me. She'd welcome you just because you're *you*."

Her expression softened, became something even more bittersweet with nuance he couldn't figure out. What had he said to make her look like that? He was always saying the wrong thing when it came to her.

Her brows drew together. "Have you ever brought anyone home?"

He glared up at the ceiling. Shook his head.

She hummed softly. "How do you want to play this? I don't want you to have to lie to your family."

"We don't owe them any explanations." Chris cleared his throat and shuffled his feet closer to hers. "But you're my girl. Just so you know."

"Am I?" She stepped in close.

He closed the rest of the distance. "News flash."

The nice thing about no longer carrying the bags was it was easy to put his arms around her. She fit him perfectly. He liked that she never felt small even if he could tuck her head under his chin. Her fingers splayed on his chest, warm and tingling softly as her charm flared in response to the wards.

He angled his neck to look down at her and found her already looking up at him.

The corner of her mouth tasted sweet, the remnant of lip gloss she'd had on earlier that day. Not as sweet as the rest of her.

A throat cleared in the doorway.

"What do you want, Professor?" Chris pulled away, casting a lingering glance at Ofelia's lidded eyes before he turned a glare on his middle brother.

Tobias had the nerve to look offended. "I'm looking for my wife."

"Well, she's not here." Chris made an exaggerated sweep of the landing that ended with a hard look.

Ofelia broke the staring contest, offering her hand. "Ofelia Adjei."

"Professor Tobias Vogel." He shook it firmly, as though she were interviewing for a position on his research team.

Chris almost groaned. What the hell was wrong with his family? Couldn't they just be normal for five whole seconds?

"Pleased to meet you." Ofelia seemed remarkably unbothered.

"Likewise." Tobias studied her a moment, then turned to Chris. "Dad's waiting to serve dinner."

"Just a fucking minute," Chris ground out, unable to keep the growl out of his voice.

"You have two minutes." Tobias's brows rose. He nodded politely. "Miss Adjei."

"Ofelia," she said, "or Fifi."

"Toby," he offered before aiming his next words at Chris. "You'd better warn her about Mom and nicknames. And Issy."

Then he disappeared back into the apartment, leaving the door open to make a point.

"What about nicknames?" Ofelia whispered.

Chris rubbed his forehead. "You sure you want to do this?"

"No one's tried to abduct us yet." She smiled resolutely. "I think it's going well."

She started for the doorway. He hooked her arm.

The words tumbled out in a rush. "My sister doesn't know."

"About what?" Her eyes widened.

"Us. My brothers. Mom and the sisters."

Ofelia stared at him for a beat longer than was comfortable. "How is that possible?"

"Long story."

"What are you two still doing out here?" Barbara came up the stairs, hands in the pockets of her linen duster. "I thought dinner would have started by now."

"We had to go over a few things." Chris kept his eyes on Ofelia.

Barbara aahed and ducked around them to get in the house. "It will be fine. Just don't grow ears at the table. And don't take too long."

"Barbara?" Ofelia said tentatively.

The smaller woman beamed as she leaned in to whisper, "You can call me Bebe."

Ofelia swallowed audibly. Something about that small concession seemed to reach her in a way he hadn't over all these weeks. He wondered at it.

"Thank you for looking after me," Ofelia said, "the other day."

Barbara's brows knit in concern as her gaze flicked to Chris, but she nodded. "We take care of each other. It's the only way we survive."

Ofelia blinked when she disappeared inside. He wondered what she made of their commitment to each other. Maybe the sight would convince her as he hadn't been able to. He could only hope. Then her focus returned to Chris. "You're serious. Your sister has no idea?"

"She's lived at her school since she was eleven. She doesn't have any gifts—er, charms or notions or whatever you guys do. She's normal."

"She's a godsdancer," Ofelia countered, unable to hold back her disbelief at how preposterous this all was.

"Except for that." He winced. "The necromancer is the academy's patron. She's too close. It's for her own good. That's the only thing I need... I need you..."

Ofelia gave him another tired smile. "I promise. We've got this. And if I didn't say it before, thank you for today. For everything."

Chris nodded grimly and tried to unlock his jaw. "Don't thank me yet."

CHAPTER THIRTY-SIX

As THEY STEPPED into the great room from the entryway, Lukas Vogel handed off his puzzle piece to one of the two nearly identical girl twins on the floor. The soft-spoken German man was the source of Chris's smile and height, and he took Ofelia's hand in both of his with that same focused gaze.

"Like the play." Ofelia gave him her name, finding herself a touch shy. "It was my father's favorite. But with an *f*. My mother changed the spelling to give me a happier life."

"Wise woman." He repeated her name thoughtfully, as though he was committing it to the deepest part of his memory. "Welcome."

He gave off nothing of the dual nature of his sons, nor Beryl's power.

In addition to the twins with the puzzle, there was another set in the dining room and a boy of not more than five who greeted Chris like he personally hung the moon in the sky.

"Missed you too, Zacky." Chris went to one knee to meet that hug, and her chest tightened.

The boy's wolf was such a distinct presence beneath his skin, she'd almost greeted it. When she met Chris's eyes across the room, he nodded with a fierce pride.

And then there was Isela, the sister who was neither witch nor wolf. She moved too quietly, and there was some distant light in her earthy gray eyes, as though she'd tapped into a vein of power and could no longer shut the connection off. She might not have charm of her own, but perhaps her bloodline had created a void that something else had filled. Ofelia wondered if any of them had an idea of what she had become.

His brothers were as different in looks as they were in personality, but similar for all that in the important ways. They doted on their wives, adored their children, and seemed to agree on very little except that their youngest brother was wasting his life. Through her exhaustion, her nerves rankled. Could none of them see him for who he was—especially for everything he did for their family?

It should have felt like a packed house, but by some magic, the top-floor flat seemed to expand to hold them all without the sensation of being crowded. Despite her exhaustion, the room full of boisterous, stacked conversations kept Ofelia's eyes bouncing between them.

Chris didn't appear to mind the endless jabs, carrying on cleaning his plate. But over the course of the meal, his shoulders tensed and his lips tightened around the edges.

"That's enough," Beryl announced finally, a wrinkle of concern between her brows.

Markus, the eldest, took after her most closely, at least in looks. "Ma, he's dropped off the face of the planet for the past few weeks."

Ofelia understood the dynamic well enough—being seen not for who he was but for their expectations of him—and bristled on his behalf. The primary complaint seemed to be he just wasn't there *whenever* they needed him.

Mind your own damn business, Ofelia.

"He's been working in the shop," she blurted out. "Before... well, what happened in the shop."

Chris's eyes rose from his plate, one brow lifting. She hadn't meant to speak, except she couldn't just sit still while Markus and Tobias pecked at him endlessly.

Ofelia took a sip of water, emboldened. "Lots of customers and orders. I haven't had time to hire someone new or train them. And Chris —Christof—well, he learned the product line so fast. And he's very good with people. His experience with barbering makes him great with the hair-care lines. It doesn't hurt that he's incredibly handsome."

"Is that why you keep me around?" He grinned, some of that cheerful flirtation restored.

A grin tugged her mouth. Had she ever told him that? She would tell him more often, starting now, in front of his whole ridiculous family who clearly loved him but did not know him at all.

"Secret's out, Charming."

Markus guffawed. "Charming. As in Prince?"

"Exactly." Ofelia stared him down, daring a challenge.

A long foot nudged against her own, calf pressing hers. She snuck a glance to find Chris offering the pasta bowl. Taking care of her. And now she knew how to take care of him too.

"Yes, please." She served herself. Then she slid her hand onto his thigh, squeezed, and addressed his mother. "Everything is delicious. Thank you for having us."

Markus's jaw bounced. "Barbara and I cooked since that one was too busy selling soap."

"Markus." Barbara sighed. "It was our *turn*."

Ofelia changed the subject with her sweetest smile. "I understand you're in construction?"

After that, Ofelia stayed on guard. If the conversation turned to Chris's failings, she simply rerouted it. Markus was a two-word-answer guy, but Tobias could talk about books forever. Barbara owned her own store and occasionally traveled the territory to do rare-materials appraisals or lecture at universities.

When dinner was cleared, Evelia began stacking plates. "Uncle Tal sends his love and dessert. He was sorry to miss dinner, but he's been overdue for a vacation."

According to Chris, Evelia's uncle ran the business side of her studio and had become a fixture around the building since the twins were born, talking jazz with their dad while teaching the little ones how to bake. Chris owned up to hanging around on those days, determined to prove by appetite that a lopsided lumpy cake tasted just as good as properly finished one.

The youngest set of twins—Barbara and Tobias's—began pounding the table simultaneously. Witch, wolf, or something wilder—Ofelia's guess was out on those two. Mark and Evie's girls had been babbling back and forth in their own language most of the night, sneaking glances at her. She was pretty sure the one with Mark's golden eyes was building a hex under the table. The other sized Ofelia up like a predator.

"Lilach, table manners." Mark's sharp command confirmed her suspicion.

His daughter's bright eyes narrowed at him as her small hands returned to the silverware. He frowned and shook his head sharply, flicking a quick glance at Isela.

Isela, who was busy arguing in low tones with their father at the other end of the table.

Ofelia rose to help with the dishes.

Chris hooked her pockets and tried to pull her onto his lap, but she twisted loose with a wry grin. "I need to feel useful."

Plus she wasn't giving Lilach "Buttons" Vogel a second chance or a clear shot.

She followed Evelia into the kitchen. As she set the dirty plates and silverware in the sink, she paused, trying to form her question carefully in case Isela had ears as sharp as her brothers'. "How is it possible—"

Evelia gave a tentative smile. "They decided it was for the best that she not know the truth. She has no power of her own."

Ofelia blinked, alarmed.

"I was supposed to pretend I had no idea what you were talking about so that you could fully express your outrage, wasn't I?" Evelia's brows lifted as she floated the kettle into place on the stove and flicked the burner on without leaving the sink.

Ofelia hesitated.

"You know the danger we face if we are revealed outside this house." Evelia collected the silverware by sweeping her hand over the open drawer. She directed Ofelia with her chin to the small plates. "And she can't even light a candle. If you could raise a child never knowing that fear, would you do any different? It's not my place to ask the question, never mind try to answer."

The air stuck in Ofelia's throat. She wanted to tell them the truth, but what good would it do? They'd lived their whole lives under the weight of the necromancer's laws. The truth now might be harder to live with than the lie. She watched Evelia take a tart out of the oven.

Before she could gather her wits, Isela stepped through the door. All through dinner she'd seemed distracted, but every time Ofelia spoke, her attention returned as if she were trying to understand something.

"The train station," Isela said, without preamble, leaning against the refrigerator.

Evelia stared at her, frustration knitting her brow. "I need to get to the cream—"

"You're the girl from the train station." Isela folded her arms over her chest.

Ofelia straightened her spine. "I am."

Evelia looked between them, lost. "What does that have to do with the cream?"

"He was twelve years old." The quiet in her voice was the stillness before thunder. "Do you know what they did to him?"

Ofelia's throat closed.

"He came home—alone." Emotion scraped Isela's voice raw. "He cried when he threw up gummy bears—because they had been a gift from you. And you just… disappeared."

The hot wedge of tears Ofelia had been denying all day expanded in her throat. "I had to—" Ofelia bit her tongue on the words she could not say. *My parents were afraid the boys would reveal me as a witch. They had too many questions they could not answer about who they were.*

"And now you're back," Isela snapped.

"This is not the time," Evelia murmured, wide-eyed.

Silence descended in the other room. A chair scraped the floor.

Tobias came in with a few forgotten plates, trying to look innocent. "Everything okay?"

"Do you remember the train station?" Isela demanded.

Tobias shrugged. "When Chris got beat up over some girl—"

Evelia hissed.

Tobias blinked as if he were trying to figure out how to retract the words as he met Ofelia's eyes.

"You're the girl?" He grinned, shook his head, then grinned again.

"Broken ribs." Isela ticked off fingers. "Stitches. Bruises."

Ofelia saw the way Tobias bit his lip and thought of what he would say if left unfettered. *We heal fast.* But because he could not, he simply stood, frozen in place.

"That was a long time ago," Evelia said carefully.

"You weren't there," Isela barked.

Evelia flinched, but her lips tightened.

Isela rounded on Tobias. "And you were away at school, trying to forget we existed, so what do you know?"

At once Ofelia saw behind her anger to the pain. Chris said she had been a baby when the family immigrated, and he was born a year later. They had shared a bedroom until she left for the dance academy. Every time he talked about her, his face lit up, and contrary to their older brothers, she seemed to doubt he could do any wrong.

"Okay, are we gonna do this tart or what?" Markus burst into the room, his voice too forced.

The panic rose in Ofelia's throat.

Markus continued through the room like a wrecking ball, taking the dessert plates from his partner. "What the hell are you all doing standing around?"

"Not until I say this." Isela's voice cracked.

Markus leaned toward Tobias. "What are we fighting about?"

"Train station." Tobias coughed, blinking.

Markus made a sound of understanding, looking at Ofelia as though something now made sense. "Isela, that was a while ago. And Chris is—"

"You made *me* feel like a criminal for trying to help him hide it from you for two days," she snapped, "because he was afraid you'd get mad and do something stupid like go after them."

Ofelia looked between them, forgotten. All this time she'd been so worried that Chris thought she was someone she had been years ago. She hadn't thought to consider that in some small way, he'd been the one trapped in time, locked in the moment she'd tried to forget by the people who loved him most.

Isela pinned Ofelia in her gaze, ignoring her brothers.

"You hurt him once." Her voice gathered the kind of gravity that if she had been witch-born, Ofelia would have built a defensive ward against. "Do it again and I will—"

Chris burst in, cheerful and oblivious. "Markus, we've really gotta help Dad with those shelves in his office. I just looked, and they're about to come down."

When his gaze settled on her, Ofelia was startled to find her eyes were wet. She blinked furiously. She would not cry, not here.

He crossed the room in three huge strides. She'd forgotten how tall he was sometimes, leaner than either of his brothers but towering over them all. "What happened?"

She shook her head once, hard, unable to meet his eyes even as she tilted her chin up. The pressure in her throat was hard as a marble and slick with emotion. There was no getting words into her mouth from her chest.

He spun, putting himself between her and the room. "What did you assholes say?"

"We—" Markus began.

"Assholes?" Tobias finished, brows up.

"I was looking for dessert." Markus laughed in disbelief.

"They don't have anything to do with this." Isela's growl rivaled any of her brothers.

"It's been a long day," Evelia said as though they were late for an appointment and must be moved along. "We're all tired. I can't even imagine what you've been through today, Ofelia. How about I cut a few slices of tart, and Chris, you take Ofelia downstairs? You both could probably use rest."

Ofelia sucked in more air, felt it whistle down her throat.

Chris spun in time to see the first tear roll before she could turn her face away. Her mouth formed the empty words—*no, no*—but he had already turned to the rest of the room.

"You started this?" Chris asked his sister, and Ofelia's heart cracked at the love that softened his voice. She grabbed for him, but her fingers slipped over the loose T-shirt and slope of muscle beneath. Everything in him tensed with certainty. "The fuck did you say, Isela?"

Ofelia had never heard anything like that come out of him.

Apparently none of the other siblings had either. The next silence was full—shock, surprise, horror.

"It was my fault." Ofelia gripped his arm, making the words come because she could not be the cause of this family fracturing.

The look Chris gave her over his shoulder made her flinch. "The fuck it is."

Then he turned to the rest of the room. "I expect these two to have too much to say about my life, but you, Issy? You can't even be bothered to come home once a month, and now you got something?"

"I said what needed to be said." Isela didn't back down. "You missed a week of school, and she just disappeared. Now she's back and you almost get burned up in her shop."

"Burned up?" He snorted. "We weren't anywhere near the shop. And she was a kid then."

"You went to the hospital, you oversized idiot," she shouted.

"You need to get your fucking head on straight, Is, before you come at my girl for some bullshit that happened fourteen years ago," Chris roared.

Markus's voice rose. "Don't talk to your sister like that."

"I don't need you to protect me, Mark," Isela grunted, voice muffled.

Ofelia dared a glance around Chris's biceps.

Markus stood between his youngest siblings. Tobias stepped into the charged space between Markus and Chris. The scent in the room was heavy with the echo of wolves.

At the kitchen sink, Evelia's eyes bounced between them, her hands flexing. The silverware in her hands began to shiver imperceptibly.

The kitchen door opened, and Ofelia wanted to melt into a puddle on the floor.

Beryl Gilman Vogel marched in, hands on hips. "What is it about my kitchen that seems like a good place to have at each other?"

Silence.

"Dessert, now." She kept her voice low, which was somehow more threatening. "You're scaring my grandchildren."

Now Ofelia heard Barbara's voice from the other room, consoling a chorus of high-pitched, worried voices.

Oh Seven, she'd forgotten the kids.

Tobias and Evelia dropped everything and hustled out of the kitchen.

Mark turned to face Isela, his eyes narrowed.

"Sorry for yelling, Ma." Chris's shoulders drooped, and he took Ofelia's hand. "It's just been a nightmare of a day. We're going to turn in."

On the way to the door, Ofelia let go. She stepped toward Isela, but Markus lifted his head. For a moment she thought he wouldn't move.

She felt for Isela Vogel, who had been wrapped like fine china and sent away to protect her from the one thing that bonded the rest of her family.

Ofelia was angry at all of them for denying their sister her birthright. Could no one see how hurt and isolated that left her? She wanted to be part of them, to protect them as fiercely as they did each other.

Ofelia met Markus's eyes. He must have seen her anger wasn't directed at Isela, because his gaze slid away and he cleared the path.

Ofelia faced Isela, hoping she finally had the right words. "I can't imagine what that must have been like… to see someone you love in so much pain. I've thought about that day over and over. I'd do anything to go back, to fix it. But I can promise that I will do whatever it takes to never let him get hurt like that again."

Isela was silent.

Ofelia nodded, accepting. Then she took Chris's hand like an overboard sailor grasping at a lifeline and let him lead her from the kitchen. The dining room was empty.

Lukas Vogel emerged from the long hall. "Is everything okay?"

"We're beat, Dad," Chris muttered. "Gonna get some sleep."

"Are you sure you want—"

"We're fine." Chris cut him off. Ofelia squeezed, wanting him to know she was there.

"Your room is—" The elder Vogel tried again.

"We're good downstairs, Dad." Chris grabbed the key off the hook near the door.

"It's been a pleasure to meet you, Ofelia with an *f*." Lukas walked them to the door.

"Thank you," Ofelia managed to squeeze out of her aching throat.

Another oblivious one, she thought. Except he couldn't be, not entirely. And he too stood outside their world. Unlike his only daughter, he had a view in but could never truly be part of it. Ofelia couldn't decide which must be worse.

On the staircase, they caught up with Evelia first. One of the twins was listing sleepily on her hip, the other holding her hand. The one walking was crying about the lost dessert.

Chris scooped her up without letting Ofelia go. "Sorry about that, Pinecone."

"I'm not Pinecone." She sniffed, affronted. "I'm Buttons."

Chris made a show of being confused. "Buttons?"

"I'm Pinecone." The sleepy one on Evelia's shoulder looked up with an unfocused gaze.

He looked back and forth between them until even Evelia smiled.

"I'll make it up to you lot," Chris said at the apartment door on the next floor. "Gelato after school this week, okay?"

The girls nodded eagerly as Evie hustled them inside.

"Us too, Uncle Chris?" Isaac's small voice piped up from across the hall as he tugged Barbara's hand to stop their progress inside.

"Come on, Zacky, time for bed," Tobias called from the open doorway, two small drowsy bodies on his chest as he propped open the door with one foot for his wife and eldest son.

"I think we'll leave the monsters out of it," Chris whispered. "Sugar turns them into gremlins."

The boy grinned and hurried inside. "Papa, Uncle Chris is getting us gelato next week after school."

"So I heard." Tobias laughed softly, nodding to them.

Barbara hesitated a moment in the open doorway. Ofelia thought she might say something, but she only nodded good night and closed the door behind her.

Chris led Ofelia down the stairs.

"It's not pretty." His keys unlocked the second-floor apartment. "But it will do for a couple of days until we figure what's what, right?"

"I'm sure it's fine," Ofelia began.

She stopped inside. It was not fine.

It was a construction zone. Bare walls and exposed wires and tools stacked up on the counter amid sawdust, boxes of nails, a level, and a saw.

The room closest to the front windows overlooking the park must have been a bedroom, or at least that's where the inflatable mattress was. It had been made up nicely, a sprig of lavender on the pillowcases. Someone has also tried to clean up the kitchen. But half of the inside walls were missing, and the floor was torn up. She could see the plumbing in places.

"What happened to this place?"

"It's mine." Chris let her hand go to shove his into his pockets. "That is, it will be. If I can ever get my shit together and focus on finishing it. We each got one."

"Your parents—"

"Bought the building, which isn't as great as it sounds considering most of it looked like this when they moved in." He didn't seem to be able to look at her. "Dad managed the renovation—the plan was to turn most of them into rentals until we were old enough to need them. Issy was supposed to be across the hall from me, but she lives at the academy—which, for the first time in my life, I am completely happy about."

"And they forgot this one existed for twenty-six years?"

"Nobody needed it till then." He shrugged. "They just left it for me. I mean, Mark helped me get started after I finished school, but I just ran out of steam. Didn't see the point. I like being close to Mom and Dad. And seeing the kids all the time is so great. They grow up so fast."

And being two floors down with a door between him and the others would have been like being on another planet. He and Isela had shared a room until she left for school. More than any of his siblings, Chris was a pack animal.

He huffed. "I don't know what got into her—"

"You're her favorite brother," Ofelia said. "And I'm the first girl who broke your heart. And a few ribs apparently."

He touched his chest as if he could still feel them. "*You* didn't break anything. Those boys—"

"Would have kept giving you a hard time at school until you hit your growth spurt and they realized they should be afraid of you." She sighed. "But you were still small. They saw you cared about something, and they felt powerful."

"Where you come from, our kind protects your kind all the time," he said. "No big deal."

"No àjé worth her charm leaves an uninitiated shifter to the mercy of bullies." She took a shaky breath. "I took responsibility for you when I showed you your wolf. You were mine to protect."

She caught her lip in her teeth, realizing her slip. She'd claimed him. When had she begun to think of him as hers? Seven knew she had no right to him. Not after everything.

Chris was silent, jaw working.

She turned away. "Is the bathroom—"

Not a hole in the floor and plumbing over bare wires, she wanted to ask. But she had gotten her livelihood burned down and her heart smashed twice, and she had no right to question the condition of the sanctuary she'd been granted.

Chris held out a hand. "The one in—through—the bedroom wall is in the best shape."

The demolition crew hadn't yet discovered it. It was an antique but charming for all that. She took a shower and found the stack of clothes.

Chris was standing by the bed when she emerged, hands in his pockets. Had he been there the whole time?

"This was a stupid idea." His brow knit at the sight of her. "Let's go upstairs. My bedroom is small, but it has walls and doors."

"I'm fine." Exhaustion had cored her and left her a shell of herself. "I can sleep anywhere."

He looked doubtful, and a ghost of a smile tickled his lips. "I've slept in your bed, Princess—that's an expensive mattress."

She skirted past him and slipped into bed, determined to make this work. She held back the covers, patted.

He hung his head. "After the day we had, Woof is going to claw his way out of my chest if I don't run for a bit. I'll just be in the park with the boys for a few hours. You're safe here."

"Of course," Ofelia said, trying to keep her voice light. "You should go. I'm fine."

He hesitated, clearly torn. He dropped to one knee beside the bed, and after a brief, awkward tussle with the duvet, she realized he was trying to tuck her in. It should have been endearing. Instead, she felt like she was going to scream. Is that how he saw her now, like one of the children?

"My family is— I didn't think—"

"You tried to warn me." She tried to make a joke of it, but her heart wasn't in it.

"I did." He angled his lips down.

She tucked her chin at the last minute, and his lips landed on her hairline.

"Look, if you change your mind, head upstairs. Issy will go back to the academy tonight after Mom finishes with her."

"She's really going to love me," Ofelia said.

He shook his head. "She and Mom have been going at each other for a while. It's their thing lately. And she's just under a lot of stress at work. This really isn't even about you."

She nodded, trying to make him stop defending the people who weren't afraid to love him. She reached up to cup his cheek, remembering her promise. "Be safe, Charming."

She'd made a promise to Isela. One she intended to keep.

CHAPTER THIRTY-SEVEN

CHRIS EXHALED as he let the building door ease closed behind him, listening for the ring of his mother's wards chiming over the physical lock. Ofelia was as safe as she could be without him right next to her. He hated knowing that fire hadn't been an accident. He liked knowing she thought she was keeping that from him even less. Once the flames had been suppressed, he'd smelled magic under the smoke. It was fragmented, but he thought it might have been Manhammer.

Mark was already outside the main door, leaning against the pillar at the top of the steps. "Well, that was fun."

"Can we not?" Chris sighed, starting for the sidewalk.

His older brother's brows rose, and Chris braced himself for a lecture. Mark had never held back before.

The door opened again, and Tobias stepped outside, squinting a little without his glasses. "So, we going to talk—"

"No." Mark shook his head. "Unless you've changed your mind, Tof?"

Shocked, Chris decided to press his sudden advantage. "How come you didn't call me in on the job for the guys at Tresor?"

"Oh, you're doing construction again?" Mark asked. "Last time I checked, you were picking up chicks at drop-off. But I guess that got old, so now you're playing shopkeeper with *this* chick. I can't keep up."

"Hold on a second." Tobias sighed. "Let me call Issy down, and then you can all shout at each other again and get Mom riled up. And terrify our children. Having to reassure my eighteen-month-olds that no one was getting hexed in their grandmother's kitchen was the high point in my night."

Chris joined Mark in staring at him. Tobias faced them, hands on hips, doing his best to glare without his glasses. Even squinting like a mole, he was the image of their father.

"Legit," Mark muttered. "You saw Lilach at the table? If I have to warn that kid one more time about doing that shit in front of Issy. Being honest with them was a mistake. I see why Mom and Dad straight up lied."

Tobias frowned. He'd suffered the most from being unprepared for his wolf.

"Oh, lighten up, Professor, it's a joke." Mark scowled.

Chris laughed. "Nice knowing the monsters are afraid of something."

"I know, right? Easiest bedtime ever." Tobias grinned briefly. "But we're too old to be doing this crap. Stop baiting each other and learn to control your tempers around the family. Understood?"

Chris agreed. After a moment of sharpening his glare, Mark did the most startling thing of all—he nodded. "Understood."

The tension eased out of Chris.

"Now are we running or what?" Mark jogged down the steps, leading the way toward the park.

"You were intense in there." Tobias slung a hand onto Chris's shoulder. "Mom said you really stepped up today."

Chris frowned. "Issy—"

"Will come around," Tobias said. "In fact, once she cools off, she's going to like Ofelia. A lot. Ofelia stands up for you. And she's not afraid of that jerk."

They tracked Mark in the darkness, already climbing the hill and stepping off the path into the trees.

"She did, right?" Chris smiled, remembering how she'd spoken up for him at dinner with a calm confidence of someone sure of their words.

Tobias was watching him, his ears beginning to point and the squint relaxing as his wolf began to push for liberation. It spoke of how far he'd come that when he took a deep breath, his wolf settled behind his human features, leaving his squinty smile. "This girl—woman—means a lot to you?"

"I love her." Chris met his brother's eyes.

"Another witch in the family." Tobias's smile turned wry as he slapped Chris on the shoulder. "That makes us three for three. Look at you, all grown up."

Chris rolled his eyes, though his heart filled his rib cage with sudden lively warmth.

A flush settled on Tobias's cheeks. "That was awkward."

"Leave that paternalistic big-brother shit for Mark." Chris grinned.

"Paternalistic?" Toby drawled. "Big word for a little fish."

Chris narrowed his eyes. "Try *patronizing*."

"I knew you had vocabulary hiding under all that swagger." Tobias left him to jog ahead in the effortless, easy lope of a runner.

Chris stared after him, hands on hips, calling, "Do you even know what *that* word means?"

He broke into a jog to catch up, and he'd never felt more at home.

THREE FOR THREE. Ofelia rolled onto her back on the too-squishy mattress, staring up at the wreckage of the ceiling. She hadn't meant to overhear it, but the spell from the club was still active—she hadn't had a quiet moment to untangle it.

With a deep breath, she broke the charm's connection between them, angry at herself. *Three for three.*

She couldn't unhear it.

Maybe that was the root of his determination to be with her. She couldn't even blame him. His desire for their approval was obvious even if he pretended like he didn't care what they thought of his choices.

But these weren't concord-bonded pairs. They had not trained for combat, nor did they have any idea of the danger this world held for their kind beyond the necromancer Azrael's laws as Ofelia did. Her vow to her own necromancer remained. Torching her shop was an act of war. A sign she was getting closer. She was done slinking around, waiting to sneak up on the witch hunter. She would find Legs and force him to give up what he knew.

She grabbed her phone, swallowed her pride, and dialed.

"Fifiti!" Ayele's voice rose with barely concealed worry. "I saw the shop on the news, and you haven't answered your phone, and then you dropped off the map."

"You have a tracker on me?" Ofelia rubbed her forehead as frustration bubbled up against her resolve.

"You're a daughter of the àjé," Ayele confessed. "It's your blood."

Ofelia bought herself time and patience with a deep breath. All this time, she'd mistaken a long leash for freedom. "I need a ride."

Ayele's silence prickled.

"You will do your duty as a daughter of the àjé." The words felt oily in her mouth, unnatural.

Ayele sucked her teeth. "Give me an address."

Ofelia was already levering herself off the too-soft mattress. Was there a hole in this awful thing? "Fast."

Ayele grunted. "Okay, okay. Boss."

"Don't call me that."

"Don't pull rank on me."

The brief silence no longer stung.

Ofelia could hear Ayele smiling and the little intake of her breath.

Since she had returned to Prague a year ago, Ayele had been her constant. Ofelia hadn't left the àjé on good terms, but no one had *really* tried to stop her—and they could have. The jaded part of Ofelia assumed Ayele had been assigned to keep tabs on her.

But maybe it had always been more than that.

Ayele was a Spider like Ofelia's mother had once been.

As Violet's replacement, she'd been embedded in Prague for years. If the àjé knew where Ofelia was, Ayele had no need to do more than just keep an eye on her. Instead, Ayele must have orchestrated their little crash in the café where they "met," the excuse to get her number and follow up on replacing Ofelia's ruined jacket. They'd started meeting up for coffee after, and the rest was history.

Ofelia remembered the hurt in Ayele's eyes at her rejection. It had been easy to deny her pain when Ofelia thought of herself as an assignment. Ayele knew her heart as well as their inside jokes.

Ofelia had not had many true friends in her life, and Ayele had been the truest of them.

"I am sorry," Ofelia began, unable to finish the sentence for the sudden tightness in her throat.

Ayele had no problem supplying the rest. "For pulling rank on me. And treating me like garbage because you were angry at our mothers."

A laugh did wonders to ease the burn of tears. "All of that."

"Okay. I accept." Ayele took a deep breath. "And I am sorry that I lied to you about who I was, but I will not regret it since you have become like my sister. Now, since you have dragged me out of bed, let me go so I can make myself passable in case I meet the boy of my dreams on the way. In which case, you will have to find your own ride."

"You *are* my ride." Ofelia's laugh was watery.

"Well then, you'd better hope he does not appear." Ayele disconnected.

Ofelia watched the window anxiously, not sure whether she was more worried about seeing the wolves emerge from the woods or Ayele's car. Maybe part of her hoped Chris would come back first and insist on going after Legs together like he always did. But the bigger part of her wanted him safe in this enormous old building, with the family who loved him a little too much for his own good. She'd promised Isela to keep him out of danger.

She sighed with relief at the sight of Ayele's Mercedes rounding the corner. On the landing, she slipped the door closed behind her and tiptoed down two flights to the front door.

"Going somewhere?"

Ofelia jumped.

Isela stood inside the building door, phone in hand.

"I have to run out for a few things." Ofelia tried to sound casual. "The apartment is…"

"A disaster area," Isela finished. "I hear about it all the time from Mark and Toby. He really is trying though. They just keep him so busy chasing their kids, when is he going to have time to finish the apartment? He can't win."

"I haven't been much help with that the past few weeks," Ofelia confessed.

"They want him to be just like them." Isela's brow furrowed. "But he's not. He's—"

"Different," Ofelia filled in automatically, then caught herself at Isela's wary expression. "I've lived in a lot of places in my life, met a lot of… people."

Isela's brow didn't ease.

"Your brother—" At Isela's unmistakable "which one" expression, Ofelia added, "Chris. He's magic."

The word just slipped out, but her tongue burned sharply. Her eyes widened in surprise. She'd never suspected Beryl's wards were nuanced enough to help preserve her daughter's naivete. She hurried to clarify. "He sees the best in people all the time. No matter who they are or where they've come from. Or what they've done. That's special."

She blinked as the truth of her own words returned the warmth of tears.

"Exactly." Isela grinned, and Ofelia knew why gods paused to watch her. In joy she was luminous. She rolled her eyes. "He *is* pretty special. But magic? Let's not go too far."

"Deal." Ofelia laughed as the ward subsided, wanting to hug the woman.

Isela opened the door, and they stepped outside together. Ofelia glanced back once as she crossed the threshold and thought she saw the outline of a familiar hair wrap on the top floor. She silently thanked the witch who had given her shelter.

From the car, Ayele watched them.

Ofelia waved. "Can we give you a ride?"

"I'm headed back to the academy." Isela fidgeted, wary.

"We go past it." Ofelia nodded.

Isela looked at the car, then back at Ofelia. "It might be a bit of a spectacle. Even this late. Sometimes the cameras are intense. You can drop me off a couple of blocks away."

For the first time, Ofelia saw her not as Chris's sister. This was Isela Vogel, Prague's most celebrated godsdancer. Ofelia knew how it felt to have people think they had a right to your life and an opinion about everything that went in on it.

"Absolutely not."

"A SPECTACLE," Ayele drawled as Isela disappeared into the building under the arm of the academy security team. The remaining flashes died down.

If there were fewer than usual, it was because at some point the paps had noted it was a famous socialite heiress behind the wheel, and their attention had been divided.

Isela had looked almost grateful for the distraction as she waved goodbye.

"I am glad I bothered to put on my face." Ayele preened. She took a good look at Ofelia as they pulled into traffic. "What's the plan?"

"We're going out," Ofelia muttered as she endeavored to type with her thumbs.

"Look at you, stepping into the modern age." Ayele laughed when she glanced over.

"Shut up," Ofelia muttered. It was slow going until she got the hang of it, but she was already faster than using her fingers. "Chris does it this way."

"Ah, Chris does." Ayele hummed softly under her breath. "Wait until you discover swiping."

Ofelia looked up. "What?"

"Aye, nothing." Ayele smirked. "Unlike *some* people, I know when to hold my tongue."

"You heard about what happened with Amanirenas?"

"The Spiders' Web carries information quickly." Her brows lifted. "Especially when it's shockingly good gossip about a rebellious àjé with a smart mouth."

Ofelia narrowed her eyes. "You mean there's nothing better to share on a secret worldwide network of spies than gossip about a Cadre dropout?"

"Times are slow." Ayele shrugged. "And there's no such thing as a dropout. We call this your gap year."

The laughed burbled in Ofelia's chest, fizzy as champagne.

"And what of your lover?" Ayele asked.

Ofelia shook her head once. "He's out."

"Fifiti?"

"I will not say it again." Ofelia refused to look up from her phone. "He's not ready; he has no place in this. He's not my concord."

"But he could have been," Ayele said quietly. "Fi—"

"It's not his job to die for our mothers."

Ayele fixed her gaze out the windshield.

"And avenging mine is my responsibility," Ofelia finished as though her friend had spoken. "If I fall, it will be up to him to protect his, as it will be yours to get word to Serwaah that I have failed."

They were quiet the rest of the way.

Ayele's penthouse looked like something out of a glossy magazine, but Ofelia recognized the touches of home and family in the bright colors and designs that evoked both the Aegean and her homeland.

"Why do you even bother pretending to attend school?" Ofelia was relieved for the moment's distraction.

"I am an artist, you wouldn't understand!" Ayele withered her with a look. "Come along, rebel. I have some things that might come in handy."

She led Ofelia down the long hall—just how many bedrooms were there?—and opened a door to a room that shouldn't exist at all. Perhaps it didn't. Ayele seemed to be good at making spaces where there had been none. Ofelia had witnessed it enough when she was stocking products in the store and never thought to attribute it to her charm.

Ayele muttered a word, and the room illuminated from all corners. It was small but well stocked with herbs and tinctures, poisons, and weapons. Ofelia recognized many labels from her own store.

Ofelia hugged her.

"It's not much—" Ayele grunted, tensing like a squashed cat.

"It's much more than that," Ofelia said. "So much more."

"I've been collecting what I've seen in your store." Ayele extracted herself, patting Ofelia's shoulders awkwardly. "And a few extra things I thought—well, I'd hoped you might never need—but times are as they are. Well. It's better than nothing, I suppose."

They stared at the room together, Ofelia categorizing everything she had access to. Even with her charm still recovering from the poisoning and the fire, she might actually stand a chance.

"I've put a call out to Kenneth, let him know we'll be at Tresor," Ofelia said.

Ayele mock-sighed heavily. "I will kiss a *Great Euro Bakeoff* marathon goodbye and rally the troops."

She was halfway out the door before Ofelia thought to stop her. "And under no circumstances are you to contact the wolf. Am I understood?"

Ayele stuck out her tongue. "Understood."

CHAPTER THIRTY-EIGHT

Was he surprised to find Ofelia gone when he returned? After dinner and the drama with Isela, he was lucky she hadn't caught the first private plane to the hidden city and forgotten he existed. But he knew she wasn't running from him. He'd seen her face watching the store. Beneath the shock and the grief, rage simmered.

He'd hoped she would do the smart thing: rest, regroup, and call in her allies. The àjé would want to know about this, and maybe Baako could send some reinforcements.

But no, she was off half-cocked and alone. Again.

He got his confirmation when his phone buzzed with a text.

@Klausmodious: YO. I don't want to get in your shit,
but I got a rally call from your girl's girl. Everything
okay, man?

Chris's thumbs hovered over the screen in frustration before he realized that Ayele was on their side.

@BigBird: Always. You guys up for a night out or what?

The group text buzzed, and Chris switched over.

They'd been going at it for a while. Someone finally tagged him in. Luca.

@Luca3000: told you she'd quit your ass @BigBird

@Ondrej: Why are you such a dick?

@Luca3000: Somebody has to keep the man's head from getting too big for his shoulders.

@Klausmodious: silencio. we ride in 30. @Luca3000 since you're being an ass, you can call the car. Pick me up. Drej, be at the curb. Tof… wear whatever Henny likes best. Gonna need that pretty face to get in the door…

@BigBird: You can all go fuck yourselves. See you in an hour.

Chris locked the door to the apartment behind him and jogged up the stairs. When he poked his head in the kitchen to grab a bite, Toby and Mark were already there, plates piled with leftovers.

"So your lady friend had another appointment?" Mark suggested around a mouthful of pasta.

"We're headed out." Chris ignored their narrowed gazes. "The apartment is a shithole—as you keep reminding me. Told her she could get a head start."

Toby paused mid-bite. "You're going to a club. You and your… girlfriend? The night after her shop burns down?"

Chris slapped a deli packet of sliced meat into a baguette. He ripped off a bite, chewed for a moment. "Wanna go?"

"Are you fucking kidding?" Mark coughed.

"She likes to dance, blow off a little steam," Chris said, shrugging. "Can't hurt."

Also, she was probably going after her ex to put the heat on finding out where Legs was holed up. He could catch up, shake some sense into her—maybe grind a little too—and then they would head out together and put this shit to bed once and for all. He wouldn't take his brothers on that last part.

Tobias shook his head slowly. "What the fuck is going on? Really, Chris."

Mark stared at their middle brother, mute with delight.

"Language, Professor," Chris chided.

Mark chuckled, folding his arms over his chest and focusing on Tobias with something like admiration. "What have you deduced, Sherlock?"

"They're hiding something." Toby lifted his index finger. "Both of them. She's lying. But you're in on it."

Chris rolled his shoulders, uncomfortable. Part of him longed to tell them about the witch hunter. But even if he'd not taken his vow, this was not their responsibility. It had been different when it was them. His brothers were parents now. There wasn't going to be any more magic duels in churches or mob rescue operations.

"What's she got you into, Tof?" Mark's humor faded. "I like this girl, but—"

"What did Evie get you into?" Chris swung his gaze to Tobias before he could decide to have an opinion. "Remember the haunted four-hundred-year-old book? Right. So come with me or get the fuck out of my way, but let me take care of my business. I am not your little brother anymore."

He paused on the way out the door. "Well, I am. But you don't get to run me around anymore. I don't give a shit whether either of you approve of what I decide to do with my life. With all the love in my heart, you can both fuck all the way off."

He was halfway down the hall when he registered a presence in the living room and backtracked, leaned in the doorway. "Hi, Mom."

"Hello, Christof." His mother looked up from where she was curled around a novel on the couch.

"Did we wake you up?" He tried to keep the tension out of his voice.

"I am going to have to smudge my kitchen again—all this bickering makes the food taste funny." She shook her head. "I couldn't sleep after Isela left, so I decided to read for a bit. Do you need help with anything?"

Chris took a deep breath. She wasn't insisting. She was asking. "I have to see something through."

She slid a dried flower into the pages of the book before rising to join him in the doorway. She smiled up at him, and the tension in his chest eased. When she lifted a hand, he lowered his chin. She rested her fingertips on his brow, her palm against his cheek.

There was no touch more familiar than this, and the Heartlight flared between them, like to like.

He closed his eyes. "It's dangerous."

"I know."

"I can't tell you anything about it."

"I can see that," she mused. "The vow that closes your throat is a very shrewd mechanism. Old. But I can't undo anything you undertook willingly. I won't."

"I would do it again." His eyes met hers. "A hundred times."

"Which is why there is no point in trying." Her lips pressed together tightly.

He waited patiently. A blessing, warning, or words of wisdom had accompanied them every time they left the house since they were old enough to go alone. He was sure this would be just like any other time. He started to smile, urge her to get on with it.

When she blinked, he was startled to see tears in her lashes. "When you were small, you knew the old songs, had a sense of people. And Heartlight is a witch's gift. It's always been in ours, but never so strong as in you. I was sure you would be like me."

"It must have been— I'm sorry."

"Never apologize for what you are." She shook her head once and he froze, terrified, not knowing what he would do if one of those tears fell. But she blinked hard, and her chin stilled. Her eyes went nearly as wolf yellow as Mark's. "You are more than both, not less than either. You carry the moon on both sides."

His nose itched, and his throat was seriously scratchy. He swallowed hard. "Ma."

She put her hands on her hips. "Son."

They grinned at each other, and when she bared her teeth, he thought that she was more wolf than all of them put together.

"Your heart is always in the right place." She patted his chest in a dismissal. "Now keep your eyes open, remember to be more clever than strong, and never forget who you are and what you come from. See you in the morning."

"Yeah, not too early, eh?" He huffed a sigh and turned down to the hall to his bedroom.

The murmur of voices followed, but he tuned out Mark's protests and Tobias's concerns and their mother silencing them both. When he finished—fresh khakis, red Nikes, and his second-favorite T-shirt—he rubbed a little product in his hair and let the memory of Ofelia calling him *Charming* at dinner buoy him to the door.

The rest of the flat was quiet, the spot his mother had been reading empty. The kitchen was spotless. He checked the time on his phone. Perfect. He could catch the tram and be at Tresor just a little late.

He paused on the front porch as déjà vu swept over him. This time his brothers weren't dressed for a park run. Evie had tried to help—Mark only looked a little less like he was headed to a jobsite under the collarless black leather jacket. There was no helping Tobias, who could have been headed to one of those fancy twenty-five-dollar-a-drink cocktail bars with his shiny shoes and oh my gods—

"You gotta lose the tie, man." Chris sighed.

"I told you." Mark laughed.

TRESOR HAD BEEN PUT on alert if the line was any indication. If Ayele seemed a little antsy, Ofelia put it off as her being nervous with the fact that Ofelia was armed for a battle. None of their friends seemed to notice anything amiss—Ayele's hidden spaces were impeccable.

When Ofelia bussed cheeks with Henny on the way in the door, he held her arm a moment longer. "What trouble, milady?"

"No harm will be done on your grounds." Ofelia knew he saw every bit of the wards she wore like armor.

Henny narrowed his big slate eyes on her, reminding her for a startling moment of Chris. "I heard about the shop."

"A terrible accident," Ofelia said steadily, though her heart felt anything but. "I'm just here to relax. A bit of extra protection seemed like a good idea."

He nodded once but didn't look relieved. For a moment she thought he would deny her entry.

"Ange is on the floor tonight," he said finally. "Call her if anything—and I mean anything—is off."

Ofelia lowered her chin.

Henny held on. "Your word."

She narrowed her eyes.

"I am no fool," he reminded her.

"I give you my word I will contact you if anything I can't handle happens in these walls."

He sighed heavily, and she could see him resist the urge to tug at his horns in frustration.

She took pity on him and dropped a real kiss on his cheek.

"You are king among rubble." She murmured the first gargoyle phrase of affection she'd ever learned. When the stubble twitched against her lips, she knew he was in real danger of smiling. "I am thankful for your protection and your kindness. And I promise I won't fuck up your club."

When she drew back, his frustration had been replaced by concern. "It's not the club I'm worried about."

Inside, she thought she glimpsed Kenneth's new girlfriend. When she turned for a second look, Brigitte was gone.

She checked her phone.

> **@KenDoll:** Be there in

She stared at the unfinished message. She tapped furiously back. It *was* much easier to type and walk when she used her thumbs. Chris was onto something.

> **@Fifiti:** This is important, K. Where are you?

No answer. She shook her head. She shouldn't be surprised. There was nothing between them anymore. No reason for him to show up because she called.

On her way to the table, uneasiness prickled her spine. She turned, searching the crowd for the source of the gaze that lingered on her skin.

Legs sat at one of the more prominent tables, in a suit and open button-down shirt. His dark skin glowed in the low light, and his teeth shone when he smiled at her. He lifted a champagne flute, and though she couldn't quite see his eyes, she felt the pressure of his gaze.

The phantom taste of poison flared on her tongue. Sick rose in her throat. Her fingers twitched with a longing for a defensive spell.

She thrust her chin up, shoulders back, and let the gauzy silver top settle over her like armor as she headed to the dance floor.

Ofelia tried to find her rhythm, but the staccato beat seemed to refuse her access. The scratching electronics grated her ears. She wondered what Chris would have made of it, if his ears needed extra reinforcement on nights like this. Now was not the time to think of him.

She exhaled, allowing herself to be swept into the music even though it made her heart stutter and her breath catch. She scanned the crowd where Ayele indicated. It seemed impossible that he could get from a booth to that position so fast.

There.

Legs moved at the edge of the dance floor as though to a rhythm only he heard. Surprise made her pause even as unease gripped her. He certainly knew better than to try to deal under the watchful eyes of the thralls. She'd come hoping Kenneth would lead her to Legs. Now here he was. A more sinister thought gripped her—what if he was here looking to identify witches for their blood?

Ofelia was squeezed in on all sides. Suddenly the press of bodies was no longer just an inconvenience. She pushed through the crowd, ignoring protests and shouts of disapproval.

When Ofelia skidded to a stop beside the bar, he was already moving down the hall toward the door. Whatever had brought him out now, she wasn't letting him slip away again.

"Wait!" She imbued her word with power. The chance that an intentional charm drew Ange was a risk she had to take. "Stop."

Neither word should have been audible at that distance, given the noise the club was calling music and the size of the crowd. But the short man turned, a knowing smile on his face. In the light, his teeth looked sharper. Ofelia squared her shoulders as she strode toward him. She sent an illusion bubble of empty space around them the human club goers would avoid instinctively and the supernaturals would know to dodge.

"You were looking for me?" He had the gall to look surprised.

"I need a word." Ofelia lifted her chin imperiously, ready to compel him if necessary. She could get him into one of Ange's security rooms. Ange owed her one.

He shook his head sadly. "I'm afraid I don't have time for a parlay no matter how beautiful the lady. A mutual acquaintance of ours has encountered some unpleasantness."

Ofelia released the start of an immobilization charm, her breath catching.

"Your Kenneth fancies himself a self-made man." His brow rose as if in answer to her unspoken question. "I suspected you kept him out of much trouble. Without you, I'm afraid he's become quite… *lost*. I tried to help, but he insisted he didn't need it. And now it seems your concerns were justified."

Ofelia's world shifted on its axis. "I'm going with you."

"We all have our roles to play." He took a step back, one long hand splayed to his chest. It was a strange hand for a face so young, she registered distantly, wrinkled with long, knobby fingers. He seemed no more than a few years her senior. But the leathery skin said otherwise. How had she missed it? When he handed her the sample, she should have noticed. "I'm afraid your minders have already come to see you safely returned to being an opiate for their masses. Ironic, isn't it, hunting a drug when you've been used as one all this time."

She glanced over her shoulder as Ange emerged from the crowd. When she looked back, Legs had almost disappeared. She hesitated. She should let Ange stop him, but if Kenneth was in danger, she might lose the chance to get to him in time.

"Some trouble?" Ange appeared at her side.

When Ofelia looked back, Legs was gone. She tried to keep her expression even.

Ange called her name, this time with a note of warning.

Ofelia forced a smile. "I just thought I recognized someone I knew."

"Where's your fur-face?" the Garg inquired too casually.

"He decided to skip tonight." Ofelia smiled. "Yele is keeping tabs on me."

"I'm glad someone is." Ange's gaze narrowed. "And Fi?"

Ofelia blinked innocently.

"I was sorry to hear about your shop."

Ofelia's heart slammed against her ribs. The pain was still too fresh to stifle or disguise. "A terrible accident." The words felt like ash in her mouth.

"There you are!" Ayele burst between them, grabbing Ofelia's arm. "I've been looking for you. Ange! Who is this guy? He's amazing."

Ofelia stared at her friend. The DJ was playing some hardstyle garbage Ofelia was certain was not her taste at all.

Ange didn't drift off as she usually did to resume her circuit. Instead, she watched Ofelia carefully.

Ofelia calculated ways to shake the Garg. If Kenneth was in trouble, every moment counted. Before she could signal to Ayele for a distraction, Ofelia caught a glimpse of that same brilliant light, shining through the crowd like a beacon. Just like the first time she'd seen him. "You didn't."

And Chris wasn't alone. She recognized his usual crew—sour-faced Luca, giant Klaus, and doughy, innocent Ondrej. And behind—

"So those are his brothers, yes?" Ayele laughed nervously. "Handsome boys."

Mark and Toby, annoyed and wildly out of place, hung at the edge of the group.

Ayele had broken her word. It should have triggered a warning in Ofelia, but then—

"You said not to call *him*." Ayele tugged at her earring. "But Klaus—"

She glared at Ayele. Seven help her, they *were* friends. "You *knew* what I meant."

"Of all people, you know the importance of specificity," Ayele countered.

Ange folded her arms over her chest, suspicious.

She almost confessed everything and begged for the Garg's help. Historically, Gargs were insular and less involved in the goings-on of other magical creatures, but the younger generations—Henny and Ange among them—pressed for more involvement after the godswar. The problem was, as the strongest beings in the room, a Garg's default setting was protection. Their idea of helping might be locking her in one of

Ange's security rooms until they estimated the danger had passed. Legs would be long gone by then.

She couldn't get the Gargs involved.

Chris, too, oriented himself around protection, and that meant putting himself between her and danger.

Ofelia had indeed allowed herself to be caged, no matter how gilded. She was not the one to be kept coddled, safe, protected. She was her mother's daughter after all.

CHAPTER THIRTY-NINE

"About damn time." Chris grinned from the curb as his boys tumbled out of their taxi.

Klaus straightened to his full height with dignified dismay, dusting off his slacks and rolling his eyes as Luca bitched about his knees being in the dash the whole ride.

Ondrej paid—of course—then jogged over to join them. His eyes lit up at the sight of Mark tugging his collar. "Boss?"

"Don't get excited," Mark grumbled.

Chris made introductions, and they headed down the long alley to the club. He hooked Luca on the way. "Hey, are we okay, dude?"

Luca spun on him, yanking his shoulder free. His pupils were huge.

Chris sniffed. "You high?"

"Mind your business, golden boy," Luca muttered.

Chris let him walk ahead and found himself side by side with Tobias. His brother frowned. "That guy—"

"I know," Chris murmured. "Hey, the club is going to be shit on your ears."

Tobias nodded. "Bebe took care of Mark and me."

Chris nodded and tried not to feel a twinge of jealousy. Once he caught up with Ofelia, he was going to have a word about her taking off without him. Again. Eagerly, he stepped to the front of the group, ignoring the looks from the line.

Heinrich fixed him in a long, stony glare. Before Chris could open his mouth, he twitched a finger and his flunky grabbed the chain. "Next time tell her I need better numbers."

Thanks, Ayele.

"It kind of grew on its own," Chris said. "My bad."

"Welcome back, Mr. Kučera," Heinrich said as Ondrej and Luca passed.

Klaus took his time with a wink at the line.

Heinrich raised a brow, studying Toby and Mark. "The famous Vogel boys."

Mark stared back, unflinching. Toby stuffed his hands in his pockets, more than a little out of place but blinking at the scene from behind his glasses like he was already planning a thesis on social rituals in underground clubs.

"You've gotten quite a reputation in certain circles." Heinrich's clan was part of a larger network that ranged from northern Scotland to southern Spain. "Possessions. The mob. You do good work."

Seeing both his brothers speechless was a moment Chris would never forget.

Mark recovered first. "Good to meet you."

"Thanks for—uh—accommodating us," Tobias said, his cheeks bright under his glasses.

Chris couldn't help himself. "They're okay. You should meet their ladies though. Those chicks are real badasses."

"And you are a menace who needs to learn some respect." Heinrich's laugh rolled like thunder. The crowd wavered like it was on the verge of hysteria at the sound. "Enjoy yourselves, gentlemen. Anything you need, ask for Ange. She'll take care of you."

Mark bumped Chris's shoulder with his own as he passed. Tobias nodded, curt and awkward—as always—and followed.

That left Chris staring up at the bouncer. For a moment it was just the two of them, old times, and so much fondness swept Chris he almost gave the Garg a hug.

Heinrich warded him off with one long finger. The corner of his mouth tipped up. "Gods only hope Her Royal Highness in there has more luck with you than I did."

"Thanks, Henny."

"Have a good night, Fur Face."

Chris went cheerily into the dark hall, ignoring the pounding throb of music. He'd find Ofelia and she'd set his ears up. Then they'd get to the business of whatever lead she was on now.

"Sorry we're late—things went long in the park." When Chris slid behind her, it took more determination than Ofelia expected not to press her shoulder blades into the expanse of his chest, tune her sense for the steady beat of his glowing heart as he called to Ayele, "Hope you don't mind if I brought a couple of tourists."

"Henny will never forgive me." Ayele's grin was too wide. "But of course not."

So he'd told his brothers and friends they were going for a night out. The inkling of a plan to get rid of Chris and Ange crawled up her consciousness, driven by desperation. What she did might break both of their hearts. A sick feeling rose under her rib cage.

The groups began to mingle.

How much time did she have left?

You can't protect him. And you don't need anyone else to worry about. She dodged the hand he moved toward her waist.

She turned slowly, bracing herself for what came next. "What are you doing here, Chris?"

"What is this all about?" Frustration tightened the edge of his smile.

"We had a nice run." Ofelia kept her voice light, ignoring the way her heart shrieked in protest. "I think we should let it go before things get weird. Don't you?"

Chris's brows drew together as she stepped back.

His boys were looking now, her crew too, likely. Not quite knowing what was happening, just that it couldn't be good.

"I mean, it was a *really* good time while it lasted." She spoke as if she was trying to keep the conversation between them but a little too loudly. "Friends?"

Chris reached for her.

Ofelia jerked away with the terrible fear that she'd forgotten to exclude him from her protective wards and he'd be hurt. But the words she spoke did more than enough damage. "I'm not your three for three, Christof."

Chris let his hand fall. "You heard that?"

Behind him, Tobias jerked, a flash of guilt in his eyes.

Ofelia hated herself for letting the words slip out even if she couldn't have planned it better. His brothers would talk sense into him, keep him from coming after her. He would be safe.

Ayele slipped a shoulder between them, wide-eyed. "Hey, you two, somewhere private maybe."

"I have nothing to say to him." Ofelia thrust her chin up, a little too defiantly. Tears burned her throat. "*You* shouldn't have asked them to come. But they're here now."

She spun and almost crashed into Ange. The gargoyle looked more harried than Ofelia had ever seen her. "What in all hells is going on, Fi?"

"I see the club is letting in whatever riffraff hits the door." Ofelia sneered, took a glance back at Chris. "I'm going home. Please don't let him follow me."

Ange looked like she would argue but thought better of it. Instead, she stepped into the space behind Ofelia as she swept past.

She half expected the thralls, or Ange herself, to trail her, but after the first few steps unaccompanied, she exhaled relief and picked up her step. At the commotion behind her, she glanced over her shoulder to see Chris pinned to the wall, Ange's smaller frame easily immobilizing him. She hesitated. What had he done?

No time. Kenneth was in danger. Legs was getting away. She headed to the closest unwired emergency exit.

Out on the street, she took a big breath, swallowing the horror of what she'd just done. She'd dumped him in front of all their friends—in public—and left Ange to do the dirty work of cleaning up her mess.

Witches are dying, and you're about to be alone with a being you're pretty sure is in on it—or at least profiting off it. Get your shit together.

She boosted her wards and shut off the part of her that wanted to race back into the club for Chris. The part that would have groveled and begged him to come with her because she was alone and she was frightened and she didn't know how she was going to make it out of this alive.

Legs had said Kenneth was in trouble. She hailed a cab and gave the driver Kenneth's address.

CHAPTER FORTY

ANGE'S EXPRESSION was dangerously close to pity when Chris tore his gaze away from Ofelia as she disappeared into the frenetic light show.

The effect of music assaulting his unblocked ears had begun to take a toll. The throb began in the base of his neck and climbed up his skull. He had to get out of this club. He had to catch Ofelia. He recognized that stride. Ofelia was on the hunt.

Chris ducked, but Ange was faster and stronger. Stupid him for assuming that because she was smaller than her little brother he had any chance of getting past her. The hand on his chest was like running into a brick wall.

"Don't make me do this, Fur Face." She sighed.

He glanced over his shoulder. The rest of Ofelia's crew looked like he'd stepped in dog shit and tracked it all over the fancy rug.

Only Ayele had moved away from the group and was attempting to fade into the background. But there was only one way around, and that was currently blocked by a gargoyle and Chris.

Whether this was just her charging off on her own to save the day again or she was upset about the shop, Ofelia needed help. She'd come with Ayele—that had to mean something. He managed to catch Ayele's eye, praying she understood what he was going to do next and would use the distraction to get to Ofelia.

As if he thought he had half a chance of trying get past Ange, he lunged. Shock caught her by surprise, but not for long. Ange planted him face-first against the nearest wall, her forearm pinning his back. His face was squashed on a surface that he shuddered to think about what else had touched. She had a grip like a boulder. His shoulder was going to hurt tomorrow, wrist too probably. But she was clearly trying not to hurt him. She could have easily snapped his arm.

Mark started forward, but she shook her head. "Please don't."

Three other Gargs emerged from the crowd.

The atmosphere had gone from train-wreck gawkers to mildly horrified with everyone looking like they wanted to be somewhere else but also to watch.

"I'm okay," Chris muttered, trying not to let his mouth touch the grimy, graffiti-covered paint.

His brothers and his crew seethed. Except Luca.

Well, that settled it. That smug asshole was getting his walking papers from the group chat.

But in the commotion, Ayele had slipped away unnoticed.

Chris tapped out.

Ange released him instantly. The look on her face made him regret pushing her. But if he had been some creep who thought he had a right to Ofelia's time and attention, she would have put a stop to that too. He respected her even more for it.

Hugging her now would not be the best move though, so he simply nodded, rubbing his wrist with an apologetic little smile. "Sorry, Ange."

"Me too, Fur Face." Ange looked mournful. "Beer on the house?"

"I should probably call it a night, huh?" Chris headed for the main doors on the opposite side of the club.

Ange fell in beside him, one hand resting on his not-fucked shoulder. "That's a good plan."

Mark and Tobias looked so confused he almost pitied them, but they followed. Ondrej and Klaus resolutely fell in. Only Luca stayed, following Ofelia's blond friend back to the booth.

Yep, his membership in the chat was canceled.

"I had my fingers crossed for you two," Ange murmured.

"Sometimes things don't work out the way you plan, I guess," Chris said, distracted and wondering where Ofelia had gone.

"I love that girl, but she's young and foolish," Ange said wryly. "She'll figure out what a mistake she made someday."

And maybe I won't be around when she does. Chris startled himself with the thought.

After all, she'd done it again—run off to fix things and treated him like he wasn't capable of standing with her. He was tired of trying to prove himself to her, trying to love her when she was so determined to leave him behind.

If Heinrich looked surprised to see them back so soon, he said nothing. He and Ange exchanged a glance. Chris wasn't sure if Gargs were telepathic or if it was just a sibling thing, but the younger Garg nodded obediently and closed the door behind them.

"I'm sorry about your shoulder," Ange said as they stepped away from the line. "Ice it and rest."

He winced, rolling it. "You've got a good grip."

"Runs in the family." She gave a lopsided smile. "No hard feelings?"

Chris opened his arms. "Come on."

Ange chuckled and stepped in. It was like hugging one of the statues in the park, except warm and it hugged back.

His back popped in three places when she squeezed.

"Take a break, give it a couple of weeks. But don't be a stranger, okay?" When she stepped away, she fanned her muscular fingers at the others. "Night, boys."

Ondrej and Klaus grumbled something like good night. Mark and Tobias nodded, the latter hunched with his hands in his pockets. Guess he wasn't getting a research paper out of this after all.

"Thanks for coming out, guys," Chris said they reached the tram. "Sorry about… acting like an ass."

Klaus clapped him on the shoulder. "Nah, man, you're good. Big heart. I told you, that girl didn't know what she had."

He backed toward the edge of the curb as the guys got on. "Night."

When the tram pulled away, Chris faced his brothers. "Let's go."

He was halfway down the block when he realized his brothers weren't following.

"Go where?" Tobias asked delicately. "Exactly."

"After Fi," Chris said.

"I think that pencil-legged ninny made herself perfectly clear," Mark snapped, hands on hips.

Chris closed the distance fast enough that even Mark jerked. He showed teeth and let Woof back him up. "Don't. Talk. About my girl. Like that."

Mark's eyes flashed yellow, but he held up his hands and backed up a step. "You're right. Sorry. But tell me why I shouldn't think—"

"She's going after him alone," Chris said, continuing his way before muttering, "again."

"It's either the person that burned down the shop or the one they've been trying to find. Maybe both." Tobias jogged to catch up. "She does this often?"

Chris snorted. His temples throbbed.

Mark sighed and brought up the rear. "I'd say she fits right in."

"Isn't that the friend?" Tobias asked. "Ofelia's. The one who invited you."

Turned out having a mega-observant brother came in handy. Chris scanned the street to see Ayele getting into a sleek cherry-red AMG.

Chris wolf-whistled loud enough to catch her attention. "Nice ride."

"I'm afraid I can't help you anymore, Christof." Ayele shook her head.

"I figured you got busted calling us in," he said. "But maybe if, while giving a couple of guys a ride home, you had to make a stop on the way..." He spread his hands.

Ayele considered him. "You know your way around words very well."

"We had to learn or nobody was having any fun growing up," he said, jerking a thumb in either direction to take in his brothers.

Markus looked pointedly at Toby. "Well, this guy didn't believe in fun for a long time."

"Shut up, ingrate," Toby said cheerfully, striding ahead. "We would appreciate the ride, Miss—"

"Yele is fine." She unlocked the doors.

"I'm up way past my bedtime." Mark slapped Chris on the shoulder on his way past. "You owe me a haircut."

Chris exhaled, laughing. "Deal."

CHAPTER FORTY-ONE

Ofelia's cab let her out in front of the glittering, glass-walled high-rise apartment building.

The doorman was absent, double panes of glass sliding open unattended as she approached. At the desk, the night watchman slumped over his station. Asleep. Legs? She leaned over to key in the code for the private elevator—nothing happened. She swore. Without the fob for access to Kenneth's floor, the main elevator wouldn't be of use.

She was hunting for the master fob when elevator doors opened, bearing a middle-aged cleaning woman pushing and her small cart of supplies. A linen handkerchief was wrapped around the front of her dark hair, but the rest of it cascaded over her shoulders and down her back to her waist.

Ofelia didn't hesitate. "Hold the doors, please."

Inside the small space with the cleaning woman, a wave of familiarity washed over her. "Do I know you?"

"What floor?" the woman asked in strangely accented Czech. Old; it sounded so very old.

"Penthouse," Ofelia murmured.

"You are sure?" The woman stared at her, one tough, stained finger hovering over the button.

Ofelia frowned, annoyed. "I'm expected."

"That is true." The woman pressed the button, using the master fob on her belt. "Though be wary of the one who waits."

Ofelia blinked. Were they in the elevator anymore? She could hear birds and beasts moving through a forest that she could not see. The scent of herbs she could not name rose from the woman's cart.

She met the woman's eyes. Those strange pale irises seemed to change continually, like waters of a pond rippling in the wind. "This is a dangerous road you walk alone. Even I took my sisters with me, young though they may have been."

Ofelia tried to rouse herself, but her attention was fixated on trying to remember where she'd seen the woman before.

"You are already brave." The strange woman smiled, her ancient Czech lilting and sure. "Be clever, witch. Be clever."

Ofelia stepped out when the doors opened. She gave one final look to the name tag half covered by long dark hair and was only able to make out the first three letters.

The doors closed. When they opened again, the elevator was empty. She blinked. Now she recognized her. The face from her postcard on her altar, the one that had stared at her from a window in a tourist shop her first week in town. Kazi. Herbalist and healer.

Kenneth's apartment was a wreck. But it wasn't a ransacking or a robbery. It looked like it had been a fight. Ofelia hurried through the rooms, calling his name. She stopped in the bedroom.

Kenneth lay on the floor by the windows, bruised and bloodied, his neck at an unnatural angle. He'd been dead for hours. His phone was just out of his reach.

Ofelia exhaled softly, bile rising in her throat. She hadn't hated him even at his worst. Only wanted better for him, for him to be the man she thought she'd known in those early days.

"Too late." Legs sucked his teeth, stepping from the hallway.

Ofelia jumped, whirling on him with an immobilization charm ready.

He held up his hands in a gesture of innocence. "Arrived a few minutes before you. Wanted to check if the place was empty."

"Why should I believe you?" Ofelia snarled.

There was nothing hurried or furtive in his gaze.

He didn't answer. Without taking his eyes off hers, he carefully stepped around her, crouching by the body. He spread his hands over Kenneth's battered face.

"What are you doing?" Ofelia snapped herself out of her stupor, horrified.

His magic smelled like dried roots and upturned soil, dusty corners, and the sickly-sweet flavor of old liquor.

When he rose, knees popping, at first glance it appeared nothing had changed. Kenneth was still dead, except the bruises were gone and his neck was fixed.

"What did you do?" Ofelia froze, her gaze stopping, horrified at the sight of the syringe and the vial beside his arm.

"A lot less questions get asked when things look a certain way, no?" Legs sat back, satisfied. "Another dealer done in by his own vices. For the good of the public if you ask me."

"Covering your tracks," Ofelia countered, steadying herself.

Kenneth was dead. The initial shock faded, and she was left with the cold certainty that she was close now. She had to see this through.

"Easier to find who did this without any competition from local law enforcement." He smirked.

Ofelia turned to him. "And you would avenge him."

Legs snorted. "I may not have thought much of him, but Kenneth was one of mine. People knew what he carried. I can't have someone interrupting my chain."

Disgust curdled in the back of her throat.

"Think what you like, Miss Ofelia," he said mockingly. "But I'd say we both have much to lose if there's too much mystery around Kenneth's demise. Your shop burned down today, no? That shop he claims you started together." He went on when she was silent. "Now you've broken up and he's dead."

Ofelia's limbs tensed and a chill raced through her. "He said he wanted no part—"

"Who heard him?" Legs murmured, cupping his ear. "One of your little spy bees? The gods?"

"We don't need gods—we have necromancers." She glared at the man. "Let him summon Kenneth to give up his killer."

"Meanwhile you're stuck in an interrogation room, trying to hide your gifts from that death dealer's people." He snarled. Then his face relaxed and he smiled again, sanguine. "Anyway, the only necromancer I care about is not on this continent."

Her mind raced through all the hidden city's known enemies from the àjé records. Most of the world didn't know the witch state existed. But Amanirenas had been around for thousands of years. Had she made enemies this generation wasn't aware of?

She needed to know if he was working with anyone and soon, because if Ayele alerted the àjé that she was with their prime suspect, they might sweep in before she could confirm his connection was to the witch hunter.

She couldn't let him go now. "How did you and Kenneth—"

"Kenneth was looking for something new to offer his clients."

"And you gave him Hexenblut."

He spread his palms. "Ask and you shall receive."

"The sample you gave me was tainted. You could have killed a mortal."

His brows lifted. "Was it?"

"You knew." Ofelia watched him. "Why?"

"Testing the strength of potential allies is an old habit."

Ofelia coughed with surprise. "Allies."

Did he think he was recruiting her?

He stared at the lifeless body before meeting her eyes. "I should have known better than letting him talk me out of getting you involved in the first place."

"Me?"

"I took his word that you were nothing but a pretty face. He had no idea what he had in you, did he?"

Ofelia looked away.

"But *you* would never have wound up like this."

Ofelia stilled. "The bees."

She flexed her fingers to recall them.

A faint hum preceded the two small bronze figures wavering through the air as they found her wrist. One at a time they stung her, and her mind flashed with images.

He'd started his text to her six hours ago. She projected what she saw on the wall, slowing down shortly after the time of the unfinished text.

"There," Legs said.

A hulking figure crouched over Kenneth's body on the floor of the bedroom, and Kenneth went from being still to flopping weakly. She scrolled back, slowly reversing through the whole apartment being ransacked as he was dragged into the bedroom and beaten, his early attempts to fight off his adversary, all the way back to him letting his killers in the front door.

She recognized one face. "Warlock."

"Gesundheit," Legs said, amused.

Ofelia narrowed her eyes, pointing out the tall, pale man. "Calls himself Manhammer. Creepy fundamentalist. Doesn't believe witches should be 'fraternizing with shifters.'" She swallowed. "But he's not a killer."

Legs stared back innocently. "Technically he only watched."

She turned to him. "Kenneth wouldn't have been dealing blood if you—"

"We can play the game if you'd like." He looked at the image, bored. "But Kenneth is mort. And this warlock, as you so hilariously call him, is getting away."

A knowing toggled her awareness. What had Cilka said about the coven's plan to do something about the witch hunter? She exhaled, letting her body relax and the emotion fall away so that memories could slide into place. She didn't close her eyes, not trusting Legs. It took longer than usual, but at the end she gasped. It couldn't be tonight. New moon.

When she returned to her senses, Legs watched her, a bit too much like a child considering whether they would trap or squash an interesting bug for her comfort.

Mistaking him for an ally might get her killed. Or worse. But they had an enemy in common now. And staying close to him might get her to the witch hunter and give her valuable information to pass to Baako.

"I know where to find them." On her way to the door, she grabbed Kenneth's keys. "Do you know how to drive?"

"You don't drive?"

"My parents died in a car crash." She cast one last look toward the open bedroom door, thoughts shivering around the body within.

He tutted at her like a disappointed grandmother but took the keys. But she turned in time to see a glitter of something like recognition in his eyes. "Did they now?"

CHAPTER FORTY-TWO

YELE DROVE like she'd been born behind a wheel, catching his brothers up the entire time. Tobias looked like he might be mildly ill by the time she pulled off the ring road to the fancy high-rises in the newer part of town.

"I think she's gone after that Leggo guy," Yele finished. "There's only one place I can think— Oh shit."

Police and emergency vehicles lined the street ahead, lights flashing. Mark leaned forward, pointing out the nondescript black cars. "Azrael's security."

"This is her ex-boyfriend's apartment?" Tobias asked as they all hunched a little.

Ayele nodded.

Chris leaned forward slightly to peer out the window at the glass building. Had Ofelia stayed here at some point? He really needed to get his shit together.

The EMTs were wheeling out a stretcher and a body bag.

"Slow down and open a window on this side." Mark leaned between the seats to take in the scene. "Please."

Ayele muttered a few words as the window descended, and Chris felt the tingle of magic against his skin. Some kind of shielding. She glanced into the back seat curiously.

Mark inhaled, and his eyes went nearly yellow in the dark. He opened his mouth slightly and sniffed. When he sat back, he nodded. "Keep driving. They're gone."

Ayele accelerated, checking him in the mirror a few times. Chris knew what she would find. A perfectly human face, hazel eyes, and a know-it-all smirk.

"They were there," Mark said. "Ofelia's scent is tangled up with something old."

"Musty?" Chris asked, suspecting.

"Like something out of an old bottle," Mark said. "Poison pretending to be wine."

"And Kenneth—" Ayele said.

"Dead," Mark said, considering. "Did he use?"

Ayele shook her head. "Not while he was with Fi."

"Then either he started up or he was murdered." Mark nodded, then added, "OD'd. Hours ago. Doesn't fit our timeline."

"You got all that just by sticking your head out the window?" Ayele asked.

Mark looked affronted. "I didn't stick my head—"

"He's always had the best nose." Chris glanced toward his brother. "It's gotten worse over the years."

"Libuše," Mark said.

"The dead witch?" Ayele said.

"Prague's patron witch," Chris clarified. "She gave us all a gift. Well, heightened the ones we had. The nose, the brains."

"And you?"

Chris shrugged, looking out the window. Nothing had changed for him. He didn't understand why. Maybe it wasn't like it was for his brothers. Maybe it was because he hadn't met his mate. That was what triggered the city's patron witches to appear, wasn't it? Maybe that was a sign too. Ofelia hadn't mentioned being visited by a very old, strange witch as Evie had. Maybe that was the proof he should have focused on.

He couldn't make her want him the way he wanted her. Couldn't make her see a forever. Not when she was so determined to walk alone. He'd made a promise they'd finish this together. And then... "Can you track her?"

"If I could do that, would we be driving around town with your brother sticking his head—nose—out the window?" Ayele sucked her teeth.

Chris waited.

"Lost her outside the club," Ayele admitted, frustrated and, he suspected, a little worried. "There's some kind of block on her, and I'm not strong enough— We're better off relying on Markus's nose."

"Doesn't quite work like that," Mark said wryly. "Scent's cold from here."

"Could you break through it?" Chris asked, praying Yele would know what he meant when he spoke next. "If you were strong enough."

Ayele looked at him wide-eyed.

"The road," Chris said gently. "Watch the road."

She returned her gaze, hands fixed on the wheel. But it was like she was somewhere else entirely. "I can't do that, Christof."

"You can," he said. "I know the deal, but this is— You know she can't take him on her own. I have to be there when she needs me."

"Spiders don't take concords."

"All àjé know the charms." He'd seen that much.

"What are you two talking about?" Mark's gaze bounced between them.

Tobias held up a hand, and wonder of wonders, Mark shut up for once.

"Maybe you should pull over here," Chris suggested. "Probably shouldn't be on the road when you do it."

She nodded and eased the car into a waiting zone, ignoring the valet. Or rather doing something that made the man do an abrupt about-face and return to his station without a backward glance.

"You're pretty powerful," Chris said, awed.

"Not enough apparently," Ayele said grimly. "Ready?"

She gripped his wrist and tapped him swiftly and without preamble. He remembered the sensation from the arena. He grunted, bracing a hand against the dash.

"What the fuck is she doing to him?" Mark growled.

Tobias held him back, watching Chris's face. Chris nodded in gratitude, unable to speak.

Ayele sucked in a hard breath, and the link deepened for a painful second. She severed the connection, leaving Chris gasping against the window.

"Seven forgive me," she said, fingers flexing on the wheel. "Are you—"

"Fine." He coughed. "Gimme a minute."

"Some kind of power transfer," Tobias murmured before Mark could start up again. "From him to her so that she could do something to find—"

"It worked—I've got her again." Ayele glanced at Chris, worried.

He shook his head, splaying a hand over his chest. "Go."

She jerked the car onto the road and picked up speed.

"Can they all do that?" Mark hissed. "Witches?"

"Where I come from, yes," Ayele said. "Shifters are naturally energy abundant. Transformation requires it. We have learned to utilize it."

She gave them a crash course on the concord bond and the àjé.

Chris exhaled and leaned back against the headrest in relief. Keeping secrets from his family had been much harder than he expected. He mouthed, "Thank you."

She gave him a weak smile, brows still knitted in concern. He wanted to reassure her. Already his strength was returning, pouring out from the center of his chest to his fingertips. But he still shook a little bit. He concentrated on a few deep breaths, like Ilya had taught him, remembering the great bear's hand splayed over his solar plexus to help focus his awareness.

"This is your assignment?" Tobias said, wondrous. "You come from a place with enough highly trained witches—àjé—to send out spies—Spiders?"

Ayele half smiled. "I think you know the answer to that, smart wolf."

"The African territory," he said, pressing into the gap between front seats. "Mama Mu—"

"They don't call her that." Chris cut a glance toward his brother.

Tobias's focus switched to Chris. "You and Ofelia, you did this… concord bond?"

"She turned me down."

"But you don't need a bond. Ayele just drew on you."

"It's not the best way." Ayele flexed the hand that had touched Chris as if trying to release tension after holding something too tightly. "It can be intoxicating, that much power. Easy to lose control. And with your brother it is… particularly difficult."

Mark swore. "You were gonna sign up for this shit?"

"Like you wouldn't for Evie." Chris snorted. "Tobias. If you could give that to Bebe, you wouldn't?"

"I *trust* Evie," Mark said. "Evie doesn't walk away from me every chance she gets."

"She did try," Tobias noted. "A couple of times."

"The fuck, Toby. That's not the point. You hear this shit?"

"I also heard that *she* wouldn't do it," Tobias said. "He offered. You can't compare you and Evie or Barbara and me. They aren't there yet."

Chris looked over his shoulder into the back seat. Tobias met his eyes with a little nod that said *I see you. I believe you*, then turned to Ayele again. "What makes Chris different?"

"Heartlight, you call it?" Ayele said. "It's a well of power to draw on.

It's nearly impossible to tap out. But it's very rare. And I've never heard any shifter—wolf or otherwise—to have it."

Tobias was uncharacteristically silent.

Chris finally felt steady enough to speak. "Mom told me it was my strength, that I could draw on it to protect myself, energetically speaking, but she never knew how it came to me or why."

Ayele eyed him as if she was trying to figure out if he was kidding. She laughed, shaking her head.

"That your mother—and your wives—are so powerful is a testament to their determination and resourcefulness. For us, knowledge is passed down through lineage. It may begin with a charm—a gift, you call it?"

"Barbara's grace." Tobias nodded.

"Notion," Mark murmured. "That's what Evie uses with the girls."

Ayele nodded. "But that isn't enough to reach our full power. We must be raised, so to speak, by more-powerful witches. The original covens were great schools of our craft. Many were faltering in the modern age, even before godswar. After, well, the necromancers took our records and broke the last of the circles. We believed that was the death knell for many of the great lines outside the territory."

"But not in Africa?" Tobias said.

"Publicly, Amanirenas stood with the Allegiance," Ayele said. "She had to. But the condition of her joining was that the rest of the Allegiance send magical creatures to us. And what goes on inside a necromancer's territory is their own business, yes? Ours is sanctuary."

"And they agreed?" Mark scoffed.

"Most of them," Ayele said. "Including Azrael."

In the silence, Chris wondered what his brothers were making of the knowledge the threat they lived under was still a danger, but it was also a chance at the kind of freedom they couldn't imagine.

Still, Tobias surprised him with an entirely different question. "The one-eyed Kush warrior queen? She took the name or is she the real thing—do you know?"

Chris groaned. Trust Tobias to turn everything into a history lesson. "Not now, Professor."

"She regenerated the eye about a thousand years ago, give or take." Ayele glanced in the rearview. "Yes. Fifi's ancestors, and mine—who gave her shelter until her powers were strong enough to protect all of us. In return, she gathered us—you call them witches—from all over the continent and raised a hidden city where supernatural beings are safe."

Tobias clapped his hands in delight. "She's a necromancer! Of course she is."

Ayele caught Chris's gaze with a question in her brows.

"He is *always* like this." He laughed.

"Amanirenas was a great general and strategist and a fighter." Tobias ignored them. "Rome spent so much trying to defeat her armies they eventually gave up trying to collect taxes and made a treaty that basically upheld their traditional boundary with Egypt and kept Kush an independent kingdom for another three hundred years."

"Much of that was before she came into her powers." Ayele shrugged. "Some say she might not have if it weren't for her son."

"He was wounded in battle," Tobias said eagerly.

"Not battle." Ayele's answer was grim. "A mercenary team was hired to kill her. He sacrificed his life so that she would live. In her desperation to save him, she turned him into what he is now. The shadow that never fades."

Chris thought of the figure from the council room that never left Amanirenas's side.

"She knew that the key to survival, for all of us, was unification and that someday the others would see it. The time has not yet come. And until it does, I must ask for your silence. Chris took a vow, which is why he was not permitted to tell you this himself."

"And why are you?" Mark asked slowly.

"There are many àjé who believe it is wrong to isolate," Ayele said with a little smile. "That we should share our existence, and knowledge, with powerful witches and allies outside the territory. With the knowledge that there is sanctuary for those who need it. My mothers are among them. It is a fragile cry still. It requires us to risk much. Perhaps someday I will get to meet your witches and they will see a place where their children never have to hide what they are."

Chris glanced back. His brothers were far too quiet for his comfort.

Mark reacted first. "That son of a bitch—he knew!"

Evie had escaped a death sentence the night her boss had finally gone down for all the terrible things he'd done. Azrael had allowed her to remain in the territory for the price of a single future favor.

"There is no death sentence." Tobias leaned back in his seat, and his eyes closed.

Sharing his life with his wolf had been the hardest on him. And now he had children of his own. Their parents had ensured that their family would always be a safe place, a circle in which they could be who they were without fear even if the outside world could not be trusted. Was he imaging what it would be like for the larger world to be the same?

"We're here." Ayele pulled off the road.

The old warehouses in the abandoned freight station reminded him of Vyšehrad and his long afternoons with Ofelia. He shook off the memory.

Chris leaped out of the car at the familiar snap of energy in the air. Ofelia's magic.

"Christof, where are you going?" Ayele asked.

He stopped fighting the anger he'd denied all his life. The anger that had once given him the courage to pick up a wooden board with an old rusty nail.

Woof surged in his chest, transforming his hands, his vision, his stride.

Ofelia was in the train station again, this time all by herself. But he wasn't a boy alone against bullies anymore. He was going to get his girl back and put a stop to whatever thought the witches in his city were fair game.

He ripped off his jacket.

"What about a plan?" Ayele said, hand on hips.

Mark's voice tangled with a growl. "We are the plan."

"You'd best stay here," Tobias said as he pulled off his glasses. "Would you mind holding these?"

"Stop," Ayele said, the word imbued with a power that froze all three long enough to return their focus to her.

All three wolves looked back at her, surprise lowering their ears.

"Now that I have your attention." She bared her teeth, hands on hips. "*This* is what we're going to do."

CHAPTER FORTY-THREE

Legs parked Kenneth's BMW outside a run-down warehouse. Ofelia leaned against the dash, peering into the darkness. Pressure formed against her eardrums. Powerful magic was swelling inside that building.

"This is it."

"You don't say," he drawled, climbing out of the car in front of the thick chain that served as a gate.

The train depot near the cemetery had been mostly abandoned when the freight lines were rerouted in the south of the city. The rails had been pulled up, and patches of weeds sprouted in the jagged cracks along the pavement. Any windows not boarded up had been shattered; anything of value had long ago been stripped. There was no sign of a security patrol even.

"Manhammer's leading a circle tonight," she said, swinging a leg over the chain, "to protect the witches of Prague."

Déjà vu swept over her, a reminder of another train station and another time.

Legs exhaled sharply as if catching a laugh.

"What's funny?" She slowed her approach at the deep shadows around the building.

"I suppose when Kenneth is found dead, he'll have proved the 'efficacy' of his spell," Legs mused, "and they will believe him."

The smell hit Ofelia first, sickly-sweet with a metallic edge. Blood magic. She recoiled on instinct.

Legs didn't sidestep quick enough, and her shoulder brushed his chest. Her skin reacted immediately, prickling as though a hundred tiny legs had raced over the spot in unison. For a second, she wasn't sure it was cloth she'd touched, couldn't be confident there was skin and bone beneath.

She jerked away. The glance Legs slid over her was oily and oddly possessive.

"What are you?" she asked aloud for the first time.

"I've been given to believe it was the height of rudeness to ask such a question in these perilous times," he drawled, unfurling that too-wide grin that reminded her they were not allies.

Whatever he was, he was mortal enough. She had to find out how he was getting the blood for the drug and use him to get closer to the witch killer. And that meant staying close.

"Where are you going?" she hissed as Legs lengthened his stride away from her.

She almost reached to stop him but recoiled before her fingers could brush his coat.

"Got to be a back way in," he whispered theatrically. "Wait here. We'll decide on a strategy when I get back."

Ofelia bristled, but he was suddenly out of reach, had moved too fast for her to block his path. If she raised her voice to protest now, she might give them away. She glared into the darkness where Legs had disappeared. Silence. She swore, pulling back into the shadow of one of the smaller buildings.

Alone, she reconsidered her theories. If Legs was responsible for the drug, he was on Manhammer's shit list too. Could Manhammer be the witch hunter after all—taking out witches that refused to serve his True One?

"Fuck this," she muttered. She might not be a fully trained àjé, but she was witch enough to handle Manhammer.

She left the shadows, aiming for the only visible warehouse door opposite the direction Legs had taken. If she was lucky, they would pin Manhammer between them, cutting off his escape.

The warehouses were dark, external lighting failing. She expected to encounter some resistance, magical or physical—guards or the bruisers who had done the dirty work at Kenneth's apartment, but there was nothing. Perhaps Manhammer thought he was far enough away from the city not to need a guard.

The low drone of a chant reached her first. She clung to the shadows, surveying the room. A splinter of light across the floor led to an open door like an arrow, shooting the horrifying scene.

There were no guards because the warlock had sacrificed them first. They looked pale but otherwise untouched.

On the other side of the altar, a ceremonial circle had formed. She recognized a few of the fourteen witches sitting around an enormous copper disk as being from her own circle, including Cilka. Each witch had brought their own light, and the red-gold flicker of candles punctuated by the occasional electric lantern created the odd lighting. They were too still. Each rested an arm over a depression with a shallow gash running along the skin. Most had dropped their knives. Their faces were blank, and a static gray sheen coated their eyes as their own lifeblood drained away. So that was what the guards' blood had been used for—the initial spell to overpower them.

The witches' blood flowed down a long channel to a shallow basin at the foot of the altar. Manhammer, in a gaping robe with arms raised, stood before an enormous grimoire, its pages rustling with energy. The blood pooled in a shallow tub near his feet. The chanting was his voice multiplied by the force of that spell. It was like a scene out of an old B-rated horror movie, and she would have laughed if the reality hadn't meant she was losing her witches to whatever madcap scheme this was.

Her witches.

Ofelia had returned to Prague to build her dreams because it was the place she'd known the greatest happiness. The last place she'd felt truly loved.

At last she understood why her parents had sacrificed everything to stop the witch hunter. Her mother had left active service for the life of an exile. Her father had no ties to the hidden city, no loyalties to a place he'd heard only stories of and that had abandoned the world's witches to protect their own. But when her mother had accepted, he had joined her.

Because the hunter was a danger to everything they'd built. Everything they loved.

Certainty burst in her like a wild rush. Stopping the witch hunter, and this warlock by extension, had never been about vengeance.

She loved this city, her shop and her home, and Ayele, whom she rarely deserved and was the best friend she'd ever had.

She loved these witches, and she wanted to guide them as much as she wanted to protect them.

And she loved Chris with so much of her heart it seemed impossible that there was anything left.

She longed for him and a future together with a sudden urgency that overwhelmed her. Chris and his big, beautiful family of witches and shifters and whatever amazing new thing their children would be called this city home.

You don't belong to me, but you're mine. Chris's words rang in her rib cage.

Mine to protect. Mine to love.

It was not duty that had driven her mother into action. It was love. Love was all that had ever mattered.

That was her legacy.

She was her mother's daughter after all.

"Looks like things have gotten a little out of hand." Legs must have found a back door after all.

He made his leisurely way across the room as though watching a child who had made a big mess.

Good. If Legs kept Manhammer busy, she wouldn't have to watch her back while she figured out how to free her witches.

Focus. One of the witches made a soft sound of pleading, and Ofelia noted the tears running down a few of their faces. Others wore expressions of fear or rage, as if they knew what was happening to them.

"When I rise from the blood, I gain the power of the True One," the warlock intoned, just like one of those crappy old movies.

Ofelia stilled, eyes wide. He was going to *what now*?

She felt around for wards guarding the circle, but apparently the warlock hadn't thought that far. She supposed once he got what he needed for his bloodbath, he wouldn't care what happened to the witches.

Sure enough, he'd dropped his robes, revealing a pale, flaccid body covered in odd patches of body hair and faded, amateur tattoos.

Ugh.

"Oh no. Don't do it." Legs halted, hands on hips. His smile never faded.

The warlock stepped down from the dais and into the tub.

Gross.

She waved her fingers in front of the Cilka's face. "In the name of our mothers, I bid you to hear me and break from this spell. Release."

Nothing.

It had been worth a try. The warlock had been so sloppy—no wards, dead guards—she'd thought it had a chance of working without using too much power. Time for something a little more potent.

She whispered a word, and the bandolier over her chest returned to this realm from the hidden pocket of space Ayele had made for her, bearing a series of vials nested in a neat row. Each potion was specially concocted—a taste, a scent, and a bit of magic laced with intention. She slipped the Dreaming free, followed by the Waking. She dipped her thumb into the Dreaming, then streaked a drop of oil over each forehead until she'd completed the circle, then her own brow before she closed her eyes.

The dream plane was warm but featureless. She hadn't had time for much. The witches milled about, blinking and rousing.

"What has he done to us?"

"This isn't what he promised!"

"He's killing us."

"The book is dangerous. It's not what he thinks."

Someone began to cry.

"Listen!" Ofelia called, ringing her voice with intention and command.

They stilled as one, watching her.

She wanted to wring each of their necks for following a self-proclaimed warlock so blindly into a spell. Didn't they know any better?

She looked around in the timeless bubble of space that defied real-world time. Many were young, but even those who weren't had the same look about them—harried and searching. Lost. She recognized it. A witch might choose solitude in their lifetime, but it was a choice. These had grown up alone. No one to train them, to guide them. Their spells had been taken and their lines broken by necromancers.

The search for somewhere to belong had left them vulnerable. She didn't have to lead like the àjé, but she could lead them her way. Her first order of business—if they survived this—would teach them how to discern *who* and *when* to follow.

But first they had to survive this.

"I'm going to wake you, but you must run." No time for consolation. "I cannot protect you if you remain. Bandage your wounds enough to get away. Help each other. Go to your homes. Lock your doors." Then she added as an afterthought, "Eat beets. Take Iron. Maybe some red meat. And rest. When you are well enough, come to my shop. I will give you something to restore you, and we will rebuild."

It wasn't until the words left her that she realized it wasn't the store she was talking about. Not at all.

They nodded, looking to her as one. She smiled. "You're not alone anymore. I promise."

She dropped out of the dream.

When she opened her eyes, no more than a second or two had passed but she felt as though she'd been holding her breath for hours.

Legs hadn't moved from his spot as the warlock began to descend into the shallow depression.

Was he going to let the warlock *bathe* in blood?

Never mind that. She only had a few minutes more of distraction at best before she'd have to cover their escape.

"Need some help?" Ayele said beside her.

Ofelia had never been so glad to see her. She placed a smaller vial of Waking in her hand and nodded. "Just a drop. And the chant—"

"For ending the dream," Ayele finished. "Basic charm craft, Fifiti."

Ofelia could have wept with relief. A fully trained Àjé witch was an asset she hadn't counted on.

"I've got you." Ayele squeezed her wrist.

They went around the circle in opposite directions. By the time they reached each other again, the spell had dissolved, rousing the witches. A few were disoriented, listing and blinking. But enough had heeded her warning in the dream. They moved quickly, bandaging their arms and helping those beside them.

Ofelia met the eyes of ones who searched for confirmation in her. "Go."

The strongest rose, shaking with blood loss but holding out their hands to each other. Two were too weak to stand. One was so inconsolable he listed against the floor, weeping.

A shriek tore the preternatural quiet. The sound stirred the witches around her into faster movement.

The warlock had stepped into the blood, but it wasn't the shallow depression he expected. His leg disappeared to the thigh, and he tipped forward, hands thrashing wildly at the rim to catch himself.

Something else moved in the tub, roiling beneath the surface, too big for the small depression.

The warlock kept screaming, flailing as his body was dragged into the dark liquid. "This wasn't what you promised!"

Ofelia couldn't find it in her to pity him, but her heart raced anyway. The witches were still in danger. Whatever had been created by their blood would be hungry for it now.

"I have to stop it," she shouted at Ayele over the shrieks. She urged the nearest witches on. "Run!"

Ayele braced one of the weaker witch's arms over her shoulders and whistled. "Time for reinforcements."

Before Ofelia could ask what she meant, two wolves charged through the doorway. One was midnight dark, the other so silvery pale it might have been the full moon in the sky. The pale one brushed her side on his way to his brother's side.

"Woof." She greeted him with giddy relief.

One ear flicked back in answer but his eyes remained locked on the shrieking man.

They positioned themselves between the fleeing witches and whatever was in that tub.

A tall, bookish man followed, hurrying to the last of the witches.

"What are we up against?" Tobias scooped the unconscious witch off the cement with thoughtless ease.

The blood roiled as patches of darkness denser than shadow emerged from the tub, taking impossible shapes. The head of one beast, the tail of another, some with horns and claws and others with the suggestion of scales or spines. They split as they rose, pausing to lap at the blood covering them.

"Demons." She counted six—a full clutch. She'd only heard of magic this powerful, or terrible, in stories. "No idea how a third-rate charlatan like Manhammer got his hands on the spell or how he thought a clutch of demons was going to boost his power."

Blood magic had a way of amplifying charms but could drain a witch much faster and was not to be undertaken unless the need was great. Some claimed there was no need so great. No wonder Manhammer had not used his own. She thought of her mother. Did she have to open her own veins, or was she already bleeding out by then?

The last remained in the soup, hunched over a broken figure slumped in the dark liquid.

Tobias grunted something like agreement, shifting the prone witch. "I understand you're a powerful wit—àjé."

"I am."

"I know our wolves are resistant to magic, but this…"

He knew enough about demons to understand the danger then. Good. A single touch from that oily darkness was toxic to most magical creatures and fatal to most humans.

"Normal wolves wouldn't have a chance against a demon," she agreed. "But shifters are special. It's what makes you extraordinary allies."

That seemed to satisfy him.

"Help is on the way." He didn't tell her to be careful or warn her against fighting. She respected that. "How long can you hold them?"

"Long enough," she promised.

The witch in his arms was pale, his breath a shallow flutter.

"Take care of them, please." Ofelia met his eyes.

He gave a quick glance at his brothers. "You too."

When he was gone, Ofelia stepped between the two wolves and cracked the vial for Protection, spreading the contents between her palms. The black wolf's growls rose to a new pitch.

"They're fresh—now is our best chance to stop them." She lifted her fingers and her charm flared, spreading the mixture over both. "They'll have the same vulnerabilities of any other animal—eyes, jugular, belly. Look out for the tails—stingers carry poisons."

The black wolf glanced at her, winked as if saying, *It's not my first rodeo.*

Seven bless him, she laughed.

The nearest demon's nostrils flared, edges wrinkling. When the depthless pits of eyes swung toward her, Ofelia fought the urge to step back.

Instead, she bared her teeth and flexed her will.

The demon lowered its snout, baring rows of teeth black as oil sludge. Mark broke from her side, flat out, tail up, ears up. The demon didn't notice him, not at a first. It knew only the scent of witch blood. Plus the wolf didn't attack. Instead, he seemed to miss the demon entirely, racing past the snout. In one fluid leap, he twisted in midair, latching onto the massive throat beneath the jaw. For a moment they blurred into a single dark shape, but where wolf fur caught the light and shone, the demon was an unceasing void. The wolf's momentum turned the strength of that bite into a tearing attack.

The demon let out a fox-like scream as smoky ichor poured from its jaw. It dropped to one knee, skidding to the floor.

The black wolf didn't hesitate. As soon as his paws touched down, he launched himself again, this time landing on the demon's back. His jaws closed over the back of the supernatural beast's neck, and something within gave a jarring sound of shattering glass.

The demon collapsed into a steaming mass, and the black wolf leaped away.

One down, five to go.

The black wolf threw her another one of those sly, yellow-eyed glares. He lifted his head and howled as demon blood faded into wispy smoke from his massive jaws.

Five void-dark heads swung his direction. Now they were paying attention. Mark jigged sideways, drawing three away from the door.

Woof brushed her thigh, jaws snapping. The trailing two had turned their attention back to the fleeing witches.

"Let's dance." She braced her wrists against each other and snapped out a ward to block the demon in front.

Woof raced into their midst. The one in the back had the forelegs of a deer, agile but slim. When the pale wolf's jaw snapped the first foreleg, the hair-raising sound of broken glass grinding on itself made her teeth ache.

When the demon buckled, Woof used its weight, rolling it until what passed for a belly was exposed. The demon shrieked as the pale wolf found his target and emerged from the vapor of its remains.

She cast a net of light over the remaining demon, drawing it tight with one clawed hand. It slammed into the floor, pinned.

At a yelp, she glanced back to see the black wolf hit the floor and roll, claws scraping pavement as he tried to regain his feet. The lion-headed demon swung toward him as a scorpion's tail unfurled around its hind legs.

Ofelia twisted her wrist and clenched her fist, tying off the net and sealing her demon inside. With her free hand, she pulled liquid from the floor, turning it to shards of ice and sending it slicing toward the lion-headed demon.

It wouldn't stop it, but it was enough for the wolf to regroup and launch himself at the lion. This time he went straight for the base of the tail, yanking it off with one savage shake of his head.

The demon shrieked and spun, catching the wolf across the side with one massive paw.

The black wolf flew into the bronze disk with a clang that resounded like a bell and staggered before falling.

Woof made an anguished sound from where he barred the path to the door.

"I've got this one," Ofelia shouted.

He raced between the lion-demon and his brother.

She turned her back to the wolves and the altar. The remaining demon was headed for the open door. Weapons weren't her strength—offensive magic took much more training. She had nothing on hand that would take out a demon entirely.

But not all poisons were made to kill.

She tapped Disorientation from her bandolier and hurled it to the ground at the demon's hooves. Then she stirred the air, pushing it into a funnel. The demon hesitated, spun, and ran into a wall, then backed up, spun again, and tripped over its hooves.

Ofelia clenched her teeth, exerting precious power to keep the wind circling the fog of disorientation. A burning began in her other forearm, the muscles straining to hold the light net on the thrashing demon she'd left behind. Sweat collected on her upper lip and the hollow of her throat. The demon in the net fought with increased strength.

She hoped Tobias's reinforcements wouldn't take much longer.

A wolf snarled somewhere in the room, claws scrabbled on concrete, and then the deadly silence of attack. Her heart knew it was Woof without looking.

The strain of holding two demons made her shake. Something hot dripped out of her nose—she tasted salt and iron. Blood.

"Enough," she snarled. She shoved her clenched hand under her nose, smearing blood over the spell for the light knot. She called on her ancestors, welcoming the blood debt she would happily repay to the ones who came before her if only it meant she could protect the wolf she loved. The last two names burned her heart. "Nyhira. Silvan."

Her heart stuttered as power exploded through her. A scream tore her throat raw. Then she twisted her fist as though she were wringing the last drop of liquid from a cloth.

The net flared, casting whole room in a silver glow. The trapped demon let out an eardrum-rattling howl, and the scent of burning made her stomach turn, but she kept twisting until the demon was a melting, shrieking void losing shape on the floor.

Without pausing, she whipped the net toward the disoriented demon. The strands flickered as the edges of her strength began to show, but she got most of it tangled up in the demon's forelegs. She doubled the wind and as the demon tripped in the net and dropped with a frustrated snarl.

Only then did Ofelia dare sneak a glance at the wolves.

Woof made his stand between the final demon and the black wolf. This demon had gained its full strength, casting the pale wolf in a shadow that dulled his coat.

The black wolf was still down. She felt for his pulse, the thread of his heartbeat. Brave, foolish wolf to fight without his witch at his side.

She would have to be enough witch for the both of them. Her fingers scrabbled along the bandolier as she hissed the words of a mirror spell. The vial containing Awake slipped out of her shaking grip. She swore, anticipating the shatter, but the glass held. A spiderweb fracture raced up its side, but none of the precious liquid escaped. She pinned the vial with her toe and sent a wave of power inside until the contents glowed.

The demon facing the pale wolf lowered its horned head, jowls dripping ichor that dissolved pits of concrete in the floor at its hooves.

Her arm shook with the effort of holding the disoriented demon. She whimpered. *Seven help me. Mama, lend me strength.*

Her opposite fingers twitched furiously to form the shapes needed to create the reflections.

Be patient—all good charms take time. Her mother's voice drifted out of her memory.

Timing was everything. She just needed the right moment. The light net flickered; the wind died down. She let them go, setting her demon free.

At the seventh repetition, she kicked the vial and cast the diamond that had formed in her palm. The vial shattered against the concrete at the black wolf's side as the demon lunged. But instead of two wolves, there were now fourteen. In every facet, the black wolf lifted his head. The demon hesitated, wheeling as the flicker of movement appeared at its flank. Confused, it spun again.

Woof lunged at its exposed jugular, teeth bared.

Ofelia turned to see the demon she'd been holding shaking off the tatters of her light net. Soulless eyes fixed on her as its nostrils flared. Scenting her blood, no doubt.

Fantastic. At least it wasn't looking at the door. Where was Legs?

Hands occupied, Ofelia wiped her shoulder under her nose. The bleeding had slowed to a trickle. But using her own blood had slowed her down.

The demon charged.

She dropped to one knee—it would be better than falling when the full force of the charm tapped her—and lifted her arms over her head, summoning a shield.

The impact never came. Instead, metal sang through the air overhead. A half dozen spears, hastily formed of twisted rebar and railroad track, pinned the demon to the wall. It groaned. A sheet of metal slid in like a discus a second later, slicing the demon's head from its neck.

From the doorway, Evelia Acaz braced on bent knees, fingers clawed in the follow-through of the telekinetic throw. Sweat darkened her hair, and a flush rose high in her cheeks. Beryl came half a beat later, her focus making it clear she was funneling her strength to the younger witch. Remarkable. Ofelia had only seen anything like it among the àjé and their concords.

Evelia barely missed a stride, arrowing toward the altar and the remaining demon.

When she lifted her hands again, the bronze disk rose, shaking slightly before steadying. "Clear!"

Woof started his retreat. The demon struck, sending the pale wolf sliding. The dark wolf lurched to cover his brother's back.

The disk hurtled along the floor on its edge. The demon tried to dodge, but the disk caught its hind leg, shearing it away in a smolder of vapor.

Ofelia broke two vials in her palms as she ran—Strength and Resilience.

She skidded to her knees between the wolves, a hand in the coat of each, and let the last of her charm amplify the potion. Glaucous eyes met hers briefly, a flash of surprise.

"Take it to pieces," she muttered, tasting the blood in her teeth.

The wolves leaped in unison. The demon went down between them, and their snarls filled the air.

Relief took the last of her strength. She braced her hand on the floor as her vision wavered.

Slow claps filled the silence that fell when the last demon had evaporated.

Legs made his way to the front of the altar, his palms hitting one another with a dry, rasping sound. She'd lost track of him in the struggle. And there he stood, untouched.

Manhammer hadn't been surprised to see him. Cold sank into her core as suspicion bloomed in her chest.

"A full clutch of demons," he said. "Quite impressive, young lady."

"I had a little help." Ofelia reached for her charm, alarmed to find it nearly tapped out.

Across the room. Beryl and Evie had closed ranks just inside the door, the black wolf pacing a tight circle around them.

Ofelia hoped Tobias and Ayele had gotten the injured witches far away.

Legs stepped over what was left of the warlock in the stinking pool of old blood, and his lips unfurled into a smile too big with teeth too sharp to be human. "Kenneth had no idea what he had, did he?"

"Nor whom he dealt with." Ofelia stepped between the witches and Legs. "But I do."

Woof crowded against her, coat rippling with the tension of muscles beneath. She slid a hand into the thick, pale strands. His ear flicked back once, but his gaze didn't break from the figure growing impossibly taller before them.

"Papa Legba." Beryl's voice rose in the silence. "Master of the crossroads."

Ofelia almost gasped.

No one knew what came first—the human gods or the powerful beings that took their names and faces to walk among humanity. Elegba had been one of the many once held as gods. And in diaspora, gods traveled with their faithful to new lands and took new shapes, legends, and names.

Papa Legba was one of his. Legs. Perhaps his being revered as the opener of the gateway between worlds had been the key.

He was neither witch nor necromancer. But a god? It should have been impossible. Human possession by gods was not unknown, but human bodies could not contain the power of gods for more than a few days without burning out. And once the Allegiance of Necromancers had ended the godswar by barring gods from the earth, even those brief possessions ended.

Legs began to laugh, head thrown back and jaw unhinged like a snake.

His head snapped forward suddenly, and there was nothing human in that face. Words slurred around lips that were not built for the torrent of sound passing through them. "Not quite, mistress witch, but very good guess."

"Name yourself so that we may have honest dealings," Beryl demanded.

"Who are you to claim my name?" Legs challenged, still amused. "You who abandoned your people to coven here among these imitations. I've brought more powerful than you to their knees, mother witch."

Memories cycled through Ofelia's awareness like puzzle pieces. Legs knowing Kenneth was in trouble. What had the warlock said before he was incapable of more than screams? This wasn't what he *expected*.

"You set this up," Ofelia said. "The drug, the warlock, my shop. You sent him there to burn it down just like you sent him to kill Kenneth. You knew I would be at the club."

"You are a credit to your duplicitous kind." Legs spread his palms like a ringmaster and took a deep bow. "Well done—your mother would be proud."

Ofelia's heart was beating too fast, lungs too tight for the breath her body demanded as the certainty boomed in her chest. "You killed them."

"A worthy opponent." He chortled. "I have her to thank for everything, you know. She showed me the way. Well, her blood did."

"Why?"

"I think you know that, *àjé*," he purred.

"Ofelia," Beryl called, a low warning note in her voice. "Do not let him—"

"Why!" Ofelia shook her head against the warning, unable to tear her eyes from the creature in front of her. Her parents' killer. Witch hunter.

Her vision blurred. The pale wolf pressed into her side.

"Cry for your mother like a little girl if you wish." His smile was a tiny, amused thing, as though they shared a secret. "I watched my mothers forced into bondage and worse"—his voice rose and the smile died—"while that death-dealing bitch holed up in her sanctuary among her sycophant witches, all of them strong enough to fight the chains and the colonizers but choosing not to protect those outside their precious forty-two. Instead, they *hid*. Some warrior queen." He spat out the words. "I bred myself into the stolen ones, whittled myself down to this *nothing* to survive in the generations filled with pain, loss, displacement, my dreams bloody with hunger for vengeance. And now the time is at hand. Now that I have you."

"Me?" was all Ofelia had time to gasp before he swept a hand as if clearing a playing board.

All of them, witches and wolves, fell like discarded game pieces. Ofelia toppled into the wolf beside her and he braced, somehow managing to catch them both.

"Your mother's charm wasn't as strong. But she gave me my first clue. They snatched you from me at that boarding school. But then you returned, even stronger than before, reeking of àjé."

Disgust and hatred coated his voice.

Ofelia scrabbled at the edges of her drained charm for a shield, a deception, anything, as her fingers tugged at the remaining vials on her bandolier. Clarity rang through her like a bell.

Serwaah and the àjé had unknowingly saved her life when they took her from boarding school after her parents' death. At seventeen, she wouldn't have stood a chance against him.

She'd been overconfident, and her insistence on going it alone had isolated her, as had her fear of leading others into danger instead of using her knowledge to protect and empower them. He'd used her attachment to Kenneth to lure her, perhaps started him on the path of dealing Hexenblut to draw her out—maybe even to distract her. Surviving his attempt to poison her had revealed her charm. Even Manhammer had been a pawn, using her witches as bait, letting her and the Prague coven drain themselves fighting the warlock's demons.

Beryl and Evie were recovering. Ayele was with the witches. Witches who could have been her allies. Legs might be a demigod, but together, they probably could have stood a chance against him.

Now she was tapped out, facing the being that had slaughtered her parents. That her lover and his family stood with her made it the horror of her worst nightmare.

Woof transformed into that truly terrifying werewolf. His arms locked around Legs, dragging him off-balance.

"Fi, run!" he roared.

The echoes of another train station fourteen years ago chimed in her. A boy putting himself in harm's way to save her. She'd been running ever since. Maybe her objection to the concord was a really an unwillingness to let anyone sacrifice themself for her again, the fear that she wasn't worth that kind of oath.

Protection, not possession.

But the bond worked both ways: I will protect and fight for you. You will protect and fight for me. Together we are stronger for our vow.

She was done running.

"Eyes closed!" she shouted instead, throwing the vial for Confusion.

Chris tucked his chin. It exploded inches before the demigod's chest.

For an instant, as Legs staggered, she was sure it would work. If Markus and Chris could get him down, she and the witches could regroup—

Legs slid sideways through time and space, passing from Chris's hold like a phantom. He solidified and flung Chris to his knees. He flicked his other hand as if casting off an insect and sent Markus into the wall. The black wolf crashed with a yelp and lay still.

Chris's hands scrabbled at the demigod's wrist, but the grip was unyielding. As he fought, he began to shift, his body contorting unnaturally. Woof's howl became an agonized shriek as Chris was forced from any semblance of his wolf.

"The secret," Legs continued conversationally, as if forcing a shifter from his chosen skin hadn't cost him anything at all, "is in the blood. I've been collecting it, you see. Each bloodline has a different gift." His gaze settled on Ofelia with a smile that was almost tender. "Alone, thin and fragile, but combined, the possibilities become endless. Easily turned into a poison, as you well know. Or a drug to fund my efforts. And with your ability—changing to adapt to anything that counters it—a scourge of Hexenblut could be strong enough to kill that god-born whore you call a necromancer."

Chris sagged as if the strength had gone out of him. It threw Legs off-balance just enough. When Chris lunged, cracking his head into Legs's face, the demigod's nose shattered. Still human enough for now.

Legs wrestled Chris back under control, and the fingers of his free hand became slender talons. He lifted them over Chris's chest. "I have a taste for mongrel heart."

"Power!" Ofelia screamed, desperate. This was all about power.

Legs paused.

"The power fades quickly when we die, doesn't it? That why it's taken so long, collecting your bloodlines? It's why you can't just kill me for my blood to make your scourge."

Legs watched her, considering.

Chris's eyes opened wide, gaze locked on her face. "Fi—"

"You need a way to preserve it, don't you?" She could not look at him. If she did, she would break down, she would beg, she would fall apart, and Legs would rip Chris open before her eyes. She had to buy them both time.

"It's quite a pickle." Legs nodded.

"You need a carrier." She licked her cracked lips, tasting dried blood and sweat. The words scrambled desperately up her throat. "He's the key. He's witch blooded."

Ofelia didn't dare look at the sound of Evelia's curse or Beryl's gasp. Bile rose in her throat at what she was doing. If revealing a shifter went against everything she'd been taught, betraying him to their enemy was an unforgivable violation.

Legs shook his head once. "Impossible."

"Then kill him now," she said, counting on the fact that he'd never seen Mark in human form and would not know they were brothers. Legs might not guess Beryl was his mother, that there were other wolf-witch hybrids in the city. "But you'll never get another chance like this."

Legs brought one talon to Chris's neck. Ofelia fought the urge to scream. He drew blood, and Chris sucked in a hard breath but did not cry out. Legs brought the bloodied talon to his lips. His teeth shone in the low light, edged with red. "And this one will do my bidding?"

"He'll do mine," she said, feeling sick. "And if not, I'm sure you can find a way to motivate him."

Legs lifted Chris by the back of the neck, grinning into his face. "You see how treacherous these creatures can be. How little it takes for them to reveal their true nature."

"Touch her and I will use you to paint the walls." Chris spat in his face.

Legs ignored the threat and wiped his cheek, still smiling when he looked at Ofelia. "Why should I believe anything you say, witch?"

Ofelia rose to her full height but let her shoulders slump. She was not a spy like her mother had been, but everything was riding on her ability to pull off her next gambit.

"They sent my mother and father to their death and then tried to brainwash me into serving the necromancer who gave the order. I ran for a reason. I've seen the world and the ones they abandoned. Let the witch city burn for all I care. But Chris—" She didn't have to fake the crack in her voice. "He's everything to me."

Legs stared at her for too long. Ofelia swallowed but did not lower her eyes.

Finally he held out his hand. "Come and he lives. For now."

Without looking back, Ofelia walked to Legs's side.

He clutched her shoulder, squeezing so hard the bones ached, but she held her tongue. Then he led her to a back exit, dragging Chris behind them like an old doll. A van waited, and she recognized the driver as the hulking bruiser of a human who had led the ambush in Kenneth's apartment.

"Keep them away from each other." Legs flung her into the back of the van himself and shackled her wrists to the wall.

"No!" Ofelia struggled.

He grinned in her face. "If you think I'd trust a word you say, you're dumber than you look. But you will serve. For his sake."

She met his eyes, baring her teeth.

He patted her cheek. "I like you, girl. Perhaps I'll keep you."

Chris struggled, a kick slamming into the wall and almost succeeding in knocking the human down.

Legs hissed and twisted his talon wrist.

Chris slumped to the floor, gagging.

Legs smiled at Ofelia. "He'd better be worth my while, witch. Or you can watch while I end him very slowly."

The van doors slammed. The front doors closed, and the muffled sound of voices floated back as Legs gave instructions. The motor engaged with an electric whine, and they began to move.

"Chris," she whispered in the flickering light from the passing street-lamps, straining against the chains. "I'm sorry."

His voice emerged, hoarse and defeated. "Save it."

CHAPTER FORTY-FOUR

CHRIS SAGGED against the transport wall. Even with Ofelia a few feet away from him, he'd never felt so alone in his life.

He banged his head against the van a few times. Sometimes Woof responded if he was injured. But making himself see stars brought no sign of the wolf.

Woof was still a distant echo of a howl in his chest. There was nothing he could do to bring the wolf back.

And she'd just revealed his secret.

"I'm so sorry." Her voice broke, and the salt of tears reached his nose.

"You kept his attention on us."

Did she think after all these weeks he didn't understand her well enough to see it?

"You said it's about power." He pushed—they needed her smart and strong and fierce, as angry as she'd been when she had sent him and Mark after the demon with her charm surging in their chests, guarding their fierce hearts. Because he wasn't going to be good for much until Woof came back. "How do we get enough to end this guy?"

Silence. For the first time it occurred to him that they might be well and truly fucked.

"Ofelia," he said, the words coming from that same place that his wolf lived inside him. "You were the first magic I ever knew, and you're still the one that makes everything else feel possible. We take this thing to the end, you and me."

He took a breath, trying to come up with something else. He was shit at motivational speeches.

A second later came the sickening crunch of bone and her soft cry of pain. Desperation filled him.

"Fi!"

"I'll live," she muttered through teeth clenched in pain. "We need to touch for this— I need…"

He could have finished that sentence himself. He needed her. He crowded against her. "Yes."

"Listen to what I'm asking first—"

"Doesn't matter," he said stubbornly.

She sucked her teeth in the dark, and he imagined her expression. The one that said *I can't decide if I'm going to hex you or kiss you.* She exhaled sharply. He figured right now it was hex. He almost smiled.

"I have an idea," she said. "But I need to make sure he can't stop us. Even if he separates—or incapacitates—one of us."

This time the silence was full of something. He could feel the words stuck behind her lips, her hesitation to say them out loud.

"Would you still take me as your concord?"

The hesitation in her voice, laced with longing, splintered in his chest. It tempered the relief at the words, the quiet contentment of knowing that this was his path.

He knew how hard this was. How desperate she must be to reach for this. "Come here."

She slid as close to him as she could, one shoulder leaning into his side, her broken wrist cradled between them. She whimpered when they hit a rough patch of road. There was a roar growing in him, words clamoring from his heart, up his throat to his mouth and filling his head.

"When you saw the wolf in me—it changed my life," he whispered. Her breath stuttered against his skin. He wished he could put his arms around her. "Because of you, I never feared what I was. I've been waiting my whole life for someone to see me the way you did then. The way you *do*. It's always been you. I was made for this. I love you, Ofelia."

"And I thought it was just because I was the first girl who ever kissed you." She sniffled.

"Oh you *now* you got jokes?" He laughed. "Anyway, who said you were the first?"

She coughed a single bright chuckle.

His heart settled contentedly in his chest. "Now concord me, Princess."

She inhaled sharply as she forced the fingers of the hand with her broken wrist along his chest. It wasn't until the third pass that he realized she was tracing a sigil.

Erandi had shown him the mural honoring the concord bond; the sigil and the words taken in every vow were no secret. She sang them now under their rasping breath binding her power to his life, as surely as his was now bound to hers.

They whispered the words in the dark in unison. "Until we are called to the earth from where we came."

Blood and sweat blurred, heating wherever they touched until the sensation crested through him like a tsunami. When it broke, he felt the threads between them it left behind, anchoring them to one another. The steady pulse between them thrummed beneath his sternum. He realized that her heartbeat wasn't coming from the rib cage pressing into his. It came from within him. They inhaled together, each breath moving through them as though they were one animal. Her pulse sang in his veins. At last she rested her forehead on his collarbone, and they breathed out together.

"It feels… " he said, trying to capture something that denied words.

"Like it's always been this way between us."

Yes. That was it. Exactly.

Wonder clung to her voice, even gritty with determination. "Legs—whoever he is—has power that doesn't belong to him. We're going to take it back."

"Good plan," Chris said, tugging at his wrists. "Burn these off. He opens the door, I jump him, and you do the witch thing."

"He's going to be ready for that," Ofelia murmured with a little head shake. "We need to distract him."

He growled her name, not liking where this was headed.

"The charm needs time." Her eyes were bright with the defiance he recognized from their audience with the necromancer. She seemed to be speaking to herself now. "Patience. The best charms do."

Not this shit again. Once again she was plotting her next steps and leaving him behind.

"What does this have to do—"

"You must stay focused." She sounded distracted and the scent of her magic thickened. "No matter what happens to me. Ground yourself as soon as you can. You'll feel it when it's ready."

"Feel what?" Nope, he didn't like this at all. He was supposed to be protecting her while *she* did the big things. "What happens to—"

"A charm." She paused to correct herself. "Spell. And he won't see you coming because shifters don't have that kind of magic."

"Me?"

"I didn't lie to him—you *are* the key to everything," she said, smiling. "You're a wolf with Heartlight—witch enough to cast a spell, I think."

Before he could argue, she pressed her lips to his. His body responded automatically, angling to take control of the kiss in the way that made her breath catch. She slipped the spell into his mouth. It spread over his tongue, and Heartlight flowed up from the center of his chest to meet it.

He wasn't going to be able to stop her. And given the condition of his wolf, maybe it would be stupid to try. But she was right. He was a wolf with Heartlight. And whatever she was going to do next, she needed to be whole and stronger than before. He held on when she would have parted them, and when she gasped, he flooded her mouth with it. If it was all he could do for her now, it would have to be enough.

He felt the bones in her wrist knit in his own.

She stared at him in wonder as she rolled her newly repaired wrist. Her eyes widened when she wrapped her fingers around the chain and yanked the shackle from the wall with a speed and strength that was decidedly wolf. "Is this what it feels like… all the time?"

He showed his teeth with a nod and flexed until the weak link in his own chain gave. "Give him hell."

The transport jerked to a stop.

Chris scented chemicals and airplane fuel.

"What have you two lovebirds been up to?" Legs chuckled as the doors opened. "Time see if you truly hold the secret to my veng—"

Ofelia flew past Chris and flung herself at Legs, whipping the shackle ahead of her. He dodged, but it cracked him across the cheek. He reeled backward. She followed up with a kick to the chest. Legs skittered across the floor like a spider, but she gave him no quarter, striking out with the shackle as she stalked him away from the van.

Chris tackled the flunky to the ground before the man could jump in. His strength was back even if Woof was still painfully absent in his chest. The bigger man didn't stand a chance.

Chris abandoned the unconscious man and staggered after Ofelia, the charm unfurling rapidly in his chest. His knees buckled as it sang in his veins and he let himself be knit to it.

Chris looked up. Ofelia was on the defensive.

"Come on." He urged the spell with more intention as threads connecting charm and Heartlight doubled. Almost there.

Legs's face transformed in rage as he looked between them, realizing that he'd been tricked.

Ofelia cried out in victory. "Take back what doesn't belong to him."

Legs got ahold of the shackle and yanked. Ofelia hit the ground. He loomed over her, clawed hand raised.

Chris lurched to his knee and preparing himself for a desperate scramble to protect her. But her eyes froze him in place. So he closed his and grounded himself.

She was right—he *could* feel it.

The charm tore from his chest as his mouth formed words he'd never be able to recall later. A dry wave of heat swept the room.

The blaze of Heartlight winked out everything else in his vision. When it cleared, Chris found himself in the woodland glade she'd built in his mind on those long afternoons in the train station. He felt hollow, half himself, the way he had been before he'd ever met his wolf. The brush shifted and Woof stood across from him, tail swinging in greeting.

Legs might have separated them, but as always, Ofelia had led him home.

He dropped to one knee. The wolf closed the distance.

Okay. Give her everything we've got.

Woof rose and rested his front paws on Chris's chest. Light shone beneath the pads, and Chris closed his eyes. The pressure of the paws eased as the wolf slid back into him.

When he opened his eyes again, Ofelia stood across the clearing. She wore a violet silk sheath bordered in gold that dropped off her shoulders, billowing around her chest and spilling over her body like a waterfall. Her hair was loose, bound back by fat gold rings so it circled her face like a halo of springing coils. He recognized her family's crest in the pattern stamped into the waist chain and the bands dripping with diamonds and gold encircling her biceps. He looked down, saw matching violet and gold belting his tunic, the ceremonial garb of a shifter going to his concord match.

His wolf howled in his chest, and the light died.

CHAPTER FORTY-FIVE

ONCE, Ofelia's charm had bored into Chris's chest and drawn enough power to make rain on a cloudless day. This time her charm taught his Heartlight the song of the desert, each searing grain of midday sand and endless stretches of gold informing the power between them what it was to be arid, unforgiving.

Bound together, they turned that power on a demigod.

Legs staggered back as a sirocco of magic enveloped him.

Ofelia scrambled to her feet, swaying toward Chris. She felt his wolf return, the bridge between them, and she finally understood what it was to know the unity she had denied so long.

When Heartlight surged, Legs's protests became a feeble wail. The charm bound him in desert wind, unleashed the full sun on what remained, and drew every drop of moisture away from him—including the blood he had stolen over the centuries. With it came his power, soaking into her pores and her bones. She lived his memories in those moments. So many bodies, ones he rode until he figured out how to make himself small enough to survive, littered his path. Each of those burned-out husks had been lives, loves, dreams of their ancestors.

She closed her eyes against the horror of his quest for vengeance, sickened, and prayed that the Seven would guide his victims to peace.

When she opened them again, she stood in a glade she'd only heard about. Chris stood on the other side. As on the first day, she could see the wolf shining under his skin like a beacon.

They wore the ceremonial colors of a concord match. He smiled in recognition, and he looked so beautiful in the aubergine and gold, a wolf king, that she ached with longing.

Her concord. Her everything.

She would tell him she loved him until he was sick of hearing it. But first... She needed to see it through to the end.

She took his hand. "Ready?"

He winked, canines too sharp to be purely human, and rippled into that fearsome wolf-headed beast from the arena. Her beast. "Let's finish this."

They stepped out of the clearing and into the airplane hangar as one.

The thing that had been Legs lay as shriveled as a desiccated corpse on the pavement.

The spark of life lingered. Even together they weren't strong enough to kill a demigod, but he was too weak to do more than issue a wordless scream of impotent fury. She whispered a binding, sealing him up.

Then she wavered, new power no match for simple physical exhaustion. Chris was there, an arm around her.

The hangar doors slid open, the black and gray wolves bounding into the space only to skid to a stop at the sight. Her towering werewolf whined softly in greeting and his jaw opened, tongue lolling in a canine grin.

A second van skidded to a stop a moment later. Evelia and Ayele leaped out, a defensive spell growing between them. Barbara put the van in park, and Beryl slammed the passenger-side door.

"I told you they like to run off together and fix everything on their own." Ayele laughed but leaned back against the van in relief.

Chris slid back into his skin, and his pack crashed into him like a tide.

Ofelia's heart ached at the sight of him surrounded by his brothers.

Ayele levered herself off the van wearily, and Ofelia slumped into her arms.

"There, there," Ayele chided. "At least you already mussed your makeup. No loss."

Ofelia hugged her with all her strength. "You are my best friend."

"Feeling sentimental now, eh?" Ayele grinned. "Come. Even when you make me crazy, I love you with my whole heart. More like sisters then, eh?" She pressed a kiss to Ofelia's cheek and lowered her voice. "Someone would like to speak with you."

Beryl had broken away from her children but kept a respectful distance. When Ofelia met her eyes, she saw only acceptance, welcome. "Brave girl. Your mother would be proud."

The dam broke in Ofelia's heart. The grief she'd pent up and pushed aside for years swept her all at once. Sobbing, she let herself be drawn into Beryl's arms. Ayele circled her from behind. Barbara came next.

Evie rested her hand softly on Ofelia's shoulder. Ofelia looked up. The other woman mouthed, "Thank you" with a glance at Mark. One of them had found an old towel for Chris, and she took a moment to appreciate the bare-chested and exuberant sight of him.

"We missed all the fun," Barbara said lightly, stepping back to take Tobias's hand. "But the witches are safe. We sent them—"

The drone of helicopter blades drowned out the rest of her words. A light scanned the ground before them, turning the ground into swirling ribbons of dirt in the air.

"Necromancer." Mark inhaled, then snapped, "Everyone in the van."

Ofelia considered their options as the light swept over them. There was no way they would all escape. She would not run. Heartlight surged against her sternum as if from her own chest, begging to be used.

Chris met her eyes and nodded, his hands pale-furred and clawed, his teeth too big.

Ofelia glared up into the vortex of wind and then back at the family. "Go—we'll hold them."

She flexed her fingers, preparing to draw up a wind to blow the helicopter back long enough to give the others a chance to escape. In his beastly form, Chris stalked to the wall and yanked an enormous metal pipe free, joining her as he hefted it like a javelin over one shoulder.

"Wait!" Ayele cried. "It's not… what it looks like. I called them."

Ofelia blinked, and the charm died at her fingers. "What have you done?"

"Trust me?" Ayele smiled hesitantly.

Ofelia allowed the helicopter to land. The blades whirred to a stop.

The doors opened, and Baako leaped out with three other àjé and their shifters. The last to step out was a compact, muscular woman dressed like a warrior, unremarkable except for the power that made her slightly blurry around the edges.

When the tall, dark-skinned healer stepped to Baako's side, Evie gasped. "Violet?"

"Eves." When Baako nodded, Violet broke rank. She and Evelia met in the gap between groups, arms around each other. "You never did know how to stay out of trouble."

The bear shifter, Ilya, shadowed his àjé, exchanging wary glares with Mark. The two women pulled back, a torrent of words between them.

The necromancer surveyed the hangar, her eyes stopping on the shriveled husk. Her shadow rose—man-shaped but only just—and it bore a glittering obsidian spear. All eyes went to Ofelia, but their attention no longer made her uncomfortable. She saw wonder in many of them, even a touch of awe.

"Is it true—he's a demigod?" Ofelia murmured.

"Not quite." Amanirenas cocked her head, studying the creature. "But he is something we have never seen before."

She lifted her gaze to take in the Prague witches and their shifters. "Twice your family has done great service to mine, Mother."

"Our duty is to protect those in need"—Beryl inclined her chin— "and help those who need us."

A shiver raced through Ofelia. Beneath the reprimand was a kernel of familiarity. There was no way the Prague witch could have known the code of the àjé: *First duty of the powerful is to protect those who are not.* Perhaps they had failed only by limiting that protection to their own. But it was the right place to begin.

A place she could begin with her own coven if they would have her.

"It has been a mistake to think there are none worthy of regard outside our lands." The necromancer's mouth twitched. "I am in your debt. Our borders are always open to you."

Beryl inclined her head in gratitude.

The àjé took what was left of Legs into the cargo area of the helicopter. Only Baako and Violet remained.

"Ofelia, you have honored your mothers." The necromancer's gaze moved. "We welcome you and your concord home."

"My place is here." Ofelia said, touching the furred arm beside her. He met her eyes and nodded. "Our place is here."

The necromancer's eyebrow rose. "No bound pairs live outside our city walls."

In response, the Prague witches closed in as one, and Ofelia found herself craning to see through a gap between Mark's and Tobias's shoulders. In his beast form, Chris towered over the others, fur on his shoulders rippling over the muscle beneath as his lips peeled back to reveal impressive teeth.

"A witch is her own sovereign." Beryl spoke calmly from Ofelia's side. "Her path belongs to her."

The necromancer showed teeth, pitiless. "This is for their own safety as well as our protection."

"My children and I have made our lives here, Your Highness," Beryl said. "Azrael is no stranger to us, and though we do not call him a friend, he has been just. I find empowerment is better protection than possession."

Ofelia's chin rose as a path of leadership became clear to her as it hadn't been before—not to possess but protect, not to control but empower. She wished her mother could have met Beryl. The two women would have loved each other.

The àjé tensed. Ofelia thought Amanirenas would not risk triggering Azrael's wards with any substantial use of her powers, but she had many ways to compel them.

"As you can see, Great Nana, this territory is full of surprises." Ayele slipped to Beryl's side, smiling brightly.

"It is far too much for a single àjé," Violet admitted, stepping back to her place amid the Cadre team. "And this family has proven itself beyond trustworthy allies."

Ayele winked at Ofelia. "I'll keep an eye on them."

When Baako stepped to Amanirenas's shoulder, the necromancer inclined her head to hear the council of her future First Àjé.

Ofelia held her breath, searching for some sign of how Baako's mind might move. The necromancer nodded, and Baako stepped back, her face impassive.

"I will have your memories to understand what happened here." The necromancer regarded Ofelia. "When the time comes, we will count you as allies."

Once, she would have railed against knowing that one day the necromancer might call her into service. But she knew what she fought for now. And that she did not stand alone. She touched Mark's and Tobias's shoulders, and they parted. She and Ayele stepped into the space between the groups. "My charm is in your hand, Great Nana."

"Shifter," Amanirenas snapped.

"Oh yeah, me too, sure." Chris was himself again—affable and completely unbothered as he retucked his towel and took a step forward.

Ofelia tugged him to one knee beside her.

The necromancer hovered her hands. The flow was a gentle ebbing tide, sliding away. When the necromancer stepped back, the events of the past few hours themselves were dull, distant.

The necromancer met Ofelia's eyes, shaking her head with distinct amusement. "You have been foolish, child. It is good that you are also so well loved."

Ofelia's chin lowered, her throat hot and dry. She couldn't look at Chris yet. But she would, and she would tell him how much she loved him and that she had been so very wrong. How grateful she was that he'd stood beside her anyway and that she would be honored to have him at her side for the rest of their lives.

"Now, my presence in this territory is a violation of the Allegiance oath," Amanirenas said, showing teeth in a feral smile. "Even if I have done Azrael a favor. Go. Your attendance in this matter will be erased."

The remaining tension dissolved. Somebody found Chris some shorts. Violet and Evelia said their goodbyes. Ayele made proper introductions. Ofelia watched it all from the outside.

"Look at you with a concord." Baako bumped her shoulder, smiling. "All grown up."

"Will Serwaah forgive me for skipping the ceremony?"

"She'll never forgive you for depriving her of a time-honored ritual," Baako said dryly. "But she was right. It kept you alive."

"She's going to be insufferable."

"Likely." Baako's mouth quirked, and when her eyebrow canted, Ofelia saw her mother's face.

Ofelia hugged her. "Thank you."

"You are welcome," Baako murmured into her hair. "When I call you—"

"I will answer." Ofelia pressed her hand to her heart. "I promise."

Baako nodded, satisfied, and hugged her tightly. "You've always done things your own way. Many àjé will be interested in the changes you have made to the concord bond."

"Tell them all I love them," Ofelia said, thinking of Alam and Erandi, her aunts.

"Come back when you can." Baako sketched a sigil on the back of her shoulder. Ofelia recognized the symbol for home and open doors. It was the one given to every Spider when she left. "Or we will come to you whenever you need us."

Ofelia's eyes blurred, but she bared her teeth. "Don't just call when there's trouble. Okay?"

"Deal." Baako grinned and followed the necromancer into the helicopter.

Riding in the back of the rocking van an hour later, sandwiched on the floor between Chris and Ayele, Ofelia drifted in and out of awareness. In the front seats, Barbara and Tobias bickered quietly over the directions.

From the jump seat behind them, Beryl ended the argument by casting a little glowing map that overlaid the dash. "Just follow the navigation."

Evelia slept against Mark's chest, his arm wrapped protectively around her. He, too, appeared to be sleeping until he blinked one yellow eye open at her.

Ayele rested her head on Ofelia's shoulder and exhaled softly. Ofelia smiled and pressed her cheek to Ayele's smooth scalp.

For the first time since she'd been dropped off at boarding school, she felt like she'd arrived. She was home.

At Ayele's apartment building, Chris opened the doors and helped her out.

Ofelia slid out with her. "I love you, Yele."

"You too, little upstart," Ayele said, squeezing her back. "So I guess we're partners now, eh? Spies for the motherland."

"I suppose so." Ofelia felt herself gravitate back to Chris. She was tired, and she wanted more than anything to wake up in his arms after many, many hours of sleep. "We can start next week."

Ayele started to walk away, but Chris called out, "Ye, hang on a minute."

Cute—he had his own nickname for her. The two of them were going to be insufferable.

Ofelia couldn't wait.

But her smile faltered as she registered his expression. He seemed to have trouble meeting her eyes.

Ayele stopped, her brows drawn.

"Just a minute," Chris called into the van, tugging Ofelia away from the others.

"What is it?" Her heart thumped painfully in her ribs. His heart? She couldn't tell the difference.

"I think, maybe, we should take some time apart." His eyes shone with emotion when he finally met hers. "Figure some things out."

Ofelia sucked in a tiny breath, the only one her chest would allow. She tried to make a joke of it. "Are you breaking up with me?"

"Can't break up if we weren't real to begin with." He rubbed his eye with the heel of one hand. They both winced when it opened the cut above his brow. Without thinking, she touched her fingers to it and it sealed. He gave a grateful half smile. "Maybe you're right—we've grown up; we have different lives. All I know is I'm tired of chasing you and trying to convince you that it's worth trying to be something new, together. I'm so fucking tired of being the only one fighting to be more than the memory of two little kids in a train station."

The first splinters webbed painfully across her heart. All she wanted was to be close to him—*apart* was a word she no longer understood.

"But our concord." It was the only thing she could think to say, but the moment it left her lips, she knew it had been the wrong thing. He wasn't talking about the bond.

Confirmation flitted across his weary face. Pain too. "Bonded for life, I know. Whenever you need me—I'm here. But that doesn't mean we have to— Well, they say it's not a love bond, right?"

It wasn't a love bond by nature. But it could have been. Only she had no idea how to do it—right or at all. She'd been alone too long. Didn't know what to say to reassure him. *I love you* felt like not enough after how hard she'd worked to maintain the distance between them. Not nearly enough.

Ofelia blinked furiously against tears. Through their connection, she felt the new strain in his chest. Some distant part of her was proud of him for standing up for himself even if it broke her heart.

He needed something she had no idea how to give. She would not fall apart on him now. But she could let him know she heard him. She understood.

"You deserve better than being left behind." She'd seen his family— their bonds hard fought and strong. No vow could match that. Realization blossomed in her chest. "You deserve a partner."

His mouth tilted in the imitation of a smile. "Yeah, I think I do."

Ofelia nodded, willing her tears not to fall. She wondered if he felt her grief in his chest as she felt his. She started to step back, but he squeezed her fingers.

"If you're ever ready for something else," he said, voice rasping now, "you know where to find me."

She wanted to scream that she was ready. But the words would seem hollow, false, a desperate attempt to keep him. He would always wonder. She had to prove it. She had no idea where to begin.

So she let him go.

He glanced over her shoulder, nodding. Ayele was at her side a moment later. She slid an arm around Ofelia.

"Bet we could still catch a couple of episodes of *Bakeoff* before I pass out," Ayele murmured as the van doors closed. She tugged Ofelia toward the building, waving at the doorman. "And you need a shower. Desperately."

Ofelia's laughter turned to tears before the door closed behind them.

CHAPTER FORTY-SIX

AT THE GRAND reopening of Charm Syndicate, Ofelia greeted customers, human and supernatural, with a smile that felt hollow as an old gourd. She was back in her business and her home. She had avenged her parents, saved the witches of Prague, earned her freedom, and found a true friend.

After all, was there a truer friend than one willing to put her up indefinitely? For weeks the building had lingered in limbo—caught between the reluctant owner and the insurance companies. Ayele installed Ofelia in one of her many spare rooms and even created an extra space for making her custom orders. As the delays dragged on, Ofelia feared Charm Syndicate would never reopen.

Until the morning she received an email from her new landlord. The entire building had been purchased by a corporation with connections to a Greco-Nigerian shipping consortium. Reconstruction started immediately.

Ofelia joked Ayele's mothers had bought the building because Ayele was sick of having a roommate.

Full Moon Construction handled the work. It had been surprisingly easy to see Mark on a regular basis. He was all business, and it was good having a contractor who understood the unique requirements of her shop.

Over the past few months, all of them—Vogels, Acaz, and Svobodová alike—had been by at some point. She had a distinct sense they were checking in on her, keeping an eye on things in a way that felt heart-bruisingly familiar and more welcome than she wanted to admit. Beryl invited her to Sunday dinner. But it would have felt wrong showing up at his family dinner without checking with Chris first. And he had not reached out.

When Mark had finished the final walk-through, he handed off the keys and a business card. "Evie asked me to give you this. If you ever want to visit the studio."

Ofelia's nose began to twitch, and Mark hurried off to finish packing the last of his tools before she went full waterworks. She didn't know what was wrong with her.

He paused on the way out the door. "He misses you."

It was the first time he'd spoken of Chris during the months of work.

Ofelia's smile wavered.

Mark smiled faintly. Nodded. "Yeah, so mutual then."

"I don't know how to *show* him I can… change. I want to."

"Thing nobody tells you is *nobody* knows." Mark hefted a final box of tools and grabbed his jacket. "But when it's worth it, you figure it the fuck out. 'Wanting to' seems as good a place to start as any."

He headed for the door.

"Tell him I said hi?" Ofelia murmured.

"Tell him yourself," Mark called over his shoulder.

And then he was gone.

She and Ayele celebrated the night before the grand reopening with a bottle of champagne and an episode of the new season of *Bakeoff*.

"Talked to him?" Ayele said.

She shook her head.

Ayele's lips tightened, but she said nothing.

The next day Ofelia stood amid the well-wishers at the reopening, making forgettable conversation, listening to Ayele ring up purchases and purr praise at people's choices. The gargoyles even made a rare daytime appearance with a contingent from the club.

She hugged her coven mates as they crowded around her. They'd begun practicing together. Well, they had bylaws, at least. And they'd voted in their high priestess. Ofelia insisted on it.

Each presented her with a plant cutting. Her eyes filled when she realized many were descendants of the ones she had given them over the year.

Ayele sucked her teeth at the sight of tears and handed her a tissue.

She was locking up after the first full week of being open, anticipating a long solitary night, when Mark's words found her heart. *Start somewhere.*

She grabbed her phone and thumbed out a text. She had the perfect excuse to see him.

CHAPTER FORTY-SEVEN

> @Fifiti: Hey. I've got to look in on a possessed building.
> Would feel better with backup. In?

HE RESPONDED RIGHT AWAY. That was a good sign. And he'd changed his contact name. She smiled stupidly into her phone for a minute after the bubble appeared.

> @Charming: I'm in.

The building was a complete shit show. But at some point she'd looked over at Woof beside her and been grateful. Ofelia fell into bed after she'd trapped the unrested spirt and removed it from the building. She slept for twelve hours. In the morning she debated her next step carefully. How to check in on him without seeming weird. First she changed her contact nickname. Two could play that game.

> @Prinzess: Ugh, still cleaning gunk out of my hair, you?

> @Charming: lol, fur.

> @Prinzess: Woof forgive me yet?

> @Charming: He doesn't hold grudges.

> @Prinzess: Good to know.

Later in the store, her phone ping revealed a GIF of a dog in a bubble bath. Laughing, she sent back an animated giraffe in the shower, washing its neck with a long bath scrubber.

He changed the chat name to Cape-less Crusaders.

She posted a GIF from some comedy superhero movie with a cape getting sucked into the jet engine.

@Prinzess: Capes are for idiots.

Every time her phone chimed with a notification, a smile tugged her lips and she hurried to finish whatever she was working on.

"I can't believe I have to tell you to get off your phone." Ayele dumped a shipment of product on the counter. "Who is in charge here? We have to stock. Move. Move."

Ofelia left her phone face down and went for the box cutter.

Most of her nonmagical products were now made by a reputable supplier, leaving Ofelia to focus on custom orders. Ayele managed contracts and quality control. She was ruthless. So far she'd been to the factory twice to supervise. To the delight of her mothers, she changed her major to business management.

"I don't need a degree to prove I am an artist," Ayele had crowed between episodes of *Buona Notte*. "But a business degree will open some doors."

It was a good thing, Ofelia thought as they restocked the next day. She'd offered to show a few of Ayele's pieces in the store and immediately regretted it. They were a literal mess. She was counting the days until she could hide them back in the storeroom.

Her phone pinged again. She glanced at it, then the box.

Ayele rolled her eyes and took the box cutter. "Go."

Ofelia read Ange's text, frowning.

She opened a new message without a thought:

@Prinzess: Gargs say there's an incubus turning up at Tresor. Would you help me convince it to work elsewhere?

@Charming: I get off at 8—meet you at the door?

@Prinzess: You back in the shop?

@Charming: Got my own spot. Borrowed a little start-up cash from Vogel Savings and Loan.

> @Prinzess: That's awesome! Congratulations.

She grinned. He was going out on his own. Her heart ached again. Pride this time.

The incubus went peaceably, but not until after propositioning them for a night they would never forget. Typical incubus shit. After politely declining, she coaxed Chris to dance. For a few blissful hours, they owned the floor again.

He rode the tram home with her and walked her to her door. Before she could get her heart out of her throat long enough to invite him up, he said good night. He was on school drop-off in the morning, earning a bit of extra money to invest in marketing.

Pride overwhelmed the flash of disappointment. Finally his family was recognizing how valuable he was and showing him in tangible ways.

On her way up the stairs, her phone pinged.

> @Charming: I thought Ange's eyes were gonna pop when we turned up together.

> @Prinzess: fr fr.

Ofelia bit her lip on a grin. She swallowed her fear of rejection, then thumbed out another text.

> @Prinzess: Hey. Tonight was good. I missed dancing w u.

> @Charming:

The dots bounced on a reply for the entire time it took her to walk up a floor. Ofelia swore as a flash of pain raced through her chest, not her own. She slipped a fist over her heart and rubbed gently, as though he might feel it and be comforted. Maybe he needed more time. Okay. She would wait. She slipped her phone into her bag and let herself into her apartment. No response by the time she went to bed. But in the morning, she had a notification.

> @Charming: That invitation to do a pop-up in your store open?

> @Prinzess: Always.

Once they set a date, she promoted the pop-up on all her socials. He showed up promptly and set up a station in the window, surrounded by plants. She put out the sign she'd had especially made for him. He saw anyone who stopped by.

Between customers, she thumbed a text.

@Prinzess: That was an incredible fade.

Chris sent a GIF of an anime wolf-headed man dusting off his shoulders. She shook her head—where did he find these things?

@Prinzess: Yup, I can see that head getting bigger from here.

@Charming: Don't hate the player.

@Prinzess: 😳

"Are you texting that boy?" Ayele hissed in her ear, startling her so much she nearly dropped her phone. "He's right *there*. Go over and talk to him."

"You sound like an old auntie. 'Go over and talk.' That's not how things are done these days anyway." Ofelia sucked her teeth and put her phone away. "What do you know? You still dangling Klaus and Sven, or have you made up your mind?"

Ayele narrowed her eyes. "Love triangles are boring. Why choose?"

Ofelia's laugh burst free when Ayele's sly, victorious smile emerged.

When she glanced up, Chris was grinning, his eyes sliding away from her as he greeted his next customer. Had he been watching them? Her?

Her heart did a little jig in her chest. She stifled it. Saw the way his palm passed briefly over his own chest as though he'd felt it too.

As they closed for the night, she tried to ignore him diligently cleaning his station, mopping and spraying everything down as his hips swayed to the beat Ayele had turned up before she left.

"Try not to get into too much trouble, you two," she'd called over her shoulder, cackling.

Chris had barely met her eyes the entire time they were alone in the shop, but his small smile warmed her as she went about packing away the last of the expensive jewelry, then watered the plants happily crowding the window. If a few of them were growing faster than expected, it must just be her green thumb, right?

He drifted over to the counter as she finished putting things in order, his duffel slung over one shoulder. "Thanks again for the pop-up."

"Anytime!" she chirped too brightly and then got a grip on herself. "I mean it was great having you. And it looked like the flow was good?"

"Better than good." He propped a hip against the counter, bringing him close enough for her to pick up the subtle scent of the aftershave she'd made him. He was still wearing it. "Hopefully a few new regulars."

She bobbed her head like a damned fool. Now was the time to say something, but words failed her.

On impulse, she plucked two bottles from a shelf and slid them to across the counter.

"You don't have to—" He shook his head.

"It's a tip," she said. "A thank-you. Anyway. You did me a favor using my stuff, and I heard you recommending it for maintenance."

He lifted one broad shoulder. "You make the best stuff."

A fiery streak of a new emotion lanced under her breastbone at the easily given compliment. She wanted him to wear her scents so no matter where he went, he would carry her with him. No matter who touched him, she would be there.

Because he was hers. Not just because of the bond they now shared. Not just because of the way their hearts fell into sync when they were a few feet apart or how her nervous system settled when he was close, as if sensing safety, welcome. Those were all physiological responses common to every concord.

This was theirs. She loved him. And she was his.

She fought the urge to pack him an entire box.

Instead, she stared at him across the counter, mouth as dry as the Sahara and heart too full to speak.

He, too, seemed unable to find words for a moment, his big eyes locked on her. He cleared his throat. "Looking forward to our next mission."

"We make a good team," she said lightly.

"We do."

She stood at the counter for a long time after the bells sounding his departure had stilled to silence. It wasn't that she needed him. Wanting was different somehow. Knowing that she would survive without him but what she wanted—to thrive—was something she'd rather do together. She was ready to figure out how.

"WELL, the wiring in the bathroom and the kitchen is finished," Ondrej said as he finished packing up his kit.

Chris stretched his back, rolling his neck for the satisfying pop. He'd been setting tile all afternoon after two days in the shop cutting hair, and everything felt stiff. He checked his phone. Nothing from Ofelia.

After he'd finished the pop-up, there'd been silence on their chat thread. It was starting to make him antsy. He'd gotten used to hearing from her—GIFs or jokes or some odd job cleaning up magical business gone awry. They'd developed a reputation among the supernatural population.

As puzzling as that last one was, he liked that she kept taking him with her. And not just because she needed Heartlight. She asked him how they should approach things, let him try diplomacy first. It had worked at Tresor, though the incubus had seemed frustrated when they turned him down.

They were starting to get jobs that paid. The Tresor gig alone had covered all his tile. And he'd gotten to dance with Ofelia again. He still wasn't over the feel of her swaying against him, hips in the cradle of his, arm around his neck. He shifted his work pants to relieve the discomfort of sudden pressure.

"Chris," Ondrej called. "You heard? The wiring—"

Chris shook his head to clear thoughts of Ofelia's salty-sweet skin and the little grin below her closed eyes. Dancing, she'd looked like she did after sex, content and satisfied. "I'm wired."

Ondrej sighed audibly.

"Sorry." Chris rubbed a palm over his eyes. That only made it worse. With his eyes closed, it was like he could smell her. "I'm just fucking beat. Thanks, man. For everything. I've got some money for you."

He found the envelope in the kitchen and grabbed a wad of cash. He counted it out on his way back. He was almost cleaned out. He calculated how many more doubles he could pull—days in the shop, taking the kids back and forth. Mark had thrown him some light work on a couple of jobs. That helped. He still needed paint, and the floors were going to cost him a kidney. He headed back into the kitchen, running numbers. He wasn't as good at that shit as Tobias. He had to focus.

And now he couldn't get the smell of her out of his nose. Almost as if—

As he rounded the corner to Ondrej, someone knocked on the door.

Chris handed over the entire envelope. "Here. Thanks. I owe you."

Ondrej tried to refuse all the money, but Chris had already left him behind, opening the door.

Ofelia stood on his doorstep, shifting a giant cloth-covered basket from the crook of one elbow to the other. Her eyes went round at the sight of him, as though flight was an option. As usual, he felt the jump in his own chest before he realized it was hers.

"I brought—" she began.

"Dinner." He sniffed and then flashed a grin as his stomach rumbled and his heart made other demands entirely. "Come in."

Ondrej's eyes widened at the sight of her. He glanced at Chris, then smiled and hustled off as fast as he could. "Night, guys."

When Chris turned his attention back to Ofelia, she was busy trying —and failing—not to stare. He followed her gaze, taking in the work. It had only been a couple of months, and he'd done most of it himself to cut down on cost. But his dad had helped; Mark and a guy from his crew, Sam, had thrown in hours here and there; Ondrej did the electrical. Even Klaus had come by and helped him with demo.

Luca had called a few times, trying to get them to go clubbing, but after Klaus removed him from the group chat, he got the message and fucked off.

It was easy to see how much more needed to be done—floors and paint and light fixtures. Decisions on the counters and the kitchen backsplash and the cabinet hardware. But for a moment he let himself see it as she might. To contrast it against the last time she had been here.

"You've been busy," she murmured.

"A little."

"This looks—" She exhaled softly, wordlessly.

He let the wave of her surprise wash over him. It no longer looked ready to be condemned. As he'd made progress, his confidence had grown and so had his focus. He still had problems getting motivated some days or got distracted and disappeared down rabbit holes. Making decisions was hard, fearing he'd choose the wrong thing or regret it. But he didn't let that stop him anymore. When he made a mistake, he forgave himself and he kept going.

"It's coming along," he said simply. "What's the occasion?"

"I should have called." She spun to face him. The weight of the basket nearly threw her off-balance, and he reached out to grab it before it slipped free or took her down with it. Her smile faded. "Thanks. It was a long day in the shop. I, ah, needed to eat. And I figured you probably needed to eat too. But is this a good time?"

"Perfect," he said, "but I don't really have a table. Or chairs."

"I thought we could have a picnic," she said brightly, tugging the blanket.

"I need to wash up."

"Okay."

He paused on the way to the door. "Breathe, Fi. I'm happy to see you."

She sucked in a deep breath, and her grin wobbled a little. "Good. Me too."

He did the best cleanup he could manage in the bathroom. He was still waiting for the glass on the walk-in shower, though the soaking tub had arrived and Sam had finished the plumbing for it last week. For a moment he entertained the idea of her in the bathtub with him. They hadn't done that yet.

When he came back, she'd spread the blanket out right there, in the shambles of the dining room. She smiled up at him, and he tuned in to her to find her a little nervous still. He didn't know what it meant that he liked that she'd come to him, that this meant enough to her to make her nervous.

She'd laid out six deli-wrapped packages.

"Aww, Princess. You made me a sandwich." He flopped onto the floor and sniffed.

"If by made you mean paid for." She laughed—bright and loud. Gods, he loved when she laughed like that. When he met her eyes, he saw she knew it. He couldn't help himself—he caught her wrist. Experimenting, he tugged. No resistance, only her slow smile as she leaned into him.

Kissing her was every bit as good as he remembered. Her fingers slid into his too-long hair, tugging him closer.

"Wait," she said a little frantically as she drew away. "I have to tell you something."

He rolled onto one elbow, tasting her on his lips and feeling himself getting hard at the thought of how the rest of her would taste. Fantasizing hadn't been enough. Time and distance had done nothing to ease his longing for her.

"You are," she said, "the best thing that's ever happened to me. I won't let you go. I can't. I need—"

He licked his lips, and she seemed to lose her train of thought. "Go on."

"Stop it," she said frantically. "I'm trying. And I can't think with you all... over there."

"Over here?"

"Being sexy!" Her cheeks brightened.

"I'm sexy?"

"You are distracting."

He laughed. "Make up your mind."

"My what?"

"Sexy or distracting?" He liked feeling her in his chest as he watched her. Her heart beat double time. His tried to keep up. As an experiment, he took a deep breath. Both beats slowed and slipped into balance.

"All of the above," she said finally, exhaling. "Both. I need you to hear me. I am trying— Why is this so fucking hard?"

He sat up. This was important to her. "Okay. I'll stop being distracting."

"Fat chance," she grumbled.

He hauled her across the blanket onto his lap and pressed her palm to his chest as though she couldn't already feel what she was doing to him. "Just say what you came to say."

"I need… I want you. For real this time." Eyes open and fixed on him with unmistakable clarity. "I can't promise I'll be any good at it at first, but if you can just let me try—"

"Yes." He shifted her to straddle him.

"That's it?" She sat back, perplexed.

He hiked the light summer dress over her knees and groaned softly. Her thighs were like warm silk—he couldn't stop running his fingers up and down, digging in lightly to feel her squirm. "What else?"

"I promise not to hide things anymore," she panted, resting her forehead against the curve of his neck. "Not to keep you guessing what I'm up to. I've been trying. With Cape-less Crusaders, you know?"

"You have been."

"Unless it's your birthday, and then I fully intend to throw you a completely over-the-top surprise party." She kissed the skin above his T-shirt, and her fingers scrambled for the hem. When her palms made contact with his skin, he exhaled sharply. "Maybe on a Greek island somewhere if Ayele has anything to say about it."

"You gonna wear one of those tiny bikinis?"

"Depends on how this conversation goes." She chuckled low in the back of her throat, husky, which was his other favorite laugh, and he remembered she was as tuned in to him as he was to her. "I might skip the top."

He groaned, mashing his eyelids shut. This was important. It was everything he'd longed for, and now all he could think about was the firm mounds of her breasts, shiny with sunscreen and sweat on a beach somewhere where the water was too blue to be real.

"I like the sound of that." He gripped the back of her neck in one palm, her hip in the other, and dragged her mouth to his. "You gonna keep running off on your own?"

"You gonna keep chasing me?" Her lips curved, teasing now.

"Definitely." When his thumb slid along the inside of her hip, she arched into him, shivering as the rough pad slid over the center of her slick heat.

"So maybe." He shivered when her breath stuttered on his skin.

A low, greedy sound escaped her. Her nimble fingers popped the fly on his work pants, but he caught her hand.

"Make you a deal." She whimpered. "I'll always call you before I go run off on my own. So you can protect me when you catch up, and since your legs are longer, it won't take long."

He shook his head, unable to keep from laughing, and let her go. "Girl, I'm never going to be able to let you out of my sight, am I?"

"I hope not." She met his eyes. "I love you."

"That was never the question." He grunted when her hand closed around him.

"Oh you!" She drew back, eyes narrowed before her sly grin returned. "Is that a wolf howling in your chest, or are you just happy to see me?"

"Yes." He barked a laugh, arms around her, drawing her in. "I adore you, Princess."

She ground into him, and every scrap of restraint fled. He couldn't bear the distance any longer. She rode him to the floor, and she was all the magic he would ever need.

THANKS FOR READING

Reviews help other readers find their next favorite book. Please consider recommending it to a friend or leaving a review wherever you purchased this book.

Want more Vogel Brothers?

Be the first to find out about new releases at www.jasminesilvera.com where you can also find deleted scenes, extras, and other goodies!

ACKNOWLEDGMENTS

I am enormously grateful for the earliest readers and location experts who helped give this book a sense of place: Lucie Greenidge, Beth Green, and Geoff Engle.

Thanks to Eva Moore and Bethany Robison, who are always in on the beginnings, and Erin Evans, Rhiannon Held, Shanna Germain, Corry L. Lee, Kate Marshall, and Susan J. Morris, who deftly advised on the final polish.

Victory Editing helmed a dramatic rescue operation for all my poor abused commas and helped me to find the word I *meant* to use every time. Sylvia and the Book Brander team came through with another stellar cover.

Writing may be a solitary act, but being a writer doesn't have to be. And having other writers in my circle somehow makes the whole endeavor seem a *lot* less shriek-worthy most of the time. Heartfelt thanks to the Ponies! Elle Beauregard, Kelly Blake, Jen Comfort, Melora Francois, Alexis de Girolami, Lin Lustig, Kate Maybury, and Jo Segura for shared meals, writing games, and memes.

And last but never least: Dearest readers, thank you for continuing to take this journey with me and for giving each story the chance to win your heart. Every time you buy, read, review, or otherwise share the love, you help make my dream of being an author come true. Thank you.